The Viceroy's Captain

The bandits never saw Caspasian coming. His finger squeezed the trigger and the gun burst into life. The barrel tugged to the left but Caspasian held it fast, spraying short controlled bursts into the bandits. A fourth man who had been concealed on the far side of the rock sprang up and let off a shot in his direction. Ganga's rifle cracked and the man fell back.

Now that the dead men's companions had been alerted to the presence of an enemy on the ridgeline, they ceased firing on the people below and closed in with unexpected fury. Two of them burst around the corner, coming at Caspasian from the side. He swung his MP18 onto them, pulled the trigger.

The gun fired and jammed. Hard behind Caspasian, Ganga's line of fire was blocked. He darted aside to get a clear shot but it was too late. The bandits were upon them.

About the author

Anthony Conway has been a Gurkha officer and has travelled extensively in the East. He has been a bestselling thriller writer under a pseudonym. His second novel featuring Captain John Caspasian will be published by Hodder & Stoughton in 2001.

The
Viceroy's Captain

Anthony Conway

CORONET BOOKS
Hodder & Stoughton

First published in Great Britain in 2000
by Hodder and Stoughton
First published in paperback in 2001
by Hodder and Stoughton
A division of Hodder Headline

A Coronet Paperback

10 9 8 7 6 5 4 3 2 1

A catalogue record of this book
is available from the British Library

ISBN 0 340 76857 6

Typeset by Hewer Text Ltd, Edinburgh
Printed and bound in Great Britain by
Mackays of Chatham PLC, Chatham, Kent

Hodder and Stoughton
A division of Hodder Headline
338 Euston Road
London NW1 3BH

For the Gurkhas
who taught me far more
than I ever taught them.

Acknowledgements

Firstly I would like to thank my agent Heather Jeeves, who took me in from that particular cold so familiar to writers. Her encouragement and support thereafter warmed like a tot of best Gurkha rum.

To Carolyn Caughey, my editor at Hodder and Stoughton, I owe an immense debt. Her professionalism throughout, and the timeliness and perspicacity of her numerous contributions have been remarkable. I count myself extremely lucky to have benefited from her experience and her wise counsel.

I would also like to pay tribute to the officers and men of the old Indian Army Gurkha Brigade and, since 1948, of the Brigade of Gurkhas into which part of it metamorphosed. From the time of Waterloo, they have comprised a military formation to rank amongst the finest in history. More importantly, it has been an enduring and extraordinary friendship between men of two nations, based on mutual respect, brotherly affection and a very great deal of humour. I hope they will exercise the latter to forgive any inaccuracies or exaggerations in this book, whether intentional or not.

Chapter One

The cut on his hand would never heal. Healing required time. Time and little else.

There was just enough light to see the short gash on his left palm, slanting downwards left to right on the pad below the forefinger. His blood was more black than red in the starlight. In moonlight it would have had a colour truer to its own but they had picked their moment well. The moon had set by the time they struck and he knew he would never see it again.

The sun was another matter. Ryan tilted on to his side and watched the east. He knew exactly where to look, for it had been his direction of travel for the past week. The top of the ridgeline on the far side of the valley showed as the jagged seam joining two worlds. Above it, a broad belt of space arose with thickening stars, the familiar patterns almost lost in the rim-to-rim profusion. But below was nothing but blackness, impenetrable all the way from the ridge-line to the rocks a few yards in front of his nose. There space had contracted as if exhausted by the effort of maintaining the spectacular display over-head. It had tightened upon itself, closing about him like a fist.

The man who had cut him lay to the left. Within reach, had Ryan wanted to. Impatience had cost him his life, closing in before Ryan's ammunition was expended. Even so, he had got near enough to swing with his blade as he went down. The tip had made contact. It was little more than a nick really, and in other circumstances Ryan would scarcely have noticed. Knowing his own death close however, it served instead to focus his attention on what would shortly come. They were counting his rounds now, not as carefully as he was perhaps, but enough to ensure they stood a better chance of reaching him than their dead comrade the next time they made a rush.

He could not hear them but he knew they were there, possibly only yards away, listening for his presence as intently as he strained to hear theirs. They occupied the darkness like evil itself. Suffocating. They were the noose round his neck, the bag over his head, the waterlogged cloth tightening on his face. Ryan shook his head to clear the rising panic. It had been brief but he had felt it coming. Some forgotten echo from early childhood, hived away until now, and then creeping out like something vile from under a stone.

He shifted the revolver to his left hand for a moment while he flexed the fingers of his right, working the blood back into them. The bitterly cold mountain air and the effort of gripping the butt had numbed them. With a bolt of alarm he realised that his feet were numb too. His body was rebelling against him, going to sleep before he had finished with it. He laid the revolver gingerly on the ground beside him and rubbed his leg muscles, drawing up his feet to massage the toes of his boots as if that might reimpose some authority over the feet inside the scuffed and beaten leather.

For a moment he felt better. He even detected the hint of a smile starting at the corner of his mouth. Instantly it was smothered by despair.

'You bloody idiot,' he mouthed silently. 'You bloody, bloody little fool.'

That was when the last of his hope died. He heard it then, a shuffling of feet out in the darkness. He snatched up his revolver and checked the cylinder, knowing all the while what a pathetic cargo it held. Three unused bullets. Three. Of course he knew he should keep the last one for himself. The men crouching all around him in the night were not the sort into whose hands one would resign one's keeping lightly. Certainly not while there was breath in the lungs and sensation in the limbs. In the fragile, fragile skin. He could imagine what they would do to his body after he was dead. It revolted him to think of it. He had seen examples of their lunatic delights with his own eyes on past expeditions. In a way though he knew it was irrelevant. The part of him that mattered would have gone by then. Gone to . . . where? To what?

Again he veered away from the line of thought. But what if in the flurry of running feet and stabbing hands the revolver was wrested from his grasp before he could turn it upon himself? Oh God, what then? Ryan swallowed hard, feeling the last dregs of strength leak from him. In that moment he felt the reality of his death for the first time, so well defined it might have been a person standing before him.

Again he drew up his knees, though not this time from the cold. His gaze fell upon the canvas haversack beside him, unregistering at first, but then with a surge of hatred and loathing that made him want to retch. That was the reason he was here. He was about to die for the contents of that. Even by dying he could not keep it safe from his enemies. They would get it whatever happened to him. He felt like taking hold of the bag and flinging it out into the night beyond the cover of the rock, shouting 'Here it is, damn you. Take the blasted thing!' And they would. And they would kill him all the same.

If he swallowed it – and it was far too big for that – but if he could, they would simply rip open his belly and retrieve it, steaming and warm from his entrails. If he took it in his fist and flung it with all his might out across the dark mountain slopes, they would chuckle and search for it after daybreak until they found it. Nor could he smash it with rock or revolver butt. After all, everyone knew that diamond was one of the hardest substances known to man.

For the last moments of his life he was wedded to the stone as truly as to the skull beneath his starved and sunburned cheeks. Keeping his revolver firmly in his hand he roughly pulled the haversack open and took out a bundle of velvet cloth, worrying at it until the last flaps were shaken clear, his features set with repugnance all the while. The miserable light clutched at the object. The size of a tennis ball, its numerous surfaces had been painted for some reason. They had all been surprised to see this at the beginning, although Ryan remembered being struck by the beauty of the designs. Exquisite portrayals, a different miniature scene for every face. Hilton had refused to believe it was a diamond at all until Swift had chipped a fragment away and they had all seen the greater purity beneath. Now however it aroused only contempt from Ryan, the last of the party that had captured and brought it all that immense distance. Hilton had died mercifully quickly from a rifle shot, sniped with unbelievable skill, a head shot at nearly eight hundred yards. It had carried away half his head although he had continued walking for a full five paces before his knees buckled and he sank to the ground, twitching.

Swift had been seized as they broke away from an ambush. Ryan had seen him go down and had faced the most difficult decision in his life. Yet even so, it had been instant. He had spun about, dropped to one knee, aimed and fired, Swift's upturned face sharp and clear beyond the foresight of the Short Mark III Lee-Enfield rifle. At a distance of fifty yards he could not miss and before he turned and sprinted for his life, Ryan had been bombarded by the twin visions, the sight of his best friend, slain by his hand, and the unmistakable look of disappointment on the face of Swift's captor, robbed of subsequent sport.

Ryan hefted the diamond in the palm of his hand. So this was what all the fuss had been about. He did not doubt it was priceless, but what did that matter now that he was about to die? Value acquired an altogether different meaning. Weighed in the balance against life there was not a damned thing to level the scales. Ryan cursed himself silently for not having realised this until now.

There was another sound from the darkness. It was hard to tell what it was but Ryan's brain ran through the options by reflex. He was a professional soldier after all and even in his present extreme situation it was impossible to halt the processes of a lifetime. Eventually he settled upon a careless footfall. Someone had scuffed a stone but it alerted him to the coming end. Any moment now. They were closing in for the kill.

For one more moment the panic returned, washing over him like the waves on the shore where he used to bathe as a boy. Tentatively he placed the revolver's muzzle in his mouth, pressing the cold hard barrel up against the roof. It tasted of gun oil and cordite. His finger was on the trigger, ready. Was this, then, it? He had three shots left. If he left it until the last one, there was always the chance it might be a blind. The thought of the hammer slamming home onto a dud round made Ryan's head swim. At least this way he would have three chances at a painless death. Why go through the heroic charade of taking another one or two of them with him? Who would ever know? Who would ever care? All they would know is that he and the others had failed. What else mattered?

A flood of memories streamed out of nowhere, as if his brain, sensing evisceration, was thumbing through old chapters. The effect on Ryan was two-fold. His finger froze on the trigger, hard up against the final pressure before the hammer's release, and a sense of wonderment surged up out of the inner darkness. Peace almost. Here he was at the very edge of death and he had never seen life and the world so clearly. It was quite extraordinary. He had heard it before many times but here it was at last happening to him. His life flashed before him. It really was true. Unbidden, his accumulated years unfolded their pattern for his private inspection and he could do nothing but spectate. It was not a coherent exposition of childhood, adolescence and adulthood, but rather a montage of scenes, and not even displayed chronologically. Yet in their parade before his inner eye they made an astounding sense of his life. A muddle somehow adopting shape and form.

His parents were there of course, and his brother and sister. Ryan himself, the eldest, appeared in all the guises his life had dressed him in. Birthday celebrant and centre of attention, comforting sibling after a wrong put right, grieving adolescent before his mother's grave. It was all there, mercilessly comprehensive.

He was so mesmerised by the inner pageant that he almost missed the footfall beyond the ring of stone. Almost, but not quite. Years of soldiering snapped him instantly into the present, slamming to attention every nerve and sinew. His eyes pierced the darkness for shapes and found one coming up stealthily from the right. With all thought gone of conserving ammunition, Ryan levelled the muzzle of his revolver, paused until the shape became a man, and fired.

After the peaceful interlude the noise of the round exploded in his ears, reverberating across the invisible mountainside. Beyond the cordite smoke he saw the shape crumple and fall, struck dead centre chest. Two rounds, Ryan thought automatically. Do I do it now? I must!

But now they were running at him. This was it. Two of them, this time from the left. Again, the two deepest instincts in him conspired to thwart his suicide, the inborn instinct of survival and the trained instinct of the professional soldier to destroy an enemy. He fired once, hitting one man and then, as the other was almost upon him, he fired at him too. Both went down. He had timed it perfectly, holding his fire until the closest possible range.

There was silence. To get in his last shot he had stood up and now, for one moment, hope flooded through him. Perhaps he had killed the last of them. Maybe this was to be his reward for all the long years of training, that he should come to the very edge of death and, like some character from the Old Testament so beloved of his heavenly Father, be rescued at the brink having passed the ultimate test.

The cascade of stones from behind smashed into his consciousness with hammerblow force. He glanced around desperately, trying to measure the remaining seconds before these new assailants closed. Clenching his left fist as if screwing up his courage, with his right he put the gun in his mouth and pulled the trigger, knowing the result even before the hammer snapped down on the base of an expended round. His counting had been right. The Webley revolver that had stood between him and death was suddenly more useless than the cursed diamond in the haversack. He darted out towards the closest of the bodies, rolled it over and searched amongst the loose clothing for a fire-arm. All he found was a short dagger and the scabbard of the sword that lay a couple of feet away.

Before he could move to the dead man's companion, he heard their comrades approaching. Confident now, they were calling to one another. One of them shouted out, addressing one of the men just killed, Ryan guessed. There was a muttered curse when the cry was met with silence.

Ryan scrabbled for the haversack, slung it over his shoulder and, clutching the dead man's dagger, ducked away into the darkness heading away from the voices. He had gone barely a dozen paces when shouts erupted from behind him. The men had reached his position and found their dead friends.

Without faltering, Ryan drove himself on down the mountainside. It no longer mattered that he was going in the wrong direction, heading west back into enemy territory. He could always double back later, if there was a later. For now he was spurred on by the terror that nothing stood between him and the most painful and lingering death imaginable.

The ground suddenly dropped away before him, veering sharply downwards into a slope of almost vertical scree. Unable to check himself, Ryan leaned back, letting the loose rocks take him. He felt himself accelerating and spread his hands for balance, losing the dagger as he did so. A bullet snapped past his head, but he didn't care. It would be a mercy. But in any case, he was going fast now, away from the danger above him. More bullets cracked through the night, sparking on stones, ricocheting wildly. Behind him he could sense them following him, but more carefully than his own reckless descent. Unlike Ryan, their expectations had not parted company with life.

Seconds passed, more shots were fired at him, but

Ryan felt himself pulling away from his pursuers. He knew the gap was widening. Down and down he went, ever faster yet just managing to keep himself upright. He was taking giant strides in the scree, bounding down the mountainside at a ferocious pace. Mixed with his fear was exhilaration. It was unavoidable. There was a scream behind him as someone tumbled out of control, cart-wheeling in a tangle of limbs down the precipitous slope.

Without warning Ryan was at the bottom, crumpling in a heap, the air knocked from his lungs. In an instant the excitement was gone. He was up and running, lifting his feet exaggeratedly high to avoid tripping on unseen stones in the darkness. He heard shouts, but his pursuers had reached the foot of the slope some way to the left, so Ryan angled away from them. He seemed to have come out on to some sort of flat plain, although it was impossible to tell how far it stretched. A glance at the sky showed it brightening. He cursed. Darkness had become his only remaining ally and that was shortly to be taken from him. He lengthened his pace, trying desperately to put as much distance as possible between himself and the men behind him.

Ryan took the emerging shapes in front of him for bushes until one of them rose. He skidded to a halt, panting hard, unable to quieten his breath. The man spoke to him calmly. Ryan thought it was Urdu but the tribal dialect was so thick that he could not understand it. Instead he backed away. The man advanced slowly, the other shapes to right and left of him also rising to move forward alongside.

This is it, Ryan thought, fighting the panic with

every ounce of his willpower. Footsteps from behind alerted him that his pursuers had caught up. He was trapped, surrounded, and completely defenceless. It did not even enter his mind to beg for mercy. It would only heighten their enjoyment. The one single thing he had left was his cunning. That and the diamond.

As the tribesmen closed in a circle about him, their faces now palely visible in the growing light, Ryan clutched the haversack to his stomach with both hands, selected his man, and slowly approached him. When he was almost within reach, Ryan sank to his knees and whimpered. He saw an expression of disgust flash across the man's face. Ryan held out the haversack to him, slowly so as not to alarm him. The man drew forward, interested. Around the circle others spoke, urging caution, Ryan presumed. But he had chosen well. The tribesman grunted and took a step towards him. Again Ryan whimpered. Behind him someone laughed. Derisive. Contemptuous.

Laugh all you want, Ryan thought. He proffered the haversack again, but still keeping his hands close to his chest. The man took another step. In his left hand he held his rifle by the stock, an old German Mauser. With his right he reached out for the prize. Behind him, the sky was brightening along its whole eastern rim. Ryan forced himself to keep his eyes fixed on the man, however much he longed to see the sun one last time. But he was living in seconds now. Time had become just that. Less even than a single minute.

With every ounce of his being focused, as he released his grip on the haversack for the man to take, and sensed the attention of his captors fractionally shift from himself to the canvas bag, Ryan propelled himself forward, reaching out with both hands and snatching the revolver tucked loosely in the man's belt. It was a Webley, much like his own, but rusty. There was a cry of alarm from the others and the man staggered back out of reach. But he was too late. Ryan rolled over onto his back, the Webley secure in his hands. With the muzzle up against the roof of his mouth, held firmly in place with both hands, his right thumb pulled back the hammer until it locked in place and he glared triumphantly about him. The morning star was just visible at the periphery of his vision, all the others melting quickly in the growing light. The last thing Ryan saw was the thinnest sliver of orange creeping out from below the bleak horizon, as his forefinger tightened on the trigger, slamming the hammer down on to the base of the .455 inch round, sending the bullet powering up through his brain and out into the cold early morning air around him.

Chapter Two

To Caspasian, it seemed as if the hour hand was cemented to the clock face. The minute hand was dragging lead weights. For the umpteenth time that morning he glanced up from his desk, cross-checked with his own watch, and let out a sigh from the depths of his considerable impatience. He ran his fingers through his sun-bleached sandy hair that, over the years, many a senior officer had complained was too long. Forlornly he scanned the array of papers spread out before him, and then looked up at the clock again.

'Come on, for God's sake,' he muttered bitterly.

'I heard that, sir.'

He turned in his chair at the sound of the bemused voice. The Chief Clerk, plump, pink-faced and looking as if he had stepped into uniform for the first ever time that morning, ambled towards him and tossed a fresh sheaf of papers into the tray at the top left-hand corner of Caspasian's desk.

'Little present from the boys on the third floor, sir.'

'Quartering?'

The Chief Clerk gave an exaggerated smile. 'I'm impressed. You'll get the hang of HQ life in no time at all.' He turned away, putting some distance between himself and Caspasian before adding, 'I can see you're a natural here.'

Caspasian glowered at the man's retreating back. 'One day, Chief, you'll find yourself posted to the real army, and when you do, I hope I'm around to show you the ropes.'

'You're all heart, sir. But you won't ever catch me poncing about with a pack and rifle. In any case, this is the real army. I would have thought you'd have learned that by now. This is where the generals are made.' He turned in the doorway, considering himself safe. 'Not out there.' He waved a fistful of files at the latest Captain to find himself with a job on the Headquarters Staff and at his mercy. 'Paper. That's what makes a real soldier. Paper. You'd do well to remember that, sir.'

Chortling with delight, the Chief Clerk darted aside as the sheaf he had just deposited on Caspasian's desk slammed against the wall beside him, the slender pink ribbon bursting open, freeing the papers inside to flutter down in a confused jumble.

'Now, sir, it's no use blaming the messenger.' He bent down to gather them up. 'Quartering wants an Ops response to the new barracks building plan by close of play this afternoon.'

'Well they won't bloody get it. Not from me, at least.'

The Chief Clerk raised an eyebrow.

'The Simla train goes in two hours' time,' Caspasian continued, 'and I'm going to be on it. My leave's got clearance from Colonel Readman and that's good enough for me.'

'What shall I tell Briggsy when they send him up to fetch your brief?'

Caspasian pushed back his chair, stretched out his long legs, and gripped the sides of his desk as if gauging whether or not he might be able to launch it out of the tall window opposite. 'You can tell him the plans raise certain issues which Ops needs to consider in greater depth.'

Clucking like a truculent hen the Chief Clerk went back to his office, his footsteps echoing down the marble flagstones of the empty corridor. Left to his own devices, Caspasian stood up and sauntered across to the window, sinking his hands deep in his pockets. He shook his head to clear it. Only weeks into his new posting and already he felt crushed by an invisible weight.

'Two years,' he said to himself. 'Two bloody years. What the hell was I thinking of to accept this bloody job?'

Rooted in the centre of the ceiling, a fan slapped the thick damp air with broad lethargic blades. Everything in the office, in the building, in Delhi, was stagnant. Caspasian could feel himself going mad. No, worse. He could feel his senses shutting down. Comfortably tall, he was lithe and fit, his muscles exercised by the hard life of an infantry regiment, and of all the infantry regiments in the Indian Army, the Gurkhas – to whom Caspasian belonged – were accepted as the finest.

He had recently found himself wondering what he most missed about regimental life. It certainly wasn't the Mess. That least of all. He avoided official functions whenever he possibly could, absenting himself on the slightest pretext. He hated the heavy joviality, the strictness of dress and form. All of it struck him as a complete sham. The Great War had burned all that out of him, leaving him unable to come to terms with it ever again. However, in the seven years since the Armistice, a new generation of young officers had appeared, men who had not endured the mud of Flanders or the blood and dust of Mesopotamia. For them the role of imperial policing sat easily with the rigid social structures of British life in imperial India, and they relished both. But then for them it was merely an exaggeration of the public-school existence that had spawned them.

By contrast, the young Caspasian had arrived at school in England from more tangled roots, sent from abroad by his grandfather to a country he had never known, to be educated alongside people with whom he had little in common. Without intention, he had acquired the stigma of exile while still a boy, and it had stuck to him like a shadow ever since. It wasn't surprising therefore that he found himself most missing the company of the Gurkha soldiers themselves, for it was amongst them that he had found his true regimental home, an exile amongst fellow exiles, they from their Himalayan homeland, Caspasian from the status expected of him by his peers. As one of the majors had once dared to put it, Caspasian simply wasn't their sort of chap.

What he most missed was being out in the hills on operations. That was where he felt most alive. For Caspasian there was nothing else like it. Out on a lonely patrol against the Pathans, watching the sun come up at daybreak, selecting a defensive position for the night, these were the things that had enabled him to remain involved in life once the war had destroyed his ability to lead a normal humdrum existence.

He leaned his forehead against the window pane and looked down into the gardens below. His natural expression was serious, meditative, as if wrestling with some conundrum, insoluble to others. It was less rigid than a frown, and was seen in its purest form when he was daydreaming – which was often – his pale blue eyes staring at nothing in particular with the sharpest, most penetrating focus. Casual acquaintances thought him rude. Those a little closer interpreted it as shyness. Both were wrong, but these two categories of people swept up everyone he knew these days. The slaughterhouse of the Western Front had taken care of the rest.

In a corner of the garden a labourer was shovelling earth from a towering pile into a small wheelbarrow. Whenever the barrow was full, the man would carefully lay down his long-handled shovel, grasp the handles of the barrow, wheel it painfully to the far side of the garden and empty the contents before returning to repeat the performance. He had been there at first light when Caspasian had arrived in the office to clear his desk before departing on leave. He was still there several hours later, the enormous pile barely reduced by his Herculean efforts.

'Damn this,' Caspasian said suddenly, turning on his heel and striding out of the office, plucking a large leather valise from beside his desk as he went. In the squash courts changing room on the ground floor he slipped out of his uniform, hanging it in his locker, putting on slacks and a loose shirt instead. Before closing his locker, he took a jacket and a battered felt hat from the peg, smacking the dust from both as he left the room and the building behind him.

An hour later he was sitting on the station platform, an island of calm now that he was away from the desk he had come to loathe. Waves of humanity lapped around him, leaving him untouched, regarding. Legs crossed, he felt relaxed, a well-worn copy of Arrian's *Campaigns of Alexander* lying open on his lap. The hat that he wore in preference to the more usual topee lay beside him on the bench, and each time he turned his head to watch the frantic comings and goings of the crowd that was proving more captivating than the battle of the river Granicus, he would reach up to mop fine beads of perspiration from his forehead.

For the first time since the rumour of the approaching train had swept along the platform, the sound of the whistle was heard in the distance. The effect on the already bustling crowd was electric, as if a machine gun had suddenly opened fire and was busily hosing the platform from end to end. A great cry arose and the packed mass of people flowed this way and that, pressing into each other, some surging forward, others struggling to the rear, all with arms laden with every manner of bundle, bag or baby.

Amidst this great cacophonous maelstrom Caspasian stretched out his legs and leaned back, hands behind his head, luxuriating in a stretch of pure ease until his joints cracked. He was out of the office and he was loving every minute of it. He liked India. He

18

liked it a lot, perhaps more than anywhere else on earth, and he had seen a great many places in his thirty years. It was so utterly different from England. It was not the rawness of life that attracted Caspasian; there was more than enough of that in the mill towns of England's north-west or the mining communities of the Midlands and Wales. Rather it was the response of the people to that rawness. There seemed to be an acceptance that, however unpleasant, it was appearance only. They could detect what lay behind. Whether or not they were deluding themselves Caspasian thought was irrelevant. The fact was that it gave them an immense inner strength and joy in life that he admired and envied. The inner strength he could match, having worked hard at it over the years. Joy, on the other hand, was another matter.

Of course, most of Caspasian's fellow countrymen were all too quick to point out that this spirituality, for want of a better word, also hamstrung the native population when it came to effecting change. That and the rigid Hindu caste system locked the country in a stasis that would take many years to shake off, although there were some emerging who were at least prepared to try.

He closed his book, slipped it into the side pocket of his valise, and stood up. He had no trouble seeing over the heads of the crowd. The train was now in sight, the engine belching steam into the fetid air, washing the pale blueness from the sky until it was colourless. The hot weather was on the way. Soon the station would be jammed with British wives and children off to the hill stations, leaving their husbands to the slavery of office life in near unendurable temperatures. The sun on the plains at those times struck like a physical blow, knocking the energy out of even the strongest man. Left to their own devices, men would have their servants drag their beds outside on to a verandah at night to sleep, but only in the early hours would it cool sufficiently to doze off. There would follow a short respite of peaceful slumber before the sunrise and a return of the ferocity. Beds would be taken back indoors where the air was still hot from the previous day.

Caspasian reached down for his hat but found it being offered to him by a small boy.

'Carry bag for ten annas, saheb!' he shouted above the noise.

Caspasian took the hat and put it on, pulling the brim low over his eyes. 'Five.'

The boy scowled and clutched the bag even tighter to him, although Caspasian was making no effort to retrieve it. 'Eight, saheb. My father is dead, my mother is blind, my sister is . . .'

'Yes, yes, I get the picture,' Caspasian chided. 'Your sister is probably crippled or a leper, and you're in debt to the moneylenders who are going to cut off your nose. Make it six and you've got a bargain.' Without waiting for the boy's answer he turned and strode away as best he could through the dense mass. The boy cursed and struggled after him, both hands tugging at the bag's handle.

Caspasian was the sort of person for whom people usually gave way. When he was in a hurry, he squared his broad shoulders and lowered his head like a big cat set to fight. One look at his eyes was cnough to make anyone in his way move themselves. An Indian station platform was another matter, for however much anyone might want to move, there was rarely anywhere to move to. In such a case therefore, Caspasian would dodge and weave like a boxer, rolling his shoulders as he slipped through a wall of packed bodies that had previously seemed impenetrable.

The train pulled into the station, the driver hanging from his cab, revelling in the sense of urgency created by an unnecessary series of piercing whistle blasts. The steam swirled and eddied, blinding everyone. Screams and shouts, laughs and cries climbed to a crescendo as Caspasian forced his way towards the carriage where the office transport clerk had reserved him a berth. After much pushing and shoving, he fought his way to the door, grasped the handle and swung himself up, being helped by the attendant. He glanced round and saw the boy miraculously close behind him, the large valise firmly in his grip. The attendant reached down and took it with one hand, raising the other ready to swipe the boy away as if he was a stray dog.

The boy looked up at Caspasian, shouting, 'Six annas, saheb! Our bargain. Six annas!' He held out his hand. He was met by a burst of invective from the carriage attendant. Caspasian dug into his pocket, pulled out a coin and tossed it to the boy who inspected it, ready to harangue him if it was not enough.

Instead his eyes widened. 'But this is a whole rupee?' he marvelled.

Caspasian shrugged. 'It's the smallest I've got. Take it or leave it.'

Before his benefactor could change his mind the boy turned and disappeared into the crowd. The attendant shook his head from side to side, looking at Caspasian with disapproval, but then brightened at the prospect of what his own reward might be.

'Come, saheb, I will show you to your berth. If you need anything on the journey just call me. My name is Krishna. I am at your service.'

He led the way down the narrow corridor and slid open one of the doors. Inside, one of the other four seats was already occupied by a well-dressed Indian gentleman, some years older than Caspasian. Caspasian took off his hat and nodded politely at the man who returned his greeting.

'Going all the way to Simla?' Caspasian enquired, surprising himself that he had bothered with such an unnecessary pleasantry.

The man smiled. 'If the engine gets us that far.'

'The driver's blown all the pressure on that damned whistle,' Caspasian said. 'Nearly deafened me.'

With his bag safely stowed on the shelf overhead, Caspasian settled himself for the journey, but a moment later there were shouts and curses in the corridor outside, the door slid open and a red-faced Englishman struggled in, followed by two porters both carrying at least two cases each.

'Damn your black blood, put the blasted cases up there!'

The porters, dripping rivulets of sweat after what had obviously been a long battle, tried to obey but Caspasian's valise and the single bag belonging to the Indian prevented it.

With barely a glance at either of them, the new arrival waved his hand at the offending luggage and shouted, 'Just bloody shift them out of the way.'

The porters glanced nervously at each other and started to carry out the orders.

'Leave the bags alone,' Caspasian said in perfect Hindi. The porters mumbled their apologies and turned to the other Englishman with helpless shrugs.

'What did you say?' the Englishman barked.

'I told them not to move my luggage,' Caspasian answered levelly, starting to leaf through the pages of his book.

'Who the blazes do you think you are countermanding my orders?' the man stammered, apoplectic.

'I'm not under your orders,' Caspasian said, slowly closing his book and placing it to one side as he felt his gorge rise.

'Do you know who I am?'

'I don't give a damn who you are,' Caspasian answered, his jaw setting like rock.

'How dare you!' The man looked Caspasian up and down, noting his shabby clothes. 'I suppose you're some damned box-wallah, are you?' He thrust past Caspasian, knocking his leg hard. He reached up and snatched at the handle of Caspasian's valise, muttering as he did so, 'Bloody shopkeeper.'

Before he could stop himself, Caspasian had fired his balled fist into the man's gut level with his eyes, little more than a jab but enough to empty the lungs of air. In the confinement of the carriage the man grunted and crumpled forward onto him. Caspasian caught him under the arms, pushed himself to his feet, and dropped his new burden heavily onto the seat opposite. The man gasped and wheezed, his eyes bulging and lips trying to form an expression of outrage.

The Indian gentleman shot to his feet. 'Gentlemen, please, I implore you! What are we? Beasts or men? Here . . .' He lifted his own case down and placed it at his feet. 'I think you'll find there's ample room for your luggage in the rack now.'

The man stared up at him, gasping, 'And you can bloody well get out too. This carriage is for Europeans only.'

The Indian's face tightened. 'I beg your pardon?'

'Ask the attendant. Europeans only. I specified it when I ordered my ticket.'

'I think you might find that a lot of things are changing nowadays,' the Indian answered as calmly as he could.

The man started to speak again but Caspasian leaned forward, grabbed him by the lapels and pulled him to his feet. 'That's it. I've had enough.'

'What are you doing?' the man stammered, struggling uselessly against Caspasian's iron grip.

'You're leaving the train.' Caspasian pulled him to his feet, swung him out of the compartment, down the corridor and with one mighty shove, propelled him out onto the platform. Only the press of people still attempting to board the train prevented the man from sprawling on the ground and by the time he had picked himself up, the train had started to move. He made one unsuccessful rush in an effort to climb back aboard but his own bags met him full in the

24

face, hurled down at him by Caspasian who stood framed in the doorway. As the train picked up speed and moved out of the station, the two men locked eyes, each imprinting the other's face on their memory.

When Caspasian returned to the compartment there was an embarrassed silence between himself and the Indian gentleman. As his blood cooled Caspasian felt the first twinges of remorse, not for having hit the fool, but for having lost his temper. It had got him into trouble before.

Eventually he said, 'I'm sorry. I apologise for my fellow countryman, and also for my own behaviour.' He forced a smile. 'I hope you don't think all Englishmen are like that.' He coughed, embarrassed, and added, '. . . like us, I mean.'

The Indian shook his head in consternation. 'I would like to think I am more broad-minded than that, but I think I'm still a little shocked. It's not every day that one sees a brawl between two of our imperial masters. Is it, Captain?'

Caspasian looked up in surprise. 'Is it that obvious?'

'That you are a Captain? Yes. And the parts that are not obvious,' the Indian said, gesturing to Caspasian's outfit, 'can be deduced with minimal exercise of logical reasoning. You should be flattered. It was a combination of your excellent Hindi and your general bearing that gave you away. At least to me.' He looked down at his clothes and brushed away some dust. 'You clearly fooled our friend however. What was the term he used? Box-wallah.' He smiled thoughtfully at Caspasian. 'That angered you, didn't it?'

Caspasian shrugged and changed the subject. 'Might I not be a Major?' he chided good naturedly.

'If you always react to insults like that I would imagine your behaviour has kept a Major's rank beyond you,' the Indian said with prescience. He smiled. 'We, on the other hand, have long become used to insults. In any case, you should be relieved,' he continued. 'We all grow old soon enough. Captain sounds somehow younger, less stodgy.' He stretched out his hand. 'My name is Rajesh Sivraj. How do you do?'

They shook hands. 'How do you do? Captain John Caspasian.'

'Of. . .?'

'The Twelfth Gurkhas.'

'I thought so,' the man said triumphantly. 'Either Gurkhas or Sikhs. I knew it.'

Caspasian shrugged modestly. 'Only the best.'

'So what calls you to Simla?'

'Some leave. Just a couple of weeks,' Caspasian answered. 'A bit of walking. Some fishing perhaps.'

'Joining your wife?'

'Not married.'

'Next furlough, I expect.'

Caspasian laughed, uneasy again at the turn of the conversation, starting to answer but then thinking better of it.

The Indian persevered. 'I hope you're not considering . . . what's that wonderful phrase? . . . the fishing fleet.'

'Not my type.' Caspasian had always found it a depressing spectacle, as every year before Christmas the P&O liners would arrive in Bombay with the latest crop of eligible young ladies from the homeland in search of equally eligible husbands. Staying with friends or relatives, they would attend all the dances and parties, the number of the unattached slowly dwindling until those remaining single boarded the liners in the spring. He winced whenever he heard anyone in the Mess refer to the 'returned empties'. It was an annual cattle market that he did his utmost to avoid, however much trouble it got him into with the Mess committee and the senior majors of the regiment.

He sat back and stared out of the window. The train had left the Delhi outskirts and was racing through the flat surrounding countryside heading northwards. His regiment was quartered far away in the west while he himself served out his sentence at the headquarters in Delhi.

He reached into his valise, took out the paper he had brought with him and started to read. Across from him, the Indian spluttered with disbelief. *'Young India*? Good heavens, I only made your acquaintance minutes ago and once again you have surprised me.'

Caspasian peered over the top, brow furrowed. 'Oh?'

'Do you always read Mr Gandhi's paper?'

'Whenever I can get it.' Caspasian smiled. 'It's none too popular in the Mess.'

'I dare say.' Mr Sivraj leaned forward, intrigued. 'And what do you think of his ideas?'

'Common sense really.'

'Well, I never!' Mr Sivraj laughed. 'You, a military

man, agreeing with the Mahatma's policy of non-violence.'

Caspasian lowered his paper, realising he was not going to be left in peace to read it. 'I was thinking more of his ideas on the caste system.'

'Ah. That is a little more difficult.'

'I thought it might be. I used to think the British were the most class-conscious race on earth until I came to India.'

Mr Sivraj nodded from side to side. 'You are right, of course. So is the Mahatma. All that will have to go in due course but it will take time.'

'How much time do you think you've got?'

Mr Sivraj sighed. 'Not enough, I expect. Your fellow countryman who we left behind on the platform probably thinks that the Raj will continue forever, but you and I both know that the end is coming.' He paused, and then asked as tactfully as he could, 'Did you serve in the Great War?'

Caspasian nodded.

'Well, then. You know that the old world has gone. Gone for good.' He brightened. 'Today everything is possible. The mid-twenties is an exciting time to be alive, is it not?'

Caspasian looked out at the Indian countryside pounding past the window. He rubbed his knuckles, but did not answer. He lay back his head, closed his eyes and pretended to sleep. Eventually, he did.

Colonel Readman was in his office when an orderly came to announce the arrival of his visitors.

'Shall I show them into your office, sir?'

'Yes, you'd better,' the Colonel said reluctantly. He had been listening to the noise of the city beyond the garden walls, pleasantly muted in the midday heat, and enjoying what little breath of air crept timidly through the open window. The punka turned steadily overhead, and everywhere on his desk and the surrounding tables a variety of weights held down piles of papers whose corners lifted rhythmically with each pass of the giant fan, like pinioned butterflies trapped on a collector's tray, not quite dead.

The clip of brisk booted feet echoed down the corridor and a moment later the orderly ushered in two men. One was in uniform, the other in a light-coloured suit. The Army officer saluted casually, a ritual for which he obviously had little time. He stepped forward, hand outstretched. 'Brigadier James Percival. Colonel Readman, isn't it?'

Colonel Readman stood quickly and took the proffered hand, trying not to wince as the senior officer ground his fingers in a vice-like shake, smiling coldly into his eyes as he did so.

'I believe you already know Sir Oswald Masterman of the Viceroy's office?'

The Colonel nodded. 'Of course. I haven't seen you in these parts for a couple of years, Oswald. How is Jean?'

They shook hands as Sir Oswald replied, 'Still trying to cultivate a decent rose out of Indian soil. Personally I think they all look the same.'

'Do give her my regards, won't you?'

'Of course. She'd be delighted if you'd call on us the next time you're in Simla. She's gone up early this year, something to do with . . .'

The Brigadier went across to one of the vacant tables and took a sheaf of papers from his briefcase, shuffling them unnecessarily to make the point.

Colonel Readman glanced across at the Brigadier's back. There was no excuse for rudeness, even from someone of the Brigadier's reputation. In his own department he was used to a certain deference. He did not care where Brigadier Percival had come from or what secret mission he was now engaged upon. The signal warning him of the party's arrival had been sparse in the extreme, simply requesting him to offer them every assistance. He was not fooled for one minute by the polite delicacy of the language. He had been a soldier for too many years not to recognise a direct order, in whatever language it was couched.

He bit back the rebuke, forcing a smile instead. 'So tell me, Brigadier, how can my staff and I be of assistance?'

The Brigadier handed him a typed sheet of paper. 'We have encountered a little problem. Something brewing in the tribal areas, I'm afraid. It's all detailed here. The main assistance will be handled by the commanding officer of the fort in Peshawar, but I had to see you before I left Delhi.' He smiled icily, flashing a row of white teeth.

Colonel Readman tried to return the smile but was aware that his own version was notably weaker. He was puzzled as to his role in the affair.

'Naturally, I will do anything required of me.' He glanced at Sir Oswald standing on the sidelines. 'Anything to assist the boys in Military Intelligence.'

The Brigadier blanched. 'Probyn's Horse, Colonel. On loan to Military Intelligence.'

It was on the Colonel's lips to say that James Percival looked remarkably like Probyn's Horse, and he stifled a titter at his own imagined witticism. 'I know, I know,' he said, gesturing to the insignia on the Brigadier's uniform. 'I was referring to your current employment only.' He looked from one to the other. 'Well,' he pressed, 'what can I do for you?'

'You have an officer working here under your command,' the Brigadier stated.

'Oh? Which one do you mean?'

'Captain John Caspasian,' the Brigadier continued.

For a moment Colonel Readman's mind was a complete blank. His department handled numerous weighty operational matters, and since learning of the Brigadier's impending arrival he had been wondering which of these he might be required to brief his guest upon.

'Caspasian, Colonel Readman?' the Brigadier prompted.

'Ah, the new staff Captain. What about him?' A frown suddenly creased the Colonel's brow. 'What's he done this time?' His expression darkened as he contemplated disciplinary hearings, courts-martial, Boards of Inquiry, scandal for the department. He had taken an instant dislike to the young man the moment he had set eyes on him. He had arrived with the reputation of a loner, the most damning label that could be attached to an officer. A fine operational record, it was true. Quite remarkable, in fact. But Colonel Readman had seen his sort before, not often, but enough to know he meant trouble. Goodness knows what he was doing at Army Headquarters in Delhi. Some well-meaning mentor had obviously persuaded the good Captain that the move would be sound for his future career. Not if Colonel Readman had anything to do with it.

The Brigadier and Sir Oswald swapped glances. 'He hasn't done anything,' the Brigadier continued. 'I want him.'

'Want Caspasian?' the Colonel stammered, incredulous. 'Whatever for? He's a staff officer, for God's sake! And the most junior in my department at that.'

The Brigadier paused a moment and then strode across to the wall map. 'A couple of weeks ago, a team of mine failed to return from an expedition into the tribal areas beyond Dir.' He slapped a rigid finger on the map and the Colonel noted that it was spot on the correct place, although the Brigadier had not seemed to look. 'They were carrying something of great importance to the Empire.'

'Why would anyone take anything of such great importance into the tribal areas in the first place?'

The Brigadier smiled indulgently. 'They didn't take it in. They were bringing it out. Or to be more precise, through.'

'From?'

The Brigadier frowned. He had hoped the Colonel would nod sagely and shut up. He knew the Colonel's reputation for being colourless but if at all possible he wanted to avoid snubbing the fellow. Colonel Readman might have been passed over for higher promotion and left to serve out his time before retirement to some flower-bordered cottage in the Home Counties, but right now James Percival needed the man's cooperation. He had the authority to give a direct order, but he would rather the Colonel's cooperation was given willingly.

'From Afghanistan,' he said, congratulating himself on the cleverness of his half-truth.

Pushing his luck still further the Colonel said, 'So you fear that these documents might have fallen into unfriendly hands?'

Brigadier Percival smiled broadly. 'Did I say they were documents?'

The Colonel shrugged. 'What else then?'

'You're right, of course. They were some papers that could prove embarrassing to His Majesty's administration here in India if they fell into the wrong hands.'

'From what you say, Brigadier, it sounds as though they already have done. Aren't you shutting the door after the horse has bolted?'

'Not at all. It is my belief that my team might have come up against a simple band of robbers. If so, they probably don't know the value of what they've captured.'

'There's no such thing.'

'I beg your pardon?'

'A simple band of robbers. No such thing. At least not in the areas you're talking of. The Pathans are the best mountain fighters in the world.' He smiled, congratulating himself on his display of knowledge. 'How else would they have managed to eliminate one of your teams?'

The Brigadier gritted his teeth. The last thing he wanted was a lecture from this fool on the merits of the Pathans. He might have spent a large part of his later service behind a desk, working his way rapidly up the promotion ladder, but in his younger days he had done his share of soldiering on the North-West Frontier. He knew a great deal more about the Pathans than Colonel bloody Readman.

Sir Oswald stepped forward, ever the diplomat. 'The Viceroy specifically told us to come here and see you, Colonel.'

The Colonel almost choked. 'You know I will render every assistance.' He frowned, perplexed. 'But what possible interest can the Viceroy have in a mere Captain?' He noted with irritation the smile that flickered between the Brigadier and Sir Oswald Masterman.

'All we need is Caspasian,' Sir Oswald said softly. 'Let us say that the Viceroy has a certain regard for this particular Captain. It probably won't have come to your notice that he is . . . how shall I put it? . . . unusual. The Viceroy . . .'

The Brigadier quickly cut in. 'So can we have Caspasian?'

The Colonel threw wide his arms. 'He's yours.'

'Excellent,' the Brigadier said with a sigh more of exasperation than relief. 'I have to find out exactly what happened and, most of all, I have to retrieve the lost papers. But a certain subtlety is required. Although we'll have a battalion-sized column on stand-by from Peshawar, that's not the ticket in this case. If at all possible we don't want to draw attention to ourselves. Quietly in and quietly out. A small hand-picked team should be able to do it. For that we need Caspasian.'

'Yes . . .' the Colonel stammered, '. . . but surely, if one team's already been eliminated . . .'

'We don't know that for certain,' the Brigadier cut in.

'Then why haven't they returned?'

'All right. We probably have to assume that they were all either killed or captured.'

'I sincerely hope for their sakes that they all died cleanly. Capture by the Pathans doesn't bear thinking about. So what's Caspasian's role to be in all this?'

'No one knows the tribal areas as he does,' the Brigadier said simply. 'You might not realise it, Colonel, as the Captain has only been on your staff for a few weeks, but he's got more experience of this type of operation than anyone else I know. And,' he added enigmatically, 'no one else has his special skills.'

'Skills?' the Colonel said, not really following the Brigadier's meaning at all. As Caspasian was only a Captain, the Colonel hadn't bothered to give more than a cursory glance to his confidential file. Caspasian's war record had briefly impressed him, but at the time there had been more pressing matters in the Colonel's in-tray.

There was a pause before the Brigadier ventured, 'Well? When will you be able to release him?'

The Colonel suddenly felt as if a thunderbolt had struck him. 'Oh my God,' he muttered.

'What is it?' Sir Oswald asked.

'I signed a leave pass for the fellow.' Colonel Readman stared at his visitors stupidly. 'The fellow's just gone on a spot of leave. He's going up to Simla, but where he is now, God only knows.'

The Brigadier scowled savagely as the Colonel

rushed out of the room calling for his Chief Clerk, returning a few moments later to say, 'The fellow left early, damn him. Otherwise he'd still be here. Taken the train, apparently.' He shrugged helplessly. 'His discipline isn't quite what I'm used to from captains.'

The Brigadier consulted his watch with mounting irritation. 'We can probably intercept him if we hurry.' He swiftly stuffed his papers back into his briefcase and, after saying the briefest of farewells, left the Colonel's office with Sir Oswald following in his wake.

When his guests had gone, the Colonel strolled across to the map and stared at it for a long time. It all looked so neat on paper, the tidy lines, the shaded areas, the careful lettering. He knew that some people said it could be the most unpleasant and terrifying hell on earth, but they were probably all exaggerating. What baffled him most however was why the Viceroy had chosen Caspasian for the job. At his initial interview Caspasian had struck the Colonel as surly, withdrawn and insolent. The man simply didn't know his place.

Colonel Readman sighed and turned his back on the map, reflecting as he looked at his busy desk that he had far more important things to deal with. The Brigadier and Caspasian could both go to hell for all he cared. In truth, he was glad to be rid of the young Captain. It would all come to no good. He was sure of it. The Pathans would see to that.

Chapter Three

An early mist lay above the trench line. Damp twists of it eddied down into the dugouts, freshening the stale air and coaxing tired lungs to breathe it in deeply. Men coughed and spat, their feet squelching on the duckboards beneath which a rank viscous liquid oozed. Caspasian turned his thoughts away from considering what the liquid might consist of. Exhausted, he glanced down the line of the trench. As far as he could see, soldiers were being assembled, shuffling into some semblance of order. It reminded Caspasian of cows being led to the milking sheds. Heads were down, feet moved mechanically, divorced from an operation of the conscious will. Sergeants and corporals dragooned them with quiet words, encouraging rather than goading, almost fond. They themselves struggled to keep awake. Not for long, Caspasian thought, not for long.

He checked his watch. Two minutes to go. An urgency had encroached upon the gathering. Somehow it quickened men's minds while leaving their limbs inert and leaden. Caspasian could see it through their eyes. That was where it most showed. Frightened, reddened eyes. In the eyes and in the fingers that fiddled with belt buckles, webbing straps, wrist watches, anything.

One minute to go. Caspasian felt he could reach out and touch the fear now. It had got in amongst them like a rat creeping into a dugout. It slithered between their wet clothes, stinking like the corpse-soaked earth. It took possession of them, one by one, and once again Caspasian was amazed by the silent fortitude with which each man met it. In a thousand breasts, up and down the line, ordinary men from ordinary places fought the most extraordinary and private of fights. In one man close by, it emanated in a muttered prayer. In another, a young farm lad, it found expression in a crude joke. To Caspasian both were holy.

The first whistle blast sounded from far to Caspasian's right, a thin reedy sound, ill-suited as a signal for what he knew was to come. It was taken up by a score of others throughout the assembled ranks. Caspasian went to put his own whistle to his lips but stopped. He glanced to left and right and found everyone's eyes upon him. He smiled. What the hell was the point? Everyone knew what they were expected to do. Why play the bloody game? Next to him his sergeant smiled back.

'Best be off then, sir,' he said.

'Right.' Caspasian grasped the wooden ladder in front of him and hoisted himself up the rungs. It felt like climbing into the attic of a haunted house. Like sticking your head into the vacant slot of a guillotine.

Over the rim of sandbagged earth, visibility was down to a matter of yards. Caspasian smiled. It was better than any smoke screen the gunners could have arranged. With luck it would shield them all the way across no-man's-land. But the whistles that had sent them over the top had also alerted the enemy and they had gone barely a dozen yards before the German machine guns opened fire. Although the machine gunners were unable to see the advancing infantry they knew exactly how they would be coming. Their guns had been laid on fixed lines, pre-adjusted in good visibility, and the moment the murderous fire started, all around Caspasian men began to fall.

Patrols had been out in the night to mark clear lanes through the wire, but in the fog their markers were lost and men floundered about, wandering up and down the dense mass of wire, searching for the breaches.

'Don't bunch!' Caspasian yelled above the noise. He had come upon a group of a dozen men huddled next to the wire. Two of them were trying to tread it flat and a gaggle of followers had gathered behind them.

'Spread out and keep low,' Caspasian said, grabbing hold of one of them and pushing the man aside. Bewildered eyes turned on him. Some of them edged away, but they were reluctant to leave the company of fellow human beings, preferring death with comrades rather than in the loneliness of the mist.

Moving along the wire, Caspasian found one of the cleared lanes, but there was no one with him now. Alone he passed through, holding his Webley revolver tightly in his fist. The air crackled with bullets, whipping and snapping past him. He felt as if every machine gunner along the German line was aiming at the centre of his chest and stomach. He could feel his guts waiting to burst out of his tunic and involuntarily moved his free hand to cover his buttons. Every instinct commanded him to curl into the tightest of balls and hug himself out of existence.

Instead he sidled forward, leaning into the unseen lines of fire as into a stiff wind. Suddenly, in front of him, the mist parted, and staggering back towards the British lines he saw a man heading right for him. He had lost his rifle and as he stumbled he rolled his eyes. He opened his mouth like a fish and Caspasian realised the man was unable to breathe. He drew closer. Caspasian made to go towards him but the man was completely unaware of his presence. He was blind.

'Gas Gas Gas!' The words exploded from Caspasian as he spun round and ran back the way he had come. When he had gone a dozen paces he crouched down and tore at the haversack around his neck. He pulled out the small box respirator, knocked off his steel helmet and pulled the mask over his face. He held his breath all the while and clenched his eyes tight shut, his fingers working from long hours of practice.

He spat out the remnants of air in his lungs and gasped through the mask, fighting the inclination to retch at the fetid mustiness. Someone bumped into him and he turned to find the man's hands working across his back, trying to establish if he was living or dead. Through the choked gurgles Caspasian could just make out the words, 'Help me.'

'Oh, Christ. Jesus Christ,' Caspasian muttered to himself. He stood and took the man by the shoulders, guiding him back towards their own line, but they had only gone a few yards when the man's legs gave way and he sank to the ground. Caspasian hoisted him over his shoulder and weaved his way through the wire and bodies. There were a lot of them now. As the mist lifted he could see the survivors and the walking wounded streaming back to the British lines right across no-man's-land. Some with leg or belly wounds dragged themselves through the mud. The attack had failed, just like the one before it and just like the one before that.

With a superhuman effort he staggered the final yards and slithered over the lip of the trench, landing in a heap on the duckboards in the bottom. A huge rat, startled by his sudden arrival scuttled away, disappearing down into one of the dugouts. It held something fiercely in its yellow teeth. It looked like an eye. Caspasian was disoriented, unable to recognise where he had arrived back in the trenches. Someone was bending over him, his face obscured by a gas mask.

'I wouldn't bother about him, sir,' the figure said, pointing to the body Caspasian had carried back from no-man's-land. 'He's a goner.'

Caspasian turned to look, squinting through the misted eye-pieces of his respirator, and felt himself go cold. The man he had brought back had changed and in his place lay another. Caspasian rubbed with his thumbs at the opaque eye-pieces, smudging aside the sweat and grease. He stumbled back, falling against the rear wall of the trench as he did so. The face on the body was his own.

From behind him, his companion laughed. Caspasian turned and looked up at him. The man reached down, grasped Caspasian's mask and wrenched it off his head, his laughter soaring as he did so. Caspasian felt his lungs fill with the noxious fumes. His fingers scrabbled at his throat to keep them out but they had already seeped into his lungs and corrupted them. Fire burned inside him and he felt as if he was turning inside out, as if someone had placed thumbs behind his eyes and was popping them from the sockets.

'Why?' Caspasian gasped, fighting for each breath.

The man's laughter stopped as abruptly as it had begun. He reached up and removed his own mask and Caspasian found himself staring into the scarred and tortured face of the gassed man. His eyes were no longer blind but gazed intently at Caspasian.

'You would be Lazarus,' he said bitterly, as if that should be explanation enough. 'You would rise from the dead,' he said, gesturing at the surrounding landscape of filth and horror, 'for this.' He thrust his face into Caspasian's, eyes hard as flint boring into him, breath stinking of the grave. 'Then let's see you try. Come forth, Lazarus. Let's see you live.'

No one knew when the mountain fortress had been built, or by whom. It had always been there, back to the furthest link in the necklace of generations, present in the earliest tales handed down ever after. Like the tales, it had grown with time, being added to by every occupant, a new wing, a tower, an extension to the rampart. Piece by piece it had grown, as if devouring the rock that bore it, consuming and then transmuting it into some new fabrication of itself.

One legend held that renegade mercenaries from the army of Alexander the Great had assembled the first fortification, recognising the defensive strength of the strategic position, astride a ridge dividing two valleys. From the heights they had supposedly observed their war-weary comrades pass by on the return journey to Greece, their eastwards expansion having been quenched in the vastness of the Indian sub-continent, beyond which, they had believed, the edge of the world tipped into an all-encircling ocean.

Thereafter conquerors, bandits, warlords, all had played their part, culminating at last in the latest occupant, Prince Mahsud of Beshandu. Standing at the window of his bed chamber, he looked down from the tower at the battlements beneath him. It was night, and the moon's glow stretched back the crenellations into long shadows, like the strings of so many bows drawn taut and ready to fire.

From the dark depths of the room came a soft moan. Prince Mahsud turned towards the bed where the woman lay sleeping. He frowned. She had been good. Very good. He knew what his late father would now have done. He would have given her to one of his commanders as a reward, but then his father had been like that. A bastard. For himself he was not sure what to do. His Oxford-educated mind conflicted sharply with his inherited qualities, diluting the ruthlessness to something more akin to savage petulance. He was learning however. The old temper, restrained whilst a boy and under his father's domineering shadow, was fast returning.

His hair was neatly groomed. He had tried growing it longer since his return from England in an effort to fit in better with his new surroundings but he had felt it becoming scruffy and had it trimmed back again. A caravan that had passed the previous week had made a gift to him of some precious oils as a tiny part of the tribute he had exacted in return for an untroubled passage. He had used some on his hair and the perfume pleased him greatly as he ran his fingers through it, smelling the scent with his aquiline nose like a fox sniffing the night.

Before stepping up to the window he had slipped into an ankle-length silk robe that had come from an earlier caravan. In that case the tribute had been proffered less willingly. His father would have left the sides of the track decorated with the skulls of the menfolk until pecked clean by vulture and crow. Mahsud had shrunk from such bestiality however, although at the insistence of his subordinate commanders he had allowed the leaders to be mutilated before being released. He had declined the offer to carry out the sentence himself.

He was fairly certain that the woman now in his bed had also come into his possession along with that last caravan, but it was all very confusing, ruling over a medieval fiefdom with a twentieth-century sensibility. He wondered if he would ever feel fully at home again. It would probably take time and he had plenty of that. Unfortunately. Now that he had succeeded to his father's position he would be expected to remain in this miserable wilderness until death in one guise or another caught up with him. He shuddered at the thought. If nothing more dramatic than old age was to be his final lot then he could expect to wither in this mountain fastness for decades to come. There was one hope however. On that he was prepared to stake everything.

The woman murmured something in her sleep. Mahsud glanced at her again, reflecting that it would indeed have been a great pity if she had fallen into his father's hands, to end up littering the roadside or else being passed from commander to commander until ending up as another tribal whore. He allowed his imagination to wander momentarily, picturing as he did so the way she would have struggled as his father's men took her. Doubtless she would have screamed. Writhed.

Beneath his gown Mahsud felt himself stirring, but his excitement was cut short by the sound of footsteps. Someone was climbing the long spiral staircase that led to the bed chamber door. They were taking the stone steps two at a time and Mahsud wondered what urgency so emboldened the messenger as to disturb him at such an hour. The man paused behind the door, listening, and then knocked lightly. Mahsud straightened his robe, fastening the cord tight about his waist before marching to the door, unbolting and swinging it open.

The messenger took a step backwards, caught unawares by his Prince's quick response.

'Well? What is it?' Mahsud snapped irritably.

'We have had word of the stone, my lord. The Eye of the Storm.'

Mahsud darted forward and grabbed the man's sheepskin jerkin, drawing him closer as his father would have done. He saw the alarm and fear in the man's eyes and almost released him but checked himself in time, tightening his grip. It would not do to have his men thinking he was soft. 'You have it?'

'We will have, my lord.'

Mahsud's temper flared and he shoved the man away, muttering curses at his followers' stupidity. 'Why have you not got it?' he whined. 'I will have it! I will have the stone!' The base of his fist slammed into the door, making it reverberate on its hinges. He liked the sound it made and the feeling of authority it gave him. On the bed the woman awoke and called out in terror, gathering the bed clothes to her when she saw the messenger standing in the doorway, his outline cast into the room by the light of the burning torch fastened to the wall behind him. Mahsud waved a comforting hand at her. She misinterpreted it as a command to leave and slid her legs off the side of the bed.

Mahsud sighed. 'I meant for you to stay!' he called impatiently. Everyone was so obtuse here. He turned back to the messenger. He took a deep breath and gathered himself before saying, 'What happened?'

'We set the ambush just as you said, my lord. Everything was in place. Our best men. The infidels wouldn't have stood a chance. We would have had them.' He closed his fist to illustrate the intended outcome.

'And?' Mahsud said bitterly, loathing the man as much for his shabbiness as for his failure to bear good news.

The messenger opened his arms wide. 'They never came.' He shook his head in consternation. 'We had covered every possible route, a network of am-bushes. A spider's web. There was . . .'

'Then what happened? Where are they?' Mahsud said, not bothering to hide his exasperation.

'One of our patrols heard firing.' He screwed his eyes tight in an effort to report precisely what he had been told. 'Rifles and a pistol. By the time our men got there it was all over. The stone had gone. All they found was the body of one soldier. It had been mutilated but it was a British infidel all right.'

Mahsud felt the anger surging through him like molten lead. He clenched and unclenched his fists, turning this way and that as he paced the room.

'Who has my stone?' he hissed, his voice barely audible.

'We are not sure, my lord, but we think it must have been bandits.'

'Bandits?' Mahsud stared wide-eyed. 'Operating in my father's . . . in my territory? Without my permission?' He was incredulous, alarmed at the ramifications. 'I will have every one of them,' he said, his voice rising with his indignation. 'Do they think that now my father is dead they can do as they please? Do they think I am not as strong as my father? I'll show them. If they want a demonstration I'll give them one. I will take their village and raze it to the ground. My father would have slaughtered every man, woman and child. He would have burnt their cattle and salted their fields until nothing grew there for a generation! Did they think I would not do the same?' His voice started to crack and he reined himself in.

He spun back to the door where the messenger cowered. He shot a pointing finger at him. 'Find them. Whoever they are. The British were to have been mine.' He held out his open hand, palm upwards, the taut curled fingers quivering. 'The stone should have been lying here by now. Here!'

A thought suddenly occurred to him, filling him with horror, a thought more terrible even than the notion of someone else temporarily possessing the precious stone. 'If they have damaged it . . . if they have . . . lost it,' he said in a whisper, as if uttering the word aloud might be sufficient to bring about the event itself, '. . . I will ensure they are all taken alive.' He drew himself up to his full height, calming himself, ordering his thoughts. 'And then they will see what kind of man I am. It will take them many, many days to die.' He turned to the messenger and added in a moment of inspiration, 'and one in every ten of my ambush parties will join them.' To himself he said, 'That at least is one thing my father did teach me. How to suffer at great length.'

Prince Mahsud folded his arms across his chest, calming after the unexpected rage. The drama of it had excited him. Almost pleasantly he concluded, 'Go now. Pass the word. Find the perpetrators of this crime and find the stone and you will avoid all this unnecessary suffering.'

The messenger disappeared as if conjured out of sight, cascading down the spiral steps and out into the courtyard far below where his steaming horse still waited. When the door was closed and fastened Mahsud marched slowly back to the window. The moonlight had lost its beauty for him now. The night had become a vast emptiness, an inestimable yearning.

A noise from the bed reminded him of the woman. She was putting on her clothes.

'What are you doing?' he asked soothingly.

She shrugged and lay back on the gathered pillows. Mahsud walked across to her, smiling. At least she was still beautiful, he thought.

She returned his smile nervously. She had accustomed herself to him since capture. He had treated her well which had surprised her. But then she had earned it. She knew that he liked her. She had learned quickly how to delight her new master.

He sat heavily down on the edge of the bed. The woman sidled up to him. She reached up a hand and stroked his hair, brushing a wisp back from his face. Tenderly she kissed his cheek, noting that he probably only needed to shave every other day. He tipped back his face and sighed.

With an assurance born of practice, the woman slid her hands beneath his robe and parted it, worrying free the knot in the waist cord. She wondered at the absence of muscle. His belly was softer even than her own. He was so unlike her late husband. He had been a cruel man. With the Prince she was not sure. She was surprised how much she had minded when she had watched, all those weeks ago, as the Prince's men had severed her husband's hands from his lean, hard arms. Death had followed, although it had not been intended. She supposed she had been fearful for her own fate at the time, but the Prince had quickly noticed her. She had been washed and groomed and then delivered to his household where she had remained ever since, his favourite. First amongst the many.

Mahsud stirred. His eyes were shut and she knew he was waiting. She ran her palms across the pale mound of his stomach, descending ever lower until she took him in her hand, teasing him until he was ready.

She let slip the gown with which she had covered herself when the arrival of the messenger had woken her. She watched as Prince Mahsud opened his eyes and turned towards her, gazing at her breasts and belly. She smiled, and gently eased herself on top of him, wriggling into place.

Her movements were slow and tender, ministering expertly to Mahsud's rising excitement. She felt his hands tighten about her waist, the fingers digging into her flesh. Looking down at him, she marvelled that she could master him so easily, if only for so brief a span of time. She knew that her life hung by a thread. She had heard the stories about some of her predecessors seized by the Prince's father, stories told to her with evil relish by those who envied her, those who had either long since passed from grace, or who wished to usurp her position.

She knew Prince Mahsud cared little for her, but only for what she could do for him night after night. She nevertheless dreamed that, given time, she might somehow become more to him. She would kill anyone who threatened her relationship with him.

Chapter Four

The train had picked up a good speed and was pounding across the countryside. Caspasian had walked down the carriage corridor and was standing at the door leaning out of the window. He had gone there immediately upon waking, pushing past the dozing Mr Sivraj, careful not to disturb him. He wanted to be on his own.

The gassed man. How many times had Caspasian seen him? He had lost count. He cropped up every few months, stayed for several nights and then as suddenly took his leave, exiting Caspasian's dreams with the mystery of a Tarot figure. Caspasian had wrestled with him since his first appearance in a convalescence home shortly after the Armistice. He had heard the name Lazarus before as well. It was highly appropriate. The man risen from the dead. As he recovered from his injuries in the English south coast resort, Caspasian had surprised the nurses by asking for a Bible. He had turned up the passage in the Gospel of St John after a search through the unfamiliar pages, and had read it for the first time since leaving boarding school and the compulsory scripture classes he had endured there.

Lazarus had been a stinking corpse, dead for four

days. Caspasian well knew how a body could smell after such a length of time. Like Lazarus, he too felt as if he had been called forth from a tomb. He had survived the war. Four years to Lazarus' four days. What was the difference? Death was death. The problem was to cleanse himself of the stink. The body could be scrubbed. Bones would mend. Wounds would scar over. But what of the spirit?

He thrust his head and shoulders clean out of the window. The rush of air hit him full in the face. He closed his eyes and mouth and luxuriated in the buffeting it gave him. He could feel his whole head shuddering on his shoulders. He opened his mouth and breathed in the world. Christ but he was alive!

In the moment of that thought came others. A sea of faces rose up to meet him, the vast host of the unnumbered dead. They paraded out of no-man's-land, rank upon rank, officers and men, men and boys. One of the doctors at the home had tried to help by explaining to him that feelings of guilt were natural.

'Guilt? What for?' Caspasian had asked in surprise.

The doctor had been abashed, not having expected to have his glib explanation put to the test of Caspasian's scrutiny.

'Well . . . you feel guilty for having survived when others didn't.'

Caspasian had stared at the man dumbstruck. He had nodded thoughtfully at the time but had woken later that night shaking his head with wonder. What a stupid notion! He felt lucky, whatever that was. He felt immense grief at the enormous waste of life. But guilty? Not in the least. It was more likely the doctor who felt guilty for being unable to explain away something which could not be so easily dismissed. How easy, to unload the crippling effects of battle-shock back on to the victims as if it resulted from some defect within themselves. Sure enough, Caspasian had met many men who would never again come to terms with ordinary postwar civilian life. In a way he was one of them. But in all of their misery, confusion and loss, he had never once encountered guilt. Regret, perhaps, at not having died, but not guilt. He encountered regret in several old soldiers.

He remembered one he had come across two years after the end of the war. The poor wretch had been selling matches outside a music hall. His clothes were little more than rags, and on his chest the row of campaign medals hung askew. Caspasian had sat in the gutter next to the fellow, ignoring the disapproving glances of the passers-by, and heard him out. The telling of his tale had been obscured by cheap alcohol but Caspasian well remembered the man hanging his head when he had finished and saying, 'I wish I'd bloody copped it. I do.'

Caspasian had said something that instantly sounded trite and patronising, something about bearing up and muddling through. The man had looked at him and smiled, a smile of deep and endless sorrow. 'My brother died on the first day of the Somme,' he said. 'Mother put his photograph in the window with pride. It broke her heart but she was still proud.' He looked away, shame clouding his vision. 'She won't even speak to me now. I mean, look at me.'

He looked at Caspasian again. 'What she doesn't realise is, I died too.' He slapped his chest. 'There's more than just this to kill, you know.'

Now, a handful of years and several thousand miles further on, Caspasian opened his eyes and wondered at the maelstrom he carried inside him. India bolted past him, village after village snatched away, and the huge plains and rivers filling the space in between. He knew that he had reached a stage in life when most men would be finding a kind of peace. What he had discovered on the other hand, was that for him there would never be any peace. The war had set him running, and his feet did not know how to stop.

'Captain?' a voice prompted from behind.

He turned without pulling his shoulders back inside the window. Mr Sivraj was watching him, concerned.

'Are you all right?'

Caspasian grinned from ear to ear. 'Just fine,' he answered. 'Just fine, thank you.'

'Are you coming to sit down?'

'On the contrary,' Caspasian said. 'I'm going to sit on the roof.'

Before Mr Sivraj could stop him, Caspasian had opened the door and swung out of the carriage. Holding fast to the long brass handle, he dangled in mid-air. 'Come with me.'

'Good heavens! Captain, come in immediately. I implore you.'

'My name is Caspasian,' Caspasian shouted into the wind. 'John bloody Caspasian!' He grinned at Mr Sivraj. 'I have a name, you see.'

To his surprise Mr Sivraj smiled back at him. 'I don't think I'm going to be allowed to forget that.' He bent down and tucked the bottom of his trousers into his socks. 'Riding on the tops of trains is really only for Indians. I'm not sure you're allowed.'

'Just let them bloody stop me.'

Caspasian hauled himself upwards, planting his feet carefully as he scaled the side of the speeding carriage. When he had a good purchase on the roof, he stretched down for Mr Sivraj. 'Give me your hand.'

Clucking at his own folly, Mr Sivraj clambered up after him until the two of them collapsed onto the roof.

'This way,' Caspasian said. He got up and, walking at a crouch, led the way to the front of the carriage where half a dozen people were already firmly seated, clinging to bundles and cases. When they saw the new arrivals they grinned and shuffled aside to make room. Caspasian and Mr Sivraj settled themselves on the roof and stared at the speeding countryside around them.

'That man you ejected from the train,' Mr Sivraj shouted in Caspasian's ear. 'I don't think you would catch him riding up here on the roof.'

'More's the pity for him,' Caspasian shouted back. He gazed around at the endless rolling plain. A group of children beside a well squinted up at them from beneath shading hands and waved frantically when they saw Caspasian on the roof. He waved back with both hands, losing his balance before Mr Sivraj grabbed his shoulders and steadied him. Mr Sivraj chuckled. 'If only more Englishmen took the trouble to travel by roof, I think they would have a much better understanding of the country they try so hard to rule.'

'But just think of it, you might never get rid of us then.'

'True, that is very true,' Mr Sivraj conceded. 'As it is I feel somehow we will have to host you for some years yet.'

Caspasian inhaled deeply, holding the air in his lungs before release. 'I most certainly hope so.'

Ali had always been poor. Like his father before him, he was of no account in the village. He participated in the cattle raids and on one of them many years ago he had even managed to carry off a woman and keep her, the mother of his three children. It had been part of a blood feud between one of the tribal elders and a man in the other village. Ali had gone along and played his part as was expected of him. It had been a good night's work. He had personally slain two of the other tribe's warriors, cutting their throats before looting their belongings.

It had been in the hut of one of them that he had found the woman hiding. He had dragged her out and as he had liked the look of her, he had taken her back to his village with him at the end of the raid. A number of the young men had acquired wives that night in a similar fashion. Their children now ran and played in the dirt outside. A good night's work indeed.

There was only one other to compare with it. The whole village was still talking of it, though quietly. It could not be kept secret in the hills forever, but for now the arrival in their midst of the strange painted stone had been cause of heated discussion amongst the elders. Quite simply, they were unsure what to do with it. Similarly, no one could imagine what the British soldiers had been doing with it, fighting over it to the point of death. They had died well, especially the last one who had played such a trick on old Rasa. The old man would never live it down. The youngsters ribbed him about it mercilessly every day, darting at him as he passed by pretending to snatch his revolver from him. He would probably have to kill one of them soon. That alone would stop the horseplay. He would have to choose the man carefully though if he wanted to avoid a blood feud.

Being infidels the British soldiers had had no compunction about defacing the object. They had chipped away some flakes of paint and, if uninterrupted, would undoubtedly have stripped it bare. There was obviously a stone of great value underneath, probably a diamond, but that was where the dilemma arose, for although it was of more value than the tribe could even imagine, most of the elders were agreed that they should exercise caution. Each face of the stone was painted with a strange scene and appeared to be of religious significance. One of the elders thought he recognised the story as one that his grandfather had told him many years before, and he was contemplating sending word to someone he knew to see whether this could be confirmed.

All of this had set Ali thinking. He had not been able to sleep ever since the idea had occurred to him. Why should he always remain unnoticed and poor?

Everyone thought him stupid. He received respect from no one. Even his wife, once she had become accustomed to the ways of her new tribe, had lost her respect for him. Beatings did nothing to restore it.

Well all of that was about to change. The whole lot of them could burn in hell. For once in his life he would take decisive action all by himself. He would do something without an order from an elder, and he would do it for himself. He would steal the painted stone. The trick however was to get into the house where it was lodged, take it, and make good his escape.

The stone, still in the haversack of the British soldier, had been placed in the bed chamber on the upper floor of Najaf Kasim's house, the elder who wanted to send word to his relative and enquire about the stone. But that evening there was to be a marriage celebration which would be attended by the entire village on the far side, away from Kasim's house. At the very most, there would be no more than one guard, if that.

When the allotted hour came, Ali made his way along with the rest of the village to the wedding feast.

For the first two hours of the celebration he made a special effort to be seen by as many people as possible, ensuring that he would be remembered as having been present. Even after the discovery of the theft, it could be some time before anyone connected him to it. Every hour would count in his favour.

It was at the height of the celebration that he managed to slip away, moving off and heading silently up the hill in the direction of Kasim's house.

Eventually, there it was, standing like a low squat fortress tower before him, one of the most impressive houses in the village. Again Ali felt a shot of envy bolt through him, spurring him across the last few yards to the entrance.

'Ali? Is that you? Where are you going?'

The voice cut through him like a scythe. He spun to the side from where it had come and saw Kasim's old mother sitting in the shadows looking suspiciously up at him. The ancient harridan spat thickly into the dirt, less to clear her wrinkled throat than to express her opinion of the man before her.

'What brings you to my son's house? Has he sent you for something?' She tilted her head to one side, eyeing him.

It was too late. Ali saw that. He had come this far. It would already be difficult to explain his presence at Kasim's front door. So, tightening his stomach muscles and mustering his resolve, he walked towards her, grinning broadly.

'Can I escort you back to the party?' he said pleasantly, one hand slipping inside his jacket. 'Or perhaps your son is here?'

'No. I was tired. I came alone . . .' the old woman answered, realising her fatal mistake the next second when she saw the stone cold look in Ali's eyes and the glint of the dagger's blade as it slid from his jacket.

'Then we shall have to make certain that this raddled old hen never crows again, won't we?' Ali darted the last two yards and sunk the knife deep beneath her left breast, going for the heart. As he lunged, he put the weight of his body behind the thrust. The old woman gasped, her eyes bulging, locking on his. A fist like a walnut came up at him but he knocked it aside with ease, twisting the blade until the breath wheezed from between her toothless gums, a gobbet of spittle dribbling down her chin.

He pulled out the knife and watched as she sank into an even smaller heap, her head dropping forward on to her sunken chest, making her look as if she was asleep. Ali was breathing heavily now, the understanding of what he had just done sinking into him. For a moment he felt as if he might be overwhelmed by panic, but he steeled himself and ran into the house.

He found the stairs and went quickly up to the bedroom. And there it was, the same canvas bag that Ali had seen that night when the British soldier had shot himself. A small oil lamp burned limply in one corner of the room, casting eerie shadows into the corners. Ali swallowed hard. He reached for the bag and lifted it off the nail.

It was surprisingly light and for a moment he was terror stricken that the stone might be hidden elsewhere. He fumbled with the buckle and pulled open the flap and to his immense relief saw the bundle lying there, safe and sound. Thinking it only prudent to check that the stone was still inside the cloth, Ali sat down on the side of the bed and delicately unwrapped the soft velvet, feeling his heart pound as he did so. A moment later there it was, the painted stone.

He picked it up, turning it over in his hand. Now

that he held it he wondered what all the fuss was about. It was not as big as some gems he had seen, and the pictures showed scenes that he found rather boring. There was an old man walking with a stick beside a river. In another, he was holding up both hands to the skies. Another showed his face, and as Ali squinted at it, turning it towards the pale yellow flame of the lamp, he felt his heart go cold. The man had only one eye. It was extraordinary.

As he focused on it, staring hard at the face, Ali became aware that the fingers of his hand where he held the stone were wet. He cursed Kasim's mother under his breath. He thought he had wiped her blood from his hands but obviously he had missed some. He shifted the stone to the other hand and rubbed his fingers on his trouser leg to dry them. It was surprisingly hot in the room. Kasim had probably left a fire downstairs for a mug of tea when he returned. Ali wiped his forehead. Beads of sweat fell into his eyes. He wiped them away, rubbing his eyes quickly. He would have to be going.

He put the stone carefully back on the velvet, but then discovered that his other hand was now wet. He looked at it puzzled. He wiped it on his chest, then ran his fingers through his hair. Again he rubbed his eyes. His cheeks and chin were itching and he rubbed them too.

It was only when he stood up that Ali realised that his skin was burning. It was as if he had put his hands in a liquid of crushed chilies, but much, much worse. He darted across to the lamp, picked it up and brought it across to the bed so he could inspect the stone more closely. In the ghostly light he could see that the liquid was not blood at all, but seemed to be coming from the stone itself. A few drops of the thick oily substance had oozed from the place where the infidels had chipped away at the paint. It was almost as if the stone was weeping.

The sudden thought of it sent a shock of terror through Ali the like of which he had never felt before. He backed away from the bed, starting to shake, his fear taking full hold of him.

'Forgive me,' he mumbled. 'Forgive me, whatever you are. Whoever you are.'

His skin felt as if it was on fire, but worse, for his eyes had started to smart and again he thought of the times when he had accidentally wiped them after eating raw chilies. But this was a pain that seemed to have no end. It intensified with every second. He bit down hard on his lip to stop himself from crying out. Water. He had to find water.

Finding it ever more difficult to keep his eyes open, he stumbled downstairs and hunted for a pitcher, finding one at last beside the hearth. There was barely a cupful in the bottom but even so he upended it, pouring the liquid over his face. That was when the fire struck him with full force. As the water combined with the tears of the stone, it frothed and fizzed, spreading across his skin and running down inside his shirt and over his chest. Ali threw back his head and screamed, his hands scrabbling at his flesh to try and tear the pain away from him.

He looked down at his hands and saw a mass of blisters forming. He staggered towards the doorway, screaming with all the power of his lungs. In his desperation he scrabbled inside his jacket for his knife. The pain was too much to bear. He would have to turn his weapon upon himself. Like the British soldier. He would have to take the same way out. Inside his jacket his fingers encountered only the same blisters, growing like mushrooms where the water had carried the tears of the stone.

It was several minutes before anyone heard his screams. By the time the first men arrived on the scene Ali was gabbling incoherently, mad with the agony, and no one could recognise him. Then someone found the body of Kasim's mother. Kasim was summoned and when he saw her prone form, he fell on the ground at her feet and wept, great sobs wracking his chest.

Ali had fallen silent by the time Kasim was helped to his feet. Someone had recognised Ali's clothing and identified the hideously disfigured human shape as him. The stone had been found, moist on its cloth, a pungent smell filling the house, driving people away, hands covering their mouths and noses.

Outside, Kasim raised his head solemnly and addressed the assembled village, all of whom had by then arrived. 'It is as I have said. The stone is sacred. See, it weeps for my dead mother. It weeps to witness such a crime.' He glared at Ali with contempt. 'There lies a thief. He would have dishonoured us all. But even that was not enough for him. He had to commit this most heinous murder as well.' He pointed to the upstairs window of the room where the stone lay. 'But the stone would not allow such a crime to go unpunished. Look what it does to those who seek to dishonour it. This is how it punishes them.'

He kicked at Ali with the toe of his boot but the blow was met with barely a whimper. 'There can no longer be any disagreement. Not now. Not after such a clear demonstration as this. Tomorrow we will send messengers to seek out the true and rightful owners of the stone.'

So saying, Najaf Kasim, elder of the tribe, drew the knife from his belt, knelt down beside Ali and cut his throat.

Chapter Five

When the train made an unscheduled halt and Brigadier Percival's man climbed aboard, Caspasian knew that something was up and for a moment considered giving him the slip. It would not have been difficult to do. He had been looking forward to his leave but, as the carriage attendant drew back the door to the cabin, Caspasian sighed deeply and gathered his belongings. Before he went, he said farewell to Mr Sivraj. They had stayed on the roof until shortly before dark, returning to their carriage to sleep.

Mr Sivraj handed Caspasian his card. 'Do look me up if you are ever in Delhi and in need of a companion to travel with you on the roof.'

Caspasian smiled. 'It has been a memorable trip. I hope you enjoy Simla.'

Mr Sivraj frowned. 'You will not be making it after all?'

'So it seems. Duty.'

'Ah,' Mr Sivraj said simply. 'Until we meet again then.' He held out his hand and Caspasian shook it warmly.

Caspasian stepped out into the corridor to see who was after him this time. A young man, barely in his mid-twenties, stood waiting at the end of the carriage. When he saw Caspasian approaching he glanced quickly down at a photograph in his hand and then smiled, his cheeks reddening.

'Sorry, old man,' he said waving the photograph. 'It's all I was given.' He held out his hand and then as an afterthought offered his identification papers which Caspasian studied suspiciously. 'Channing. Douglas Channing. Indian Civil Service. I've been sent to fetch you, I'm afraid. Leave's cancelled and all that.' He looked at the valise in Caspasian's hand. 'But you've obviously guessed that.'

Caspasian grimaced. '*Plus ça change.*'

'What?'

'Never mind. Who wants me? Readman?'

'No, but he's given his clearance, old man.'

'That's big of him.'

They had stepped down from the train which slowly started off again as if in great agony. There was a car waiting and as Channing reached for the valise to swing it into the boot, Caspasian took him lightly but firmly by the wrist, smiled sweetly and said, 'Just one thing, I'm not your old man, all right?'

Channing took one look at Caspasian's eyes and decided not to try and pull his hand away. He swallowed, adopting a supercilious expression that reminded Caspasian of a camel. 'All right. No offence.'

'None taken.' Caspasian slapped him on the shoulder a little harder than necessary, the two of them got into the car and Channing signalled the driver to start.

'You never answered my question,' Caspasian said almost immediately.

Channing smiled. 'Quite right old . . . erm, my dear chap . . .'

Caspasian frowned meaningfully.

'. . . erm, Captain Caspasian. I believe you know Brigadier Percival?'

Caspasian stiffened. 'Percival. Of course. What does the old bastard want with me this time?'

Channing laughed, ill at ease. 'That's hardly the way to speak about a senior officer. In any case, I'm afraid I'm not at liberty to say. Not yet. The Brigadier was explicit. He wants to brief you himself. Sorry old . . . sorry, Caspasian.'

'Do you work for him?'

'Not really. I'm assistant to Sir Oswald Masterman. He and the Brigadier are cooperating on this one.'

Caspasian's eyes widened. 'The Brigadier cooperating with someone? He can obviously smell promotion again.'

Although he knew his escort would have told him more, Caspasian decided not to press him. Any information imparted would only serve to bolster the young man's ego and would not satisfy Caspasian's curiosity. Channing had already said that the meat of it was to be presented by the Brigadier himself, so he decided to wait until then. He sat back on the red leather seat and gazed out of the window, trying to suppress his irritation at having had his leave cancelled.

For his part, Douglas Channing waited in silence for Caspasian's next question. He was enjoying his assignment immensely and had looked forward to playing the role of intermediary between Brigadier

Percival and the man whom he had been told was going to be central to the forthcoming operation. Instead Caspasian's seeming lack of interest puzzled him. He himself would have been bubbling over with questions. Caspasian on the other hand had every appearance of being thoroughly bored at the prospect of the excitement to come. But then Channing supposed he must be used to such things. After all, a man who had survived the Great War and then numerous operations on the North-West Frontier and elsewhere throughout the Empire and beyond, must have seen it all. He sighed, disappointed that his companion had apparently drawn a line under further conversation. With the heat of the day and the rocking motion of the car, it was not long before they were both asleep, heads lolling. Every so often the car horn would wake them as the driver negotiated a bullock cart or other obstacle, and when at last they tumbled into Peshawar, dust-covered and rumpled, the driver headed straight for the British cantonment, drawing to a halt in front of a large bungalow that sat in the middle of a fence-ringed garden.

Channing sat up and rubbed his eyes. 'Ah. Here we are,' he said. 'Bit of a hike, wasn't it?'

Caspasian looked at his watch. 'What time does the Brigadier want me?'

'He said he'd be along here once you've had a chance to sort yourself out.'

'The briefing's going to be here?' Caspasian asked surprised.

'Yes. He doesn't want you up at the fort. He wants to keep your presence here a secret.'

Caspasian looked around at the passers-by. 'There aren't many secrets in Peshawar.'

'Well, secret for as long as possible. The fort's watched all the time. Every local bandit knows exactly who goes in and who comes out. They know our strengths, armaments, everything. This bunga-low belongs to one of the missionary groups. No one takes much notice of them. That's why the Brigadier selected it. Of course, the missionaries don't know what he's using it for. In any case, we only need it for a day and a night.'

Caspasian stared at him. 'A day and a night? What about the planning? All the preparation? Presum-ably whatever you're up to will need time for that?'

Channing shrugged. 'I'll let the Brigadier explain. We don't have any more time on this one.' He let Caspasian out of the car, directing the driver to carry his bag inside. 'I've got to go and report to Brigadier Percival now. He'll be along later. We'll give you an hour or so. Will that be enough for you to wash off the dust? The driver will tell the houseboy to fill a bath for you.'

When the car had gone, Caspasian went inside to find his valise in one of the bedrooms. As usual, the term houseboy was a poor description for the wizened septuagenarian who grinned maniacally at Caspasian as he waved him towards the bath-room where various underlings were already at work with buckets, filling a large enamel tub with a brackish looking liquid. Nevertheless, when Cas-pasian had undressed and lowered himself in, the water was beautifully cool, and as he lay back he felt the dusty miles fall away, while yet being aware that a good many more probably lay just ahead.

True to Channing's word, an hour later, as Caspasian was shaking out a clean shirt in the bedroom, he heard a car pull up outside. The doors slammed and a moment later a voice called out from the entrance hall. Tucking in his shirt, he bent to lace his shoes, quickly ran a comb through his still wet hair, and padded through to see the new arrivals. Channing was there, washed and groomed like himself, and three others whom he quickly introduced. Caspasian and the Brigadier exchanged cold glances of recognition. The other two were announced as Sir Oswald Masterman and Lieutenant Colonel Patrick Gibson, a battalion commander from the Peshawar garrison.

'Thank you so much for joining us at such short notice,' Sir Oswald said as if there had been some element of choice on Caspasian's part. 'I hope Douglas looked after you on the journey up from the railhead.'

Brigadier Percival stepped forward and shook hands stiffly. 'Hello, Caspasian. Good of you to come. Glad you're here for the ride.'

'The ride?' Caspasian smiled politely. 'You know me, Brigadier. My own worst enemy. Never could resist a tempting offer. But then no one's yet told me what sort of ride you're planning.' He narrowed his eyes. 'Let me guess. An expedition into the tribal areas perhaps?' he said sarcastically.

'Spot on,' Sir Oswald said, impressed.

The Brigadier shot the older man an irritated glance. 'Let's just get on with it, shall we?'

He went across to the large table in the centre of the room and began to unroll maps and papers. Caspasian noticed that Channing went quickly and methodically round the doors and windows checking that there was no one within earshot. When he was satisfied that they were completely alone, he nodded to the Brigadier who ushered them all to chairs before continuing.

'Have you heard of the Eye of the Storm?'

It was not often in his life that Caspasian found himself caught completely off guard. He rocked back in his chair and blinked. 'The statue of the eighteenth-century prophet Abdul Rashid? Yes, of course.'

The Brigadier swapped a glance of satisfaction with Sir Oswald. 'The eye of the statue, to be more precise.'

Caspasian thought hard. 'It was fashioned after the prophet's death and stood above the gates of the old Mughal fort at Patna.'

'That's the ticket. When the fort was stormed by the soldiers of the Honourable East India Company, the statue was destroyed, but not before the Eye had been prised from its socket by some enterprising young subaltern. Legend had it that whoever held the statue would be protected from all harm and would rule India, so when the defenders saw what had happened they fled in terror and the fortress and town fell into British hands.'

'And India too, eventually,' Sir Oswald contributed.

'Thereby giving the legend some credence, at least to simple minds,' the Brigadier said. 'However, the story doesn't end there. Time passed and the legend was forgotten. The fortunes of the East India Company declined, the British Government took direct control of the country, and the Raj as we now know it came into being. The Eye of the Storm languished forgotten in a Calcutta museum until it was sent back to London along with other artifacts for display there.'

'I remember,' Caspasian said. 'So what's happened now? Presumably it's still there?'

'Unfortunately not,' the Brigadier continued. 'In a little known gesture of largesse it was given by Queen Victoria as a wedding present to Tsar Nicholas of Russia.'

'Oh,' Caspasian said bluntly, starting to get the drift.

'Exactly. From there it went to the Hermitage in St Petersburg where it remained until the Bolshevik Revolution of 1917. In the chaos and civil war that followed it disappeared, along with a number of other priceless treasures, lost until a force of White Russians recovered it by chance. As you know, there are still groups of them operating in the Caucasus, although they are slowly being eradicated by the Reds.'

'And?'

'It seems the Bolsheviks were intending to make use of the Eye. As their power becomes more established, they are starting to look beyond their borders.'

'The old Russian expansionism,' Sir Oswald said. 'Doesn't matter what political label it travels under, it's the same dangerous bear.'

'They were planning to resurrect the old legend and use the Eye of the Storm to destabilise India and foment revolt here. It was going to be passed to some suitably influential Indian Prince . . .'

'Someone with a grudge,' Channing interjected.

'Exactly, someone with a grudge, and leave superstitious belief to do the rest. You might wonder who would fall for such a trick . . .'

Caspasian shook his head. 'Not me. I've seen what legends can do. Morale and belief are funny things, no matter what people say about this being the modern world.'

'Good. Well, it was just lucky for us that it fell into White Russian hands. Desperate for arms and ammunition, they contacted us through intermediaries and a deal was struck. Of course, we were willing to oblige. As a treasure itself the Eye is worth a small fortune, but as an instrument of political manipulation it is worth a great deal more to us. If it were to fall into the hands of the wrong person, they could claim that the power of Abdul Rashid was with them and that they were the destined ruler of India and before you know it we'd have a full-scale frontier war on our hands, or worse.'

Sir Oswald leaned forward. 'I need hardly remind you that the Congress Party is becoming a dangerous force in the land. Since Mr Gandhi was released from jail last year he has increased his influence. It might be that some day there will have to be a peaceful transition of power, but . . .' he shrugged, 'these things take time. Something like this could upset the whole apple cart. It could even lead to another Mutiny.'

The Brigadier paused while Channing was sent in search of refreshments, returning a few moments later with a large pitcher of iced lime-flavoured water and a tray of glass tumblers. Once again he did a check of the doors and windows.

Caspasian twirled his glass in his hands, watching the cubes of ice and the slivers of lime jostle for position. 'So what went wrong?'

The Brigadier smiled ruefully. 'We're not exactly sure. All we do know is that the team that was returning with the Eye never arrived back. The White Russians took delivery of the arms and they continue to fight on.'

'Did they honour their part of the bargain?'

'To the letter. They gave the Eye to my own man. Captain Ryan. He and his men set off on the return journey and that was the last we heard of them. It seems likely that they fell foul of Pathans along the way, but whether it was a chance attack by bandits or something more sinister we just don't know.'

'More sinister?' Caspasian said.

The Brigadier shook his head, staring down at his clasped hands. 'We know who the Bolsheviks intended the Eye for. If it has fallen into his hands, then we've got big trouble.'

'So? Who?'

'Prince Mahsud of Beshandu.'

Caspasian stared. 'Beshandu? He isn't still around, is he?'

'Not the old man. This is the son.'

'Ah, yes,' Caspasian said slowly, dredging his memory. 'I remember now. Didn't he . . .?'

'Go to Oxford? Yes, and incredible though it might

seem, I believe he did rather well. We don't know a lot about the fellow but my contacts at Oxford tell me he spent most of his time there living the good life. Acquired quite a taste for fast cars, women and ragtime. All that and he still managed to do well academically.'

'And yet he's after the Eye of the Storm. A bit odd, don't you think?'

The Brigadier shrugged. 'Perhaps he acquired more than an education at Oxford. Political ambitions for instance. His father was a politician in his way.'

'His father was the biggest thief, brigand and murderer on the North-West Frontier,' Caspasian added laconically.

'Exactly.'

'We launched more punitive expeditions against him than anyone else in all the tribal areas, all to little effect,' Colonel Gibson interjected. 'Every time he simply withdrew to his fortress, fell silent for a while and then came back to stir up more trouble later on. Frankly we hoped we'd seen the last of the troubles in that region when the old boy died.'

Caspasian thought for a moment. 'Well whatever the son's got in mind, presumably he doesn't yet have the Eye. If he did the frontier would be alight by now.'

'That's our one cause for optimism,' the Brigadier said, 'the one thing that leads me to believe the Eye is in the hands of bandits who don't know the value of what they've captured.' He drummed his fingers on the table. 'But it won't be long before they find out. And when they do, so will the Prince.'

'And when he finds out,' Sir Oswald said, 'it will be a very short time before he gets his hands on the Eye.'

The Brigadier pushed back his chair and stood up. 'There's yet another complication to all this. My informers in the hills tell me that a party of foreigners crossed the Afghan border a few days ago.'

'No need to ask who they are, I suppose?' Caspasian said grimly.

'Russians. Bolsheviks. Here for the same reason as us. To get to the Eye and see it into the right hands. For them that means Prince Mahsud. For us, the Viceroy. It's as simple as that.'

Caspasian ran his fingers through his hair, ignoring the disapproving frown from the Brigadier whose own head was cropped at the back and sides almost to the bone. 'Simple isn't exactly the word I'd have chosen, sir.'

'No. Of course not. But you see the predicament we're in. We have to prevent the Eye from falling into the hands of Prince Mahsud, or anyone else for that matter. Except us. A column's out of the question. For now at least. Too blunt an instrument for a task like this. It would raise a great stink right across the frontier, which is exactly what we don't want. The tribes would all wonder what we were up to. As matters stand, for the moment I don't think many people know. What's required is a very small expedition, a handful of men only, to go into the tribal areas, locate the Eye, retrieve it and bring it back.'

He quickly held up his hand before Caspasian could protest. 'And I'm not pretending for one second that it's going to be easy. Quite frankly we'll be lucky to get back alive, but there's no alternative.' He stopped his pacing and turned to face Caspasian. 'You know the tribal areas better than any other British officer. You know the people and you know the type of operation I'm planning. That's why you're here. I suppose I shouldn't order anyone to come on a mission like this, but I need you, so that's all there is to it.'

Caspasian grinned sardonically. 'Well, thank you for making that clear. I believe Readman . . .'

'You mean Colonel Readman,' the Brigadier said sternly.

'I believe Colonel Readman has already released me for this assignment, sir?'

'That's correct,' the Brigadier answered. 'More specifically, the Viceroy himself is backing the plan.' He paused. 'And your part in it. I believe he knew your father.'

Caspasian stiffened. The Brigadier smiled harshly. 'Of course, if you don't feel up to it . . .' he added sarcastically, ignoring a cautionary stare from Sir Oswald.

Caspasian glanced away. 'Do you have a plan?'

'What would you say to entering the tribal areas in disguise?'

'Absolute nonsense. I tried it once in my subaltern days. Most stupid thing I ever did. I'd been reading too much Kipling. I stood out more than if I'd been in full Regimental Mess dress. I was lucky to escape with my life.'

There was a choked cough from Channing as he was caught in mid-sip and sprayed water down his shirt front, from which Caspasian deduced that infiltration in disguise had been his own particular brainchild. To his relief he saw the Brigadier and Sir Oswald exchange a quick smile.

'That was my suspicion,' the Brigadier continued rapidly. 'Which is why I've decided we'll try another tack.' He ignored the hurt expression on Channing's face and said, 'Bernard Spencer, the Political Officer responsible for the Beshandu and surrounding area, is going to attend a tribal assembly.'

'A jirga?' Caspasian said in some surprise.

'That's right. There's some issue over a blood feud that he is trying to help the locals resolve. Anyway, it gives us an excuse to go with him. As observers.'

'Will he know the real reason?'

'No. Not at all. Nor must he. The fewer people who know about this the better.'

'But we'll be putting his life in jeopardy. He has a right to know, surely.'

'The man's the local Political Officer,' the Brigadier replied. 'It's his job to . . .'

'It's his job to know everything that's happening in his area of responsibility.' Caspasian said quickly. 'I do think he should be brought in on this, sir.'

'Leave Bernard to me,' Sir Oswald cut in. 'He's under my direction. I'll square it with him if he finds out.'

'The jirga should last for several days, enough time for us to make contact with one of my informers who will also be there. Nothing travels as fast in that region as rumour, as you are aware. It is my belief that by then he will have established who has the Eye.'

'And then what?'

'That's where you come in. If it is relatively straightforward and in an area with which you are familiar, we will ourselves go and retrieve it, bartering if necessary. If not, then it might be necessary to summon a column, which is where Colonel Gibson and his men come in.'

'The Dorset Light Infantry will get you out,' Colonel Gibson said. He smiled warmly at Caspasian, indicating as best he could that he sympathised with him.

Caspasian looked around the table. 'How many of us will be going to the jirga?'

'Myself, you, and Channing,' the Brigadier said.

'So it's just us and Bernard Spencer?'

'Bernard might have another one or two in his party but that won't interfere with our mission. Probably the agency surgeon and perhaps a guard or two from the local militia. He always likes to make use of such visits to set up a small clinic while he's there to treat a few minor ailments. It's all good for relations.' The Brigadier slid a notebook across to Caspasian. 'I want you to jot down a list of everything you need for such an expedition. You're the most experienced of us at this sort of thing. Colonel Gibson will pass it to his Quartermaster at the fort.'

Caspasian took the notebook and started writing immediately. Without looking up he said, 'There's a man I'd like to take with me, if I may, sir. Someone from my old battalion.'

'This isn't a regimental picnic, Caspasian.'

'That's exactly why I'd like Ganga with me. Sergeant Gangaprasad Limbu. He's the best shot on the frontier and just the man I'd want beside me in a tight corner.'

The Brigadier sighed, but nodded his consent at Douglas Channing. 'Get him, Channing.'

'But Brigadier . . .'

'Douglas, just get him, please. There's a good fellow.'

'Yes, Brigadier,' Channing answered sullenly, glowering at Caspasian.

'Send a wire to his battalion immediately. He may have to rendezvous with us at the Spencers' at Madanchot. We can't wait for him here. Time's pressing.'

He stretched. 'I think that about wraps it up for the moment, gentlemen. We'll have a proper coordinating meeting to discuss the detail this evening, back here. I'd like to be able to set off tomorrow morning before first light. Channing has organised the transport, two cars as far as the roadhead at the Spencers' from where we'll be using horses. We'll be there for one night, hopefully no more, and then across the border, out of the North-West Frontier Province and into tribal country. After that we're on our own.' He beamed at the others. 'Any questions that can't wait until this evening?'

Channing put up his hand. 'Do we know what the Eye looks like, sir?'

The Brigadier shook his head crossly. 'Forgive me. I completely forgot. Of course we do. Here.' He dug in his briefcase and produced a photograph which he passed across. 'This was taken when the Eye was in London, just before it was sent to Russia.'

Couched on a deep velvet cushion, the Eye of the Storm stared defiantly up at the camera.

'As you can see, on each of the stone's surfaces there are painted scenes from the prophet Abdul Rashid's life.' The Brigadier grinned. 'Apparently there was one story that, although the Eye would confer immense power upon the destined ruler of India, upon others it would bring a curse. But I don't think we need let that deter us.'

'It didn't bring the Tsar much luck, did it?' Caspasian said laconically. 'Nor Ryan and his men, come to that,' he added.

The smile fell from Channing's face. Caspasian reached across and put a hand on his shoulder. 'Just joking. Old man.'

Sergeant Ganga was praying to all the gods that he occasionally believed in that the man would put his head above the rock just one more time. Once more and he would have him. Either that or he himself would remove the crossed rifles marksmanship badge from the sleeve of his tunic and burn it. To miss once was bad discipline. To miss twice was unforgivable, a slight on one's name, one's regiment, one's family. To miss a third time . . . well, it did not bear considering. He tightened the grip of his right hand on the Lee-Enfield's smooth, nut brown wood, flexing his thumb along the grain, and testing the trigger pressure so he knew exactly how far to pull it without snatching. To be caught unawares and snatch at it would jerk the rifle fractionally off his point of aim and undoubtedly result in a miss. A third miss.

Beside him, Lance-Naik Rambahadur started to

whisper something but Ganga cut him short. 'Ssh! Leave a man to think!'

But that was the problem. He was thinking too much. He had to cut the mind out of the equation. The shot had to flow naturally. From his eye, the length of his rifle, through the smoothest of shots, all the way to the target. The Pathan sniper who had dropped Sergeant Birprasad that morning. One minute good old Biri had been walking towards the tent with his mess tin of steaming sweet tea, and the next he had been lying face down in the dirt, the tea pooling with his blood from the bullet hole in the centre of his chest. He had died before the minute was out.

Birprasad had been one of Ganga's oldest friends in the battalion, which was why, Ganga reasoned, he had been unable to remain dispassionate about revenging himself on the Pathan. Until then it had been just like any other frontier tour for Ganga. The battalion had marched up to the area of operations over a two-week period, camping along the way, and once in hostile territory they had set about building fortifications sufficient to keep them safe from a major assault. Pickets had been put out on the surrounding hilltops, each of at least section strength, but somehow the sniper had slipped through the net. It never ceased to amaze Ganga how proficient the Pathans were at fieldcraft.

The sun on the back of his grey flannel shirt lashed at him like a whip. Once again his companion tried to reason with him.

'Sergeant guruji, this will not work. He is too clever.'

For the first time Ganga had to admit that Rambahadur was right. The Pathan knew exactly where they were and had probably crawled away by now. The last thing he would do would be to show his face again when he knew what was waiting for him. A .303-inch bullet drilled through his forehead. Ganga sighed and relaxed his grip on the rifle. The palms of his hands were wet with perspiration.

'Come on then. We'll return to camp. But I've not finished with that bastard yet.'

When they got back, the duty officer listened to Ganga's request with a wry smile. Sergeant Ganga's persistence was legendary in the battalion, but Birprasad had been a popular NCO so when Ganga laid out his plan, Major Willingdon decided to give it a go.

Two hours later, with all due pomp and show, a patrol of platoon size ventured out of the camp in a simple sweep along the valley floor to the north, working their way in the direction of the sniper's last known position. Out on a flank, Sergeant Ganga and Lance-Naik Rambahadur moved stealthily forward, searching every fold of the ground for the sniper, knowing all the while that he would long since have made good his escape. But for now the show was all that mattered.

The platoon stayed out for an hour, clearing a large area, but towards dusk made its way back to the camp, the men being allowed to bunch carelessly. There was even some good-natured banter, which to any observant Pathan would have marked the unit as being hopelessly undertrained for frontier operations, and fair game for further chance snipings.

They reached the camp as the light faded, hopped over the makeshift walls and sangars, and disappeared amongst the tents.

Out in the gathering darkness, Sergeant Ganga and Lance-Naik Rambahadur settled into their carefully selected fire position, feeling vulnerable as they watched the last of their comrades vanish from sight, for whereas thirty soldiers had ventured out of the camp at the start of the patrol, only twenty-eight had returned, Ganga and Rambahadur having been left behind in the position that Ganga had selected himself earlier. In the muddle of the disorderly withdrawal back into the camp, he hoped that anyone watching would have failed to notice that he and the Lance-Naik had ducked down into the narrow cleft between two large rocks and remained there, a position that gave them a clear line of fire on to the most likely site of any future sniping.

Sergeant Ganga removed his broad felt hat and laid it beside him. From his haversack he wrestled free his khaki pullover and slipped it on. He positioned his rifle, the sights adjusted meticulously. To avoid any noise he had already put one bullet in the breech and cocked the weapon, the safety catch on. Now all that remained was to wait. And to hope.

The first hour passed slowly. The second even more slowly, and the third and fourth more slowly still. Next to the sergeant, Rambahadur shifted uneasily. His movement attracted an instant and painful dig in the ribs.

It was in the early hours of the morning that Ganga felt his hair bristle. There was something out there. Someone. For him, the night had suddenly come alive, although to Rambahadur beside him nothing seemed to have changed.

'What is it, guruji?' Rambahadur hissed.

Ganga's elbow fired into his ribs.

Ganga took up his rifle, his hands enveloping it, his body insinuating itself around it like a snake, making it a part of himself as if it was another limb. His right thumb silently moved the safety catch into the armed position leaving nothing but his will-power between the touch of his finger on the trigger and the impact of the firing pin on the base of the round.

Then even Rambahadur heard the voices, soft and very low.

'How many?' he whispered nervously.

'Two. Maybe more.'

The new arrivals had moved into a position that was on higher ground than the waiting Gurkhas, just as Ganga had intended, for in the growing moon-light they were silhouetted in front of him. They were good. He already knew that. The sniper that had shot Birprasad – for Ganga knew in his blood that it was the same man – had brought along a friend for the easy sport. Ganga smiled.

Through the darkness he could hear them. The ploy of earlier in the day had clearly worked. The Pathans had formed the opinion that this particular Gurkha battalion could be treated with contempt. They were taking their time, moving into position for a night's sniping, and exchanging gossip as they did so. Their voices carried across to the two Gurkhas lying in wait off to their flank.

To Rambahadur's surprise, Sergeant Ganga gently

reapplied the safety catch on his Lee-Enfield, released his grip on the rifle and slithered backwards away from it.

'What are you doing?' Rambahadur hissed desperately, eyes wide with fear.

Ganga's whisper came out of the darkness like the low growl of a mountain leopard. 'I want them in my hands. This is not for my rifle.'

In the darkness Rambahadur understood. 'Do you want me to come too?'

He felt Ganga's hand on his shoulder. 'No. They are mine.'

'How do you know it's the sniper?'

'It's him,' and despite the darkness of the night he saw the flash of Ganga's smile.

Ganga slithered backwards away from the fire position, moving across the rocky ground with practised ease. He felt like a boy again, at home in the foothills of the Himalayas, stalking a wolf or a bear or a leopard. He was the equal of all of them. He was their master. With every yard he felt the blood surging in his veins. His legs and arms propelled him across the intervening ground, inching ever closer to his quarry. He felt completely in control, wholly confident in his pursuit.

Ahead of him he could hear the Pathans. There were two of them. He had been right. They were over-confident, at ease. He could hear the sound of one of them drinking from a gourd, the water lapping over an upturned face and on to stone. He drew closer. His breath was so silent it had almost stopped. In the final yards, his right hand moved to the belt at his waist, the fingers making contact with the smooth walnut grip of his kukri. Closing about it, they drew the thirteen inches of steel blade from the leather-bound wooden scabbard, drawing it like drawing a line under a problem, like crossing a T.

Ganga's line of approach had brought him up behind the two Pathans. Beyond them, raising his eyes he could see the fires of his camp, where his comrades were waiting, waiting for the rifle cracks that would signal his success. Ganga smiled to himself. It was to be far, far simpler than that.

He gathered himself. Every muscle and sinew drew taut as he pulled his knees up under him and settled himself for the rush. In his mind's eye he could see his old friend Birprasad. The two of them as young recruits, fresh from the hills. The two of them being awarded their first stripes together. The two of them being welcomed into the Sergeants' Mess on the same star-filled night, the pipes and drums playing and the whole future bright before them. Birprasad lying face down in the dirt of some nameless valley, his blood spilling into the earth from which he had been created.

Ganga held his battle cry in his throat until his first blow had fallen. He exploded across the last yards out of the darkness. His thigh muscles powered him the last paces on to his enemy, his arm swinging high above his head, the savage blade arching down onto the man closest to him. The honed steel found bone and cleaved it through. Before the swing had reached its end, Ganga was turning to his next target, and now his cry cleared his lungs, emptying them. It came from deeper still, from his gut. The Pathan threw himself back against a rock, swivelling sideways to bring his rifle to bear on the terror confronting him. But it was too late. His fate had been decided the moment Ganga had crawled backwards away from his own rifle. His fate was in Ganga's hand, the hand that swung the kukri.

With a backwards swipe, Ganga slashed the blade across the man's throat, laying it open to the spine behind it. He watched as the Pathan's eyes bulged and glazed, his hands scrabbling as if they would hold the breath within him.

When he was certain that both men were dead, Ganga sat down beside them, checking them for weapons. Each carried both rifle and pistol and was swathed in cartridge bandoliers stuffed full with spare ammunition. They had clearly been planning a busy night, sniping at the camp and perhaps accounting for yet more Gurkha dead.

He reached across to the nearest body and wiped the blade of his kukri on the loose cotton shirt, drawing the steel between his cloth-covered thumb and forefinger to expunge from it the last trace of blood. When he was satisfied he returned it to its sheath, tapping it fully home before standing up to greet Rambahadur who came padding up carrying their two rifles. He squinted at the dead Pathans in the darkness, peering closely first at one and then the other, and whistled softly.

'Well they won't be eating much breakfast, will they?'

Chapter Six

The Spencer bungalow was an impressive structure, standing at the top of a gentle hill, at the base of which a broad fast-flowing river marked the boundary between the administered territory of the North-West Frontier Province and the unadministered tribal areas for which Bernard Spencer was the political agent. Around the main bungalow, other buildings housed the agency surgeon, Dr Angus McCloud, and the officer commanding the small detachment of militia also quartered around the site, Major Henry Allenshaw. To a military eye it was plain that the bungalow had been sited as much for defence as aesthetics. The walls were thick but the windows narrow, each of them offering a clear field of fire down the hill's bare slopes as far as the river and beyond. Each possible direction of approach towards the group of buildings was covered by at least two windows, usually more, the interlocking and over-lapping fields of fire providing a comprehensive lattice work of potential defensive fire that would have rendered even the most sustained assault a remarkably dangerous undertaking.

At the front of the bungalow the driveway swept up to the main entrance which stood beneath a low roof supported by two columns. In front of that there was a circular lawn bordered by flowerbeds of marigolds and bright purple bougainvillaea bushes, none above waist height and thereby not impeding the view of the ground beyond. To the sides and rear there were close-cropped lawns and, facing the spectacular view of the mountains, a paved terrace with rattan chairs and two rectangular coffee tables. Seated around them, Brigadier Percival and his team were deep in conversation with Bernard Spencer, discussing the coming tribal council.

The cars that had brought them earlier in the day had departed, leaving their bundles of supplies stacked close to the stables where the grooms were busily preparing the horses for the next day's journey. In the kitchens the chief cook had summoned his relatives from the village to help him with the evening meal. It was not often that Bernard Spencer entertained such a number of visitors, and the cook was terrified lest they be disappointed with his preparations. However, despite the sudden increase in numbers and the significance of the occasion, the menu would remain as it was for all special functions. Mulligatawny soup, curried chicken, followed by steamed sponge pudding and treacle. It was virtually all he could produce to an acceptable standard.

Bernard Spencer was enjoying the company immensely. It was seldom that the station received visitors and he and Dr McCloud were making the most of it. In normal circumstances Major Allenshaw, the OC of the local militia company, would have been with them too, but he had been called away on some military errand or other, and his return was overdue. Bernard Spencer was anxious lest this lateness delay the departure for the jirga.

He raised his hand and looked around for the houseboy.

'Burra-peg, Salim.' He turned to his guests. 'Anyone else for a whisky?'

Douglas Channing tentatively waved a hand. 'Just a small one if I may, Mr Spencer.' The first double had gone straight to his head and, although he could feel his cheeks redden, he was rather enjoying it. Besides, it would probably be the last for quite a while.

Bernard Spencer smiled indulgently at the young man. 'And a chota-peg for Channing Saheb.' He could see so much of himself in the young fellow, much as he had been when he had come out to India all those years ago before the Great War. The other characters were all a bit quiet. Brigadier Percival had given only the barest of justifications for their attendance at the jirga.

The other officer however was quite intriguing. He had little small talk and had spent most of the evening staring at the mountains with that misty faraway look that Bernard Spencer recognised as the mark of the adventurer. He was the sort of character that the British seemed to produce above all other nations. Had Bernard been aware of Caspasian's origins he would have been amused by the irony of his observation. Caspasian appeared to him to be a man searching for something, probably without realising it. Great Britain, being a small, compact, concentrated little island, was wholly incapable of satisfying such a great hunger. It was a hunger that fed on wide open spaces, borderless deserts, rim-to-rim mountain vistas.

Spencer had enjoyed the honour of meeting Colonel Lawrence in 1919 at Versailles for the Treaty negotiations. He had been such a man, although Spencer had been left with the impression that in addition to Lawrence's hunger there was also many a hidden demon driving him out into the deserts of Arabia and beyond. He had not been overly surprised when Lawrence had disappeared from public view shortly after the war. The rumours were that he had even enlisted as a ranker in the Royal Flying Corps, a harsh reminder that such a hunger could sometimes turn and feed upon itself.

There was another way in which this Caspasian reminded Bernard Spencer of Colonel Lawrence. He too gave the silent impression of an unexploded bomb.

So what were they all doing here, he wondered? To the Brigadier's face Spencer had accepted the explanation that they were travelling as observers to the jirga. Some nonsense about gauging the temperature of tribal affairs and disputes in the district in case it might prove necessary to reinforce the local garrison. Had that been the real mission, Spencer himself could have furnished them with a report more detailed than anything such a party of newcomers would be capable of producing after one single expedition.

Their presence clearly had some clandestine purpose. It did not particularly surprise Bernard Spencer. Such shenanigans were far from uncommon on the North-West Frontier. In his younger days he might have felt a bit affronted by such a lack of trust, but now he merely smiled inwardly and left them to get on with their little game. So long as it did not jeopardise his own position with the tribes. It had taken him many a year to reach such a position of trust. There was one further thing which now caused him concern, so much so that he was about to raise the issue when he was pre-empted by a voice from inside the house heralding the arrival of his daughter.

Judging from the effect she had on the seated guests, when she stepped out onto the terrace, Rachel Spencer felt as if she might have been a fully armed Pathan tribesman with blood dripping from his dagger. All the assembled men shot to their feet, mouths agape, eyes staring stupidly. She stifled her enjoyment of the spectacle and adopted a carefree smile.

'Rachel, my dear,' Spencer began, getting to his feet with more control. 'I was just about to tell our friends here about your visit.' He turned to the Brigadier and said, 'It's Rachel's first trip back to the old place since my wife died two years ago.' He beamed proudly at his daughter. 'Rachel graduated from medical school last year. She's taking a short break before settling down to work for a living.' He put his arm round his daughter's waist and presented her to each of his guests in turn. The Brigadier was stiffly polite, Douglas Channing alcoholicly incapable, and the enigmatic Caspasian wholly inscrutable.

For his daughter's part, Spencer could sense that

the only one in whom Rachel evinced any spark of interest was Caspasian. Bearing in mind his own recent thoughts he was not surprised. He had always known that she had no time for most of the old India hands, seeing them as brainless fossils from a bygone era. She had inherited her mother's temperament all right. Dorothy Spencer had been similarly uninspired at Bernard's first meeting with her all those years ago, and it had taken him a good deal of time and effort to convince her that he was different from the crowd. It had been worth every second.

Rachel had just returned from riding and still wore her white shirt, sweater and jodhpurs. She did not particularly care whether her father's guests approved or not. She had untied the ribbon fastening the ponytail she wore when riding and her long dark copper-coloured hair fell to just below her shoulders. She disliked, just as her mother had, the term that her father sometimes used to describe her. Petite. He had learnt his lesson now, but if ever it slipped out, she would fix him with her penetrating green eyes and freeze him into silence. Her arrival back in India, the sunlight, the proximity of the mountains and the fresh air they brought with them, had all nurtured the freckles that gave her tanned face an even greater youthfulness than it already possessed. Nevertheless, she derided the use of make-up as a vanity reserved for Civil Service and army wives with no better use for their time.

Spencer ordered another chair to be brought so his daughter might join the party.

'You had better make it two. Major Allenshaw's back,' Rachel said.

'Henry? Thank goodness for that. Where is he?' Spencer looked over her shoulder as a stocky man in a crumpled suit marched gruffly out of the house, scowling fiercely and clutching a drink in one fist. 'Henry, my dear fellow,' he continued, noting with some surprise his unusually dishevelled appearance. 'Whatever happened to you? You look as if you've walked all the way from Delhi! Come and meet our guests.'

Spencer had just started the introductions, beginning with Brigadier Percival, when there was a choked snort as Henry Allenshaw sprayed a mouthful of gin and tonic down his grubby shirt front as he caught sight of Caspasian.

'You!' he rasped, raising a quivering finger in Caspasian's direction like an Old Testament prophet casting out a demon.

Caspasian clenched his eyes shut and cursed under his breath.

'It's him . . . by God! Him!' Henry Allenshaw stammered.

Afraid that this latest arrival at his house was about to assault one of the guests, Bernard Spencer placed himself between the two men as Rachel stared with barely concealed amusement. The evening was showing signs of unexpected promise.

'Now then, Henry, calm down and tell us what happened,' Spencer said soothingly like a mother with a distraught child.

'This . . . this . . . man, ejected me from the train. Threw me off, God damn it! Had to wait a day for the next one, sleeping on the blasted platform, and then travel third-class, jammed in with all the bloody locals. He . . . he . . . struck me!' He seemed uncertain whether to launch a physical assault or burst into tears. Instead he sank down heavily into the chair that Spencer pushed behind his knees.

Brigadier Percival stepped forward. 'Is this true, Caspasian?'

Caspasian winced at the question. 'I didn't realise . . .' He shrugged, looking around in mute appeal.

'Well, I never,' Bernard Spencer said, looking at Caspasian with renewed interest. 'What did the good Major do to deserve such an assault?'

Henry Allenshaw was on his feet. 'Deserve?' he screeched with outrage.

Spencer placed a hand on his shoulder and thrust him back into the chair, keeping his eyes firmly on Caspasian.

Before Caspasian could think of an appropriate answer there was a gentle cough from the back of the agitated circle and Rachel indicated the houseboy who stood formally at the door ready to announce with great ceremony that dinner was ready.

His invitation was met with silence until the Brigadier said, 'Gentlemen, I suggest we clear this up later.' He turned to Caspasian. 'I'll speak with you after dinner.'

'You will have to excuse me,' Rachel said, indicating her riding clothes. 'I couldn't possibly join you all like this.'

'We can wait for you if you like,' Spencer said. He glanced at the cook, ignoring his stricken expression of panic. 'I am sure the food can be kept hot.'

But Rachel was already taking her leave, waving her hand in blank refusal. When she had gone,

Spencer shrugged to his guests. 'A wilful girl. Just like her mother. I blame that damned school I sent her to in England.'

By casually taking his seat again he indicated that the confrontation was over. The Brigadier followed his lead. 'They don't know how to drum it into them these days.'

Spencer shook his head vigorously. 'Oh, no. On the contrary. They tried too hard to do just that. The only effect on Rachel was to turn her into the biggest rebel they had ever had. I used to receive letter after letter from the headmistress, almost begging me to remove Rachel. I think she couldn't bring herself to shame the school by expelling my daughter, however much she must have longed to. God knows how Rachel made it through. By the skin of her teeth, I imagine.'

As he had been speaking a stream of muttered invective issued darkly from Henry Allenshaw who stared into his gin as if he was watching Caspasian drown in it.

'A doctor, you say?' Caspasian persevered innocently.

Spencer glowed with pride. 'And a very good one at that.' He paused thoughtfully for a moment, sensing his opportunity to broach a new subject, and was about to do so when the gardener came running round the side of the house. 'Saheb, saheb, there is a man come. He is waiting.' He jerked his chin, pointing it at Caspasian. 'He says he is waiting for you, saheb.'

'My goodness,' Spencer said, mildly disappointed at being interrupted. 'This is turning into an evening of unexpected arrivals.'

Caspasian broke into a smile of pleasure and relief. 'If you will excuse me for just a moment, gentlemen. Please go in to dinner without me. I will join you shortly.' Before waiting for the Brigadier's leave he turned on his heel and followed the mali back around to the front of the house. There, beside a large pack, stood Sergeant Gangaprasad Limbu of the Twelfth Gurkha Rifles. He beamed when he saw Caspasian, clicked his heels to attention and saluted rigidly.

'Caspasian Saheb. Here I am. You sent for me. Thank you. I came as quickly as I could. The Colonel Saheb sends you his salaams. He says he hopes you are enjoying your staff job.' He looked around at the bungalow, then across to the looming range of mountains. 'But I do not think you will be doing much paperwork now,' and his grin broadened still further, showing a row of glistening white teeth.

Caspasian helped him to pick up his bags, ignoring Ganga's furious protests. 'Come on. I'll show you round the back. You can dump your kit in the stables with the rest of ours and then I'll see you get a bed and something to eat. You've had a long journey.'

When they reached the stables Ganga took one look at the horses and blanched. Caspasian laughed. 'Don't worry. They've got an especially docile pony for you. So small your feet will still be touching the ground.'

To his surprise, when they entered the stables Caspasian almost walked into Rachel. She smiled back at him, bemused. 'Why, Captain. I thought you'd all be tucking into your mulligatawny by now.'

Aware of Ganga's eyes boring into him, Caspasian stood aside to introduce the new arrival. To Ganga's discomfort Rachel held out her hand. 'How do you do?'

'How do you do?' Ganga said, shaking her hand tentatively as if afraid of breaking it.

'Sergeant Ganga's accompanying my colleagues and me with your father.' Caspasian said unnecessarily.

'I gathered as much,' Rachel answered. 'There should be quite a stir at the jirga. What with your party, my father and Dr McCloud's clinic, there'll be a veritable caravan up there.' She turned to Ganga. 'And what will you be doing?'

Ganga swallowed hard, glancing at Caspasian for help.

'Sergeant Ganga and I are old comrades in arms. I heard he was in the neighbourhood, on his way back to the battalion, so thought we might use him.'

Rachel's green eyes bored into Caspasian with barely concealed amusement. He could not avoid the comparison of a cat with a mouse. 'In the neighbourhood, you say?' She squinted theatrically out through the stable doors at the surrounding emptiness. 'Out here?'

Realising that he was in danger of digging himself in further, and resenting the Brigadier's insistence on secrecy from Bernard Spencer, their host, Caspasian decided that a part truth was preferable to a complete and insulting lie.

'I am sure you know the reputation of the tribal areas, Miss Spencer.'

'Rachel,' she corrected. 'Please call me Rachel.'

'Rachel,' he said reluctantly. 'The customs of a jirga require our numbers to be kept small. Yet with the possible dangers, we thought it only prudent to have at least some protection for our party.'

She widened her eyes at Ganga. 'Then you must be an extraordinary man indeed, Sergeant Ganga. A jirga can be attended by as many as a thousand or more tribesmen.'

Caspasian stared at her in amazement. 'You've been to one?'

'Of course. Since I was little. My father often used to take me. I'd never have given him a moment's peace if he hadn't.'

'But, the restrictions on British women across the border?'

Rachel shrugged. 'A special pass was necessary. But my father's the one who issues them.' She beamed at him happily. A second later she saw the penny drop.

'You don't mean to say. . .'

'Yes?' she prompted, tilting her head on one side.

They were interrupted by a slurred voice summoning Caspasian from the bungalow. Caspasian made his excuses and, leaving Ganga grinning awkwardly at Rachel, stepped back into the yard to find Douglas Channing moving with great concentration towards him.

'It's a damned mess. The whole blasted thing. One damned fine mess.'

'What is?' Caspasian asked, guessing the answer but dreading to hear his suspicion confirmed.

'Have you heard? That blasted young filly's coming with us. Damnedest thing I ever heard. Highly irresponsible of her father, I call it. The Brigadier's thinking of calling off the whole thing. Won't blame him if he does.'

His eyes almost popped out of his head when he heard Rachel's voice over Caspasian's shoulder. 'Call what whole thing off, Mr Channing?'

'Miss Spencer!'

'Dr Spencer, actually. I'm accompanying Dr McCloud to assist with his clinic.'

Channing spluttered. 'But . . . but . . . Pathan tribesmen being seen by a female doctor?'

'I might be wrong, but I think they have women in their villages too,' Rachel answered. 'I'm well aware of the sensitivities of the region, Mr Channing.' She glared at him suspiciously. 'I wonder if you are? It's taken my father many years to build up the tribesmen's trust. I'm sure you wouldn't want to put that in jeopardy, would you?'

Bernard Spencer peered round the side of the bungalow. 'Ah! There you all are. I was wondering where you'd all got to. Now I really must insist that we eat. If not, I'm afraid Rachel will have to resuscitate my cook. The poor fellow's almost having heart failure watching the soup go cold.'

'They're just coming,' Rachel called. She smiled at Caspasian. 'Captain Caspasian and Mr Channing here were just saying how much they were looking forward to our expedition.'

Knowing defeat when he saw it, Caspasian returned her smile. 'Can I leave Sergeant Ganga in your capable hands?'

'Of course. I'll be glad to see he is fed and given somewhere to sleep.'

Caspasian put a hand on Channing's shoulder and steered him around. 'Come on, Douglas. Dinner is served,' and when they were out of earshot he added, 'and I think we both know that the Brigadier's not going to cancel anything. There's far too much at stake. Isn't there, old man?'

Alexei Karpov turned in the saddle. 'We'll break here,' he called back to the nine mounted men behind him. 'Vassily, get the porters to brew up some tea. I don't want to hang around too long.' He felt uncomfortably vulnerable down in the open valley and was keen to reach the thickly wooded slopes on the far side that he could see a couple of miles ahead of them. But nor did he want to push the little party too hard. His own men, the three nearest to him, were all right, but the six porters who had been detailed to join them when they first crossed into Afghanistan had proved to be far from dependable. They moaned at every opportunity, complaining at the tough pace he had set from the first day, and they disliked beginning each day's journey before filling their stomachs with tea and bread.

The pace had been hard, Karpov conceded, but he had his reasons. He had also made it clear to them that they would be rewarded according to the effort they put into the mission. It did not seem to cut much ice with them. Vassily Novikov had suggested paying them a percentage of their wage up front, but Karpov knew that the moment they saw any money they would be off. They would disappear into the night and that would be that. In some ways he

wondered whether that might not be the best option.
The guide had proved to be less than useless, leading
them up one wrong valley after another, and it was
only due to Karpov's skill with map and compass
that they had made such good progress.

He shifted in his saddle. They had been riding for
only an hour but already his backside was numb. He
detested horses and everything to do with them. A
strong advocate of mechanisation, he could not wait
for the dumb stupid beasts to be completely sup-
planted by cars, trucks and trains. In this present
backward country however there was no alternative.

He slipped his feet from the stirrups, gripped the
front of his saddle and slid to the ground, sighing
with relief at the touch of firm earth. Two of the
porters had quickly set to work unloading one of the
packhorses, while the others gathered the reins of the
remaining mounts and led them to the banks of the
river. Karpov looked around, pleased with the spot
he had chosen for their first halt of the day. Against
the more usual practice of setting out only after a
morning cup of tea, he preferred to get an hour or so
of travel under his belt before stopping and lighting a
fire. It set the pace for the day, he felt. The break
thereby became a brief interlude in the journey rather
than an excuse for dallying before getting started. It
also put distance between themselves and their night
camp. Karpov was always tense when stationary,
feeling vulnerable to discovery and attack. Every
evening he found it difficult to relax after advertising
their position for miles around by lighting a cooking
fire, and then sleeping in the same location until
shortly before daybreak. He had tried to change this

custom too, insisting at first that after eating their evening meal, the party should pack and move on through the darkness for another hour before camping for the night. The porters had threatened to leave him and Novikov and the others had prevailed upon him to relent, much against his better judgement.

Dragov came up to him grinning. 'Oleg's been complaining to me about his buttocks for the last two days. I think I know more about his arse than his own trousers.'

'I know how he feels. Unfortunately we've got a long way to go yet,' Karpov replied smiling. He took out his compass and readjusted the dial to check the bearing he had set at first light after measuring it from his map with the protractor. He held the compass in the flat of his palm, oriented it until he had aligned the north pointer with the markers on the face, and then squinted through the eye-piece to discern the line of travel, looking ahead for a landmark to use as a reference point. A line of jagged peaks marked the horizon. Between two of the highest, a patch of forest crept up between them, marking the line of a re-entrant leading up to a pass.

He pointed it out to Dragov. 'See that? Make sure that Oleg and Vassily know. That's where I want to be by nightfall. Earlier if possible.'

Dragov whistled softly. 'With this lot?' he said, jerking his thumb at the porters. 'They won't like it.'

'I don't care what they like. I'm tempted to shoot the lot of them. Our maps have proved far more reliable than I supposed, and with this,' he said hefting his compass, 'I think we'd be better off without them.'

'I heard that.' Vassily Novikov came up and stretched lazily. 'You're an unforgiving man, comrade,' he said, a mischievous twinkle in his eye.

'I'm in no mood for joking.'

'You never were,' Novikov continued undaunted. 'You could never see the funny side of anything. The German war, the Revolution, the war with the White revisionists.' He clapped his old friend on the back, almost knocking the compass from his hand. 'If it wasn't for me keeping you on the straight and narrow you'd have become a narrow-minded little commissar by now, ensconced in some dark and dingy ministry in all the grimness that is Moscow these days.'

Alexei Karpov scowled at him. 'That's dangerous talk. It's lucky we're a long way from hungry ears.'

'Yes, aren't we?' Novikov said, hands on hips, gazing contentedly around at the mountainous wilderness. 'Don't you feel how good it is to be alive in a place like this?'

Karpov turned away from him and continued with his scrutiny of the far mountain range through his compass eye-piece. 'Not particularly. We're here to carry out the mission and as soon as it's completed we return home.'

'Yes, but so long as we have to be here why not make the most of it? Open your eyes to new sights, new places, new people even,' Novikov continued, gratefully accepting a mug of steaming sweet tea from one of the porters.

They heard a chuckle and looked round to see the porters pointing at Oleg Zykov who had pulled his trousers down and was sitting with his backside in a pool of icy cold water at the river's edge.

'Dragov, go and tell him not to be such a bloody idiot,' Alexei said. 'If he gets pneumonia out here who does he think is going to look after him?'

Dragov sauntered away. 'Let him. At least I won't have to listen to his complaining. He sounds more like an old woman every day. I'm going to get something to eat.'

'There you are, you see,' Novikov said. 'The old discipline has gone. You could have had him shot if he'd spoken to you like that in the trenches. The Imperial Army did have some merits.'

'You know, Vassily, I get the impression sometimes that you yearn for a return to the old days.'

Vassily Novikov smiled, but not as easily as before, aware that he was stepping on dangerous ground, even with his old friend from numerous campaigns. After all, Karpov was widely regarded as a rising star in the Party, and Novikov knew that although the loyalties of an old friendship mattered to Karpov more than to most, there were limits to what even he, Vassily Novikov, could get away with. It had not taken long for the old innocence to go. It had been burned up in the first couple of years after the Revolution, when the flush of victory paled into a cold realisation that it was one thing to overthrow a rotten government, but quite another to run a vast and disparate country peopled largely with impoverished and superstitious farming communities.

A porter came to inform them that water had been heated for shaving. Karpov had insisted on strict discipline being maintained at all times and that included personal hygiene. He carried his bowl of steaming water to the riverside and hunted around until he found a suitably flat-topped rock. Placing the bowl down carefully, he unrolled a small canvas shaving kit, lathered his face and set to work with his razor. From the small mirror beside the bowl, his thin stern face peered suspiciously back at him. Beneath a head of thick hair – prematurely grey, although he preferred to think of it as silver – his dark brown eyes were deep-set. He was a small man, compensating for his lack of physical stature with an energy that, when not directed at some particular task, made his movements seem almost erratic.

Less than a dozen yards from him, Novikov could not have been more different. Tall and big-boned, he made Karpov think of a Cossack, his broad moustache curling up on either side of his smiling mouth like a buffalo's horns. They made an unlikely pair but had nevertheless been friends since first meeting in the early days of the Great War when the Kaiser's divisions had marched against Mother Russia, pulling her into a conflagration that had turned the country inside out. In the midst of all the horror he and Novikov had found themselves in the same unit. Without supplies of food or ammunition, and driven to ever greater extremes of deprivation, the men had finally mutinied. It had not been organised. There were not even any ringleaders at first. The revolt had arisen spontaneously in response to the conditions.

Order had been reimposed with a brutality that had shocked Karpov, even after his experience of the great battles of attrition. The commanding officer had been a classics scholar and took a certain delight in resorting to the Roman method of decimation, selecting at random one man in every ten who was then separated, led out in front of his fellows, and executed by firing squad. That night, both Karpov and Novikov had deserted, making their way east and back towards Russia. Neither of them seriously expected to make it. Both were convinced that capture and death would overtake them at any moment. But it was 1917. When they were eventually spotted and surrounded by a troop of mounted cavalry, they were stunned into shock, followed by tears of relief at the news. The Tsar had been taken prisoner. The old order was overthrown.

It was during those days on the run that the bond had been formed that had bound Karpov and Novikov ever since. After the seizure of power by the Bolsheviks, they had both risen rapidly through the ranks, Karpov's sharp mind soon bringing him to the attention of the new leadership. Through every promotion he made sure that he kept his old friend at his side. In the turmoil that had engulfed Russia he realised that a trusted ally was worth any amount of political influence.

He rinsed the soap from his face, dabbed his cheeks dry, and repacked his razor. He looked across at Novikov and for the first time in a long while felt his heart lighten. There was a man he could trust. He had no doubt of it. Together with Dragov and Zykov they would complete the mission successfully, return home the same way they had come, and . . . then what? He sat back on his heels and allowed himself a short daydream. Success would bring further promotion, naturally. It would probably mean a move to the very centre of things. He already knew that a place in the government was not his aim. His own particular ambitions lay in the field of intelligence. For Alexei Karpov it was the greatest lure he had ever come across. He was attracted to it like a moth to a flame. Sometimes he wondered if it was a result of having spent those years in the trenches as an infantryman, constantly kept in the dark, ignorant of the greater processes going on about him and yet upon which his very life depended.

The intelligence game, Novikov called it, but then to him everything was a game, or so he pretended. Karpov knew the truth. He had seen Novikov in battle. Karpov's friendship with Novikov was not wholly altruistic. Novikov was a fearsome soldier. He revelled in combat and was the best Karpov had ever seen. If he was going to rise as high as he intended, Karpov knew that he would need not just a trusted ally at his side, but someone other men feared. Someone capable of ferocious action when required. That man was Vassily Novikov. What did it matter if sometimes he got on Karpov's nerves with his little jests? Karpov could forgive him that. He was going to be too useful to Karpov for such trivialities to matter.

Fifteen minutes later the party moved off, the horses stepping lithely through the fast flowing but shallow water of the river, refreshed after the halt and as eager to be on the way as Karpov. Having confirmed the direction, Karpov pushed two of the porters out in front about fifty yards. If they encountered trouble he wanted the hired porters to take the brunt of any ambush and not his own men. It was going to be hard enough to make do with only the four of them as it was. Even after the rendezvous, when the manpower at his disposal would be almost unlimited, there would still be only the other three Russians that he could really trust.

The sun had now risen above the line of the hills and Karpov could feel the growing heat of it in the prickle of sweat running down his back. He regretted not having used the halt to take off the thick woollen pullover he wore under his jacket and he did not want to present the others with the spectacle of their leader on horseback struggling with his clothing, undoubtedly only to suffer the ignominy of dropping something or other. He would have to wait until they stopped for their midday meal. He sighed. He was certainly not a natural soldier. He never had been. Not like Novikov. Nor like Dragov or Zykov for that matter.

To take his mind off his growing physical discomfort, he turned his thoughts to the mission and all the associated dangers ahead. He felt a smile creep across his lips from side to side, a thin, private smile. Soon, Alexei, soon, he said to himself. He could see the prize before him as surely as the mountain pass ahead that would take them closer to India. He could almost feel the weight of it in his hands. Once he had got it there would be no stopping the new regime. No stopping him. He turned in the saddle and smiled openly at the others.

Novikov beamed back and waved at the surrounding mountainscape. 'You see? You too feel liberated here, don't you?'

Karpov shrugged, nodding to please his friend. Nothing could stop him now. He had come so far. Nothing could stop him. Nothing and no one.

Chapter Seven

Within a day of setting out on their journey, Brigadier Percival, Bernard Spencer and their entourage had crossed into tribal territory and left behind them the relative safety of the British-administered North-West Frontier Province. Riding near the front, with only two scouts from Henry Allenshaw's militia ahead of him, Caspasian could feel his spirits soaring higher with every mile he put between himself and the office he had left behind in Delhi. He sat straight in his saddle, one fist on his thigh, surveying the surrounding mountains that grew in height the further they travelled.

Though hot, the air was pure, without the dust and foul smells of the city. As they climbed, the sandy stretches of the plain gave way to grassland, sparse but nonetheless green. Boulders of all sizes were strewn around them, having tumbled from the mountainsides in rockfalls long ago, and eventually, towards late morning, they came across the first trees, stunted and windblasted on the lowest slopes, but gaining in height and number as the hours wore on.

Although Bernard Spencer was nominally in charge of the expedition, Brigadier Percival had quietly directed Caspasian to move near the head of the little column. Caspasian, in turn, had placed Ganga at the rear, close to the two packhorses that were carrying the team's weapons, discreetly concealed in canvas satchels and strapped beneath other non-contentious packs of rations and camping equipment. In all, the column numbered about twenty. The two militiamen moved at the head, with Caspasian a little way behind them. Bernard Spencer and Brigadier Percival came next, chatting congenially, each concealing their private suspicions from the other.

Douglas Channing, Rachel, Dr McCloud and Henry Allenshaw rode in a tight huddle, the three men competing good naturedly for Rachel's attention, while she tried not to glance too often or too obviously in Caspasian's direction.

A short way behind came Ganga, cursing and clucking at his docile pony, hands clasping the reins far out at his sides, urging on the confused animal with knees that were already beginning to smart from the effort. Immediately behind him were the packhorses, half a dozen in all, managed by two grooms. Four or five porters scurried along on foot beside the animals, with another two militiamen bringing up the rear. When the party stopped for a meal, or for the night, it would be the porters who would erect shelters, light fires, fetch water and prepare the food.

Anticipating a short, uncomplicated round trip, Bernard Spencer had ordered provisions for a week. Even though he expected it might be a little longer than this, he was certain that they would be able to bargain for more provisions once they arrived at the jirga. They would probably be presented with gifts of a couple of goats or sheep, and these could then be slaughtered and eaten. In addition, the country through which they were passing offered excellent opportunities for shooting game of various sorts, and the rivers higher up would feed them with fish. He had brought his gun and his rod, and did not doubt that his military friends had done likewise.

In fact, he had been somewhat alarmed to note the amount of weaponry that they were carrying between them, and he was experienced enough to suspect that they probably had more secreted amongst their baggage. Both Caspasian and the Brigadier carried handguns, and the Gurkha Sergeant had a Lee-Enfield Mark III rifle. The Brigadier's weapon was a Webley revolver and, while certainly no expert on the subject, Spencer thought he recognised Caspasian's as a German Mauser pistol. Spencer had only seen one once before. Caspasian also had some strange sort of carbine attached to his saddle, the thick metal barrel perforated with small holes from stock to muzzle. It was not like any weapon that Spencer had ever seen carried by British troops. Beside it hung several canvas sacks, each holding a round metal container much like a canteen. It was all very odd and he resolved to tackle the Brigadier about it when the moment was right. It would not look good to arrive at the jirga looking as if they were spoiling for a fight.

It was on the evening of the second day when the party had stopped to make camp for the night that Caspasian decided to slip away from the main body.

He had had enough of Henry Allenshaw's muted insults and was afraid that if he heard one more he would lose his temper and drop the man in front of everyone. So as the grooms took charge of the horses and the porters set about pitching camp and preparing the supper, he left the others to their own devices, nodded to Ganga that he was just taking his leave for a while, and set off towards a clump of trees on a hill nearby.

They had selected a spot beside a broad but shallow river. The water was crystal clear and ice cold, burbling and hissing over the brightly polished pebbles where the porters crouched with pots and pans, gathering sufficient to brew tea, boil rice and prepare hot water for washing. A lush meadow stretched from the sprouting tents to a scattering of boulders, and it was beyond these that the first of the trees grew, mostly pine. The higher he ascended, the quieter it became as the noise of the river and the chatter of his companions receded. Eventually he came out into a small level clearing. The sun had fallen below the line of the treetops and it stood in a rapidly cooling shade.

'Perfect,' he said to himself.

He stripped off his sleeveless leather jerkin, and leaned against a tree to remove his riding boots and socks. He massaged and flexed his toes, squatting down several times to stretch his thigh muscles, taut after the day's riding.

When he felt himself sufficiently loosened up, he shook his legs and arms and moved into the centre of the clearing where he stood erect and silent. He steadied his breathing, focusing on it, concentrating on each breath as it flowed in, held, and then went out. Then, as he inhaled, he raised his hands, palm up, all the way to his armpits, keeping his elbows rigidly to the rear, thereby expanding the lungs' capacity, increasing the intake of oxygen, and its flow to the brain.

Next he slid his right foot forward and sank into a low stance, his right knee bent but his rear leg firm and straight, the tendons stretching. Resembling a fencer's thrust, but with the hips and shoulders square to the front, the back upright, Caspasian preferred the Japanese name, zenkutsu-dachi, the forward stance. He then slid forward with the other leg, keeping low, his hips moving at the same level and his feet sliding quickly and smoothly on the soft grass. It was the first method of attack he had learned as a boy in the days when his grandfather had been alive, and long before the young Caspasian had been sent away to school in England where his fighting expertise had set him in good stead, but at the same time isolated him from the other boys who had come to look upon him as a freak. The monkey, they had nicknamed him. Eventually he had worn the tag with pride.

Blotting the painful thoughts from his mind, he brought his hands into play, couching one clenched fist tight beside his chest, elbow hard to the rear, while the other shot forward in a forefist punch aimed at the solar plexus of an imaginary opponent before him. As he punched, slowly at first, Caspasian focused the power on the base knuckles of the punching hand's middle and forefingers. Together they created the weapon, the seiken, a one inch broad rectangle of bone capable of smashing through wood, tiles and brick. The idea, explained to him by the man who had taken the young Caspasian under his wing in those early years, was to focus a couple of inches beyond the point of impact. That way the force of one's blow would carry the fist clean through the target, shattering the wood or whatever else in the process.

Caspasian could almost hear his tutor's voice, soft and gentle when explaining something, but changing to a ferocious roar when executing a demonstration in front of the young boy's startled eyes, transfixed on the splintering boards or the smashed roof tiles. He had known immediately that this was a power he wanted to master. What he had not realised at the time was that it would take years of hard training to achieve, and when he eventually reached an acceptable level of competence, like the ever retreating rainbow's end, he would find that there would always be higher levels to which he would aspire.

He drove himself hard for half an hour, becoming so enrapt in his exercises that he failed to notice the approach of someone through the trees, their footfall muffled by the grass and carpet of pine needles. Unaware that he was being watched, Caspasian changed position, drawing back his front foot and shifting his weight onto his rear leg, crouching down into the cat stance, kokutsu-dachi. At the same time his fists opened to form shuto, the sword hand, executing as he did so a circular double block, the gentle flowing movement sweeping aside an imaginary punch, opening the way for a counter-attack in the form of a kick with the ball of his front foot.

As he spun to face a new quarter, his eyes met Rachel's. She was leaning back against a tree watching him intently, a slight smile on her lips. When she saw his horrified expression she stifled it.

'Don't stop,' she said quickly as Caspasian shot upright as if he had just trodden on broken glass. 'Please, go on. I didn't mean to interrupt you.'

'No, really, I'd finished anyway,' he lied badly. He could feel his cheeks turning scarlet and strode rapidly to the far side of the clearing to retrieve his boots and jerkin.

Rachel silently cursed herself. 'What were you doing anyway? I've never seen anything like it.'

'Oh, it's nothing. Just fooling about.' From somewhere deep inside him, Caspasian could hear the taunts of his school fellows. The monkey. That's what he was. A blasted monkey dancing on a barrel organ, his chain jerked by an unseen hand. Even after the war and everything he'd been through, the boy was still there, his loneliness and hurt pride as raw as ever.

Rachel fought for something to say, sensing the damage she had unwittingly done. At last she said, 'Where did you learn that?'

'Nowhere really,' Caspasian replied brusquely, staring down at his boots as he pulled them on. 'You know, just things I've picked up here and there.'

'It looked far more proficient than that. Come on, where was it? Was it here in India?'

He had finished dressing and sprang to his feet,

brushing the pine needles from his riding breeches. 'We'd better be getting back. Supper should be ready,' he said with a lightness that he certainly did not feel. He walked quickly past her and started off through the trees in the direction of the camp. Rachel waited a moment and then went after him.

She thought she would try one last time. 'Captain Caspasian, I'm sorry I interrupted you.' As he continued to march ahead she felt herself growing angry. 'What's the matter with you? Can't you be civil with anyone? It's not my fault I came upon you in the wood.'

'Isn't it?' he called back coldly over his shoulder.

Rachel felt the sting. 'You arrogant . . .' she blurted out. 'Of all the pig-headed, self-important imbeciles! I bet you think I crept after you to spy.'

'Who knows?'

'How dare you!' She could feel herself reddening with fury. 'And I thought you might just be different from the usual lot I meet out here.' She shook her head in exasperation. 'How wrong I was. You're as dead as the rest of them. Wooden-headed and completely lacking in imagination.'

'Look, just forget it, shall we?' he called back. 'It's not important.'

'Not important? You're rude and abrupt, and all but accuse me of eavesdropping on your woodland antics, and I'm supposed to accept it? Actually I think you owe me an apology!'

Caspasian stopped in his tracks and turned, hands on hips. 'I owe you an apology? How did we get to that? I didn't ask you to follow me . . .'

'I didn't follow you!' Rachel almost shouted at

him. Her hair had come loose and was spread over her shoulders, and her eyes burned with fire. Caspasian felt the force of them drill into him. He blew out a deep breath and hung his head, chin on chest. When he looked up again she was still glaring at him and he was startled to see hatred there.

'Look,' he said as calmly as he could, 'can we just. . .'

His words were cut by a shout from the direction of the camp and he turned to see Ganga trotting easily up the hill towards him. The squat, muscled sergeant stopped, his breath not even labouring after the steep jog, and looked from Caspasian to Rachel and back, puzzled.

'I think you should come, saheb.'

'What is it?'

'Some men. At the camp. Traders, they say, but I think they are lying.'

With a resigned glance at Rachel, Caspasian followed Ganga back down the hillside. She looked after them, shaking her head and then, with a deep sigh, went as well.

When they got back to the camp, Caspasian saw that several small tents had been erected and a collection of pots was already steaming over a large cooking fire, attended to by the porters. The grooms had unsaddled the horses and were rubbing them down by the river. To one side, Bernard Spencer was in a lively and apparently good-natured conversation with a group of half a dozen men in Pathan dress, the loose baggy shirts and trousers topped with headcloths. They were all bearded and looked as if they had been living rough for some time. Brigadier Percival and the others were sitting drinking mugs of tea and Caspasian could see that, although Henry Allenshaw paid no attention to the newcomers, the Brigadier kept glancing warily in their direction. Caspasian saw the relief on his face when he spotted him returning with Ganga.

'Where are the militiamen?' Caspasian quietly asked Ganga.

Ganga sighed. 'Allenshaw Saheb sent them off to try and shoot something for the pot.' He spat with disgust. 'If you ask me, they couldn't shoot their own shadows.'

The traders had seen Caspasian and Ganga and a couple of them exchanged words.

'They're counting our numbers,' Ganga said. Together with Caspasian he moved over to the packs, trying hard to appear unconcerned.

'Ganga, relax,' Caspasian said with a smile. 'You'd never make an actor.'

The Gurkha sergeant grinned. 'Shall we get our weapons?'

'No. The less we show them the better. They won't try anything now. If they're bandits they'll learn all they can and then hit us later.'

'Tonight?'

'Perhaps. Or maybe tomorrow. It depends what the country ahead is like.' Caspasian looked around. 'It's too open here.'

Rachel came into the camp and was about to walk straight over to join her father when the Brigadier got quickly to his feet and intercepted her. 'Ah, there you are, Rachel. Nice walk?' He took her by the elbow and steered her away from the men and towards the fire. 'Mug of tea?'

She was startled, but he kept a firm hold of her, bending his lips closer to her to whisper. 'Your father's doing a splendid job. Probably best to leave him to it, eh? They probably haven't seen an English woman before.'

She was on the point of telling him not to be so absurd when there was a burst of laughter from the traders and they split away from her father, with cheery waves of farewell.

'There you are,' Rachel said. 'No cause for alarm. You and Captain Caspasian will be quite disappointed to have missed out on a fight, won't you?'

The Brigadier stared at her in surprise. 'Caspasian? What's he been saying?'

'Nothing, of course. None of you have really said anything since you arrived, have you? Just pleasantries.'

Before he could take issue with her, she had walked briskly away to her tent. Bernard Spencer came up to him. 'What's the matter with her?'

The Brigadier sipped his tea as if nothing had happened. 'I think she's tired after the hard ride today.' He was thoughtful. 'Listen, Bernard. It's not too late to send her home, you know. Henry and a couple of the militia could escort her.'

'Send her home? Whatever for? She'd make my life a misery if I were to try that. In any case, she wouldn't go. She might be my daughter but she gave up obeying me a long, long time ago.'

Seeing his chance to broach the subject, Spencer continued, 'James, it's good of you to have come with us. I always like company, you know. But is there anything else you can tell me about the real reason for your being here.' He jerked a thumb at Caspasian and Ganga. 'Particularly with those two. It hardly seems like a bona fide fact-finding mission to me.'

'The real reason?' the Brigadier said ingenuously. 'I've told you the reason. As for Caspasian, he's simply under my command. Call him my aide-de-camp, if you like.'

Spencer smiled tiredly. 'All right. I understand. I'll just say that as Political Officer for the region I really ought to know if there's anything going on that could compromise my position.' He quickly held up his hand as the Brigadier started to protest his innocence. 'I'll leave it at that.' He sniffed the air. 'And now I think supper really must be ready. Shall we go and eat?'

Prince Mahsud had been steadily increasing the size of his father's army ever since he had hatched the plan for the Eye of the Storm in conjunction with his contacts in the Bolshevik government in Moscow. It had been hard work but he had found himself warming to it. Perhaps his father's blood did run in his veins after all. Drawing men from all the local tribes, he had watched with immense satisfaction as the numbers swelled. Initially weapons had been a problem. His forces were armed with a mixture of captured British weapons and home-made rifles from the bazaars of Peshawar, which were sound enough for hunting, but too unreliable for a prolonged conflict against a professional army.

The solution had come once again from Moscow. The Bolsheviks had been only too ready to send arms shipments through Afghanistan, paying off the tribes along the way for safe passage with smaller quantities of armaments. But whereas the Afghan tribesmen received only rifles and sparse quantities of ammunition, to Prince Mahsud they sent not only rifles, but light and heavy machine guns.

There were Danish Madsen light-machine guns that the Russians had been using for several years. There were German MG08s, as well as a handful of British Lewises captured from the White Russians. There were French Maxim heavy machine guns. There were medium mortars and grenade launchers. The Bolsheviks had even sent some mountain artillery. The rest was stored in the heart of the fortress, along with case upon case of grenade, bomb, shell and bullet to feed it.

Some of the simpler weapons had already been passed out to the tribes most trusted by the Prince, but for the heavier equipment Mahsud knew that he would need help from the Bolsheviks to direct and advise his men. First of all they would prepare cadres of the best and the brightest, teaching them how to operate the machine guns and artillery and how to deploy them to best effect.

Then, when they were satisfied that these select few were ready, they in turn would train others, the knowledge and expertise cascading down through the ranks of the Prince's followers. He was determined that when they finally met the British in battle, they would be prepared. It would take only one victory for news to spread down into the plains, and then Mahsud would watch as the people rose up in revolt to throw off the imperial yoke, with himself,

Prince Mahsud, as the chosen leader. Just one small victory would suffice, if he was able to display sufficient British dead to his followers.

As he watched his men practising that morning he was impatient for the arrival of the Russians whom he knew to be on the way. He stood at the edge of the makeshift rifle range that had been constructed outside the fortress walls and looked up at the towering mountains. When would they be there?

To build the range, a shelf had been cut out of one side of the ridge extending for nearly six hundred yards. At hundred-yard intervals, firing positions had been marked on the ground so that his men could practise firing at the targets from a variety of ranges. Up to twenty men could fire side by side at a time, more if they closed shoulder to shoulder.

For targets they used dummies in mock-ups of British army uniforms, but this morning he had other plans. Some village elders had been tardy in sending their tribute to the Prince. When they had finally appeared at the fortress gates at daybreak, Mahsud had accepted them with kind smiles, taken their tribute, and then promptly had them arrested. In this he had earned the instant approval of his commanders, although at the same time he had put himself in an awkward position, for what was he to do with them now? At first it had been suggested to him that they should be beheaded, but then, as the rifle range had only recently been completed, Mahsud surprised himself by coming up with what he thought was a far better idea. The elders were taken down to the butts. The target dummies were removed and, in their place, the elders, a dozen in all, were lashed to posts.

To increase the entertainment appeal of the spectacle, Mahsud had selected his newest recruits, given them rifles they had not used before, and started them at the six hundred yards firing point. Each man was issued with thirty rounds, the agreement being that any of the elders left alive by the time all the rounds had been expended would be free to leave. Mahsud himself had taken up a position on the slopes above with his commanders to watch. When everything was ready he gave the order to fire. As the minutes went by it proved to be excellent sport, so much so that he had ordered his midday meal to be brought out to him rather than miss the fun. He quite forgot the Russian advisors.

At last, after a large number of rounds had been fired, the first strike occurred. An old man on the end of the line furthest away from the Prince was hit in the knee. The bullet, a .303 inch, virtually severed his leg, leaving it hanging by shreds of blood-soaked flesh. The commanders cheered and the recruit who had fired the shot grinned delightedly up at them. Mahsud winced at the sight but nevertheless felt unable to take his eyes from it.

Seeing one of their number hit, the other elders screamed all the louder while their companion slowly bled to death, his body slumped forward, pulling against his ropes. Their pleas carried up to Mahsud through the sound of rifle fire, but his attention was on the firers. He was admiring how, as they fired, they were gradually improving. Several of his commanders, becoming bored with the spectacle, had gone down to the firing point and taken it upon themselves to coach the recruits, showing them how to use the rifle sights properly and hug the weapon tight into the shoulder.

Then a second man was hit, this time struck in the stomach. Ironically, having stood there unharmed from the beginning, when he was finally hit, it was by a fusillade of at least five bullets all from different firers. The force of the blows was such that he was split open like a water melon, his intestines tumbling to the ground to lie in a steaming heap at his sandalled feet. The man stared down at them in silence, his mouth working like a fish plucked onto the river bank.

It was a further quarter of an hour before the human targets had been reduced to three who were still living, and each of these had been hit, one almost to the point of death. By now Mahsud had tired of the whole event. He was also a little shocked that the whole affair had been his own idea. The realisation that he was no longer answerable to anyone and that he had supreme power of life and death over people had furrowed his brow with deep interest.

It was hot sitting on the hillside. The sun had moved round and there was no longer any shade to cover him. His attention wandered and in a fit of impatience he suddenly got up to leave. One of his commanders looked at him questioningly, but Mahsud gestured that the entertainment should continue until the job was done, rejecting an initial inclination to clemency for the survivors.

He had just started to walk back up the hill to the

fortress when something came to him. It was a sound. He frowned, wondering, and turned back to the rifle butts where most of the village elders now hung at their posts, doubled over in death. One of the survivors had tilted his face to the sky and was screaming something. He was crying out for help. But what had caught Mahsud's attention was the words he used. Amongst the man's pleas that were aimed at the heavens, the word 'stone' was repeated over and over again.

Mahsud froze on the spot, his spine tingling, first with excitement and then, the very next instant, with terror.

'Stop!' he screamed at the top of his voice. 'Cease firing!'

He raced down the hillside heading straight for the man, shouting all the while at his men to hold their fire. The first man to notice him was one of the commanders at the firing point. He stared open-mouthed at his leader who was running at full speed into the line of fire. He shot to his feet and ran along the line of recruits, snatching at their rifles, kicking them and shouting for them to stop firing.

'If any of you kill this man I will have you fed to the vultures!' Mahsud screamed.

At last the fire became desultory and then stopped, a final bullet cracking dangerously close to Mahsud. The next second the firer was clubbed to unconsciousness by the commander.

At the butts, Mahsud rushed to the village elder. The old man was hysterical with fear and had not noticed that the firing had stopped.

'Silence, old fool!' Mahsud yelled in his face. He

slapped him until the cries subsided into sobs. He had been hit twice, but neither bullet had struck bone, artery or vital organ. The bleeding was slight and Mahsud heaved a huge sigh of relief. He stood before the man and lifted his face so he could look him in the eyes.

'What is this stone you speak of?'

The man started to blubber. In irritation Mahsud shouted for water. One of his men sprinted to his side and handed him a water skin. Mahsud tipped the contents over the old man's head.

'Cut him loose,' he commanded.

The old man slumped to the ground and Mahsud poured more water into his mouth and down his shirt, cooling him. In return the old man seemed to notice at last that his ordeal was over. He seized Mahsud's hands and began to mumble his thanks, kissing Mahsud's fingers which Mahsud snatched away in disgust.

'Listen, old fool. Tell me of this stone and I will let you go free. You and any others of your number can return to your village and tell of what has happened here today. Maybe that will teach you to be more prompt in future. But first, tell me of the stone or you will be tied up again and my men will continue with their target practice.'

For the first time the old man understood what Mahsud was saying. His eyes struggled to focus and he fought to clear his brain, shaking his head to clear the ringing in his ears from the bullets.

'The stone has saved me. I prayed to it and, see, it has delivered me!'

Mahsud gripped the man by his shirt, pulling his

face close to his own. 'What does this stone look like?'

'Pictures . . . strange pictures.'

Mahsud threw back his head and laughed. 'More. Tell me more! You have this stone in your village now?'

'No. Not my village. My cousin. He has the stone.'

'What is his name? His name, damn you?' Mahsud roared, shaking the old man violently.

'Najaf Kasim,' he said finally.

Mahsud spun round on the men who had come to his side. 'Does anyone know this man?'

One of his commanders put up his hand. 'I do. I know Kasim's village.'

Mahsud grinned in triumph. 'The stone is there now?'

'It is there, my Prince,' the old man stammered, hovering on the edge of consciousness.

Mahsud frowned suddenly, remembering the past insult. 'And how did it come to be there? Tell me that.'

'I do not know. I have heard of it and of its power. That is all.'

'You are lying,' Mahsud said, getting to his feet and stepping back from the man. 'You were a party to this theft.'

'No,' the old man said, starting to gabble, realising that events had suddenly turned against him once more. 'It was Kasim. I had nothing to do with it. I promise you.'

Mahsud shook his head. 'It is of no importance. You are of the same blood. If he is guilty then so are you.' He started to walk away. 'Kill him,' he called back over his shoulder. 'Kill them all.'

'The recruits?' his commander asked.

'No, just finish it.' He waved a hand dismissively in the air, noticing with satisfaction as he did so the smiling glances his commanders exchanged.

On the ground the old man blinked, trying to focus on the retreating back of Mahsud. 'But . . . but you said you would spare my life.'

Mahsud did not hear the old man's words. His mind was racing. He knew the location of the stone. It was safe. Soon, very soon it would be in his hands, and then it could all begin.

The old man sank back against the wooden post as one of Mahsud's commanders took a revolver from its holster, pulled back the cocking handle and levelled it at the old man's face, sighting between the eyes. Further along the line of posts there was first one shot and then another as the other remaining elders were executed.

The last thing that entered the old man's mind as he waited for the end was a feeling of satisfaction. He knew that the Prince would indeed hold the stone in his hand, and when he did, the old man knew that he would achieve a measure of revenge. He had heard what the stone had done to Ali the thief. His last prayer was that Prince Mahsud would meet the same end as that.

Chapter Eight

While the porters broke camp the following morning, Caspasian and Ganga prepared themselves for the encounter they were anticipating with the bandits. Ganga sat cross-legged on a rug, stripping his rifle and studiously scrubbing each of the tiny metal parts with a lightly oiled rag, ensuring that no specks of dirt entered the mechanism when he reassembled it, sliding the bolt back and forth, his ear cocked beside it, examining the sound.

Caspasian recharged the drum magazines for his sub-machine gun. Until now, all but two of them had been empty to preserve the spring-loaded mechanism inside. Once filled to its thirty-two-round capacity, the internal spring would be fully compressed. If left for too long at such a tension it would weaken and then it would be only a matter of time before the gun jammed when firing.

He stripped and oiled his Mauser C96 semi-automatic pistol, testing the magazine springs and making sure he had plenty of spares to hand. Ganga handed him a satchel of lightweight egg grenades. Smaller than the Mills bomb, they could be thrown further and were ideal for operations such as this. There were also several white phosphorous grenades which would be useful if they needed to produce a quick smoke screen.

When they were ready, Caspasian walked over to tell the Brigadier.

'How do you want the militia to be used?' Brigadier Percival asked.

'Same as before,' Caspasian answered. 'Two to scout in front and two to bring up the rear. It might be an idea if you tell Major Allenshaw, sir. I don't think he'd listen to me.'

The Brigadier smiled. 'All right. Where are you going to place yourself?'

'Ganga and I will ride close to the packhorses. That way we can keep an eye on the porters in case they decide to throw in their lot with the bandits, and if we're roughly central we can move in any direction when they hit us.'

'Do you think they will?'

Caspasian shrugged. 'We'll see, won't we?'

Caspasian and the Brigadier had voiced their concerns about the supposed traders but Spencer and Allenshaw thought they were over-reacting.

'You run into those kind of fellows all over the place out here,' Allenshaw said nonchalantly as they mounted the horses and gathered before setting off. He grinned at Caspasian. 'Of course, if the young Captain's frightened I'll be happy to ride beside him.'

Caspasian gritted his teeth but said nothing.

With a wave of his hand Allenshaw sent his two men on ahead and then moved his horse beside Rachel's. 'Can I keep you company, my dear?'

Rachel smiled. 'Why not?' She glanced icily at

Caspasian. 'I'd appreciate some civilised conversation.' She called across for Douglas Channing and the Doctor to join them, noting the look of disappointment that crossed Allenshaw's face.

The two soldiers from the militia set off, moving quickly out of the old camp site and turning their horses towards the rising hills. All the talk of an ambush had unsettled them and they rode side by side, glancing anxiously around at the hillsides and trees, their rifles on their laps.

For the next two hours the group made good progress. The ground was open and the horses, rested from the night by the river, were enjoying the spring in their step. The riders, overcoming their initial wariness, spread themselves out, except for the tight little group clustered around Rachel. From time to time there would be an outburst of laughter as one of the men regaled the others with a story.

From his position beside the packhorses, Caspasian looked on with contempt. Occasionally Allenshaw would glance back over his shoulder, grinning broadly with satisfaction that he had manoeuvred himself to Rachel's side, and relishing the sight of Caspasian relegated to pack escort.

For his part, Caspasian forced himself to keep his mind on the job in hand. The memory of the previous evening in the glade was like an open wound and he could feel himself smart whenever he remembered turning round and finding Rachel watching him. What was more, he was baffled by his reaction to her. Had it been anyone else he would have continued to the end of the exercise sequence before allowing himself to be interrupted. There was something about Rachel however that had put him off balance and he resented it. She was certainly very attractive. Extremely so, in fact, but Caspasian had resisted beauty before. With her it was different. There was a fierce independence about her, and a self-confidence that was wholly natural and understated. She was unlike any woman he had come across since returning to India.

This realisation reinforced his irritation that he had made such a fool of himself.

'Like a sulking bloody schoolboy,' he muttered to himself. 'After everything I've been through, I get felled by a schoolboy's hurt pride, damn it.' He shook his head with self-disgust.

Ganga looked across at him but kept silent. He had seen Caspasian like this before and knew that he was best left alone to come to terms with his own demons uninterrupted.

When the rifle shot rang out it cut through Caspasian's tortured reverie and brought him to his senses in an instant. At the front of the column one of the two soldiers sat bolt upright, one hand clutching at his chest, and then slowly toppled out of his saddle and on to the ground.

Brigadier Percival stood in his stirrups and shouted. 'Ambush!'

In one second Caspasian had considered the options. There were three. Turn round and ride back the way they had come, dismount and shoot it out, or ride on through the ambush. The bandits had chosen their ground well, as might have been expected. Had the column attempted to turn round they would have inevitably bunched together, presenting the enemy with an easy target. To dismount was also hazardous, for the cover was sparse and they were in the middle of the enemy's chosen killing ground. To ride through was also dangerous as the valley narrowed and curved out of sight and no one could know what lay round the bend. Perhaps further bandits were lying in wait. Nevertheless, it would at least get them out of the killing ground and, with luck, would be the course of action the bandits least expected.

Caspasian took a deep breath and opened his mouth to shout, but before he could do so, Allen-shaw screamed, 'Take cover!'

Caspasian saw the Brigadier look back, a look of surprise on his face. He caught Caspasian's eye.

'Ride on, sir!' Caspasian shouted above the noise of frightened horses, churning hooves and gunfire. The Brigadier nodded agreement, but as he pulled his horse around, he was met by Bernard Spencer jostling into him. The two horses locked together, the Brigadier cursing as they circled, the beasts panick-ing in an effort to break free. Further back, Allen-shaw was already on his feet pulling Rachel from her saddle, the Doctor and Douglas Channing following.

Caspasian spat. 'Damn this!' He spurred his horse to the nearest cover available, a scattering of boulders, and slid from the saddle, catching at the satchels of spare magazines and grenades as Ganga arrived beside him, sprawling in the dust as a fu-sillade of bullets snapped in the air around them.

'I hope that bastard Allenshaw gets it,' Caspasian said, but in the next instant he thought of Rachel at Allenshaw's side. He craned to see round the side of the rock that shielded him from the firers. Rachel and Allenshaw were about thirty yards away, Channing and the Doctor tucked in behind the same poor screen of scrub. All of them were hugging the ground as if willing it to open up and shelter them.

'Can you see any of the firers?' Caspasian asked desperately.

Ganga had been studying the surrounding ridgelines, his eyes narrowed with the effort. He nodded slowly and pointed. 'There, saheb,' he said. 'One of them hasn't dried the oil from his barrel.'

Sure enough, when the next shots came, Caspasian saw the telltale puff of black smoke. 'Can you hit him?'

Ganga smiled privately but did not reply. Instead he cocked his rifle and snuggled down into a solid firing position. When his body was set as if moulded to the earth, he set his sights and pulled the rifle's metal butt plate tight into his right shoulder as if propelling a screw into wood. His breathing steadied, slowing, the final breath being drawn in, and then expelled. For a moment he was empty, lungs and mind, focused on the line from his shoulder to the distant target. His finger tightened smoothly until the firing pin slammed into the base of the .303-inch round clasped in the chamber. His body absorbed the recoil with barely a flinch, the shock wave travelling through him and into the earth unimpeded.

When the shot had been released, he paused a moment, and then opened his left eye, looking hard at the target. Although a good six hundred yards away, he and Caspasian saw the barrel of a rifle lurch up in the air and fall behind the rock where its owner had just had half his face removed by Ganga's bullet. Without further ado, Ganga swivelled on his belly, hunting for fresh targets.

'Why don't you bloody well fire, Caspasian?'

Caspasian looked round and saw Allenshaw's scarlet face set in a grimace of scared anger. A bullet popped the ground at Allenshaw's feet and he replied with three rounds from his revolver fired randomly in the direction of the hillside.

'Don't waste your ammo,' Caspasian called across.

'I don't see you using yours,' Allenshaw shouted back petulantly.

Caspasian did not bother to respond, but Allenshaw was right in one respect. Caspasian's submachine gun was almost as useless at this range as his own revolver. Somehow he had to close the distance.

He reached into one of the satchels and took out two white phosphorous grenades.

'What are you doing?' Ganga asked.

'I've got to get up there,' Caspasian answered, pointing at the jagged ridgeline, heavily littered with rocks.

Ganga fired off one more shot, spat in disgust at his lack of success, and gathered himself to follow.

Caspasian pulled the pins of the two grenades, tested the wind for direction, and then threw first one and then the other so that they landed some twenty yards apart. When they burst, an instantaneous screen of dense white smoke sprang up, the wind catching it and spreading it across the front of Caspasian's position like a curtain.

'Now!' Caspasian said. Together with Ganga he broke from cover and sprinted hard for a line of trees that snaked down from the ridgeline, reaching a point fifty yards from where he and Ganga had lain. The smoke screen covered them for most of this and by the time they cleared it and were spurting across the last open yards, it was too late for the bandits to realise what was happening and bring their fire to bear upon them.

Caspasian and Ganga broke into the tree line, branches snapping about them as they thrust their way in, dropping to their knees to take stock only when they were confident that they were screened from view. A livid voice barked at them from the valley floor. 'Come back you cowardly swines! You'll be court-martialled and shot for this!'

Ganga laughed. 'Can that man get any more stupid?' but Caspasian's mind was already on other things. The first task was to get up on to a level with the bandits. Once there, they could work their way along the ridgeline, taking them on one at a time from the flank, rolling them up until either they were all dead or, more likely, they decided to call it a day and run.

'Let me go first,' Ganga said.

Caspasian cocked his MP18 sub-machine gun and started up the wooded hillside. 'Just watch my back.'

He moved quickly, judging that the ground immediately around them was clear, the bandits having placed themselves only on the ridgeline. Holding the MP18 close to his body with his right hand, with his left he brushed aside the branches. The going was steep but the two men were fit. This was what they were both trained for. This was the place where they both came alive. You could keep your desk in Delhi, Caspasian thought as he spied the trees thinning out ahead. He would be damned if he ever allowed himself to be sent back to it.

They reached the crest of the hill, the trees parting to form a clearing at the summit. Strangely, the gunfire seemed a long way off. Here at the top of the hill it was almost peaceful. The far side was also tree-covered, but from the peak it was possible to see out across the treetops to the valley beyond. For a moment Caspasian was tempted to stop and enjoy the smell of the woods. There was a light breeze and the pine boughs waved gently, wafting their scent across the clearing.

'Come on,' he said reluctantly. There was work to do.

It was impossible to tell whether the bandits had realised what he and Ganga were up to. They would have seen the smoke screen, but might have assumed with Allenshaw that they were running away from the fight.

The answer came the next second when they heard someone crashing through the trees towards them, coming from the direction of the ambush positions.

Instinctively, Ganga moved off to Caspasian's left, the two of them thereby coming into line so that they could both bring their weapons to bear on anyone approaching from the front. Ganga crouched down beside a tree. He brought his rifle butt into the shoulder but kept the barrel lowered, watching for his target, ready for a snap shot. Caspasian moved to the right, both hands on his MP18. He knew the weapon canted sharply to the left when fired, the side of the heavy drum magazine, so he braced himself to counter it, the heel of his left palm pressing on the perforated barrel, ready to take the strain.

Whoever was coming towards them suddenly stopped. Everything went quiet. Caspasian was just wondering what might have alerted him when he heard the sound of water on stone. He looked across at Ganga who grinned.

'Taking a piss,' Ganga mouthed silently.

Caspasian nodded. It was too good a chance to pass up. He crept slowly forward, noting Ganga out of the corner of his eye keeping pace on the left. Some ten yards ahead he saw a large boulder and, from around the side of it, the crimson headscarf of the bandit. He was facing the other way, the seemingly unending stream of urine splashing delightedly against the grey stone. Caspasian heard the man sigh with pleasure. Clearly he had been sent to investigate against his will, believing the flank free of enemies and taking the opportunity to relieve himself.

Caspasian flicked on his safety catch. The MP18, like most sub-machine guns, sometimes discharged itself if jolted or dropped. He then reversed the weapon, right hand on the barrel, left hand taking hold of the stock, and advanced round the side of the boulder. With each step more of the bandit came into view. He had put his rifle aside and Caspasian gauged how long it would take the man to get to it. Too long.

With his sub-machine gun at shoulder height, Caspasian closed the last three paces, placing his feet stealthily each time before shifting his weight. The man's back was to him, head down inspecting the stream snaking away from the foot of the rock. Caspasian waited.

The man finished. His head came up, the neck straightening. As it did so, Caspasian punched the butt plate of the MP18 sharply into the base of the man's skull, projecting it in deep. Just as he had been taught, he focused the blow beyond the man's spine where it joined the base of the skull, and so it went. The head jolted oddly backwards as the neck broke under the force of the blow, the body went limp and sank to the floor. The bandit had died without even noticing, as Caspasian had, that he had pissed on his own sandals.

Caspasian quickly searched the body for anything that might be of use. There was nothing. The rifle was ancient and looked as if it had been made in one of the local bazaars, so Caspasian removed the bolt and flung it away as far as he could. Anyone finding the weapon would always be able to have another one made, but for now at least it was inoperable.

Down in the valley, Rachel had at first been terrified, but the longer they remained pinned down by the sniping fire from the ridgeline, the angrier she became. Henry Allenshaw was all over the place. First he scrabbled to one side, blazing off a couple of random shots, and then he wriggled and squirmed back again, slithering over Rachel's legs to crack off another couple of equally useless shots in the other direction.

His outburst at Captain Caspasian had taken her by surprise. She had looked over to see the dense white smoke screen, the two figures snaking quickly away into the treeline. Although she was certainly no soldier, she did pride herself on knowing something about human nature. She had only known Caspasian and the Gurkha sergeant a few days and her opinion of the Captain had suffered from the meeting in the woods the previous day. Nevertheless, she was quite sure that neither of them was the sort of person to run away from a fight, leaving their comrades to thrash it out unaided.

Dr McCloud had gone to attend to the injured man and had succeeded in dragging him into cover. Rachel could see him working over the man, attempting to stem the bleeding. Douglas Channing, on the other hand, had proved to be only slightly more useful than Allenshaw. Armed with a Lee-Enfield rifle, he was cracking away randomly at the bandits. Rachel could forgive him however. He was a civilian after all, and his aim seemed to be improving the more he fired.

She could see her father a few yards away. His greatest concern was his daughter's safety and Rachel had had trouble waving aside his efforts to crawl back to her. Beside him, Brigadier Percival was the model of cold efficiency, selecting target after target, and engaging each deliberately until it fell silent. In between, he would take stock of those around him, shouting encouragement here, or goading there. Twice he had called for Allenshaw to get his men to concentrate their fire more effectively, but his effort had been wasted and he had given up trying. The militia, when they dared to shoot at all, blazed away in panic-stricken flurries, retreating behind their cover after each one to summon the courage for another ineffective sortie a few minutes later.

One of the porters screamed. When the ambush had been sprung they had at first tried to take the horses and flee the way they had come. One of the grooms, a long-time employee of the Spencers, had stopped them, fearing that once out of sight they would keep on going, leaving Bernard Spencer and the others to their fate. He had grouped them in cover as if awaiting the passing of a rain storm. When the firing stopped they would be there, waiting.

Rachel looked round to see the porter fall face down, legs kicking in spasmodic jerks. She searched desperately for Dr McCloud but he was busy and, in any case, the noise was now too great for him to hear her even if she called.

The temptation to stay where she was was immense. She could not be seen by the bandits and was as safe as the moment allowed. Furthermore, as a woman she knew she was free of the expectations of physical courage with which the men around her were burdened. Poor old Henry Allenshaw, skittering around from side to side, trying to be seen to do the right thing without really knowing what that was, presented a pathetic spectacle. Yet in some ways Rachel had to admire the man. Clearly no natural soldier, he nevertheless felt the weight of duty upon him, and was doing all he could to perform.

All her life, Rachel had scorned the pampered wives that she had seen, living out their unproductive lives, occupying themselves with little more than pastimes. It was one of the spurs that had driven her to study medicine. She could not help smiling to herself. This was the test. The moment of truth. Her bluff had been called.

She had gone before Allenshaw or Channing noticed. When they did, they cried out in unison. Bernard Spencer looked round, his face a mask of horror when he saw his daughter sprinting across the open ground towards the wounded porter. He started up, but the Brigadier's iron hand grabbed hold of him and thrust him back into cover.

'Stay down, man! Leave the girl to do what she can for the fellow.'

Rachel felt her heart pounding as she ran, though not with the effort. Accustomed to an active life, she had always been fit. She had never been in such danger however. She had never been shot at. At first, she thought that the spurts of dust at her feet were stones thrown up by her own feet. When she realised they were bullets, she felt physically sick. A momentary panic swept through her. Her limbs went weak until she felt she was going to collapse, her legs like rubber. Only her instinct for self-preservation kept her going.

With one last great effort she propelled herself forward and dived into the middle of the group huddling around the body of their comrade behind the rocks. The realisation that someone had been firing at her was overpowering. Some other human being had sighted their rifle at her, putting all their effort in ending her life. She shook her head to clear it. There was a job to do.

The man lay on his back. The bullet had struck him centre chest. From the bright red blood frothing at his lips she realised one of his lungs had collapsed. The hole had to be sealed. Her satchel of medical equipment was with the pack horses which wheeled and spun in terror in the open. It would be madness to try and reach it. All she had in her pocket was a handkerchief. She snatched at the headscarf of one of the porters. The man grabbed at it, but the groom who had held the group together understood what Rachel was doing and slapped the man's hand away. She folded it into a tight wad and pressed it firmly against the bullet hole, bearing down on it with all her might. It was not working. Blood was still pumping from the man's mouth, foaming and bright scarlet.

'Roll him over,' she said. The men around her stared dumbly. Taking the man by the shoulder, she tried to do it herself, saying again, 'Roll him over!'

The groom helped her and the wounded man flopped over on to his stomach. As he did so, his back came into view. Rachel felt herself gag. She covered her mouth with one hand, clenching the muscles of her stomach and fighting for control. The bullet had passed right through the porter, but whereas it had made little more than a neat hole when entering the chest, the exit wound on the man's back was raw and gaping. The hole was the size of a man's fist.

Rachel sat back on her heels and stared. For the first time in her life she felt utterly helpless. Thinking that all she needed were further bandages, the porters offered more cloths. Only Rachel knew that their efforts were wasted. Even with a fully equipped modern surgery at hand the man's chances of living were small. He had lost a lot of blood, and dirt from the ground was clotted around the wound. Fighting back tears of exasperation, Rachel stuffed the cloths into the hole, packing them down tight. For a moment it seemed as if the man stabilised. His breathing stopped rasping and became more even, but she knew it was only a matter of time before he bled to death from the massive internal injury. What had she been thinking of, running across like a saviour angel? Here she was, all her years of learning and effort useless. Unable to cry, unwilling to leave her patient, she bore down on the bandages and prayed for the man to die quickly.

The bandits never saw Caspasian coming. He and Ganga had worked their way along the rocks, leaving the trees behind them and clambering over the scattered rocks and boulders. When he saw the group of three men a few yards ahead, Caspasian signalled to Ganga to leave them to him. He steadied his grip on the MP18 and advanced. All three of the men were intent on the valley below. One of them had just hit something and was pointing out his success to the others.

Caspasian covered the last yard and stopped, bracing himself. His finger squeezed the trigger and the gun burst into life. The barrel tugged to the left but Caspasian held it fast, spraying short controlled bursts into the bandits. A fourth man who had been concealed on the far side of the rock sprang up and let off a shot in his direction. Ganga's rifle cracked and the man fell back.

Now that the dead men's companions had been alerted to the presence of an enemy on the ridgeline, they ceased firing on the people below and closed in with unexpected fury. Two of them burst around the corner, coming at Caspasian from the side. He swung his MP18 onto them, pulled the trigger, the gun fired and jammed. Hard behind Caspasian, Ganga's line of fire was blocked. He darted aside to get a clear shot but it was too late. The bandits were upon them.

Caspasian just had time to sidestep the first man who rushed him. As he did so he swung the butt of his gun up and around, catching the man in the chest and knocking him to the ground. Again he reversed his grip on the MP18, ready to slam it down on to the man's face before he could rise, but unlike the first bandit Caspasian had killed, this one was alert and ready for him. He rolled aside and sprang to his feet, drawing a long knife from his belt as he did so.

While Ganga grappled with his comrade, the man circled Caspasian. Their eyes locked and Caspasian knew he had a fight on his hands. The man lunged at Caspasian's chest. Caspasian parried the blow aside with the jammed MP18, metal sparking on metal. The man lunged again, this time at the face. Holding the MP18 with his left hand Caspasian knocked the blade out of the way, and with his right, fired a punch at the man's face. His knuckled fist hit the cheekbone below the man's left eye. Caspasian saw him flinch with the pain. The knife fell from his hands, Caspasian dropped the MP18 and closed in.

He feinted with a left to the face, the man's hands shot up instinctively to shield himself, not seeing the real attack which came in with a low right punch to the solar plexus. As he delivered it, Caspasian dropped his hips, putting his whole weight behind the blow and driving the fist in hard and fast. He found his target. The man's eyes bulged and he doubled over. Without a pause and without breaking the momentum of his attack, Caspasian brought his knee up into the man's face, feeling the nose bone shatter. Clenching his right hand into the tettsui hammer fist, he brought it down on to the back of the man's neck. The whole body shuddered under the force of the blow, fell and lay still.

Caspasian turned to see Ganga wiping the blade of his kukri. His opponent's neck was cut half through. Ganga's eyes however were already scanning the rocks around them. He retrieved his rifle, checked its load, and waited for Caspasian's orders.

The firing had stopped from the ridgeline, but for all they knew there might still be other men further along. Moving in short bursts, Caspasian and Ganga continued to clear the ridgeline, each covering the other as they moved. A desultory fire still came from the valley below where Henry Allenshaw and his nervous militia continued to fire up the hillside.

When they were confident that there were no more bandits in the ambush position, Caspasian and Ganga moved carefully up to the edge of the rocks. Without looking over, Caspasian shouted for the men below to hold their fire. His cry was met with a fusillade of shots. He sat back and cursed. Ganga smiled, resigned to the inefficiency of others.

'For God's sake, stop firing!' Caspasian screamed at the top of his voice.

Down below, Brigadier Percival heard him and passed the word. Allenshaw looked on doubtfully. 'How do we know it isn't a trap?'

Brigadier Percival sighed. 'Trust me, Henry. It's Caspasian all right. If he says it's safe to stop firing, then it's safe.'

'Well I don't know about that . . .'

'Major Allenshaw,' the Brigadier barked, 'Just do as I say.'

It was several minutes before Caspasian and Ganga appeared over the top of the ridgeline and made their way back down to the valley floor. Before starting down, they had seen two further bandits heading off on horseback at speed. Ganga had been keen to have a shot at them but Caspasian had stopped him. They were at the limit of the Lee-Enfield's range and it was likely they were simply fleeing, never to return. Caspasian did not admit to Ganga the other reason for stopping him, that he thought there had already been enough killing for one day.

When Caspasian and Ganga jogged down into the valley the first thing they saw were the bodies of four men, the militia soldier who had been hit first, his comrade who had been killed later in the ambush, the porter who Rachel had tried to save, and one of the two grooms. What shocked Caspasian most however was Rachel herself. She stood with her arms folded covering her chest, hugging herself.

Her head was upright and although Caspasian could see she had been crying there were no tears now, just a faraway look that he recognised all too well. He had seen it before in many a face after a first experience of combat. What shocked him though was seeing it on Rachel.

He glared at her father who should never have allowed her to accompany them, but the next moment he realised that this was nothing compared to what lay ahead of them.

He walked across to her. 'Are you all right?'

She turned away from him. 'What do you think?'

'Look, Rachel, you've got to go back. This is stupid. What are you trying to prove?'

The look in her eyes as she spun to face him was like a physical blow. 'How dare you? How dare you treat me like some . . . some. . .'

'Get away from her Caspasian.' Henry Allenshaw strode up to him, the revolver threateningly in his fist. 'While you were scampering about on the hillside before we drove them off, Miss Spencer tried to save one of the wounded porters.' He looked at her, seeming on the point of tears himself. 'It was heroic. Dashed heroic.'

If he had cleared the jam in his MP18, Caspasian felt he would probably have emptied the rest of the magazine into the Major. As it was he swung back the muzzle and was about to drive in into Allenshaw's face when Brigadier Percival grabbed it by the stock. He glared into Caspasian's eyes.

'That'll do, you two. Break it up or I'll have you both on a charge, do you hear me?'

He steered Caspasian away, keeping a firm hold

on his arm. When they were out of earshot he said, 'Good work up there, Caspasian. You and Ganga did a fine job.' He glanced over his shoulder at Allenshaw who was busy comforting Rachel, ignoring her pleas that she most wanted to be left alone.

'We'll have to watch that idiot. I wish we could have come by ourselves, but that was never on the cards. We need them as cover.' He slapped Caspasian on the back, including him in the conspiracy. 'There'll be no sending of anyone back. Our mission is far too important to be upset by the safety of any one or two people.'

'I understand that Brigadier, but Rachel . . .'

'Rachel knew the dangers. She made her own choice, as did we all,' he said. He pulled back and eyed Caspasian mysteriously. 'You're not becoming, how shall I put it, involved, are you?'

Caspasian felt himself redden. 'Of course not.'

'Good. Not like you. Not like you at all.'

The Brigadier chuckled and walked away, leaving Caspasian staring after him. So that was his reputation, was it? Cold-hearted. Ruthless. He spat the dust from his mouth and sighed. The Brigadier was right. What had he been thinking of? It was all a matter of self-discipline, of steeling the spirit and chilling the heart. Rachel was not worth bothering about. The mission was what counted, and that was all there was to it.

Silencing the dissenting voice in his head, Caspasian tugged the drum magazine from his sub-machine gun, and went in search of somewhere to sit so he could clear the jam.

Chapter Nine

The first Alexei Karpov and his party knew about the Prince's escort was when they stepped into the ring of light cast by the campfire. Novikov was on his feet in a second, cursing the porters they had placed as guards. His hand moved towards the flap of his holster, but he was dissuaded by a gesture from one of the armed men confronting them in a circle.

There was a silent stand-off as each side gauged the other, the Bolsheviks believing the others were robbers, the Prince's guards confused by the dishevelled appearance of the men they had been sent to meet. How could such as these be the Soviet military advisory team so respected by their master who had placed such faith in their assistance, as all his men knew? They had been told on numerous occasions that the arrival of the Bolsheviks would herald in a new era. Yet the men who stood uncertainly before them in the firelight looked more like escaped prisoners than soldiers.

One of the Prince's commanders stepped forward. He looked grimly from one to the other, trying to seek out a leader amongst the four Russians. He fixed his eyes on the biggest of them, Novikov.

'I have been sent by Prince Mahsud to fetch you.'

There was a collective sigh of relief and a short, diminutive figure smiled. 'My name is Alexei Karpov. I am in charge of this expedition.'

The commander looked with surprise at Karpov, the disappointment written clearly on his face. 'Oh. My name is Ahmed. You are the leader?'

A laugh came from the tall Bolshevik who wiped the food from his moustache. 'That's what he said. Are you questioning it?'

Karpov waved aside Novikov's taunt. 'Forgive my comrade, Ahmed.' He gestured to his grubby clothes. 'You must pardon my appearance. It is not how I would have wished to meet the Prince's soldiers but we have had a very long and difficult journey.'

Ahmed scowled at Novikov. 'I understand.' He remembered something and waved to more of his men who stood in the darkness behind him. 'Your guards were asleep. Both of them. I could hear their snoring. It led me straight to their positions.'

The two men were brought forward and thrown at Karpov's feet. Ahmed looked on expectantly awaiting Alexei's judgement. Karpov looked down at the cowering figures in confusion wondering what he was expected to do. His hand went unwillingly to the revolver at his belt but before he could draw it, Novikov walked over to the two men, kicked one of them hard in the face, knocked aside the arms of the other as he tried to shield himself from the punishment to come, and kicked him even harder.

'We will deal with them later in our own way,' he said, fixing Ahmed with an evil grin. Ahmed nodded, getting the measure of the Bolshevik and wondering how it was that in a supposedly civilised country such a man as this was not the leader instead of the grey-haired weasel who had declared himself in charge.

'I am glad that I have found you because you were going in the wrong direction,' Ahmed said with some satisfaction.

'Wrong direction?' Karpov stammered. 'But my map and compass . . .'

'That sort of thing is all very well,' Ahmed said. 'Here it is best to use guides.' He glanced at the porters huddled together to one side. 'Reliable ones.' He raised a hand and a score of heavily armed men stepped out of the night on all sides. 'We will sleep here until daybreak and then I will lead you to Prince Mahsud.'

'Excellent. I am looking forward to seeing his base. I have heard much about it,' Alexci said.

Ahmed clicked his fingers and pointed to the best place by the fire where one of his men instantly set about unrolling the commander's bedding. 'We are not going to the fortress. Not yet at least.' He chuckled, the sound gurgling deep in his bearded throat. 'Prince Mahsud has a little entertainment prepared for you first. A sort of welcoming gift, if you like. Or perhaps a demonstration.'

'Demonstration? A demonstration of what?' Alexei disliked having the control of the mission wrested from him, particularly in front of his men.

'You will see. For now, eat.' Ahmed's men had brought the carcass of a goat to the fire and had set about fixing it to a spit.

'I must post guards,' Karpov said despondently.

'Ha!' Ahmed roared delightedly. 'Don't concern yourself with that. Tonight you will sleep well in my protection. Besides, no one would dare attack soldiers of Prince Mahsud.'

He caught the exchange of glances between Karpov and Novikov. 'Sleep peacefully, my friends. If I had wanted to kill you I could already have done so many times over.'

Novikov shrugged. 'He's right, comrade.' He sat down beside the fire where the goat fat had started to spit and hiss, the flames hungrily leaping up to lick at it. 'I for one am going to sleep soundly tonight.'

Karpov slept badly that night, less from fear of treachery at the hands of Ahmed and his men, as from indigestion due to the greasy goat meat he had been obliged to swallow out of politeness. Novikov had delighted in eating more than the rest of them and, in his inimitable fashion, had won over the Prince's escort with conjuring tricks that even a child could see through. Nevertheless, Karpov had to admit that the man was an admirable diplomat, easing the tension between the two groups before falling asleep himself, and snoring louder even than Ahmed.

When the dawn came, scurrying the darkness from the sky, Karpov sat up and scratched the stubble on his chin. His mouth tasted foul and he longed for an enamel bath filled with hot soapy water. Instead he looked around at the prone bodies, most still rumbling in sleep, some starting, like him, to awake and enter the day.

It was a couple of hours before the group was on the move. Tea had been brewed and consumed, along with cold chapatis and goat meat. Karpov had declined the latter, feeling himself start to retch at the sight and smell of it.

In spite of his ill-humour, however, he found himself relaxing. He did not doubt the truth of what Ahmed had said. Surely no one would attack the Prince's men in his own territory. With the tension of danger removed, Karpov sat back and allowed his mind to roam. He thought ahead to the work that they would carry out with the Prince fomenting rebellion along the frontier, but most of all he thought of the stone. It was the key to so much.

It was early afternoon when Ahmed rode up beside him. 'We are nearly there.'

'You haven't yet told me where we are going,' Karpov replied evenly.

Ahmed grinned. 'Just tell your men to be very quiet. On no account fire any weapon. We must not draw attention to our presence here.'

He spurred his horse ahead, taking the lead up a thickly wooded narrow defile. Near the head of it he dismounted, his men following suit. Novikov and Karpov looked at one another. Novikov shrugged and swung off his horse.

Leaving the mounts with some of his men, Ahmed led the way upwards on foot, becoming more and more cautious as he went. By the time they reached the neck of the defile, they were on all fours, crawling slowly forwards until they came to a broad screen of scrub and tall grass. Ahmed pushed into it on his belly, waving Karpov and the others up beside him.

To Karpov's surprise, on the far side he saw a peaceful village scene in the wide valley below.

Houses were clustered around a village square where a well was the centre of unremarkable activity. Women came and went, lowering pots over its lip, and then retrieving them fully laden. Children played in the dirt, chickens scratched, a few goats and sheep were gathered in pens, and the menfolk that were visible generally sat in small groups in the shade, playing some sort of board game.

Karpov looked at Ahmed. 'Very interesting, but what is this to us?'

Ahmed grinned, his stained teeth bearing shreds of the cold goat meat he had eaten for breakfast. He squinted up at the sun.

'Soon,' he said. 'Very soon.'

Karpov sighed, wishing to express his boredom to his host in the only way he dared. He reached for the pair of binoculars that hung around his neck. In a second Ahmed's fist grasped his hand. 'No.' He pointed to the sun. 'The reflection will be seen.'

Karpov tugged his hand away petulantly but left his binoculars for now.

They did not have too long to wait. The peace of the valley was suddenly shattered by a fusillade of gunfire. Karpov, startled out of a reverie, looked down and saw lines of horsemen riding down on the village from all sides. Amongst the houses, panic spread like wildfire. People emptied into the streets to see what was happening. Then, as the horsemen neared, the menfolk rushed for their guns. Women swept their children in their arms and ran for shelter, slamming and barring doors and windows. There was no time to organise any form of coordinated defence. The surprise of the attack had been complete. By the time the first of the horsemen were entering the outer edges of the settlement, only a handful of armed villagers was there to meet them.

A few shots were fired, but Karpov did not see any of the attackers fall from their horses. Instead, the defenders were cut down where they stood, their cries reaching Karpov at his vantage point several seconds after he had watched in fascination, the sweep of sabre or the thrust of a knife. He had seen mass destruction before, plenty of it. In the Great War he had seen death being meted out to men in their thousands as they walked stolidly and unquestioningly, rank upon rank, into the withering fire of the German machine guns. He had even seen the cold butchery of civilians, both by Red Russian forces as well as by White during the civil war. Somehow though, the more he saw of it, the more he felt unable to drag his eyes away. It was as if he was staring into the depths of some ghastly pit, whose contents were at the same time both repellant and hypnotic.

Beside him someone sighed. He turned to see Novikov staring glumly at the spectacle below. 'What is all this?' he said.

Karpov shrugged uncaring, his eyes still glued to the distant slaughter.

Ahmed replied, 'All will become clear soon enough.'

Novikov spat and crawled away muttering to himself.

'Your friend has a weak stomach,' Ahmed said in surprise.

'Never underestimate Vassily Novikov,' Karpov

said. 'And I would never call him weak if I were you. At least not to his face.'

Ahmed looked over his shoulder with renewed interest as Novikov went back down the defile to the horses. 'I will remember that. Perhaps we shall have to put your comrade to the test.'

Karpov smiled. 'Don't, my friend. Life is short enough as it is.'

In one part of the village, Karpov noticed that the resistance was fiercest. All of the houses were flat-roofed and on one particular house a group of villagers had mustered with rifles and shotguns and were giving a good account of themselves. The house looked as if it had been built as a miniature stockade, possibly the domain of the village headman, and by the speed with which the guard had assembled Karpov judged that they had probably already been present there, not expecting this attack perhaps, but on guard to protect someone or something.

Alexei felt his heart go cold. He looked sharply round at Ahmed who met his wide open eyes with a knowing smile. Before Alexei could frame the question he most wanted to ask, Ahmed held a finger to his lips. 'It would be unseemly of me to say what should be reserved for my Prince. He will tell you everything soon.'

'Prince Mahsud is here?'

Ahmed scanned the activity before them and pointed. Karpov followed the direction and saw a cluster of horsemen grouped on a small hillock to one side of the village, surveying the attack. To the front of the group he could just make out a single horseman, and even from a distance Karpov could see the difference of his dress.

'Prince Mahsud,' Ahmed said simply, seeing the light dawn on Karpov's face.

'And the . . .?'

'Enough. Be patient.'

As the assault worked its way to the centre of the village, the Prince's horsemen dismounted to batter down the doors and drag out the occupants of the houses that had already been bypassed. Karpov noticed that only those who resisted were being killed. Everyone else was being kept alive, preserved for some other fate.

Several of the houses were in flames. The screams of people trapped inside swept up the hillside to where Karpov lay. A figure tottered from one of the burning houses, clothes alight. Its arms flapped at the flames engulfing it, spinning in a tight circle like a dog chasing its tail in a futile attempt to extinguish the fire. Ahmed laughed and Karpov found himself sniggering. He was shocked for a moment, but shrugged it off.

Ahmed sat up and scratched, the need for concealment no longer necessary. He belched, the stench of his breakfast wafting over to Karpov who grimaced with disgust.

'Come. We might as well go down. By the time we get there it will all be over and you can meet the Prince. He will enjoy that.'

They backed away from their vantage point and went quickly down to the horses where Novikov met them. He frowned doubtfully at Karpov. 'Seen enough, comrade?'

Alexei pouted but found he could not look his friend in the eye. 'It's not like you to take the moral high ground.'

Novikov shook his head. 'It's not for me to say. I only know I don't like watching women and kids being murdered. Soldiers in battle . . . that's another matter. But women and kids . . .?' Novikov shrugged.

Karpov pulled himself into his saddle. 'If this mission comes off as we intend, you'll have to see a lot more unpleasantness.'

'Ah!' Novikov said, as if suddenly all had become clear. 'So that's what you call it? Unpleasantness. How . . . clean. That's so like you, Alexei. Neat and tidy. Leaving others to shovel the shit.'

Karpov stared at him, shocked by the vehemence of his tone. 'Vassily, what's got into you?' He softened, reaching down to lay a hand on his friend's shoulder. 'What is it?'

Novikov shook his head, gripping the pommel of his saddle as he swung himself up. He smiled sadly. 'I don't know. I'm getting too old for this game.'

'Too old? You?' Karpov stared at him, smiling.

Novikov tugged his horse's head around to point down the defile where Ahmed and his men were leading the way down to the burning village. 'I'm sorry, Alexei. Forget it. Perhaps I'm just too far from home.'

The ride down to the valley took them round the back of the hill from where they had watched the attack, and by the time they reached the valley floor most of the fighting was over. The state of the outermost houses of the village set the tone for the rest.

All the doors had been broken down, and those that had not been set alight had been ransacked. Bodies of men, women and children littered the streets. The smell of death hung heavily in the air, mixed with woodsmoke and cordite.

Mahsud had moved from the hillock with his entourage and was nowhere to be seen. Instead Karpov and the others came across emptiness and death. It was as if a devastating wind had blown through the village, sweeping it of life. Even the animals had been slaughtered, Mahsud's men disdaining even to take some of them for food.

The first living beings they came across were three of Mahsud's men who were busy prising the rings and other jewellery from a huddle of corpses. They looked up in surprise as the group rode by, relaxing when they saw Ahmed and acknowledging his greeting. A couple of Ahmed's men shouted to them and they all laughed. One of the men who was worrying at a ring tired of the effort, drew his knife and severed the finger. He wiped off the blood and tested the quality of the metal between his teeth, smiling and then tossing the ring to one of Ahmed's men.

'His brother,' Ahmed explained. 'We share everything. Those of us who did not take part in the attack will each receive our share. The Prince is a fair man.'

Karpov surveyed the destruction on all sides, every house either ransacked or in flames. 'Yes. He's certainly been very even-handed here.'

They came at last to the house that had appeared like a stockade when viewed from the hill above. Less impressive close up, it was nevertheless clearly the best of them all, and Karpov therefore supposed it to be the house of the village headman. They were obliged to halt some way from it as there was a press of Mahsud's men in between. The door had only recently been forced, and there were shouts and gunshots from inside. One of Mahsud's men ran towards the open doorway brandishing a burning torch but a shout from the flank stopped him in his tracks.

'No fire! Not in this house, you fool!'

Karpov looked round and saw the same figure he had seen from his earlier vantage point, the horseman that Ahmed had identified as Prince Mahsud. He was sitting on his horse about thirty yards to Karpov's right, his bodyguards close around him, alert for any threat to their master.

Dressed in a white cricket pullover, jodhpurs and riding boots, Mahsud sat in the saddle keeping his back erect with an effort that even Alexei could detect. His face was full but nevertheless imperious and stern. His eyes were fixed on the house as if he might find all the answers to life's questions there.

A further flurry of gunfire echoed inside the house. There were screams and the sound of a savage struggle, and then silence. More of Mahsud's men rushed inside and returned moments later bringing with them the surviving defenders who were flung to the ground before Mahsud's horse.

'Which of you is Kasim?' Mahsud demanded.

One of them got unsteadily to his feet. 'I am,' he said bitterly. Karpov noted that the man appeared to know the identity of the Prince, if not recognising him by sight, then at least by reputation. His head hung down and he had every appearance of a man who knows he is as good as dead.

Mahsud leaned forward in his saddle, one elbow resting on the pommel. He narrowed his eyes at the man with interest. 'So. You are Najaf Kasim, the man who saw fit to steal what was mine.'

Kasim looked up, terror in his eyes. His death might well have arrived, but the manner and length of it had yet to be determined.

'I never intended any insult to you, my Prince. It was a simple raiding party. They happened upon the stone by chance. As soon as I realised what it was, I . . .'

'You what?' Mahsud asked derisively. 'Sent for me?'

Kasim shook his head. 'I was going to, I give you my word.'

Mahsud laughed, his expression ugly. 'Of course. How stupid of me.' He swung down from his horse, strode up to Kasim and hit him hard across the cheek with the back of his hand. Kasim's knees buckled but he managed to stay on his feet. Many of his fellow villagers were still alive, captives of Mahsud's men. They looked on from the sidelines and it mattered to Kasim that he meet his death in a manner befitting the leader of the village.

'Had I known the British soldiers were bringing it to you I . . .'

'Of course they were not bringing it to me,' Mahsud jeered. 'But I was going to take it from them. It was mine by right. Instead you and your miserable thieves snatched it from under my nose.'

'Prince Mahsud,' Kasim began, but suddenly he

fell silent, his mouth closing slowly as the realisation dawned on him that the charade need not go on any longer. Whatever he said his fate was decided. He hung his head, weary to his soul.

Mahsud seemed disappointed. He had been working himself to a pitch, enjoying the spectacle in front of his men. It was not fair that the wind should suddenly be taken from his sails.

'Well? Where is it then?' He looked around at his men. 'Have any of you found it?'

Kasim muttered something. Mahsud turned on him. 'What did you say?'

Kasim looked up, a new strength in his eye. 'You will find it upstairs hanging at the foot of my bed. It has been wrapped in goatskins to preserve it.'

Mahsud looked suspicious but nodded to one of his men who sprinted into the house and thundered up the stairs. There came a cry of triumph and a moment later the man emerged into the daylight holding the bundle aloft. He sank to his knees and started to fumble with the wrapping that had been fastened tightly with leather thongs.

'Prince Mahsud!'

Everyone turned on Karpov who had dismounted and approached the Prince.

Mahsud looked at him questioningly. He smiled slowly. 'My guests have arrived,' he said, advancing to meet Karpov who saluted. 'I hope Ahmed has been looking after you.'

'He has, my Prince.'

'What did you think of my demonstration?'

'Most impressive,' Karpov answered. 'But Prince Mahsud, surely this is not the place to reveal the Eye of the Storm?' He opened his arms, embracing the ruined houses, the bodies and the cowering prisoners.

Mahsud looked thoughtful, weighing Karpov's words carefully.

'You cannot doubt that the skins contain the stone,' Karpov continued. He pointed to Kasim. 'A man facing death does not lie.'

Mahsud laughed. 'A man facing death always lies! It is one of life's few certainties. He will say whatever he thinks will prolong his life.' He paused. 'But you are right. This is not fitting. Not here.' He snapped his fingers and the man holding the bundle presented it to him.

Karpov stepped forward quickly. 'Will you do me the honour of allowing my men and me to escort the stone to its rightful home,' he said, holding out his hand.

Mahsud smiled uncertainly. 'We have both been pursuing this,' he said, hefting the bundle in his fist. 'Ever since the British took possession of it. Now it is safe.' His smile broadened. 'As your government had intended to deliver it to me in any case, I am sure you will understand if I now keep it. A treasure so nearly lost is not readily surrendered. Even to an ally as loyal as yourself, Comrade . . .?'

'Alexei Karpov, my Prince.'

'Good, Alexei. I will keep it then. But I thank you for your concern.'

Karpov nodded agreement. 'As you wish, my Prince.'

Mahsud looped the bundle over the pommel of his saddle and then turned again to face Kasim. He stood with hands on hips as he pondered what to do.

'Bring all the surviving villagers to me,' he said eventually. There was a rush of activity as his men rounded up the prisoners. Many of them had been injured in the fighting and had to be helped by their companions. When they were huddled in a circle before Mahsud, he surveyed them carefully.

'Separate the men,' he commanded. Instantly the men were beaten apart from their families who screamed and pulled to go after them.

Mahsud addressed the women and children. 'You are now mine.' He turned to his men. 'Take whichever of them you want,' he shouted. 'Kill any that are left over.' A great cheer went up from his men who surged forward and snatched greedily at the prisoners until only a handful of the elderly or injured were left unclaimed.

Mahsud hesitated for only a moment before saying, 'Finish them.'

When no one volunteered for the grisly work of execution, he singled out the youngest of his men for the task. Reluctantly they went from person to person, carrying out their Prince's command as quickly as they could while Mahsud watched them closely, intrigued. He turned to Karpov who had moved back to join Novikov and the others, checking that they too were watching this latest part of his demonstration.

As the last shot was fired, Mahsud turned to the male prisoners and ordered them brought before him. 'Kasim, come here,' he ordered. Kasim shuffled towards him, his face a mask of hatred.

Mahsud turned to one of his men. 'Give him a knife.'

The man stared at Mahsud as if he had not heard him correctly.

'I told you to give him a knife,' Mahsud repeated pleasantly. As Mahsud's eyes chilled, the man fumbled at his belt, pulled out his own knife and thrust the hilt into Kasim's hands. Kasim stared at it wonderingly.

'You do it,' Mahsud said simply. 'Kill them. One by one.'

Kasim dropped the knife as if it had suddenly become red hot. His hands trembled and he shook his head, the hatred gone, replaced by horror.

Mahsud picked up the knife and put it back in Kasim's hands. 'Do as I command or I will order the women and children killed in their place. It's as simple as that.'

One of Kasim's men shouted, 'Do it, Kasim. At least let our families live.'

'With them?' Kasim roared in desperation, pointing at Mahsud's men who looked on in horrified fascination at their master's newfound inventiveness.

Kasim's man closed his eyes and nodded, the tears falling on his breast.

Slowly Kasim advanced on his men. They had been marshalled into a line by their captors. One by one, Kasim went to his villagers, looking each one in the eye before driving in the knife. He did the job well, sparing them whatever pain he could.

Finally he came to old Rasa, the man who had first laid hands on the satchel containing the stone, accepting it from the British soldier who had used the opportunity to snatch his revolver and kill himself.

Kasim looked at him and smiled sadly. Neither of them said a word until Kasim whispered, 'Revenge will be ours, won't it, my friend?'

Rasa stared back, fighting down the terror that filled him at the prospect of death. He nodded, not fully understanding. Then, just as Kasim drew back the knife the truth of Kasim's statement dawned on him and he shouted, 'Death to Prince Mahsud! May the stone turn upon you as it did upon . . .'

Before he could finish the cry, Kasim thrust in deeply with the knife. The very second his work was done, before the last glimmer of recognition had petrified in Rasa's eye, Kasim whipped the blade out and sprang away from Mahsud's men who had come to seize him.

'Hold him, you fools!' Mahsud cried. He glared ferociously at Kasim. 'What did the old fool mean? Tell me!'

It was too late. Kasim reversed the blade, the point against his solar plexus, and with all the remaining strength of his arms, pulled it into himself. He clenched his jaw shut, not against any cry of pain that might escape him, but lest, in the moment of death, some weakness in him try to claw back an ounce of dignity by spitting out his curse at Mahsud. It would not serve his best interest. That lay secreted in the goatskins suspended from Mahsud's saddle. Kasim averted his eyes from it, turning them away from all things earthly in the last moments of his life.

Mahsud rushed upon him but he was dead before his body hit the floor. An involuntary scream of frustration and rage burst from Mahsud's throat.

As he turned upon his men who had guarded Kasim, Ahmed rushed to his side to distract him.

'Come, my Prince. Let us go from this place. We have what we came for. There is nothing else to be done here.'

Mahsud glared at him. 'Oh yes there is. Torch every house. Poison the well with the bodies of the dead so it will never support life again.'

Ahmed bowed and, as Mahsud strode to his horse, waved to Kasim's guards to make themselves scarce.

Karpov, Novikov and the others had stared at the whole spectacle mesmerised.

'So our government makes allies with such men as this,' Novikov said bitterly. He turned to Karpov. 'I say we go now.'

'Careful, comrade. We will do our bit and go when we have done it. Not before.' Karpov spurred his horse to follow close to the Prince. 'In any case, I doubt our host would let us go just yet.'

Novikov cursed, and then remembered something. 'And what was all that shit about us escorting the bloody stone? Who gives a damn who carries it?'

Karpov did not answer, and although Novikov was surprised to see him blush, he decided he had not heard him, for the air was full of the cries of the women being led captive from the ruined village that had been their home.

Chapter Ten

It was a further two days after the ambush that Brigadier Percival, Bernard Spencer and their party reached the village where the jirga was to be held. During all that time Rachel had kept herself to herself, responding to Henry's anxious enquiries after her health with polite but firm replies. She had sought to pull herself together but had achieved only minimal success, all of which had led her to question her role, not only on the current expedition, but in medicine itself. How could she expect to manage, she asked herself, if she froze when faced with extreme circumstances?

It was true that an ambush and a close brush with death at the hands of men who were out to kill her were not the sort of things she expected to encounter in the course of her normal working life, but then what was normal? It raised the whole question, avoided until now, of where she was going to practise. Should she remain in England or come out to India to be with her father? As a girl she had enjoyed a life of extremes with her parents on the North-West Frontier. In many ways it had been exotic, or so her fellow medical students in England had thought whenever she succumbed to their pleas and regaled them with tales of her childhood. Nevertheless, however exotic her past life may have been she was far from certain that she wanted to continue living and working in India. There were too many restrictions on a young woman, and the idea of a female doctor was laughable to most of her father's friends. Some of them had said as much.

Even so, in some ways she felt that her upbringing had ruined for her any chance of ever being satisfied with a normal life in England, as a general practitioner in some quiet rural parish, spending her days listening to the gripes and moans of village folk who, in contrast with their Indian counterparts, had little to complain about.

Interwoven with all these thoughts, was a feeling of hollowness that she believed was some sort of shock, the result of the ambush. She had once attended a lecture on the after-effects of battle. Many people in her profession ridiculed the idea that any such thing existed, preferring to attribute it to cowardice or a simple lack of backbone. Rachel was convinced they were wrong. The lecturer had been a doctor with an infantry battalion in Flanders during the war, and he put his case with overwhelming conviction. Now, to add to the lecture, she had her own experience, however brief by comparison.

It had also cast the strange Captain Caspasian in a new light for her. She had heard Brigadier Percival telling her father that Caspasian had fought in several different theatres. Against all the odds, he had fought throughout the war, returning to one front or another after each wound, of which he had received several. Rachel was intrigued. How could anyone experiencing such horrors want to return? It was possible, she supposed, that there had been little choice involved. Once a man had joined up the only way out was through death or through some serious injury such as the loss of a limb. How else could one explain it? Unless the man was a psychopath, and in spite of his odd and withdrawn behaviour, he did not strike her as that.

He was quiet, certainly, but there could be all sorts of reasons why a man might prefer his own company. The Gurkha sergeant clearly respected him and Rachel knew that such men did not give their loyalties lightly. She could not imagine Ganga following Henry Allenshaw up the hillside to attack a party of Pathan bandits. She had always prided herself on being a good judge of character, but with Caspasian she had to admit that she was at a loss. The upshot of all this was a resolution to try and approach the man afresh. From the perspective of her new viewpoint after the ambush experience, she would tackle Caspasian anew.

Resolving to do so proved easier than finding the opportunity to carry forward her self-appointed task. Henry clung to her like the dust itself, Douglas Channing and Dr McCloud were rarely far behind, and overseeing the whole circus troupe was her father's concern, and the ever present eyes of Brigadier Percival who never seemed to miss a thing. Only Caspasian and his faithful sergeant showed no sign of interest whatever in Rachel. She realised she had only herself to blame. On the two previous occasions that she had spoken with him since leaving home, she had lost her temper. It was just about the only failing she had never successfully tackled.

A group of houses had been set aside for the use of Bernard Spencer and his party by the village elders for the duration of the jirga. Dr McCloud occupied one, establishing it as his clinic and allocating a spare room to Henry Allenshaw. Spencer and Rachel occupied another, the Brigadier, Channing, Caspasian and Ganga another, and a fourth was used as a billet for Allenshaw's militia, the groom and the porters. The houses were modest mud-brick affairs with thatched roofs, all following the same layout. The ground floor consisted of a single large room, one corner of which acted as a kitchen. A wooden ladder led to an upper floor which would be divided into individual bedrooms either by curtains or by a wattle and daub screen.

To one side of the four houses a deep fast flowing river cut past, the steep banks standing a good five feet high. To the other side, a clearing extended for fifty yards to the start of the main settlement, and it was to be here, Spencer had learned, that the jirga was to be held the next morning.

It was early evening when they arrived. The village elders met them and showed them to the houses. Spencer had met some of the men before and was surprised at the cursory nature of their greeting. They seemed to be preoccupied but he thought it best not to pry and decided to wait until the jirga opened in the morning before delicately seeking an explanation.

Allenshaw took the administration of the stay upon himself and decided that rather than use the individual house cooking fires, the meals would be cooked centrally in the porters' house. The food would then be brought to Dr McCloud's clinic which at meal times would function as a Mess. What he did not admit was that this would enable him to spend more time in Rachel's company. The only problem was that it would also mean Caspasian being included in their number, but however unsavoury the prospect, Henry Allenshaw decided it was the only way for him to see more of Rachel.

After settling into their respective houses there were a couple of hours to spare before supper. While Dr McCloud set about organising his clinic, assisted by Rachel, the Brigadier got his small team together for a briefing. Having first checked that they could not be overheard, he stressed again the urgency of establishing the whereabouts of the Eye of the Storm as quickly as possible.

'While Bernard is conducting the jirga and sorting out whatever squabble the elders have got for him, I suggest that we split up and talk with the villagers to get a feel for the situation.'

'You mentioned having an informer here,' Caspasian said.

'That's correct.'

'How do we find him?'

'We don't. He'll find us. He'll know we're here and as soon as he's sure he can do so without compromising his position, he'll get in touch.'

On the assumption that the informer would have news of the Eye of the Storm, the Brigadier then ran through various courses of action, all of which struck

Caspasian as risky in the extreme. He sat back and ran a hand through his hair, smiling.

'What's so amusing, Caspasian? Not getting cold feet I hope?'

Caspasian chuckled. 'I was just thinking that had I known this was going to be a suicide mission I'd have asked for a few hundred of Ganga's friends to join us.'

To his surprise the Brigadier said, 'They still might. You'll remember from the briefing that Colonel Gibson's Dorset Light Infantry are on stand-by. Well, there'll be a company or two of Gurkhas with them. A battery of mountain artillery as well.'

'That's all very well but how do we call for them?'

'Despatch rider, if possible. If not . . .' the Brigadier shrugged.

'What?' Caspasian asked suspiciously.

The Brigadier pushed back his chair and spread out his hands on the table. 'Sir Oswald has had instructions from the Viceroy that if they hear nothing from us within seven days of our departure they are to assume we have failed and the troops are to move in, no matter what.'

Caspasian stared at him in horror. 'Move where?'

'They are to march on Prince Mahsud's stronghold. It was a direct order. I could do nothing about it. Either we retrieve the Eye ourselves and get word to Sir Oswald or else the army goes in and takes the fortress by storm.'

'They'll be lucky if they get anywhere near it. Mahsud can hold any one of the passes with just a handful of snipers. They'll be walking into a death trap.'

'All the more reason for us to succeed first.'

Caspasian shook his head in dismay. 'This has all the hallmarks of a disaster.'

'Really, Caspasian,' Channing said, 'there's hardly call for that kind of defeatist talk.'

Caspasian shot him a withering look. 'What the hell would you know about it?' He felt a light touch on his arm and looked round to see Ganga smiling.

'It's all right, saheb. We can find this stone.' Behind the smile Caspasian recognised the cautionary glint. Do not let these people irritate you, he was saying. We have been in tighter corners before, you and I. We will do the dirty work for them again.

The Brigadier thumped the table. 'That's the spirit, Sergeant. I see now why you wanted him along, Caspasian.'

The meeting drew quickly to a close and Caspasian left the others in preference for some fresh evening air. Buckling on his holster, he went out of the house and down to the river bank, turning to follow it upstream away from the village. The air had cooled considerably and he fastened his jerkin against the slight chill. The smell of the village cooking fires was in the air, mingling with the freshness of the crystal clear water and the dust of the path that ran parallel to the river.

He had gone barely a hundred yards when he was hailed from behind. He turned round and saw Rachel hurrying after him.

'I hope I'm not disturbing you,' she said smiling. 'After the wood I thought it best to announce my presence.'

Caspasian returned the smile, a little awkwardly.

He had done his best to block her from his mind and felt he had been succeeding. The moment he heard her voice however, and saw her face, flushed from running to meet him, he realised he had been fooling himself.

They walked side by side in silence for a while until Rachel thought to ask, 'Do you mind me joining you?'

It was on his mind to answer that she had already done so, but instead Caspasian smiled and shook his head. 'No.' Then, taking courage from her he added, 'It's good to have the company.'

'Excellent,' Rachel remarked, regretting the jaunty tone that had appeared in her voice and fearing that she sounded like an eager school girl.

There were ample distractions in their surroundings to occupy them. One of them would comment on a plant, the other would respond by pointing out a certain type of bird, until at last they were silent again, each feeling as relaxed as if dressed in a hair shirt.

At last Caspasian asked her about the ambush. Rachel thought for a while. 'I expect it's nothing compared to what you must have been through.'

'What am I supposed to say to that?' Caspasian answered. 'You're not me. For you it must have been a terrifying experience. Doctor or not.'

'Terrifying is a good word for it. How did you cope? The first time you were shot at?'

Caspasian thought back.

'You can't remember, can you?' Rachel joked.

'Oh yes, I can. I think everyone remembers the first time for something like that. It's funny, but I still don't really know what I thought about it. You don't really think at all. You feel. I felt as if something had changed in the world. Somewhere, another person had deliberately pointed a gun at me and tried to end my life.' He stopped and turned to look at her. 'It's sort of like growing up in a way that no one should ever have to grow up.'

Rachel cocked her head on one side as if listening to something far away. 'Yes. I know what you mean.'

'It was as though I had suddenly stepped through a door into another version of the world,' Caspasian went on. 'Or rather, part of me had. My spirit. But this,' he said, stabbing a finger at his chest, 'this flesh and bone remained stuck in the old world, although my whole viewpoint had shifted.'

'And the second time?' Rachel said. 'And the third time, the fourth? What did all that do?'

'Simply reinforced the change that had already taken place. I was suddenly cursed with an additional aspect of sight, one that I hadn't asked for or even known existed. I could see through things.'

'Through things?' Rachel asked, intrigued.

'Yes. Not physical things, but man-made things like . . .' he hunted around for the right words as if he might find them in the dust at his feet or the water coursing noisily past. 'The niceties of social convention.'

Rachel pulled a face. 'I can understand that but surely it doesn't take a battle to make you see through those things?'

Caspasian smiled. 'No. Of course not.' He shrugged. 'I'm not very good with words.'

'Good enough. I think I know what you mean,'

Rachel added quickly, fearing lest she was about to drive him back into his more customary silence. She was relieved when he continued a moment later.

'It's a change, a shift in perspective that I wasn't aware of for a while. I suppose I realised that we're all just hanging on by our finger nails. From the most powerful politician to the lowliest servant. Life hangs by a thread and as often as not there's not a damned thing anyone can do about it.' He smiled at her. 'It's not that great a revelation, but it's the best I can do. In any case, it turned me into a moody devil I suppose. I wasn't much fun to be with. It might surprise you to know I wasn't always like this.'

'Really?' she said wide-eyed, making him laugh at her expression.

'It wasn't until much later that I realised what had happened to me.'

Rachel was suddenly aware that she was entering on dangerous ground but she pressed ahead nonetheless. 'Was there someone who helped you? Did you have anyone . . .?'

Caspasian turned aside and started to walk on. 'It was all a long time ago. Another age really. Everything's changed since the war, don't you agree?'

Rachel cursed herself. So much for a subtle bedside manner. She tried a new angle. 'So why does everyone call you Caspasian? Your first name's John, isn't it?'

'That's right. It's an army tradition. You know, all surnames and that. Mine stuck easier than most. Some people think Caspasian is my first name.'

Rachel laughed. 'Were you called John after your father?'

To Rachel's surprise the smile was shot from Caspasian's face as surely as a bird blasted out of a tree.

'No. He was called something else altogether. Edward.'

'Edward,' Rachel said, trying it out for size. 'That's a good name. "Edward Caspasian."'

There was a bitter chuckle from Caspasian that went right through her.

'Edward was his surname.'

For a moment Rachel was confused. 'But . . .'

'My father's name was David Edward. Sir David Edward.'

Rachel felt her cheeks go scarlet. 'I . . . I'm sorry,' she stammered. 'I didn't mean to pry.'

For a second she thought Caspasian had closed the whole subject, but then he let out a long breath, as if the confession had emptied him of an enormous weight of guilt.

'Caspasian was my grandfather's name. My mother's name too, of course.'

'Was?'

He nodded. 'They have since gone the way of all flesh.' He looked at her and she was shocked by the flint in his gaze. 'We humans do, you know. But you're a doctor, so you know that already.'

They stopped. They had come a long way from the village and suddenly found themselves on the edge of a spreading plain. On the far side, barren hillsides stretched up towards mountains. It was as desolate a place as any Rachel had seen.

'We'd better be getting back,' Caspasian said. He attempted a smile. 'Tongues will be wagging.'

As they strolled back the way they had come, following the dust track in which their footprints lay embedded side by side, Rachel desperately wanted to learn more. Instead Caspasian diverted the talk to herself, asking about her childhood and youth.

Rachel told him about her life with her parents in India, of her education in England, of uncles and aunts she had never seen until she returned to school, and finally she told him of her mother's death, some years before.

'That must have been very hard for you,' Caspasian said. 'Were you in England at the time?'

Rachel nodded. 'That was the worst part of it. I knew she had been ill but I never dreamed it was as serious as that.'

'You can't get much more serious than death,' Caspasian said.

Rachel stared at him, then laughed. 'No. That's true enough.'

'So you see, there are worse things than being shot at, aren't there?'

'I certainly felt so at the time,' Rachel said. 'All I got was this telegram. My father's letter arrived quite a bit later.' She held out her arms. 'I felt so helpless. So completely powerless and alone. I was thousands of miles away, and there was nothing I could do about it.'

Caspasian stared straight ahead, lost in a black reminiscence of his own losses.

Without noticing, they had arrived back on the outskirts of the village. Reluctant to go their separate ways they stood beside the river watching it rush past in a fury of sparkling foam. Caspasian seemed suddenly very distant.

'Listen, Rachel,' he said at last. 'There's something you and your father should know.'

'Oh?'

He looked furtively over his shoulder and cursed. Striding towards them was Henry Allenshaw.

'There you are, Rachel. Been looking all over the place for you. Wondered if you'd like a jolly old stroll before supper.' He scowled hatred at Caspasian. 'Too late now though. Food's ready.' He paused, looking from one to the other. 'Are you coming then?'

'In a minute, Henry,' Rachel said irritably.

Instead of taking the hint Henry remained firmly rooted to the spot, determined not to leave the two of them alone together again. 'Your father's been asking after you,' he said with all the confidence of someone delivering the *coup de grâce*.

Rachel looked up at him. 'Well we can't keep Daddy waiting then, can we?' she said, not bothering to hide the sarcasm in her voice. She turned to Caspasian, trying to think of something to say, but under Henry's intense scrutiny she simply smiled and walked away.

When she had gone Henry Allenshaw leaned towards Caspasian, arms rigidly at his sides like someone bending into a strong wind. He reminded Caspasian of a schoolyard bully mouthing abuse at a new boy. 'I know what your little game is, Caspasian. Don't think I didn't see the two of you so deep in conversation.' His voice was thick and Caspasian thought he could smell rum.

'Let me tell you that Bernard and I have an under-standing. About Rachel.'

Caspasian stared at him as if he was mad. 'An understanding?' He was not sure whether to laugh or just hit the man.

'That's what I said. Are you deaf or something?'

Caspasian squared up to him. 'Whatever makes you think Rachel would do as her father says? She's not one of your fishing fleet tarts. What century are you living in, Allenshaw?'

'It's Major Allenshaw, Captain.' He attempted to match Caspasian's stance and failed. 'It's about time you started to remember things like that. I don't know what the Brigadier sees in you, you little upstart, but if it was up to me, I'd . . .'

There was a cough from behind. Unnoticed by either of them Ganga had approached and stood rigidly to attention. He threw a perfect salute to Henry, as crisp as a freshly laundered sheet.

'Mr Spencer Saheb is asking for you, saheb.' He waited, staring fiercely into the empty space between the two men. Caspasian knew that he would not leave until he had parted them and in spite of his mounting rage he could not help smiling at the formidable figure of the Gurkha sergeant.

Henry looked from one to the other and lost his thread. Finally he muttered something inaudible and stalked off towards the houses. When he had gone, Ganga relaxed.

'Nice work, Ganga.'

The Gurkha grinned.

*   *   *

The following morning Caspasian was up at first light. It was the best time of day to be about and he was determined to make full use of it. Slipping into his clothes and a pair of boots he went quietly out of the house, closed the door behind him, and set off along the track beside the river at a steady jog. The air was sharp and crisp and a mist clung to the water, filling the sunken riverbed.

The sun was still below the eastern mountain ridgeline and he speeded his pace to keep warm. By the time he came to the turnaround point of his walk with Rachel, he was perspiring and ready for his exercise routine. He dropped onto the palms of his hands and did fifty push-ups, then rolled on to his back and did a hundred sit-ups, hands behind his head and knees bent.

When he had finished, he went through some slow stretching exercises, working through all the main muscle groups until he felt confident enough to tackle the next stage of the routine without risk of straining anything.

Standing with feet shoulder-width apart, he circled his right foot forward, bending the knees and turning the toes inwards, sinking his hips into the sanchin-dachi stance. Simultaneously his fists and arms came up in the opening double block. As they did so, he inhaled sharply through the nose, and then expelled the breath noisily through the mouth, propelling it out using the diaphragm. When the last of it had gone, he inhaled again, expelling the next breath and moving forward with the left foot, executing a slow-motion punch with his left hand as he did so.

The routine went on, Caspasian's mind opening as each movement drew him deeper in. Having executed a turn, his hands opened, each describing an arc in the air, simulating sinuous blocks, enveloping and sweeping aside imaginary blows. They were followed by a series of devastating thrusts using the edge of the hands, each aimed at a different target area. The first one scythed through collar bone, the second drove deep into an opponent's sternum, a third arched in from the side and sliced into the neck muscle, and the fourth came down upon the shoulder muscle with the grace and power of an axe felling a tree.

At the end of the sequence, Caspasian's feet came together and he drew himself up to his full height, his hands closing, raising to his face, and then lowering to his side. Caspasian exhaled gently. It felt like returning to earth after a flight among the crystal cold stars.

All his senses were alert. He felt ready for anything or anyone. He was quick to hear the distant hubbub of voices and cocked his head to one side to catch the direction. It was coming from the village. He set off, back along the track, lengthening his stride, revelling in the power he could feel in his legs as he ran.

The closer he got to the village the louder the noise became, until he reached the edge of the clearing where the four houses stood. The other members of the party had also been roused by the noise and had emerged in various states of dress to investigate. Caspasian ran to the Brigadier's side.

'What is it?'

Brigadier Percival spat with disgust. 'Bernard said

it's a blasted stoning. He's gone to try and stop it. He's supposed to be here to settle a blood feud. It seems he's come too late.'

Caspasian dashed inside and retrieved his belt and holster, quickly checking the load in the Mauser. He stuffed a couple of spare magazines in his pocket and ran outside to find Rachel. He knew she would be with her father, and if Spencer was about to put himself in between two opposing sides, Caspasian wanted to be on hand in case things got nasty.

It was not difficult to find them. The crowd had moved away from the village to an area where the stoning was to take place, beside the river with its abundant supply of smooth rocks. Caspasian could hear them, the hubbub growing to an incensed roar the closer he got. When he located Spencer he saw him talking urgently with a group of the village elders. Spencer appeared to be imploring them, talking quickly. Close behind him Rachel hovered, ready to pull her father out of harm's way.

Caspasian went up to her. She shot him a glance, noting the holster at his waist. Further behind, Ganga, Allenshaw and the others stood in a group looking on.

'Stand back, please, Captain Caspasian,' Bernard Spencer said when he saw him. 'Your presence here can only aggravate things. If anyone can save this fellow it's me.'

'I didn't come to save him,' Caspasian said, his eyes taking in the mob, gauging them. 'I came to keep an eye on Rachel.'

There was a sudden roar from the crowd and a man was thrust forward and tumbled to the ground.

His arms were pinioned behind him with twine and he had been knocked around on his way from the village stockade.

'What's he done?' Caspasian asked.

'I don't know. They won't tell me,' Spencer replied, trying without success to break into the elders' heated conversation. Eventually he gave up. 'They say the matter has gone beyond my help now. It's something to do with a killing. This man,' he said indicating the prisoner who was kneeling before them, urgently mumbling prayers, 'has killed a man over some marital infidelity.'

'Ah.'

'Is there nothing you can do?' Rachel asked.

Her father shook his head but tried again. One of the elders turned to him and spoke in a long stream, so agitated that Caspasian had trouble following him.

Spencer attempted to reply but the man had turned his back on him. Several men ran forward, grabbed the prisoner under the arms, hoisted him screaming to his feet and dragged him further towards the river. They threw him down and ran back. Automatically a space cleared around him, isolating him in the centre of a killing zone.

'For pity's sake!' Spencer cried.

He took a step forward but Caspasian saw the look on the faces of the villagers and caught hold of his arm.

'Let me go, damn you. I can't allow this.'

'You can't stop it either,' Caspasian said firmly, one hand on Spencer's arm, the other on the flap of his holster.

Rachel sobbed and buried her face in her father's chest. He tugged his arm away from Caspasian and encircled his daughter, drawing her away from the spectacle unfolding before them.

Caspasian steered them back to join the others, keeping himself between them and the mob. They were no longer of interest however. The mob had switched their whole attention to their quarry. The man whimpered, straightening to face his executioners who were bending to gather rocks from the ground.

An eerie silence fell, the more unsettling for the noise that had preceded it. A man stepped forward, drew back his arm, and hurled his rock with all his might at the bound and cowering figure. It struck him on the chest, knocking the wind out of him and toppling him over. In an instant he was on his knees again, imploring the crowd to show mercy. His pleas were met with an outburst of rage and a hail of rocks fired at him. Most of them missed, but it only needed a few to do him harm.

He was struck about the shoulders and head. Blood quickly appeared where he had been cut above the eyes. A split opened in one cheek. Then the white of bone was visible, and as if bowing in prayer, the man sank forward, his forehead to the ground as the rain of missiles went on. Each one that struck him did so with a sound that Caspasian knew he would always remember, adding it to the other horrors that he carried locked inside.

He looked at Rachel. Her face was buried in her father's jacket, her hands covering her ears. Caspasian wanted to go to her. He wanted to lead her away from that terrible place and keep on walking as they had the previous evening. Only this time he never wanted them to stop. He wanted to tell her everything. He wanted to empty the sack of ghouls he had carried for so long and share them with someone. He remained rooted to the spot. How could he ever so harm anyone as to share his nightmares with them? He could certainly never do that to Rachel.

He looked again at the prisoner. He was now virtually buried under the rocks. His bonds had come loose, severed by the bombardment, and one arm lay protruding, unnaturally twisted. As his death became evident, the mob reverted to a crowd. People looked from one to the other, clucking their tongues as if he had been a naughty child, now suitably chastised. It served to hide their guilt and the severity of the punishment.

One by one they moved away to return to the village. A dog ventured out to sniff with interest at the pile of rocks. Confused, it looked from the rocks to the departing villagers and back. It cocked its leg and imprinted the execution site with urine that steamed in the chill morning air.

'Come on my dear,' Spencer said, leading Rachel away.

Allenshaw followed close behind, looking back over his shoulder as if the prisoner's ghost might arise and pursue him. 'Bloody savages,' he muttered, just loud enough so that no one except his companions might hear him.

Only Brigadier Percival remained once the others had gone, musing thoughtfully at the body under the rocks. Caspasian went to his side, feeling empty, the exhilaration of his earlier exercise drained from him.

'Nice bunch, aren't they?' he said.

The Brigadier seemed not to hear him at first, but then said, 'Yes. Damned bad show, that. Damned bad show.'

Caspasian spat. There was blood in his mouth. While facing down the mob he had bitten his cheek without noticing. 'That's one way of putting it.'

'Hm?' the Brigadier said, starting back to the present. 'Sorry, Caspasian. I was miles away.' He shook his head sadly. 'A damned shame, that's what it is.'

'The execution, you mean?' Caspasian said, getting the drift that he and the Brigadier were at cross purposes.

'No. I mean, yes. That too.' He turned to Caspasian. 'What I mean is, that fellow was my informer. He was the chap who was going to tell us about the stone.'

Chapter Eleven

Prince Mahsud could hardly contain himself. The Eye of the Storm was finally in his possession. Every mile of the return journey to his fortress was a torment when all he wanted to do was unwrap the Eye and savour it. He had already waited too long but at last it was his and now nothing could hold him back.

He turned in the saddle and looked back at his groom riding behind him, the bag containing the stone safely stowed in his panniers.

The man grinned. 'Now we attack,' he said eagerly.

Mahsud smiled. 'Attack. Yes, of course. Not long now.' He swivelled to the front again and heaved an immense sigh of relief. Not long at all, he thought with satisfaction. He could feel himself relaxing. Life had taken on an altogether new aspect. The very mountains seemed less bleak and Mahsud found himself whistling the 'Maple Leaf Rag'.

He thought about the Bolsheviks and was not quite sure what to make of their leader. Karpov could be trouble unless he was very careful. There was something about him that Mahsud did not like. Still, they were in his country now and under his control. It should not be too difficult to make sure they fell in with his plans.

The attack on the village had gone well. Mahsud smiled. His father would have been proud of him. He felt it had been a stroke of genius to get Kasim to kill his own men. Ahmed and the others had clearly approved and his standing had obviously risen. He felt a twinge of embarrassment however when he considered what his old tutor at Oxford would have made of it all. Different worlds, he reflected, shaking his head. Since returning to his childhood home he had felt the conflict of two worlds within him, two cultures, two value systems battling for place. There was little doubt which had been victorious at the village. The corpses left behind and the keening prisoners amongst his ranks bore ample testimony to that.

In stark contrast he found himself thinking of his old lodgings in Oxford, of his college and of his frequent trips to the bright lights of London. He sighed at the memory of the theatres and the clubs. It was all in very stark contrast to his current surroundings.

A cry from the front of the column announced their approach to the fortress. Mahsud heaved a sigh of relief. He did not enjoy sleeping rough and the thought of another night on the hard ground was not attractive. He sat up straight as Ahmed spurred to his side. 'The Bolsheviks have asked if they can inspect our armoury when we arrive, saheb.'

'I don't see why not,' Mahsud replied. 'They're here to help us and to do that they'll need to know the level of our resources.'

Ahmed grunted. Mahsud smiled at him. 'I know. I don't trust them either. Have them watched every second.'

'Of course,' Ahmed said with a grin. He paused and Mahsud could tell he had left something unspoken. At last Ahmed said carefully, 'The men all respect you, saheb. You are their leader now.'

For a moment Mahsud wondered whether Ahmed was lying. He studied him carefully but Ahmed stared blankly ahead.

'Your father was a great fighter. But now he is dead. You are his son. Never fear, the men will follow you. Even to death.'

Mahsud blanched. He had no intention of leading anyone to death. Sending them perhaps, but leading? Definitely not. Nevertheless he realised that Ahmed was trying to set his mind at rest and he appreciated it. He was somewhat alarmed however that his restlessness and self-doubt should have been so obvious, but then Ahmed had known him since he had been a boy.

'Thank you,' Mahsud said awkwardly. 'I am going to need your support over the coming days.'

Ahmed looked at him in surprise. 'Days?'

'You know what I mean,' Mahsud said quickly. 'You will always be my right-hand man. It's just that the next few days are going to be a severe test for all of us.'

'Of course,' Ahmed said, nodding thoughtfully. 'At last the rising can start.'

'The rising. Exactly.'

An hour later, with his men dispersed back to their quarters Mahsud oversaw the allocation of rooms to his Bolshevik guests. He had sent the Eye to his own quarters to await his arrival, but first of all he had to ensure his guests were settled and would remain occupied and out of his way for some time.

'When you have washed and relaxed, Ahmed will send for you and show you the armoury. After that I have arranged for you to be taken to the ranges. You will find them most interesting. Not up to your own high standards I expect, but they suffice for our own purposes.'

Karpov seemed on edge. 'The Eye of the Storm, sir. If I may, I would very much like to see it to make sure it is all right. I would not like to think such an important article had been damaged in any way.'

'No, of course not. I understand and your concern does you credit, comrade. Rest assured it is in safe hands now. When the time is right and the tribes are assembled it will be shown to all. Until then . . .' Mahsud drew the conversation to a close by beckoning to an aide and indicating that he should lead the guests away for their tour. Karpov hesitated for a moment but, recognising defeat, he set his mouth in a rigid smile and left.

The moment they had gone, Mahsud went quickly out of the room and crossed the large courtyard in the direction of his quarters. Everyone he met on the way smiled broadly at him. The fortress was filled with an air of excitement now that the Eye of the Storm had been captured. A group of heavily armed tribesmen quickly got to their feet and cheered him when they saw him approaching. He acknowledged them proudly as he strode past. He could feel the precious stone summoning him and it was high time that he inspected it closely.

As he neared his tower he broke into a trot. The door at the bottom stood open and he sprang up the steps, climbing past floor after floor.

He was two floors from his bedroom when he was met by his groom running madly down the stairs. The two men almost collided and Mahsud had to grab the railings to prevent himself from losing his balance and tumbling downwards in an undignified heap.

'What . . . what the blazes are you doing?' he said, catching the man by the hem of his jacket. The groom's face was ashen and his eyes bulged in terror. He opened his mouth but no sound came out.

Mahsud shook him violently, the alarm mounting inside him. 'Speak, idiot!'

The man jabbered something but Mahsud could not make sense of it. He drew back one hand and slapped the groom hard across the cheek.

'The Eye . . .' the man stammered, 'it weeps!'

Mahsud stared at him uncomprehending.

The man looked back up the stairs as if he expected to see some terrible apparition pursuing him at any moment. 'The woman,' he continued, 'she . . . she . . .'

'What woman?' Mahsud said angrily.

The man fell to his knees. 'Forgive us, my Prince. We only meant to look upon the sacred Eye. We never meant to touch it. Indeed, I didn't. Only the woman did.'

Mahsud felt his heart go cold as he understood who the groom meant. He threw the man aside and ran up the remaining steps, spinning round the corners and finally reaching his bedroom door. It stood open and from inside he could hear a woman sobbing. He edged round the door, wondering at the strange smell filling the air, a nauseous smell that caught at the nostrils and made him want to retch.

In the far corner his woman knelt doubled over. She turned when she heard his footsteps. There were tears running down her cheeks and when she saw him her sobs burst from her.

'Don't touch it!' she screamed. She pointed at the bed where the opened haversack lay. Beside it Mahsud saw a tangle of cloths concealing something underneath. 'Don't go near it! It is evil!' With her face contorted in agony she raised her other hand, brandishing it in front of her in horror. 'Look what it has done to me.'

Mahsud stared transfixed at the woman's hand. It was horribly swollen and covered in large blisters.

'All I did was touch it,' she said sobbing. 'Nothing more. I wasn't going to take it. Do you think I would be so stupid?'

Carefully Mahsud approached her, giving the haversack and the bundle a wide berth. 'Show me your hand,' he said gently. She raised it again.

'Don't touch it,' the woman cautioned, withdrawing her disfigured hand.

'I wasn't going to.' Mahsud examined the skin, staring at it in fascination. He went across to the fireplace and took down a sword that was fixed above it, an ornament from his grandfather's time. Remaining as far from the bed as the length of the blade would allow, he reached towards the bundle of cloths, hooked the sword point under the corner and gingerly flicked them clear. Lying in the middle, the Eye of the Storm gazed into space. Mahsud pulled out his handkerchief and pinched his nose against the smell. The Eye was larger than he had expected. He crouched down to examine the pictures covering it. His eyes sparkled in wonder.

'Magnificent,' he whispered. 'Absolutely magnificent.'

He moved to the left so he could see where the liquid was coming from and there, oozing out of the chip where the British had struck it, Mahsud saw a thick dark yellow substance.

He shifted closer and the woman cried out. 'Don't! Keep away! I tell you, it is evil!'

Without taking his eyes off the stone Mahsud smiled bitterly. 'Only men are evil. Men, and the things they do. Believe me. In my father I had the best of teachers.'

When he had studied the stone to his satisfaction, Mahsud turned to the woman. 'Touch nothing with your injured hand. Don't scratch yourself, don't lick the wounds, do nothing, do you hear me?'

The woman sobbed. Her head hung down and she bit her lip to keep from crying out at the agony. Mahsud had to admit he was impressed by her courage. More gently he said, 'Do you hear me?'

Without looking up she nodded.

'Good. I will send someone to dress it. It will heal, after a fashion.'

She called out as he walked away. 'Don't send me away, my Prince. Please. Let me stay here.' She struggled to her feet, becoming desperate as the implications of her disfigurement hit her. 'You are right. It will heal. I will be as before.'

Mahsud turned at the door. 'Have I sent you away?'

The woman shook her head uncertainly. 'No,' she said slowly.

'There you are then. Guard the Eye until I return.'

'Where are you going?' she called after him.

'It is time I had a talk with my guests.'

As the sound of his footsteps faded the woman walked across to the window, keeping as far from the stone as she could. She stared across at the bed with hatred. The pain from her wound shot through her as if her hand was being roasted on a spit. She sat down, laying her arm on the windowsill so the breeze could cool the livid blisters. She would wait for the others to come and dress it, as the Prince had said they would. Tears coursed down her cheeks when she thought of the triumph she would see in their eyes. She, who had risen from nothing to be the Prince's concubine, would be put aside. Despite his protestations to the contrary she knew the fate that awaited her.

His last words came back to her. The guests. She had heard it had been the guests who had sent the stone. The men from far away, now lodged in this very fortress. They were responsible for her burns. They were to blame for her coming humiliation.

'You can't just walk up to people and ask them where the blasted stone is,' Brigadier Percival stormed.

'I don't intend to,' Caspasian replied, keeping a firm grip on his temper. The mission had been ill-conceived from the start and it was rapidly turning into a farce. 'All I'm saying is let Ganga and me go into the village and see what we can pick up. We'll just go and chat. If people don't want to open up, then we come straight back here.'

Douglas Channing nodded. 'It's worth a try, sir. Now our contact's been compromised . . .'

The Brigadier turned on him. 'Don't be pompous, Douglas. He wasn't compromised. He was caught shafting another man's wife.'

'That sounds compromising enough to me,' Caspasian added helpfully.

Seated in the corner, Sergeant Ganga was cleaning his rifle. He had stripped it and was lightly oiling the working parts. He held up the bolt and inspected the firing pin. 'We need fresh milk, saheb. Someone has to go out and buy it. Why don't Caspasian Saheb and I go.'

'Armed to the teeth I suppose?' the Brigadier said sarcastically.

Ganga smiled sweetly. 'No, saheb.'

The Brigadier relented. His fingers rasped through his cropped hair. 'I'm sorry, Ganga. It's just that I'm getting exasperated.' He turned to Caspasian. 'All right, Caspasian. You and Ganga nip into town and get some milk. Say hello to the villagers and see what you can find out.'

'Can I go too, sir?' Channing asked eagerly, keen to prove himself useful.

'No you can't. And don't look so bloody crestfallen.'

'It's fine by me,' Caspasian said.

Channing stared at him in surprise. Brigadier Percival held up his hands. 'All right take him!' He snatched up his hat from the table. 'Just don't make it obvious what you're up to.' He opened the door and went out. 'I'll be across with Bernard if you need me.'

When he had gone Caspasian spoke rapidly in Gurkhali to Ganga. The sergeant listened closely, his face serious, nodded and left the room.

'What was all that about?' Channing asked.

'Nothing that need bother you,' Caspasian answered curtly. He buckled on his pistol belt and reached for his jerkin. 'Let's go.'

'What about Ganga? Isn't he coming with us?'

'He'll catch us up.'

Caspasian set off, his long stride taking him towards the village. At his heels, Channing hurried to keep up, determined to match Caspasian's gait even if it killed him.

The village was quiet. The few people they came across seemed subdued which Caspasian put down to the stoning, reckoning that a low always followed such a flow of adrenaline. Children played in the dirt but he noticed how their mothers quickly shepherded them out of his way as he and Channing approached.

'Friendly bunch, aren't they?' Channing observed.

Caspasian did not reply, although his internal alarm system placed him on guard. Villagers were usually welcoming to people staying in their midst. This reticence was disturbing, particularly as they were a long way from help.

It was not difficult to find the goatherd who had been supplying them with milk. He lived slightly apart from the village on the edge of a wood that provided plenty of grazing. As they neared, the tinkling of bells helped them find their direction through the last of the houses. A large billy goat looked up at them in surprise when they turned the corner and set foot on the path leading to the herdsman's front door. It lowered its head and leaped at them until its neck chain ran out and jerked it to a shuddering halt.

Caspasian knocked loudly on the door. A moment later it opened and the goatherd stared out at the two men.

'What do you want?'

His dialect was thick but the tone of his response said it all. Channing chuckled. 'Is it just me, or are we unpopular today?' he said merrily.

More and more alarm bells were ringing in Caspasian's head but he forced as pleasant a smile as he could manage. 'Can you spare any milk, baje?' he asked politely.

'Who are you calling grandfather?' the old man muttered, turning away from the door and going to close it.

'I meant no offence,' Caspasian said quickly, placing one hand firmly on the door to keep it open. 'Please, we have money. We can pay.'

The old man peered out at them from the gloom. Another figure moved in the background and Caspasian could just make out an old woman who looked ancient enough to be the goatherd's mother. She squinted at them from the back of the room and mumbled something. In response the goatherd gave her a blast of invective. He turned back to the two men, glared at Caspasian's hand until he removed it, and then slammed the door shut.

'What the devil was all that about?' Caspasian said.

'I don't know but we've got company.'

He turned round. Channing jerked his chin at the end of the path. 'There.' At the corner of the nearest house where the billy goat had lunged at them, a small crowd of half a dozen men had gathered.

'Thank God you brought your gun,' Channing said.

'Can't use it though.'

Channing stared at him in alarm. 'Why ever not?'

'Don't be stupid. We're in the middle of their village. How many blood feuds do you think we'd create if I blazed away at that lot?'

'What the hell did you bring it for then?'

Caspasian grinned at him. 'I'd feel undressed without it.' He had a quick look at the gang by the house. 'Can you fight?'

Channing swallowed hard. 'Fists, you mean?'

'Fists, feet, knees, teeth, you name it. Can you fight?'

'I used to box at school but that was some time ago,' Channing replied miserably, regretting his earlier urge to accompany Caspasian. The man seemed to attract trouble.

'Time for a little revision. Come on.' Caspasian set off down the path.

'Shouldn't we go some other way,' Channing called after him, seeing Caspasian square his broad shoulders.

'Do I have to take them on by myself? Get down here.'

Channing cursed under his breath but followed. As he went he looked quickly down at his fists. They were the hands of a civil servant. He really should not have to do this. He racked his brains in an effort to recall the commands of his old school physical training instructor. Straight, jab, hook, uppercut. God, what a mess!

As Caspasian approached the men he singled out the leader and smiled broadly. 'Hello,' he said in a loud, confident voice. He pointed up at the sky. 'Lovely day.'

The man smiled back but Caspasian read his real mood in his eyes. Two of the group carried rifles but they were slung across their shoulders. All of them had knives in their belts, and as he drew closer Caspasian noted that two of them were also trying to conceal clubs behind their backs. He called jauntily back to Channing, still smiling at the men as he did so. 'What you see here is a press gang.'

'A press gang?'

'They want us alive.' He beamed at the leader as he closed the last few yards towards them. 'But you aren't going to get us, are you my old fruit?'

The man frowned, not understanding. He moved to one side as if to let Caspasian pass, but Caspasian saw it was merely to let the first of his henchmen get a good crack at Caspasian's head with the club.

'Thank you,' Caspasian said pleasantly, and burst into action.

Before the man with the club could even raise it, Caspasian darted in towards him and fired out a kizamizuki snap punch. His fist was clenched hard as iron and the two knuckles at the base of his fore and middle fingers drove into the man's upper lip where it joined the base of his nose and down he went.

With the most immediate threat out of action, Caspasian went for the leader. If he was put down he reckoned the rest might lose heart and clear off. While the man was obviously used to giving orders, Caspasian noted from the look on his face that he was less accustomed to close-quarter fighting. Nevertheless, he was well muscled from the hard life of the mountains and Caspasian had never taken victory for granted.

He feinted to the man's face with another snap punch and when the man's hands came up to block, Caspasian shot in a kansetsu-geri low side kick that sheered down the man's shin. There was a scream of pain as the hard edge of Caspasian's boot tore through the skin all the way from the knee to the instep. The man jumped backwards as if scalded.

Caspasian was prevented from pushing home the attack by the next two men closest to him. Both had their knives out and they were coming at him together. Out of the corner of his eye, he saw Channing circling the other villager who had been concealing a club. Channing's fists were raised in best schoolboy fashion and his opponent's face was a mask of mystified wonder.

A knife blade flashed in low. Caspasian palmed it down and to one side, kicking out as he did so with a kin-geri, his instep shooting up into the man's testicles. Caspasian felt his foot connect and drove it up hard. The man's eyes bulged and he went down.

The momentum of his kick carried him forward and he almost fell on to the second blade which was coming at his chest. With his left forearm, he executed a rapid chudan soto-uke block across the front of his body, his forearm picking up his attacker's right wrist and knocking it harmlessly to Caspasian's right. The force of the block was so great that it spun the man off balance until his side was wide open to attack. Without hesitation Caspasian locked into a solid zenkutsu-dachi stance, and with the full force of his hips behind the blow, swung his right elbow into the man's ribs beneath the armpit. Caspasian had timed his breathing perfectly and gave the blow the benefit of an ear-shattering kiai, the cry coming from deep in his gut. Completing the combination, he grasped the shoulder of the man's jacket and swung his own right instep sharply forward in a foot sweep, knocking the man's legs from under him and compounding the broken ribs with a vicious fall.

Caspasian looked up to find himself staring down the barrel of a rifle. The last man of the group had managed to unsling his weapon, cock it and bring it into the aim. His eyes smiled at Caspasian as his finger tightened on the trigger. Diving forward into a roll, Caspasian launched himself at the man, little expecting to cover the distance before the rifle could be fired. There was a thud, and when he came out of the roll Caspasian looked up to see the rifleman collapsed on the ground. Behind him, Sergeant Ganga stared back with a blank expression, his kukri reversed in his grip so that the man had been struck with the blunt back edge.

Slowly Caspasian got to his feet. Against a wall of the adjacent house, Channing was pummelling away at his opponent.

'For God's sake, put the man down,' Caspasian called across.

Channing muttered something. He had taken several punches and his face was red and bruised.

'Feint with the left, then right hook to the chin,' Caspasian shouted.

Gathering himself, Channing broke away from his opponent's grasp, took a deep breath and did exactly as he was told. His left fist connected lightly with the man's chin, and when the way was clear, his right fist hooked in, slamming home just below his opponent's left ear. The man stared into space for a second, his knees crumpled, and he sank to the floor.

Caspasian and Ganga looked at each other, but their astonishment was not as great as Douglas Channing's.

'It worked!' he said, more to himself. He looked at his bloodied fists, the skin broken, the knuckles swelling. 'It bloody worked!'

The gang leader sat on the ground leaning against a wall. He looked up angrily as he nursed his badly injured shin. Blood stained the front of his trouser leg where Caspasian's boot had raked down it. Caspasian went over to him.

'Why?' he asked simply.

The man sullenly looked away. Caspasian lightly kicked his injured leg and he howled in agony. 'I asked you a question,' Caspasian said calmly, working to make his dialect as clear as possible.

The man grimaced but replied. 'I was told to come and fetch you.'

'Told? Who by?'

'The elders.'

'What do they want with us?' Channing asked.

'You are to be handed over to the Prince. You are trouble for our village.'

At the mention of the Prince, Caspasian squatted down beside the man. 'Prince Mahsud?'

The man was still a moment and then nodded, recognising defeat.

'We came here with the district officer to attend the jirga. Why should we be trouble for you?' Caspasian persisted.

'I don't know. I just do as I am told.'

Ganga stepped up beside Caspasian. The man looked up at the savage kukri that Ganga hefted in his fist.

'We don't want our village to be destroyed like Kasim's,' the man continued quickly.

'Explain,' Caspasian ordered. Ganga squatted beside him, bringing the kukri closer to the man's face.

'I don't know any more than that. Kasim's village was destroyed. The elders are scared. We are all scared. If we hand you over to the Prince he will leave us alone. That is what the elders say. I just obey their orders.' He hung his head.

Ganga stared hard at him, finally conceding, 'He is telling the truth, saheb.'

They got up and knocked off the dust. Caspasian had a quick look at Channing's face. 'You'll live,' he said, smiling.

They gathered up the clubs and knives and flung

them down the hillside. Ganga stripped down the rifles, clucking at the patches of rust, and threw the bolts away as far as he could. Using the rifle slings, he tied up the men who had attacked them, adding a blindfold for good measure.

'How was everyone when you left?' Caspasian asked.

Ganga shrugged. 'Fine.'

'What do we do now?' Channing asked. 'Hadn't we better go and warn the others?'

'It'll be too late for that,' Caspasian said. 'The villagers have probably taken them prisoner by now. The best thing we can do is get out of the way. Come on.'

Ganga nodded agreement and together with Caspasian set off up the hillside, heading away from the village. Channing stared after them in astonishment. 'Where the hell are you going? You can't just leave them!'

'I don't intend to,' Caspasian called back.

'Then why aren't we going to help them?'

Caspasian stopped and looked back. 'Six men was bad enough. Do you want to take on the whole village?'

'No,' Channing admitted, confused. 'But . . .'

'Just do as I say. Any moment now the villagers are going to come and see what's happened to their mates. I think it's best you and I aren't around when they arrive.'

'But they'll also have captured all our kit. Our food, weapons, everything.'

Caspasian set off again. 'Not if Ganga's done what I told him to. Which he will have done.'

Chapter Twelve

When the door was kicked open and Brigadier Percival and Bernard Spencer looked up to see a pack of tribesmen shouldering their way in, they bitterly regretted the absence of Caspasian and the Gurkha sergeant. For one moment the Brigadier considered resistance, but for one moment only. Although fit, he was no longer a young man and the thought of a physical brawl appalled him. For him violence was distanced, a more measured, controlled phenomenon. He directed it from a higher level. The idea that he himself should get stuck in and lay about him with fists and boot was not an option. In extreme circumstances, perhaps, but oddly enough he did not yet consider the current circumstances extreme. More to the point, considering the crowd he could see gathered beyond the doorway, he realised that in this instance any sort of resistance would be counter-productive. The stoning by these same people was fresh in his mind and he had no intention of ending up similarly buried under a pile of river rocks. Diplomacy and guile were his preferred strategies here.

'Bernard, do you have anything to say to our friends?' he said calmly.

Bernard Spencer slowly pushed back his chair and stood up, being sure to keep his hands in full view of the intruders so they could see he was unarmed.

'What do you mean by storming in here like this?' He faced them square on, determined to present a brave front, even though he was deeply alarmed by the sight of the villagers. 'Is this how you treat guests of your village? What has happened to the laws of hospitality? This is an outrage!'

The tribesmen looked shamefaced but none of them moved. 'You are to come with us,' one of them said from the back.

'And why should we do that?' Spencer said sternly, filling his voice with all the authority he could muster. 'I am the District Political Officer. Do you realise what you are doing? You'll call down a column on top of you before you know what's hit you. There'll be British troops in the valley within days if you harm any one of my party.'

For a moment the Brigadier thought that Bernard's speech had done the trick. The tribesmen looked from one to another and some of them whispered doubtfully. But then their attitude hardened, someone at the rear of the group gave an order and they roughly snatched at Spencer and the Brigadier and pulled them towards the door.

'The woman. Where is she?' one of them asked.

'If you harm her . . .' Spencer began, but was cut short.

'We are not going to harm any of you. Our fight is not with you. We do not want war with the British.'

'Then what the blazes are you up to?' the Brigadier said.

They ignored his question. 'The woman?'

In answer, Rachel climbed down the ladder. She had been lying on the bed on the upper floor and had heard the commotion. She smiled at her father. 'I'm all right,' she said quickly when he moved to her side. 'They've said they don't mean to harm us.'

'Is it money you're after?' Spencer asked. 'A ransom? That's it, isn't it? Well I can tell you now the authorities won't pay. They'll give you an ultimatum to release us or face attack. You should know that well enough by now.'

It was Rachel who answered, her eyes on the Brigadier as she did so. 'It's not money, father. Tell him, Brigadier.'

Bernard looked at her and then at Brigadier Percival. 'What's that? What do you know about it?'

'Tell us, Brigadier,' she persisted.

The Brigadier shook his head. 'I don't know what you're talking about, my dear.'

'You're up to something and you should have told us. What's going on?'

Bernard Spencer stared hard at him. 'James?'

There were shouts from outside as Henry Allenshaw, Dr McCloud and their party were seized. Allenshaw's outraged voice carried above the rest. 'Take your damned hands off me, curse you!'

He tried giving an order to his militiamen but their weapons had been snatched from them and they stood with bowed heads, refusing to meet his eyes.

'Resist, I tell you!'

Dr McCloud tried to calm him but was met with a sharp rebuff.

'We'd better go and stop Major Allenshaw from

getting himself killed,' the Brigadier said, leading the way outside.

A harsh sunlight beat down. They were surprised when they stepped outside to find most of the village gathered around the cluster of houses that had been their accommodation. Even the children had come to witness the spectacle and stood clinging to their mothers, their faces fixed on the visitors in awe.

'Thank God you're here, Bernard,' Dr McCloud said quietly. 'Tell Henry to shut up or he'll get us all killed.'

Allenshaw had broken free of the arms that had been restraining him and was remonstrating with the men closest to him. One of them held a knife and the other had one hand on the pommel of a large revolver stuffed in his belt. Their eyes were fixed on the British Major and they looked ready to attack.

'I'll give you to the count of five to return our weapons,' Allenshaw was saying, 'and then I'll . . .'

'Henry,' Spencer called, 'I think we'd better hear what they have to say.'

'But . . . they've taken my gun.' Henry Allenshaw stood with hands on hips, brow furrowed and lower jaw thrust out in protest.

The Brigadier watched him with amusement, wondering if Bernard was going to calm him with a promise to buy him another one.

Going to her father's side, Rachel took hold of his arm. There was a stir in the crowd when she came outside and Allenshaw shot angry glances at the nearest of the tribesmen who were taking a particularly close interest in the young English woman.

One of the village elders stepped forward. 'You

will please gather only what you need in the way of food and clothing and you will come with us.'

'Where to?' Spencer asked.

'We are taking you to Prince Mahsud of Beshandu.'

'Prince Mahsud?' Spencer queried. 'Whatever for?' His face became ashen at the mention of the Prince. It was bad enough for him to be caught up in this unpleasantness, but he was becoming increasingly concerned for the safety of his daughter.

'The Prince will tell you. If he has no interest in you, then he will let you go. I am sure of it. But we will have done our part. We will have proved ourselves loyal to him, and for our village that is all that matters.'

Spencer shot an angry glance at the Brigadier who ignored it. 'It seems we have little choice but to comply,' he said to the elder. 'However, I protest in the strongest possible terms and I tell you now that you and your village will be held responsible if any harm comes to us, even if it is committed by Prince Mahsud.' He noticed the flicker of doubt on the village elder's face so pressed home his attack. 'It is you who have taken us prisoner whilst guests in your village. It is you who are abusing the laws of hospitality, and it is you who are delivering us into the hands of Prince Mahsud of Beshandu. Do not think that your actions will be overlooked when British troops come here to seek justice.'

There was a pause while the elder consulted with his colleagues, but after much head-shaking he returned to his captives and said, 'I am sorry. Believe me, Spencer Saheb, if there was any other way I would take it, but we must answer to Prince Mahsud before anyone else. After Kasim's village, we have no other choice.'

'Najaf Kasim? What has happened to him?' Spencer knew of Kasim. He was a renowned local bandit for whom Spencer had never had any time.

'His village was destroyed by the Prince, everyone was killed or taken prisoner. We do not want that to happen here.'

'But why would the Prince do this?'

The Brigadier stepped forward. 'Because he is planning a frontier war.'

Spencer stared at him in disbelief. 'And you knew about it?'

'Not exactly. Not about the village.' He held up his hands. 'I know what you're going to say, but honestly, Bernard, I thought it was best if you didn't know.'

'I'm the Political Officer, damn it. I have a right to know. I suppose you think that because I'm at the bottom of the intelligence gathering chain I don't matter. But, blast it all man, you've let us walk into a trap!'

'Now, Bernard . . .'

'If you knew Mahsud was planning a frontier war you should damned well have told me.'

'That's not quite the whole story.'

'Then what is? Really, this is intolerable. You let me bring Rachel into all this without so much as a warning.'

'Believe me, I could not tell anyone.'

'Why the devil not?'

'I just couldn't, and that's that.'

'That most certainly is not that. I'm going to take this further if we ever get out of here. Up to the Viceroy himself it necessary.'

The Brigadier smiled ruefully. 'You do whatever you think you have to, Bernard, but you'll be wasting your time. There's more at stake here than you know.'

'Our lives are at stake. I should think that was enough,' Spencer protested.

There was a scuffle as the villagers laid hold of Allenshaw again and led him and the others back into their houses under close escort to gather their belongings. Their weapons were removed and a few minutes later they were assembled outside again and led away. As they headed off out of the village, the Brigadier was just wondering where Caspasian and the others had got to, when he saw a man hobbling towards them. Two of the tribesmen ran towards him and he collapsed into their arms. His wrists were tied and a leather thong flapped from one ankle where he had broken free from his bindings. There was a heated exchange which he was unable to overhear and the next moment a large crowd of tribesmen ran off up the hillside heading in the direction from which the man had just come.

The Brigadier smiled to himself.

'I'm glad you find our situation amusing, James,' Spencer said.

'Not at all,' he replied. It's just good to know that in an uncertain world Caspasian's skills are as reliable as they ever were.'

* * *

After leaving the goatherd's house and the scene of their fight, Caspasian, Ganga and Channing headed up into the hills. They travelled away from the village for half an hour, before Caspasian turned and led them in a wide circle. Channing watched for a while before asking what he was up to.

'I'm doubling back towards the village,' Caspasian answered.

'Why?' Channing said, gaping at him as though he was mad.

'We've got to pay a little visit to our arms cache. Ganga's task, remember?'

Channing smiled to himself. 'How the hell did you know we'd be needing that?'

'I didn't. It was an SOP.'

'SOP?'

'Standard operating procedure. A standard drill. Never put all your eggs in one basket. Certainly not when in the middle of a tribal village.'

'But what are we going to do now? I mean, even if we have some weapons hidden away somewhere, we can't exactly attempt a rescue, can we? There'd be too much risk to Rachel and the others.'

Caspasian quickened the pace. He knew that it would not be long before the tribesmen discovered they had got away and hill people such as these were always expert trackers. If it had been just Ganga and himself they could probably have stood a chance of outrunning the villagers and getting away, but with Channing it would be impossible. The young lad was fit all right, but he had lived an office-based life for too long. It would take several weeks of rough hill living to harden him before he could undertake a successful escape.

'I agree, which is why we're not going to try and rescue them. Not here, at least. Not until we're presented with an ideal opportunity, and there's little chance of that with this lot at the moment. We'll shadow them, see where they're going, and I'll decide what to do then.'

'When?'

'When I have a blinding flash of inspiration. Right now I haven't got a clue! OK? So stop talking, conserve your energy, and keep up.'

By the time they drew near to their houses on the edge of the settlement, the village was quiet. The doors still stood open and everything that had not been taken with the Brigadier, Spencer and the others, had been looted by the tribesmen. Immediately after the escort had led them away the remaining villagers had rushed into the vacated houses and stripped them bare. All that was left for Caspasian to survey from his vantage point on the sheltered path beside the river where he and Rachel had walked so recently, was a scattering of debris that nobody had wanted. Lying out on the ground, empty food sacks, broken crockery, and some clothing were all that remained as evidence of the party's having stayed there.

The sight of the desolate remnants brought their plight home to them. Douglas Channing let out a sigh big enough for the three of them.

'Where did you hide the kit?' Caspasian asked.

Ganga pointed down to the river bank on the far side of the houses. 'There, saheb.'

'Let's go.'

Leaving Ganga to show the way, Caspasian

moved behind Channing, keeping a sharp eye on the ground behind them. He had drawn his Mauser, although he hoped he would not have to use it. They slid down the steep embankment to the water's edge and were able to skirt the houses with their heads below ground level. The only disadvantage was that they were unable to see over the top and detect if anyone was coming towards them. Caspasian reckoned it was unlikely however. The excitement at the houses was over, everything worth looting had been taken so there was no reason for anyone to be sniffing around.

Ganga led them straight to the packs. He had made a selection of weapons and other equipment, and packed it hurriedly with spare clothing and food on Caspasian's orders.

'We'll check them and repack once we're well clear of the village,' Caspasian said, tightening the shoulder straps on his pack and slipping his arms through them. As he hoisted it onto his shoulders they heard the tinkle of goat bells. They looked at one another.

'Just what we don't bloody need,' Caspasian whispered. 'Let's get out of here.'

Taking the lead, he moved quickly back the way they had come, but when he reached the place where they had dropped down to the river's side, he kept on going. The embankment gradually reduced in height so that the further they went the more they had to double over to keep their heads from showing above the top. When they could bend no more while still running, Caspasian stopped beside a spot where a thick clump of gorse grew on top of the embankment. With his face hidden behind it he carefully peered over the top, trying to see through the tangle of thorns and small delicate flowers.

About thirty yards away a small girl was shooing along a herd of a dozen goats, heading straight for Caspasian's hiding place. He cursed his luck and ducked down again, signalling for the others to lie down. Crouching close beside the bank, he waited for the girl to discover their hiding place. They would have to grab her before she could raise the alarm, but what then? He could hardly kill her. He doubted whether even Brigadier Percival could do that, although he was glad the Brigadier was not there to put the theory to the test.

Nor could they take her with them. If they were to do that, when could they release her, and how could they leave her miles from her village when they had safely outrun their pursuers? It was more likely that the tribesmen would come after them with renewed vigour when they knew that Caspasian and his men had taken one of their children hostage.

A goat nibbled its way to the edge of the embankment, concentrating on a piece of the gorse bush inches above Caspasian's head. All three men stared intently at the spot. Ganga gently laid his rifle on the ground and silently drew his kukri. Caspasian was not sure what he intended but as he himself had no better idea he left him to it. The sound of Channing's breathing had been amplified into a snore by a punch he had taken on the nose from the tribesman he had fought by the goatherd's house. He shook his head in an effort to clear it and when that failed he tried breathing through his mouth instead.

To Caspasian's horror the goat suddenly saw him and froze. Cursed with curiosity, the wretched animal leaned into the drop and peered over. It reminded Douglas of an old maiden aunt of his, examining him over the top of a book when he was a small boy. Bewildered by the three unmoving bodies whose shapes were otherwise strangely familiar, the goat leaned over further to get a better look. Suddenly Caspasian heard the pad of small feet and the girl's hand grabbed the goat by the scruff of its neck and yanked it back. In the one brief instant Caspasian caught a glimpse of the bracelet on the girl's wrist and a wisp of dark hair, but she had been concentrating so hard on retrieving the animal that she had not thought to see what it had been inspecting so studiously.

She shouted at it angrily and sent it scuttling back towards the rest of the herd. As the sound of her voice receded, Caspasian looked at the others and they all broke into smiles of relief.

The next instant a shout of alarm shot through them like an electric current. Caspasian spun round to see a tall man on the far side of the fast flowing river, little more than twenty yards away. The little girl and her goats had occupied their full attention and Caspasian swore at himself for having been so careless. The noise of the rushing water had blocked out the sound of the man's approach. Although he could not get at them, the man had unslung his rifle and was aiming it straight at them.

He shouted again, this time at the girl. She came running across, looked over the embankment and blanched at the sight of the three men.

'What's he saying?' Channing asked.

'He's telling her to run for help while he holds us here,' Caspasian said, searching around for a way out. The man jerked the muzzle of his rifle at them by which they understood he wanted them to stand up. He was alone and a fishing rod lay on the ground beside him. Caspasian wondered if the villagers ever went anywhere without carrying a gun.

Try as he might, Caspasian could not see anywhere to run. The embankment at their backs was sheer, even if no more than a few feet high. From such a short range, the man could shoot one, probably two of them before they could climb it. To both left and right the river bank stretched away for at least fifty yards before reaching any cover worth mentioning. Although a moving target would be more difficult for the man to hit, Caspasian was not prepared to gamble on the quality of his marksmanship. For all he knew they had been caught red-handed by the best shot in the village.

In front of them the way was blocked by the river. It was difficult to gauge the depth but Caspasian reckoned it might be possible to wade across, perhaps even shallow enough to run through. But if the water was as much as knee depth they would be delayed sufficiently for the man to shoot them down one by one. As an added complication the riverbed was strewn with slippery pebbles. One false step and they would be flat on their backs.

He had just about given up hope when Ganga coughed lightly. Caspasian glanced over to see the Gurkha holding his kukri down the back of his leg. He had not returned it to its scabbard after drawing it to use on the goat. Now he was seeking permission to use it on the tribesman.

Caspasian had dearly hoped to get away without killing any of the villagers. With blood on their hands their escape would be more difficult than it already was. The shout of approaching voices from above the embankment helped him decide. He nodded to Ganga.

The tribesman had also heard his comrades coming to help him and as the tension left him he visibly relaxed. The muzzle of his rifle dropped slightly and he looked away from his three prisoners, craning over their heads to catch a glimpse of his friends.

Ganga saw his opportunity and acted. Judging the distance perfectly, he drew back his hand, paused to sight along his other outstretched arm aimed at the rifleman, and threw, following through with his body and dropping to one knee as he did so. The deadly blade spun end over end like a Catherine wheel and with a dull thud, the blade lodged deep in the base of the man's sternum. The follow-through had given the throw such force that the man was knocked backwards. His rifle tumbled on to the stones and he lay still with arms spread wide.

'Go!' Caspasian shouted, and led the way across the river. They pounded through the icy water, gasping as the spray soaked them. As they struggled out the far side, Ganga retrieved his kukri, but there was a cry from behind and Caspasian spun round to see Channing flat on his stomach in the water, having slipped on the pebbles. He darted back, grabbed Channing's jacket in one fist and hauled him to the river bank. Glancing up, Caspasian saw that the first of the tribesmen had arrived at the top of the embankment. Without pausing he drew his Mauser pistol, aimed and fired. Now that one tribesman was dead, there was no longer any point in holding back. The man twisted in a half circle and toppled forward over the drop and on to the pebbles.

Ganga, who had been jogging away from the river, turned at the sound of the pistol. When he saw what was happening he cocked his Lee-Enfield, knelt, and fired two rounds in quick succession over the top of the far bank. Although there was no target to engage he knew that the crack of the shots would make anyone think twice before poking their heads above the gorse.

'Back, saheb. Go!' He shouted.

Caspasian shoved Channing hard, keeping him in front this time, and jogged back past Ganga. There was no time to extract his sub-machine gun from the top of the pack where it was strapped, but the Mauser's wooden holster doubled as a shoulder-stock. So as he ran he unhooked it from his belt and slotted the base of it onto the pommel of his Mauser, converting the pistol into a carbine. It would steady the aim and increase the range out to one hundred yards by improving the accuracy. It might have nothing like the hitting power of the Lee-Enfield but it would put a man down. For now that was all that mattered.

When they had gone twenty paces beyond Ganga, Caspasian pushed Channing to the ground, turned and knelt, bringing the Mauser into the shoulder. Cupping his left palm under the short barrel, he shouted, 'Go!'

Ganga was on his feet and jogging back while the aftershock of Caspasian's command was still ringing in Channing's ears. Ganga kept his pace steady, avoiding the novice's impulse to sprint. The last thing they needed was a fall and a sprained ankle. His eyes were on the ground, checking his footfall and seeking out his next fire position. His breathing was silent and unruffled. It was like a day on the ranges.

A head peered over the bank, followed by the muzzle of a gun. Before the man could bring it into the aim, Caspasian cracked off two rounds. One of them struck the wooden stock and the rifle spun from the man's grasp. There was a cry of pain, and the man snatched at his broken wrist, but he and his fellow villagers had got the message. The pursuit was not worth the effort, not without considerable reinforcement. Prince Mahsud would have to be content with the prisoners they had already seized.

If they could not capture them however, perhaps they could at least kill or injure them. Spreading out along the top of the embankment, the tribesmen waited until they were all in position before, at a signal, rolling forward to the lip and firing across the river all at once. Faced with numerous targets over a front of some thirty yards, Caspasian was forced to pull back. Luckily, by then Ganga was in position and did his best to provide covering fire with well aimed snap-shots. Caspasian again shoved Channing in front of him, shouting at him to keep low, and darted back for cover, weaving to left and right to throw the tribesmen off their aim. He hooked wide as he ran to give Ganga as clear a line of fire as he could.

Bullets snapped and whined at his heels, ricocheting off the stony ground and whipping up into the branches of the treeline in front of him.

'Keep on going!' Ganga shouted as Caspasian reached him. The magazine in his Lee-Enfield was almost empty but he knew there would not be time to slam in a fresh clip until Caspasian was able to put down covering fire.

Caspasian bounded the last few yards into the treeline, Channing tucked in close by his side, ducking from the bullets as if from a shower of rain. Turning on his heel, Caspasian slid out the expended magazine from his Mauser and pushed in a new one, tapping it home.

'Go!' he shouted.

Now it was Ganga's turn to dodge and weave. With thirty yards to go the tribesmen's fire intensified. The ground at Ganga's feet was pocked with impacting bullets. Channing saw a strip of the Gurkha's webbing being torn off as a bullet ripped through it, and his hat was knocked forward over his eyes, struck from behind. Ganga stumbled but just managed to regain his balance and run on, snatching his hat from his head as he went.

Once at the trees, he pounded past the two men and dropped to his knees. At the same time he ripped open an ammunition pouch, pulled out a fresh clip, opened the breech of his rifle and with his thumb, thrust home the five rounds. A second clip went in on top, thereby recharging the magazine with its full capacity of ten .303 calibre rounds.

'Keep your pack on,' Caspasian called back to him as he saw Ganga about to shoulder out of the straps.

'We're not going to get into a firefight.' He was determined to break contact as soon as they could and run for it. The danger now was to get involved in a prolonged exchange of fire which they could never hope to win. Sooner or later they would run out of ammunition, the enemy would outflank them, and this time there would be no chance of fighting their way out with their fists. If they were lucky they would be taken to rendezvous with the other captives and be handed over to the unpredictable mercies of Prince Mahsud. More likely the tribesmen, angered by the death of their comrade, the beating accorded to some of their number by the goatherd's house, and the frustration and expense of the long pursuit and firefight, would kill them out of hand, no doubt bringing their inventiveness into play and extending the torment with a variety of agonies.

'OK, when I give the word, we'll empty a full magazine each, turn and pull out. Reload on the run. Got it?'

'Yes, saheb!' Ganga shouted back.

'What about me?' Channing asked. 'What can I do?'

'Stick to me like glue.'

'Oh come on, surely I can . . .'

'Not now, Douglas. Not now.'

They stopped firing for a few seconds, just long enough to give the tribesmen the idea that they had taken to their heels.

'Steady . . .' Caspasian hissed. 'Steady . . .'

First one head popped up, and then another. The men were too far away now for Caspasian to catch what they were saying but his plan was working.

The villagers were amateurs when it came to a fire-fight and they took the bait. They stood up and one by one dropped down the embankment and started across the river. When they were halfway over, starkly silhouetted against the embankment behind them, Caspasian gave the word.

'Fire!'

Both he and Ganga rose out of the tall grass that grew thickly between the trees and opened fire, Ganga starting from the left of the enemy line and working in towards the centre, Caspasian starting from the right. Firing only one round at each man, they did not mind whether they hit or missed. A hit was a bonus, but a miss would still be close enough to give the target a nasty shock and put him on the ground in cover for long enough.

'This is like a bloody circus shooting gallery,' Caspasian said as the tribesmen went down. He could see blood in the water and a couple of bodies floated downstream. Most staggered ashore, some going back the way they had come, some stumbling forward to the near bank. But the aim had been achieved. They would think twice before advancing again.

'Time to go, I think,' Caspasian said, pulling tight his shoulder straps. He pointed the way back into the trees and grinned. 'Mr Channing, after you.'

Chapter Thirteen

Karpov was horrified by the news of the injury sustained by Mahsud's concubine. It made his task considerably more difficult.

'How badly is the stone damaged?' he asked, trying not to reveal the true extent of his alarm.

'It is hard to tell. I'm not going to pick it up, funnily enough.' Mahsud had stormed into the Bolsheviks' quarters with half a dozen armed men behind him. Zykov and Dragov sat on the edge of their beds. Their guns were in reach but both knew it would be suicide to go for them. Beside Karpov, Vassily Novikov stood his ground, a broad smile illuminating his face. He winked at Ahmed who scowled back.

'You know about the curse, I suppose,' Karpov said.

Mahsud stared at him and was about to reply but turned to his guards first. 'Ahmed, take the men out of the room.'

'But, my Prince, we can't leave you . . .'

'It's all right. What do you think they're going to do? Kill me in my own fortress?' He turned back to Karpov and glared at him. 'They would be roasted on spits and they know it. However, if it will make you feel better, take their weapons.'

Ahmed took a step forward. Novikov moved to block his path but Karpov, seeing the Prince's men raise their rifles, restrained him. 'Don't worry. Hand them over. We're among friends.'

Grudgingly, Zykov and Dragov surrendered their guns, and when Ahmed had all of them, Mahsud said, 'Go now.'

Ahmed started to protest again but, seeing the Prince's expression, he led his men away and closed the door behind them. When he had gone, Mahsud pulled up a chair and sat down, indicating that Karpov and Novikov should do likewise. Slowly they complied, surprised at the turn of events.

'Don't you dare give me that shit about a curse.' Mahsud's voice was low but his eyes were dangerous. He leaned forward, elbows on his knees. 'Do you think I'm some stupid bumpkin?' He imitated an English accent. 'Just another wog, old bean?' He smiled, his eyes narrow and mirthless. 'The British do, which is why they're about to come seriously unstuck. I'd thought more highly of you. You disappoint me.'

Karpov rushed in to heal the breach. 'I didn't mean that you would believe it, Prince Mahsud. That was said for the benefit of your men.'

'Which is why I sent them away.' Mahsud grinned conspiratorially. 'For now it might serve my interests if some of them at least, believe the old tale. Of more concern to me is what has happened to the Eye of the Storm that was promised to me by your government.'

Novikov frowned, glancing uncertainly at Karpov. His English was not as good as Karpov's but he had picked up the gist of Mahsud's question. Mahsud understood in a second. 'Ah. I see. Your men are also in the dark. Perhaps we should reconvene this meeting somewhere more private, just you and I?'

Unlike the Prince however, Karpov was not in the heart of his own stronghold, scores of men within shouting distance, in the centre of his own country. He was not prepared to surrender the slender protection afforded by his comrades. 'I have no secrets from Vassily Novikov or the others,' he said proudly.

'Fine. Then tell me, what have I just slaughtered dozens of people to capture? It looks like the Eye of the Storm, but, if I'm correct, the real Eye of the Storm that adorned the statue of the prophet Abdul Rashid, was not filled with liquid mustard gas?'

Karpov felt as if he had been punched in the face. Seeing that his words had struck home Mahsud smiled at him, this time with genuine satisfaction.

'You obviously haven't done your homework on me or you would know that among my hobbies at Oxford chemistry was one of my favourites.'

Novikov had had enough. 'What's he talking about, Alexei? Is this true?'

Seeing that he had no alternative but to admit it, Karpov nodded. 'Yes.'

'What's all this about mustard gas?'

Mahsud sat back, grinning like a cat. 'Go on, comrade. I'm all ears.'

Karpov was silent for a moment, gathering his thoughts. 'The stone contains liquid mustard gas in a highly concentrated form. It is an altogether new generation of chemical weapon and was developed by Russian scientists in the days immediately before the Bolshevik Revolution. A small sample was enclosed in a glass crystal that was disguised to look like the Eye of the Storm. It was to have been smuggled to England along with other Romanov treasures and presented to the British government as the price for a safe haven for the Tsar and his family. But everything went wrong. The Tsar, his wife and children were executed, their treasures seized before they could be evacuated, and in the mêlée surrounding those stormy times, most of those who knew of the stone's hidden contents were killed before they could pass on their secret. There were few enough of them as it was.'

'But surely there were other stocks?' Novikov asked, hardly believing what he was hearing. He grinned, uncomprehending. 'And why the glass crystal? Why go to all the trouble of . . .?'

'Let me finish!' Karpov snapped. He calmed himself, staring fixedly at his old comrade. 'Please, Vassily, everything will become clear. Yes there were other stocks, but they were all destroyed by the Tsarists before they fell into our hands.'

'And the formula? Was that destroyed too?'

'Destroyed, lost, what does it matter?' Karpov said. 'No one escaped death who knew how to manufacture the new gas. The only remaining sample lay safely in the heart of the stone.'

Warming to his subject, Alexei stood and paced the room. 'The ironic part is, the stone and its deadly gas were in our possession all the time, although we never knew it. It was only when it fell into the hands of White Russian guerillas that we learned the true value of what we had lost. It was part of a consignment of Romanov treasure that was being taken by train from St Petersburg to Moscow. The train was ambushed and the treasure seized. But, in the raid, the guerillas lost one of their men, left behind for dead. An officer. He was lucky not to have been finished off on the spot. Instead he was taken prisoner, he recovered, and then,' Karpov said smiling grimly, 'imagine our surprise when he offered to bargain for his freedom with a tiny piece of information?'

'Where was the Eye by this time?' Novikov asked.

'Out of our reach, unfortunately. By the time we closed in on the headquarters of the guerillas who had ambushed the train, the Eye of the Storm was already on its way to rendezvous with British agents. With the Tsar dead, they could still use it to bargain for enormous quantities of arms.'

Chair legs scraped on the stone floor as Prince Mahsud pushed himself to his feet. 'So let me get this straight. Your government promised me the Eye of the Storm, knowing all along they didn't have it to give. Correct?'

There was no answer.

'Correct?' Mahsud repeated, his voice rising.

'We had it when the promise was made. At that time we thought it was the original Eye of the Storm, a useful instrument for fomenting revolution in British India,' Karpov responded glumly.

'I see.'

'By the time we discovered the true nature of the stone that we had lost, it was too late. It was in the hands of the counter-revolutionaries who were dealing with the British. You can imagine how keen they were to get their hands on such a powerful new chemical weapon.'

'Indeed. But to get back to your duplicity, comrade, you knew that the British were bringing the stone back through Afghanistan and that they would cross through my territory. You also knew that there was no way you could recapture the stone before it reached India. So what you needed was some simple dupe to ambush the British agents, and then . . . what?'

Again no one dared answer.

'What?' Mahsud shouted. 'And then you turn up, pretend everything has gone according to plan, assist with the uprising that, in truth, means absolutely nothing to you, and, at an opportune moment, steal back the Eye of the Storm, and return home.' He glared at Karpov with loathing. 'Did you really think it would work?' He paused to consider. 'I suppose without the seizure of the stone by the bandits and the damage inflicted, the stone would have arrived in perfect shape. We, of course, would have handled such a priceless relic with the tenderest of care and you might even have managed to steal it at some point. Escaping back to the Soviet Union however does stretch it a little too far, don't you think?'

'What choice did we have?' Karpov said. 'Let it fall into the hands of the British? We were assured by our scientists that it would be possible to analyse the sample and reconstitute the gas, producing it in vast quantities. With such a weapon at the disposal of the counter-revolutionaries the new Soviet government could have been overthrown.'

Mahsud looked at him sadly. 'So it was just another toy you had to have, to help you spread world revolution.' His face was contorted into a savage sneer. 'How pathetic. And now, after such lies and deception, I suppose you think I am going to let you live?'

At a nod from Novikov, Zykov and Dragov stood up and moved beside him, the four of them facing Mahsud.

'What are you going to do?' Mahsud asked sarcastically. 'A cowboy shoot-out? Don't be ridiculous.'

'It doesn't have to be like this,' Karpov said. 'You can still have your frontier war. Only you know about the Eye of the Storm. No one else does. We can use the gas on the British troops. There will be enough of it for that. They will have no protection against it. It might mean that we cannot take it back with us, but at least the British won't get it.' He smiled. 'At least, not in the way they anticipate.'

Mahsud pondered this for a moment. The presence of the gas had taken him by surprise, but if it could indeed be put to some good use then something of value might have been salvaged from an otherwise messy situation.

'All right then. We will smash the stone, or crystal, or whatever it is, and extract the liquid. What then?'

'No!' Karpov cried. 'You must not break it.' He steadied himself. 'It is highly toxic, you see.'

'There is a young woman in my rooms who used to be quite beautiful. She will testify to that,' Mahsud said harshly. He would be sorry to part with her but he could hardly be seen consorting with someone with a withered hand.

'That is why I wanted to look after the stone for you at the village,' Karpov confessed.

'Having the chemical weapon is one thing, but how do I use it against the British?' Mahsud asked.

It was Novikov who spoke. 'Do you have mortars?'

'Of course.'

'Do you have illuminating rounds amongst the ammunition? Parachute flares?'

Mahsud smiled. 'Go on.'

'I can convert them to disperse the chemical over the advancing troops. The liquid from the crystal can be diluted to provide enough chemical for dozens of bombs. If the small parachute is removed from the base of the flare round, I can seal the chemical inside the compartment instead. When it is fired over the British infantry, the flare will burst, but instead of being a simple illumination, it will rain down the chemical in a spray of fine droplets.' He grinned. 'Exposed skin will blister. They will be completely at the mercy of your men.'

'Mercy?' Mahsud said smiling. 'An interesting notion, but not really what I had in mind.'

It was well into the early hours of the next morning before Caspasian felt safe enough to call a halt. While he was confident that he and Ganga had given the tribesmen a sufficiently bloody nose to dissuade them from following up their pursuit, he wanted to put as much distance as possible between himself and the village before resting.

By the time they stopped, Channing was panting

hard. He had been soaked when he had fallen in the river but had mostly dried out during the long hot forced march. Nevertheless he was exhausted. Unlike his two companions he was unused to physical hardship. Even Caspasian had felt the pace. Although he had only been behind his desk at the Headquarters in Delhi for a short period, it had taken its toll on his fitness. Only Ganga was completely untroubled by the hard hill march. Taking the lead most of the way, he strode ahead, rifle at the ready, eyes taking in their surroundings and alert for ambush.

Caspasian's plan was to circle around until they cut the route he believed the villagers would be using to transport their prisoners to Prince Mahsud's fortress. They would almost certainly be travelling by one of the main tracks. Once Caspasian had made contact he intended to shadow their progress from a distance, looking for an opportunity to launch an attack of his own to rescue Rachel and the others. What he was supposed to do about the Eye of the Storm, he was uncertain. If, as now seemed likely, it was in the hands of the Prince, then there was probably nothing to be done about it. There would be a frontier war, as the Brigadier feared, and it would be up to the British, Indian and Gurkha troops to win it.

If Mahsud had wider political ambitions that encompassed some greater role for himself in the future government of an independent India, then God help them all. He would have to be defeated on the field of battle. A victory for him would bring unthinkable consequences for the Empire, and indeed for India itself, if his reputation and that of his father was to be believed.

'Can we light a fire? I'm freezing,' Channing asked.

'Sorry. Too risky,' Caspasian said. 'How are the clothes? Have they dried out yet?'

'Pretty much.' Channing felt gingerly at his sleeve. 'It's ruined the hang of my jacket though. I feel like a scarecrow.'

Caspasian clapped him on the shoulder. 'Maybe, but you're a living scarecrow.'

'Thanks to you.' Channing looked at Caspasian. 'Look, to be frank, I haven't been much help up to now. Isn't there something I could do?'

'Yes. You can keep up, keep quiet, and keep going.'

Channing grimaced. 'Great. That really makes me feel good.'

Ganga looked across from where he sat, opening some tins of curried mutton. 'Anyone can fight, saheb. It takes a clever man like you to do the other things.'

'What other things?' Channing asked sceptically.

Ganga shrugged, prising open another tin and setting it down on a rock. 'Oh, I don't know. Make everything work. Organise things.' He nodded at Caspasian. 'Soldiers like us, we break things. You make things. That's the difference.'

He paused a moment and stared into space, a satisfied smile lighting his face. 'Yes. That's right.'

'Hold on a minute,' Caspasian protested. 'I'm not sure I like being grouped with the destroyers. What do you think I was doing in Delhi?'

Ganga laughed. 'Yes, saheb, but you hate it. Everyone in the Paltan knows it.'

'Don't talk to me about the Regiment,' Caspasian said angrily. 'They couldn't wait to see the back of me.'

'Not everyone, saheb. The sahebs in the Mess, they take much pleasure when they think of you at your desk. Only the Colonel Saheb was sorry to see you go on posting, but he says it is for the good of your career. A good job, he calls it.'

Channing was interested by this insight into Caspasian. The image of Caspasian as outcast fitted well with everything else he had read about him in the file and heard about him from Brigadier Percival. 'Don't you like people?' he asked.

Caspasian looked up sharply, ready to attack, but the smile on Channing's face was ingenuous and his tone innocent. He relented. 'I've never really thought about it.'

'Oh, come on! How many years were you in the trenches? There must have been a million times you had nothing else to do but think about people.'

Caspasian eyed him shrewdly. 'You're not always as stupid as you appear, are you?'

'Thank you. Actually no, I'm not. They don't accept just anyone into the ICS. I might not be able to dismantle four armed men in seconds, but that doesn't mean I'm not observant.'

'I know. I also know that Percival doesn't tolerate fools.' Caspasian measured his words. 'OK, then. People.' He had taken off his pack and boots and now leaned back against a large stone, stretching out his legs and flexing his toes. 'I don't dislike people. In fact, there are a number of people I actually like.' He glanced across at Ganga. 'Of course, I hate Ganga. He's utterly appalling.'

Ganga giggled and lobbed across a pebble.

'I'm not very good with them, I suppose.'

'Was that the war?' Channing asked.

Caspasian smiled. 'That would be a good excuse, wouldn't it? How wonderful if I could blame the war for blowing all sociability out of me.' He smiled. 'It would be a lie, of course. Or at least an exaggeration. It certainly did nothing to help, but if I'm honest I've just never had much to say to people.'

Channing took one of the tins that Ganga offered and sat down next to Caspasian to eat. He was intrigued by him and wanted to know more. The Brigadier was a hard man, but cold as a fish. Caspasian, on the other hand, was different. When he was with Caspasian, Channing felt like a horse wearing blinkers. Caspasian could see things he could not. Not hidden snipers or anything particularly physical. Rather, it was as if Caspasian's world was peopled by ghosts, beings that no one but him could see. Even when he was speaking with Channing, Caspasian was only there in part. Channing always had the impression that the greater part of Caspasian's mind was elsewhere. He could appear to be wholly focused on the conversation, but Channing knew that some vital aspect was far away. Perhaps it was striding over imaginary mountains, or maybe it was back in the trenches. Who could say? Maybe not even Caspasian himself.

'That fascinates me,' Channing enthused. 'Never

had much to say? Me, I love talking. What's the problem?'

Caspasian felt himself becoming uncomfortable.

'Well?' Channing prompted.

'The problem is, Douglas, that people sometimes talk too much.'

He took a mouthful of the cold mutton and reached for his water bottle, signalling that the conversation was over. Channing paused, wondering if he had missed something, then smiled. 'OK, point taken. I'll shut up. Lump me together with the rest of humanity if you like. Just another garrulous twit.' He tasted the meat and frowned. 'What's this? Bully beef?'

'Hardly likely with a Hindu Gurkha in charge of our messing arrangements, is it?' Caspasian said.

'Oops, sorry, Ganga.'

Ganga laughed. 'No matter, saheb. It is mutton. In fact I don't mind eating bully beef, but my pandit says I am not supposed to.'

'The priest, eh? No end of trouble, priests, the whole lot of them. Always telling us what to do and what not to do. I suppose I'm lucky. I can eat any meat.'

Ganga smiled wide-eyed. 'Really, saheb. So you eat snake, do you?'

Douglas pulled a face. 'Good heavens, no.'

'And dog, rat, hornet?'

'Never!'

'Well I have eaten all of those,' Ganga said proudly. 'Some on operations when we had nothing else, and some at home.' He wagged a finger for emphasis. 'Hornets especially are a delicacy. But you have to fry them with plenty of ghee. Until they are crisp.'

Caspasian tilted his wristwatch towards the moon and checked the time. 'I suggest we have a couple of hours' sleep. No more. I'll keep watch for the first hour, and Ganga, you for the second.'

Channing looked from one to the other, a hurt expression on his face. 'What about me? Don't you think I can stay awake too?'

'Frankly, no. I'm not prepared to take the chance. Later, perhaps, once we're further away from the village, but not tonight.'

Channing groaned but realised it was useless to protest. Caspasian had pronounced and that was that. They continued eating in silence and when they had finished, Ganga collected the empty tins in a small sack. 'What's that for?' Douglas asked.

'We take all our rubbish with us, saheb,' he replied. 'Leave nothing for the enemy to find. It's an . . .'

'Let me guess. An SOP, right?'

Ganga laughed. 'Correct, saheb.'

They unrolled blankets and while Ganga and Channing stretched out on the hard ground, searching for comfort amidst the hollows and lumps, Caspasian moved apart to select a vantage point which would afford a clear all-round view. He had already nominated an escape route in case they had to move out in a hurry and, before last light, had shown them all a place on the far skyline where they were to rendezvous if they became separated.

Channing pulled his woollen blanket up under his chin. He had started to shiver. There was a rock sticking into the small of his back and he shifted to one side to prise it out. He really was not cut out for all of this. On that he had to agree with Caspasian. In future he would stick to more office-bound pursuits. One did not have to endure such physical hardship to rise through the ranks of the ICS. Undoubtedly that was not the case with the army. The poor devils, he thought. But then Caspasian obviously liked it. Indeed, he thrived on it.

He rolled on to his side, tucking the blanket over his shoulder and looked across to where Caspasian sat, his back to Channing, arms hugging his knees. The big Mauser pistol lay on the ground beside him, freshly cleaned and oiled. How many men had Caspasian killed today, Douglas wondered. How many in total over the years. He shuddered. The man was a killer. Douglas marvelled at the label. It did not match any of his preconceptions however. In fact it was somehow incidental. He could believe it of Percival. Of Ganga even. But Caspasian? Obviously it was his preconceptions that were at fault.

As Caspasian stared hard-eyed across the mountainside into the night, Channing could feel his eyelids closing. In the brief clarity that comes in the moments before sleep and full wakefulness, he understood the man. He was a romantic, but a romantic disabled. As if in the conflict that was his life he had lost a limb. But what had undone him? What had blasted the hole clean through? If not the war, then what? Caspasian certainly was not saying. As a romantic he could hardly be said to be robbed of opportunity, given his chosen lifestyle. Perhaps, Channing thought, like all romantics who must live in the real world Caspasian was doomed, and, as an intelligent man, he knew it.

The journey was hard for Rachel. Where the ambush had been a brutal but short-lived introduction to the world inhabited by Brigadier Percival and his kind, captivity by the tribesmen was unending. Oddly enough, it was not so much the loss of freedom that aggravated – as a girl she had grown used to such confinement when sent away to boarding school in England. The hardship stemmed from the thought of being handed over to Prince Mahsud and also, she was not wholly surprised to discover, from the absence of John Caspasian.

Shortly after they had been taken prisoner, they had learned of Caspasian's escape. Some of the villagers had wanted to wreak their revenge on the helpless captives but fortunately a more merciful counsel had prevailed, if it was appropriate to speak of surrender to Prince Mahsud as merciful.

Caspasian, Ganga and Douglas had, it turned out, fought their way out of the trap set for them by the tribesmen, turning the tables on them and getting clean away. Her father had overheard and told her that several of the tribesmen had been killed in the process. There had apparently been a heated debate about pursuing the three fugitives, but after the gun fight at the river they decided against it. They would leave that pleasure to Prince Mahsud. He had the greater resources of manpower, weaponry and expertise to hunt them down and kill them.

When they stopped for the night, they were given

blankets but Rachel slept fitfully. Henry Allenshaw snored soundly and the Brigadier lay unmoving and silent. He might as well have been a corpse. In the brief moments when she did drift off to sleep, Rachel's dreams were filled with terrifying images. The mortally wounded groom at the ambush valley – she saw him in all his gory detail. The wound opening beneath her hands, the gaping chasm where the bullet had exited, the last shuddering breath, the glaze slipping into the eyes as life vacated the body.

At the dream's last appearance she started awake, resolving to be done with sleep for the night. She sat up, pulling her legs under her, and looked up at the sky. Beside her she could hear her father breathing evenly. A guard glanced across. His gaze settled on her breasts and he grinned. Rachel drew the blanket about her shoulders and turned herself away from him. She heard him mutter something and tried to deflect her thoughts elsewhere.

It was a clear night. The moon had set and the sky was pitted with stars, all of them shuddering as if from the bitter cold. Rachel searched amongst them until she found patterns she recognised. It gave her a certain comfort.

One of the tribesmen had said he was certain they had wounded one of the Englishmen. Of course no one could confirm or deny his account, or say whether it had been Caspasian or Douglas Channing who had been hit. Rachel found herself praying for Caspasian's safe-keeping. Was it odd, she wondered, that after so short a time and after so unpropitious a meeting in the woods, she should feel this way? Probably. But then her father had always told her she was an odd girl. She smiled and looked down to where he slept. She reached out and lightly stroked the shoulder of his jacket, feeling the coarse tweed beneath her fingertips. She knew that he was suffering doubly on her account. She regretted causing him the extra distress when he had more than enough already. The Brigadier had lied to them and was lying still. She was certain of it.

What she did not regret was the chance to talk to Caspasian and that could only have happened on the expedition. She did not regret the chance of getting to know him better. If all of that had come about as a consequence, then so be it. It made her feel that everything had not been quite such a failure.

Henry Allenshaw had loudly voiced the opinion that Caspasian and the others had bolted. 'Scarpered!' he had said. 'That's what they've done. Mark my word. I know that sort. All bold as brass on the face of it, but yellow as a dog underneath.' He had looked around at his fellow captives for agreement. Having received none he had persevered nonetheless. 'Seen it all before. War probably unhinged the man. Expect he was the sort who skulked down in the dugouts when the others went over the top. Lucky not to have been shot by a firing squad, I shouldn't wonder.'

It had continued in a similar vein for a while before his reserves of invective had run dry, exhausted by the long march and the heat of the sun. Dr McCloud had moved his horse up beside Rachel's at one point. 'I shouldn't worry,' he had said. 'The Prince won't want trouble, and if he harms a hair on our heads he'll get more trouble than even he ever bargained for. He knows that. He's no fool.'

Rachel had smiled at him. 'Thank you, Angus. I'm sure you're right.' She had only said it to put his mind at rest. There was nothing she disliked more than having others worry about her.

There was a sound from behind and she turned to find that the guard had walked up beside her. He stared hungrily down at her, the smile gone now, his intentions plain. Because of her companions sleeping around her she did not feel threatened. At any moment she could cry out and bring them to her assistance. But what if the other tribesmen prevented them? The thought chilled her to the bone and she clasped her blanket tight about her, staring fiercely back at the guard. He shuffled a step closer, his eyes roaming freely about her. He glanced at the other forms unmoving beneath their blankets. Staring hard into Rachel's eyes he jerked his head in the direction of the trees.

'You come,' he whispered.

She stared back at him, unmoving.

'Come now,' he hissed through clenched teeth, his expression savage. He drew his knife and pointed it at her father. 'Or I kill.'

Rachel shook her head, her mind racing. If she shouted for help and her father awoke, he would try to defend her. Then perhaps the guard would indeed kill him. The guard crouched beside her and reached out. He touched her hair, stroking it gently. He touched her cheek, his fingers hard and calloused. Rachel suddenly noticed that he had moved his knife closer to her father and the point now rested on his jacket collar at the base of his skull. One thrust and he would be dead.

The guard grinned, transfixing her with his eyes as his hand stroked her shoulder, feeling the round firm curve. He clasped the edge of the blanket and tugged it from her grip. He looked down and feasted his eyes on her, his lips open, his breathing shallow. He muttered something she could not understand. He slid his hand down from her shoulder and stretched his fingers towards her breast. Rachel reached up to knock his hand away but he jerked the knife close to the skin of her father's neck. He cocked his head to one side, giving her the choice. She clenched her eyes tight shut and waited.

From behind the guard there was a hushed but urgent call. Rachel opened her eyes. The village elder stood five paces away, a rifle in his hands. 'Leave the girl. Now!'

The guard scowled but stood up slowly. Before he went he stooped down to Rachel, his face close to hers. 'It is far to the Prince. We will lie down yet, you and me.' He grinned. She could smell his stale breath. 'And after me, the Prince will have you. You will see.'

'Move!' the elder repeated and the guard sloped away.

When he had gone Rachel curled into a ball. She was shivering, though not from the cold. She knew in her heart that Henry Allenshaw was wrong and that Caspasian had not run. He would help them. She was sure of it. But he would have to come soon. Very soon.

Chapter Fourteen

It was two days later that Caspasian and Ganga picked up the trail of the tribesmen with their captives for the Prince. Caspasian had hung back to urge greater speed on Channing, letting Ganga go on ahead, when the sergeant signalled from a rocky outcrop with a frantic wave. Instantly Caspasian dropped to the ground, senses alert. Beside him Channing looked around but saw nothing.

'What is it?' he asked, his voice alarmed.

'Wait,' Caspasian said, staring hard at Ganga's hand signals. Fist closed, thumb down. Enemy. A finger thrust indicated the direction. More fingers gave the range, yards in units of a hundred, followed by the numbers of men.

Caspasian smiled, his eyes narrowing. 'Found them.'

'Now what?'

In answer, Caspasian grabbed Channing by the scruff of his jacket and hoisted him to his feet. 'Now we shadow them. We'll have to be twice as careful though. These aren't just any bunch of idiots. They'll know this country backwards. Any hint that they're being followed and the game's up.'

Channing was incredulous. 'We've hardly been sloppy up to now!'

'Nonsense. It's been a stroll so far. Barely even a route march.' He bared his teeth in a mischievous grin. 'The next bit's going to be fun.'

By the time they had caught up with Ganga, the sergeant was flat on his stomach. Hearing them approach from behind, he held out his hand, palm down, keeping his eyes fixed on the target.

'Flat,' Caspasian whispered, pushing Channing to the ground.

'Not again,' Channing complained.

'Crawl.'

Flat on his belly, Caspasian crawled up beside Ganga using his elbows and knees to propel himself forward. As Channing approached, Caspasian looked back. 'Not all the way. You stay there,' he said, indicating a point level with his boots.

'Oh, come on. I want to have a look too.'

'This isn't a game. Do as I say.'

The look in Caspasian's eye was enough to silence Channing who rolled over on to his back, folded his arms across his chest, and gazed up at the sky.

'About twelve hundred yards, saheb,' Ganga said, his voice little more than a whisper. He had lived in the mountains long enough to know how far even the smallest sound could travel, amplified by the funnelling effect of the valleys along which the winds would sweep every noise.

The hillside in front of Caspasian's vantage point sloped down at a gentle gradient. Boulders covered it and, lower down, there were trees, but wind-blasted and sparse. Caspasian realised it would be impossible to make any approach towards the party from his present location. Any movement would be spotted the moment he stepped over the skyline.

He looked to his right where the ridgeline curved in an enormous arc for at least two miles, gradually descending until it met the track along which the group was moving. Where it cut level ground, the track disappearing out of sight beyond it, the trees thickened into a substantial pine wood. Ganga grinned at him. 'Good place for an ambush, saheb.'

'Perfect. If that's what we have to do.'

'Saheb?'

Caspasian nodded in the direction of the tribesmen. 'There are, what, thirty of them? That's a lot of gunfire. In all that lot some of the Brigadier's group are going to be hit.'

'What else can we do? The Prince's fortress is less than five miles past the foot of the ridge. Once they are there we will have more than thirty men to deal with. We will have the Prince's whole army. Even I will have trouble shooting as many men as that by myself.'

While Caspasian knew that Ganga was right, he struggled to think how they could deal with such a large escort party and prevent causing casualties to their friends. 'Let's get down there anyway. Maybe something will come to me on the march.'

'It always does, saheb.'

'That's very reassuring, thank you.'

There was a tap on his boot and he looked back to see Channing preparing to move. 'How do we get down there?'

'We'll contour round, following the ridge and

keeping below the skyline. We'll have to step out a bit faster than we've been going up until now or we might miss them. Once they're into that wood it will be more difficult to keep track of them. It's taken us long enough to find them. I don't intend to lose them now. Not so close to the fortress.'

'Step out a bit faster?'

'I thought that would appeal to you,' Caspasian said.

Channing cursed under his breath and then said, 'When I get back to Delhi I'm asking Sir Oswald for a month's leave.'

'Spot of hill walking?'

'No bloody fear! Fishing. Up at Srinagar. Sitting in a boat, feet up, a sack of beers cooling in the water beside me. Just you see.'

They backed away from the ridge and crawled downhill for several yards before getting to their feet. Caspasian adjusted the straps on his backpack, tightening them ready for a fast pace. He unslung the MP18 sub-machine gun and cradled it, the bulbous drum magazine nestling in the crook of his arm. He checked the safety catch was secure.

'If you really want to catch fish, I'll give you a couple of hand grenades,' he said.

'Caspasian, has anyone ever told you you're a peasant?' Channing chuckled.

'Many times, dear boy. Many times.' He smiled. 'You're at the back of a long queue.'

They set off, Ganga taking point again, followed by Caspasian some way behind, Channing within swiping reach. Ganga had also unslung his rifle and advanced with it in the ready position, hands on the stock and grip, finger alongside the trigger guard but off the trigger in case he slipped. His thumb was on the safety catch, ready to fold it forward, disengaging it at a moment's notice.

Channing had been given a Webley revolver. Initially Caspasian had decided against giving him a rifle as well, judging that he might try and use it at a range for which he was not trained and do more damage to friend than to foe. But Ganga had pleaded Channing's cause, pointing out that at least he could put down suppressing fire in a direction safely away from the captives. To Channing's relief Caspasian had finally agreed, handing him a second Lee-Enfield and a canvas bag of ammunition clips.

'But you fire only when I tell you and where I tell you, is that understood?'

'Yes, father.'

The first few hundred yards they made good speed. The ground underfoot was firm and lightly covered with a film of coarse grass but beyond that they came upon a belt of scree. A hundred yards wide, it cut across their path. They stopped at the edge to see if there was an alternative route. To the left, where it climbed up towards the top of the ridge, they would risk being silhouetted against the skyline, while to the right, it ran away as far as the foot of the valley they had left earlier that morning.

'The only way is straight across,' Caspasian said. He cursed, knowing it would slow them down. As they picked their way steadily across, being careful to avoid twisted ankles, each step sent showers of small rocks cascading down the slope. Even though it was on the side of the hill away from the tribesmen,

Caspasian knew that there could be other people about to hear them, hunters or traders. Any one of them might take an unhealthy interest in the noise and come to investigate. The last thing he needed was an enemy on two sides.

They were halfway across when there was a shout. Caspasian and Ganga spun around. Moving at the back, Channing had lost his footing and started to slide.

'Get him, saheb!' Ganga shouted. 'Quick, before he falls out of control!'

Caspasian lunged for Channing. He judged that he could maintain his own balance just long enough to reach him. Sure enough, as he came alongside him and seized his shoulder with his free hand, he went down on his backside and the two of them were sliding, accelerating down the scree out of control. Ganga was powerless to help. All he could do was sit tight and watch.

'Hang on to me!' Caspasian yelled. He slid in front of Channing, the two of them sitting one in front of the other as if on a toboggan. As Channing gripped the shoulders of Caspasian's jacket, Caspasian drove the butt of his MP18 deep into the scree, using it like a rudder and brake rolled into one. With the toe of his boots pointing skywards, his heels gave him extra braking power, but he knew he had to be careful. He had seen someone do it before. They had panicked and driven their heels in too deep and too fast. Their forward momentum had turned them head over heels and they had ended up with two broken ankles.

'Copy me,' Caspasian yelled.

Using the butt of his rifle, Channing tried to brake. Instead he drove it in too deep and almost lost it, the heavy weapon skittering out of his grasp, only the sling remaining twisted around his forearm. As he struggled to regain control he felt himself going over on to his side.

'Caspasian, I can't hold it!' he cried out.

Grasping his MP18 under one arm, Caspasian reached behind him with his free hand and gripped Channing's jacket in a fierce vice, locking the two of them together. His muscles screamed in protest at the effort of keeping them both upright, but he held. Gradually Channing regained his balance and yard by agonising yard their descent slowed.

Caspasian drove in deeper with the MP18, keeping the drum magazine well clear of the scree to avoid damage to the mechanism. By the time they finally pulled to a stop, they were both exhausted and gasping for breath. Caspasian felt as if his arms were about to snap with the strain. The moment they halted, he released his hold on the weapon and shook his muscles, massaging them in agony.

Channing started to get up.

'Don't move!' Caspasian barked. 'You'll set us off again.' In front of them, the scree slope continued down and down, eventually curving out of sight.

'It could go on for miles. There might even be a cliff face at the bottom of it,' Caspasian said.

He looked back. Ganga was now a tiny figure in the distance far above them. He waved to show he had seen they were safe. He swung his rifle to his side and pointed.

'What's he saying?' Douglas asked.

'He's saying he'll go and take a shower and then have tea and toast ready by the time we catch up. What the fuck do you think he's saying?'

Caspasian could feel Channing smarting at the rebuke but did not care. The fall would add precious minutes to their already stretched journey. They would be lucky if they managed to intercept the captives now, and in the forefront of Caspasian's mind was Rachel. That much had become clear over the last couple of days. Duty was one thing, and Caspasian was as dedicated as the next man, but this was personal. The Brigadier had got them all into this and as far as Caspasian was concerned, the Prince was welcome to him. Rachel was another matter. The thought of her at the Prince's mercy turned Caspasian's blood cold.

They edged their way to the far side of the scree run, Caspasian going first, Channing close behind. It took agonising minutes but Caspasian knew that if they went into another slide like the last one it would either kill them, or at the very least destroy any chance of catching up with the captives.

At last, with clothing torn, their bodies battered, bruised and bloodied, they reached the edge and crawled onto firm ground. For a full three minutes they lay there panting, leaning against their packs. Caspasian rolled onto his front, drew his knees up under him and got shakily to his feet, using the butt of the MP18 to steady himself. He felt a hundred years old, bent over like an old man with a stick.

'Come on,' he wheezed.

Channing gasped for breath. 'Just a minute.'

'No time . . . must get going.'

Without bothering to wait, Caspasian began the long trudge back up the hillside. He stared at the ground immediately in front of him, watching his footing, but at one point he glanced up. Ganga had already disappeared, going on ahead as he had indicated. Caspasian knew it would have been pointless for Ganga to wait for them to catch up. It would have been wasted time and yet he was sorry he had gone. They were considerably stronger as a team than when separated. He knew that Ganga would try to intercept the captives on his own. He would not be so reckless as to attack if he could possibly avoid it. Rather, he would shadow the party and bide his time until Caspasian arrived. The problem would be following his trail. Caspasian knew that the Gurkha would leave sufficient sign to enable Caspasian to track him, but he had to strike a fine balance. Ganga knew the high level of Caspasian's tracking skills, but he had to be careful in case someone else came across his path.

Caspasian set his face to the hill once again and pushed on and up. Behind him he could hear Channing panting like a buffalo. His anger began to dissipate with the effort of the climb. There was no room for it. Any novice could have slipped. He himself had done so when a junior officer. He glanced back over his shoulder. Channing was dripping sweat as he climbed, but he was trying. He was trying hard and Caspasian had to admire that. The youth was a fish out of water but at least he was giving it everything he had got. Caspasian regretted having been so hard on him.

He called back with a word of encouragement but

Channing only grunted in response. He was either conserving his energy or he was sulking. Knowing what little he knew about Douglas Channing, Caspasian reckoned it was the former.

With a supreme effort of will, Caspasian wiped out the pain of aching muscles and the fatigue nagging at him, begging him to pause. It would have been the easiest thing in the world to stop, just to stop, if only for a moment. One foot in front of the other. That was the way it went. How easy to break the rhythm, just for a second, to lift one's face and let the cool wind pass over it. But he knew that a second would become a minute, a minute would become two. Muscles and joints would stiffen, the flow of breath would realign itself for rest, and Ganga would be out there on his own. Rachel would be out there without help.

The thought of Rachel was all he needed. Caspasian surged on, powering himself up the hill, angling away from the scree towards the point where Ganga had disappeared from view. He knew Channing would have trouble keeping up and he knew the lad would think he was doing it out of bloody-mindedness. That was too bad. There would be time later for redress. Perhaps. If they got out. If they lived.

Lieutenant Colonel Patrick Gibson turned in the saddle and looked back along the length of the column that stretched out behind him as far as he could see. It was a wonderful sight. Weaving back down the dusty road, the whole of the 1st Battalion

Dorset Light Infantry marched in column of route, rifles slung, stepping out at a lively pace. In front of him, a single company had pushed ahead to act as an advance guard. Behind him, the main body consisted of the remainder of his own battalion, a battery of mountain artillery, engineers, logistic support troops and porters. At the back of the column, another rifle company brought up the tail as rearguard.

The light guns of the mountain artillery were stripped down, the constituent parts strapped onto big Missouri mules. Colonel Gibson kept them close to the front of the column and from where he rode he could hear the creak of leather, the jingle of harnesses, and the clink of metal on metal as the barrel and limbers shifted with every plodding step of their giant bearers.

He squinted up ahead, took out his binoculars and surveyed the lie of the land. A mile in front the road entered a broad valley, but from a study of his map he knew that the valley soon narrowed into a pass that twisted and turned for several miles. The hill-tops and ridges on either side rose anything between a hundred to a thousand feet, providing a series of ideal locations for snipers to hide and wreak havoc on the marching column.

Colonel Gibson sought out his runner and sent him in search of the Adjutant. When he arrived, Captain Miller looked miserable. Until recently he had been suffering from dysentery and still had to make rapid excursions into whatever cover the route afforded alongside the road. Colonel Gibson had suggested he stay behind in Peshawar, but Miller would not hear of it.

'Michael, I think it's time to deploy the pickets.'

Captain Miller saluted. 'Right you are, Colonel.'

As he rode away, Colonel Gibson called after him, 'How are the guts?'

Miller winced at the very mention. 'Rotten, Colonel. A bullet in the head would be a mercy.'

For picket duty, the battalion had been assigned two companies of Gurkhas. Picketing consisted of sending groups of men, anything from section to company strength, up the adjacent hillsides to occupy any high point from which an enemy might wish to snipe at the column. The success of the operation depended largely on speed, speed in reaching the top of the hill, and speed in coming off it once the column had passed by. If a picket was too slow reaching a high point, the progress of the column would be delayed, opening it to other dangers. If the men were too slow extracting themselves from the picket position, they were at risk from surprise attack by an enemy who had remained hidden, biding their time. Leaving a picket position was the most vulnerable moment, when the soldiers were off guard, their backs turned, withdrawing.

If speed was essential, then Colonel Gibson had to admit that Gurkhas were ideal for the job. Born and raised amongst the world's highest mountains, they were as sure-footed as mountain goats, and could run faster up or down a hillside than they could on the flat to which they were not as well accustomed.

At the signal from the Adjutant, the two companies accelerated forward from their place in the main body, their short muscular legs powering them on past their British comrades. Good natured jeers flew between the passing companies as Johnny Gurkha was encouraged on his way.

Colonel Gibson decided to ride forward with them, placing himself with the advance guard company commander whose job it would be to select the picket positions and order the deployment of the individual picket parties. Once the column had passed by, it would be the responsibility of the rearguard company commander to oversee the extraction of the pickets who would rejoin the column. They would then quick march to the front of the column again, ready for further use. The column would be moving inside a protected area formed by the advance and rearguards at the front and back, and by the pickets on either side, the whole body rolling forward like a giant tank track. Overall, the movement would be slowed, but in tribal country and in hilly terrain Colonel Gibson knew it would have been suicide to do it any other way.

For the moment he decided not to deploy the mountain artillery. He would wait and see the level of enemy opposition, if any. If the need arose for indirect fire support from the guns, he would use the battery in a similar rolling fashion, dividing it into its constituent troops. While some guns were deployed at the roadside, ready to give fire support to the picket positions, the rest would move past them with the column. When the tail of the column reached the deployed guns, they would be stripped and packed on the mules, and move forward to the front of the column again. They would not pack up however until they received the signal that one of the other troops at the front of the column was deployed and ready. Colonel Gibson would therefore have continual fire support on call, should he need it. 'Keeping one foot on the ground,' the army called it.

The sun blazed down on the Gurkhas as they strode ahead in their felt hats, grey flannel shirts, shorts, hose tops, boots and puttees. Sheathed kukris hung from their webbing, bouncing in their canvas-covered scabbards in time to the pace. Groundsheets and water bottles were strapped below their haversacks. Each rifleman carried a Short Lee-Enfield Mark III rifle, except for the light-machine gunners armed with their .303-inch calibre Lewis guns.

When the front of the lead Gurkha company reached Captain Underwood near the head of his advance guard, the Gurkha subedar received his instructions and deployed the first pickets to left and right of the column. To give the first pickets time to get into position, the column slowed. Colonel Gibson dismounted, handed the reins of his horse to his runner, and looked around for some shade from where he could watch the pickets' progress with his binoculars. Beside him, he could hear some of his own men laying bets on which of the two pickets would be the first into position.

As he surveyed the ridgelines, focusing his binoculars, he was aware of someone moving up beside him.

'Damned hot. I think you might have been right, Patrick, about my staying in Peshawar.'

Without taking his eyes from the binoculars Patrick Gibson smiled. 'You can't say I didn't warn you, Sir Oswald. Nevertheless, your close interest in the mission does you credit.'

Sir Oswald Masterman snorted. 'You're a dear fellow, Patrick, but a terrible liar. Stick to soldiering. Leave diplomacy and flattery to the professionals. We're bred to it.'

'And welcome to it too. Give me a soldier's life any day. You know where you stand with the Pathans.'

'You're joking! They can be your grinning best friends one minute and sawing at your throat the next.'

Colonel Gibson laughed. 'You know what I mean. The Pathan you see through your rifle sights. It's him I'm talking about.'

'I'm not even sure about that. From what I've heard, you rarely do see him. Too damned elusive. Scarlet blasted pimpernels, the lot of them, only not as helpful.'

The Gurkhas were making good headway and on the left flank the lead men were surging up the hill as if it was a race. The soldiers who had placed their bets were cheering them on and, noting their progress, Captain Underwood ordered the advance guard forward again.

'How far up are they going?' Sir Oswald asked, shielding his eyes and staring hard. In Panama hat and light cotton suit, Colonel Gibson thought he looked more as if he should have been sipping a gin and tonic in his club. Sweat patches darkened the armpits of his jacket and were beginning to spread between his shoulder blades.

'For now only about six hundred yards, effective rifle range. I'm not expecting anything heavier than sniper fire at this stage. Beyond six hundred yards it would have to be a pretty good shot to force me to halt the column and deploy.'

'A fellow could make a damned nuisance of himself though, couldn't he?'

'Yes, but if a sniper's going to do real damage he'd have to come in closer. The Pathans aren't ones to rely on a lucky shot. They like to go for the kill.' He handed his binoculars to Sir Oswald. 'Here, have a look. Over there.' He pointed Sir Oswald in the right direction.

Sir Oswald scanned the hillside until he found the Gurkhas. 'God, they're fast little devils, aren't they.' He chuckled. 'Look at them go!'

'That's why I asked for them. I'll save my lads for later. This way we'll make better speed.' He glanced at Sir Oswald, still busy with the binoculars, but now sweeping the mountains and more interested in taking in the scenery than in admiring the Gurkhas' textbook display of a vital aspect of soldiering in mountainous country. 'One thing still worries me.'

'Oh? What's that?' Sir Oswald said.

'How far do we push this? I mean, what if Prince Mahsud doesn't take the field of battle? Do we storm his fortress?'

'If we have to. In order to recover the Eye of the Storm.'

'It's going to look pretty aggressive to the rest of the tribes. If Mahsud doesn't start a frontier war, an action like this just might.'

Sir Oswald handed the binoculars back to Colonel Gibson, took out his handkerchief and mopped his brow. 'Do I detect a slackening of resolve?'

Colonel Gibson blanched. 'Of course not. It's not a question of resolve. If ordered, I'll bloody well invade Afghanistan! I thought it was supposed to be you political types who were the cautious ones?'

'Cautious is perhaps the wrong word, Patrick. When we identify a threat, we believe in swift and ruthless action. Nip it in the bud.' He snapped his fingers by way of illustration.

'And you see this as such a threat?'

'Most certainly I do. Unless we take possession of the Eye of the Storm, Mahsud will be down in the plains before you can say Independence, an army of howling tribesmen at his back and many, many more flocking to join him. Believe me, it is a matter of great concern to the Viceroy.' He eyed Colonel Gibson as his runner brought his horse and he pulled himself up into the saddle. 'He is taking a close interest in it,' he added pointedly.

Colonel Gibson smiled down at him. 'Then we'd better not disappoint him, had we?' He pulled his horse round and started off after the advance guard which had already set off again. He called back, 'I think, Sir Oswald, if you don't mind, I'd feel happier if you moved with the main body from here on. I wouldn't be surprised if we had a contact soon and I don't want to have to answer to the Viceroy for the death by sniping of one of his key men.'

'No chance of that, I promise.' Sir Oswald swept off his hat and fanned his face. 'I'm on my way. On my way.' As he waddled back to join the main part of the column, he reflected that he had no intention of getting shot by some grubby tribesman, not at this stage of the operation. So far everything was going according to plan. The silence from Brigadier Percival was an annoyance, but he had to assume the fellow was still in the game. He had no other alternative. He did not like the Brigadier one little bit but he needed him just as the Brigadier needed Sir Oswald and his political connections. In that respect they were partners.

The thought of it brought a smile to Sir Oswald's lips. He stood for a moment and watched the column march by. It was an awesome sight and he felt a momentary shot of alarm when he reflected that it was largely his actions that had set them in motion. Still, it was what they were there for. Soldiers loved a good scrap. It gave them their *raison d'être*. Without it they would be joining the dole queues as countless thousands of their number had done at the end of the Great War. The scum of the earth, someone had once called them. Was it Wellington? Dead right, Sir Oswald thought. Patrick Gibson was a nice enough man, but not the sort of chap a decent fellow would want his daughter to marry.

The front of Headquarter Company was approaching and Sir Oswald decided he would join them to be close to the cooks and the field kitchen. It was hot and the cooks always had a nice cup of tea on hand, though goodness knows how they managed it on the march. The army stuff was hot, thick and sweet, just the way Sir Oswald liked it.

The sooner they got to grips with Prince Mahsud, the better, Sir Oswald thought. As it was they had left well before the deadline he had agreed with Percival. Get to grips with the man, get the Eye of the Storm, and get out. The only unknown quantity was how the tribes would react. In the worst case, if Patrick Gibson was right and the army's action was seen as provocative, they could end up facing a fighting withdrawal through enemy territory, ambushed and harried all the way back to Peshawar. But Patrick was always being pessimistic. Sir Oswald thought it must be a major failing with soldiers. That was why Patrick Gibson was only a Lieutenant Colonel and Sir Oswald was one of the most powerful men in India, even if few others knew it. When Sir Oswald was being hailed in London as someone of note, Patrick Gibson would be pruning rhododendrons in Bath. When Sir Oswald was attending receptions at Buckingham Palace, Patrick Gibson would be living on memories of his borrowed splendour as a commanding officer in India, boring the local parish council with tales of life on the frontier.

But for now it all depended on the degree of hostility they encountered, Sir Oswald decided. No sooner had he done so than a single faint rifle shot echoed down into the valley, stemming from the far side of the ridgeline to the left of the column where one of the picket positions had encountered something or someone. To his surprise, Sir Oswald felt the tiniest of shivers run down his back, toying with the rivulets of sweat soaking into his shirt and jacket. A rifle shot. He pondered, concluding at last that he was eternally grateful that someone else was going to be doing all his fighting for him. Let the Gurkhas play their silly games in the hills. For Sir Oswald there was only one game that mattered, and its centrepiece was the Eye of the Storm.

Chapter Fifteen

Far away in a different valley, another rifle fired. The crack of the single shot reached the Brigadier, his party and their captors only after one of the Pathans had been knocked to the ground as if by an unseen hammer. For a moment his fellow tribesmen froze, bewildered, their eyes searching for the firer. Then a second ear-splitting crack severed the air between them and another man fell, like the first, shot clean through the heart. Everyone scattered.

'Keep hold of the prisoners!' the elder shouted, scanning the terrain for their attacker. 'Don't lose them!'

Rachel's guard shoved her to the ground, holding fast to her wrist as he too tried to locate the sniper. On the far side of the track, Spencer, the Brigadier and the others huddled in the comparative safety of a shallow dry river bed. Angus McCloud dug his elbow into Henry Allenshaw. 'So Caspasian ran away, did he?'

Scowling, Allenshaw muttered, 'Could be anyone.'

There was a shout as one of the tribesmen caught sight of a figure high above them.

'Where?' screamed the elder, craning this way and that to see.

'Up in the trees. Beside the two boulders.'

Suddenly there he was. A small figure in a broad-brimmed hat, darting from cover to cover. In between the two positions, he paused in full view and stared at them as if daring them to open fire. The next moment, as their bullets pecked their way towards him, he was gone.

'After him!' someone screamed. With two of their number lying dead they wanted blood for blood. His blood. Before the elder could prevent them, half his men had bolted in pursuit of the sniper.

'Come back you idiots!' But he was too late. They were beyond earshot, bounding up the rocks and heading for the thickening trees towards the spot where the firer had been spotted. The elder shook his head and cursed them. It was stupid to divide their force, especially in such close country. The track had entered a mountainous forest that continued all the way to the fortress of Prince Mahsud. If they became separated now they would lay themselves open to attack from all sides, and they had already seen what the men could do who had evaded capture back at their village.

He glanced at the men about him. Their eyes were upon him and he could see the eagerness to join their comrades in the chase. The young were so impulsive. With discomfort he reflected that his own position in the hierarchy of the village was far from secure. If the young men felt he had lost his hunger for a fight, he would be relegated to the ranks of the old men, to be left behind when raiding parties went out, left to mind the women and talk with the other grey beards about the old days.

Reluctantly he got to his feet and gathered the remainder of his party about him. 'All right we will go, but bring the prisoners. Without them we are lost. The Prince will finish us all.'

There was a roar of assent and the tribesmen kicked the captives to their feet and thrust them forward along the track. Allenshaw tried to protest but received a rifle butt in his stomach in response.

'Best just do as they say,' Brigadier Percival called back. One of the tribesmen had him tightly by the arm and was dragging him along, anxious to catch up with the others who they could hear whooping and calling in the forest above them. The hunt was in their blood and they longed to be after the sniper.

Another rifle shot rang out and there was a cry of outrage as another tribesman was hit. He had been wounded and his cries spurred them on, fuelling their lust for vengeance. Racing through their minds were images of what they would do to their quarry once they laid hands on him. They promised themselves that he would suffer dearly for his arrogance.

'Steady on,' Allenshaw panted as he was prodded in the back with rifles. 'I'm going as fast as I can.'

Beside him Angus McCloud stumbled from rock to rock, calling encouragement to the militiamen, porters and groom. With hands tied behind their backs, one or other of them would fall every few paces, to be savagely kicked until they struggled to their feet and continued up into the trees.

There was another shot and someone shouted, 'There he is!' Brigadier Percival looked up and high above them saw a small figure, standing on a rock in full view like a mountain goat. He glanced over his shoulder at Spencer and smiled wearily. 'That's Sergeant Ganga all right. Good for him.'

Spencer paused, bent double to catch his breath. 'I . . . wish he'd jolly well . . . slow down.'

'Nonsense. He's doing a fine job. Leading them on. Probably got Caspasian and Douglas waiting in an ambush position. Lure the buggers straight into it.'

Unconvinced, Spencer stood up and plodded on. As the oldest of the captives he had dropped behind. His leg muscles were burning, unused to such hard physical effort. He had fallen twice. The knees of his trousers and elbows of his jacket were torn and he had cuts all over him. He glanced behind him to check on Rachel. She was nowhere to be seen. He stopped dead in his tracks, his guards stumbling headlong into him. One of them jabbed his rifle muzzle viciously into his back. 'Go! Quick!'

'My daughter. I must wait for my daughter,' he protested.

'She is coming,' one of them said, glancing over his shoulder. He spoke quickly to his comrade who muttered something to him and they giggled. Spencer tried to stop but they pushed him forward again. 'Go!'

'Where is she?' he tried again, moving forward but peering desperately back in an effort to see her.

'There! She is there!' The guard said, pointing off to a flank. 'Did you not see her? She is further ahead than you, old man. Now go, or you will never see her again.'

Spencer stared hard in the direction the man had indicated. Figures darted between the trees, all of them heading up the hill where the sound of firing had started again, the single rifle shots of Ganga's Lee-Enfield, answered now by a fusillade of fire from the tribesmen. Confused, he continued on his way. Rachel must be over there, he thought. The others were all well ahead of him, and he knew that she was fit and accustomed to hard exercise. In the back of his mind however there was a nagging worry, as he could not remember having seen her since they took cover down by the track. One minute they had all been riding into the forest, enjoying the sudden respite of some welcome shade, and the next they had been tumbling from their horses, pulled down by their guards, and thrust into the cover of the dry stream bed. He thought he could recall Rachel taking cover on the opposite side of the track, but then why was she not with them now, with the rest of their party, all of whom he could see spread out in front of him?

When she heard the village elder shout the command for everyone to go after the sniper, Rachel had watched as her father, the Brigadier and the others had been beaten to their feet and dragged away with the tribesmen. Wearily she had tried to flick back her hair, unable to use her hands as her wrists were securely tied behind her back. Drawing her knees up under her she had begun to rise, but her guard had shaken his head and held her down.

'Stay. Too dangerous. We stay here. We wait.'

For one moment, Rachel had been grateful to him. Since his rebuke by the elder he had kept his distance, avoiding her eyes and she had begun to think he felt some shame for his actions. It was only with the first rifle shot that he had reappeared at her side, pulling her from her horse and tucking in beside her, shielding her from the rifle fire with his body.

As the rest of the party moved away he said again, 'We wait until they come back. They will be back soon. We are safe here.' She looked around and saw that the others would indeed have to return. The horses and their supplies stood close by and would need to be collected once the chase was over.

However, as soon as the others disappeared from view amongst the trees further up the hillside and she realised she was alone with the guard, she felt the panic start to rise. Determined not to show her fear she kept her eyes on the hillside, listening intently to try and make out what was happening. It was then that she became aware of the guard watching her. She turned towards him and the look in his eyes told her all she needed to know. The expression of concern had vanished, replaced by something far uglier.

'Now you come,' he said simply. There was no room for appeal in his voice. He stood up and pulled her roughly to her feet. Spinning her around, he marched her off in the opposite direction from the others, heading for the trees further down the track. Rachel tried to stop but he had a firm grip on the shoulder of her blouse and her resistance did not even cause him to falter. As they neared the edge of the track she realised that if she was going to save herself she had to act before he got her into the cover of the trees. Gathering all her strength she suddenly tugged away from him. The shoulder of her blouse tore, the material coming away in his fist. The moment she was free she ran away from him, spurting back up the track in the direction she had seen her companions go. As she ran she shouted for help, but at that moment there was a flurry of gunfire, the shots ringing through the rocks and trees and blotting out her cries.

She felt his hands on her shoulder. He wrenched her around and hit her hard across the face with the flat of his hand. The shock was almost greater than the stinging pain and for a moment she was stunned. He grabbed her with both hands, his rifle now slung across his shoulder, and propelled her towards the trees.

'You come.' His voice was thick and Rachel could feel his urgency as he pushed her faster, breaking into a jog. Once at the treeline he pushed her through the low-hanging branches that whipped back in her face. She closed her eyes against them, bending her head. Suddenly she tripped, starting to fall. In an instant his hands had caught her, bearing her up until he was almost carrying her.

He paused for a moment, searching around for a suitable spot.

'If you touch me . . .' Rachel began.

'Quiet.' He shoved her on again, and Rachel was aware that every step was taking them deeper into the forest and further away from the others and from any help they might have been able to offer. The elder had proved himself a man who could be trusted but he was far away by now. In the forest there was no one to hear or help her, no one but herself and the guard. And he had only one thing on his mind, plain in the expression on his face, his eyes staring hotly at the woman in his grasp.

The distant rifle shot stopped Caspasian in his tracks. He and Channing had rounded the side of the escarpment and were heading down towards the valley where they estimated they would be able to intercept the road. They had already entered the forest and Caspasian was having increasing trouble following the signs that Ganga had deliberately left for him. He was concentrating on the ground when he heard the lone report. Instantly he was on his guard. Channing moved up beside him.

'Ganga, right?'

'That's his rifle,' Caspasian answered. 'Let's go.'

They set off in the direction of the shot, Caspasian with his MP18 at the ready, safety catch off, finger on the trigger, Channing clutching his Lee-Enfield. Caspasian quickened the pace. It was a fine balance between reaching Ganga in as short a time as possible, and yet remaining sufficiently on guard lest in their haste they accidentally run headlong into the tribesmen. That would do no one any favours.

He was certain Ganga would not have initiated the contact without a good reason. The sergeant had known that it would take all three of them to stand any chance of taking on the tribesmen and rescuing the captives. In all probability, Caspasian thought, Ganga had shadowed the tribesmen until he judged he could delay no further. Unable to wait longer for Caspasian's support, he had fired on them to slow them down. Now he was probably being pursued and hunted down. Unless Caspasian could get there in time they would catch up with him and he would have sacrificed himself needlessly.

Coming out through a screen of pines, Caspasian and Channing suddenly found themselves at the top of a steep wooded slope. Peering downwards through the trees they could see at least two hundred yards. The thick growth overhead had kept out the sunlight, preventing anything from taking root in between the trunks. The forest floor was covered with a dense mat of dead brown pine needles which muffled their steps as they set off downhill. Caspasian held the MP18 snugly in the crook of one arm and with his free arm he swung himself down from trunk to trunk, keeping his balance as best he could.

There was a second shot and in the distance they heard muffled shouts. They stopped a second to orientate themselves.

'There,' Caspasian said, and set off again. The going was difficult as the needle-covered surface, while soft, was slippery and they both found themselves virtually skiing down between the trunks, going ever faster and faster.

'Steady on,' Channing cautioned, breathing hard. He stopped for a moment, grabbing hold of a trunk to steady himself while he checked the safety catch of his rifle and then slung it over his shoulder, tightening the strap so he could use both hands to control his descent.

The halt had only taken seconds but by the time he set off again Caspasian had already gained a good lead on him.

For a moment Caspasian considered firing a random shot into the air. That way, if the tribesmen were closing on Ganga, he would cause them to falter and perhaps divide their forces. It might just give Ganga the break he needed. He decided against it, trusting instead to Ganga's good sense and experience. He would not have opened fire and disclosed his position to the enemy unless he had been confident of success. He would have had a plan and Caspasian had to trust that. He had known the Gurkha sergeant long enough. There was no point giving the enemy advance warning of his approach. He would need all the advantages he could get, and surprise was always the biggest and the best advantage in a close fight with bad odds such as this.

Further shots rang through the trees, this time from an assortment of other weapons. The tribesmen were taking the bait, but what would Ganga want of him, Caspasian wondered? If he were to try and join him in the fight there would be every chance, in such close country, of each of them mistaking the other for the enemy. They could ill afford to take pot shots at each other, especially as Caspasian well knew that Ganga was the best he had ever met when it came to snap-shooting.

The captives then. That must be it. Ganga had led the tribesmen away from the captives, giving him and Channing a chance of tackling the reduced number of guards and thereby freeing their friends. The guards would have their attention on the pursuit, so he and Channing would need to come at them from the opposite direction. He stopped for a moment, giving Channing time to catch up and listening to get the direction of the distant fight.

They were almost at the bottom of the slope and in front of them the ground started to rise sharply again, still heavily wooded. Shots and cries rang out from the other side of it. Clearly the hunt was on and by the sound of the excitement, the tribesmen were enjoying it.

Caspasian tore open a pocket and flicked out his compass, checking direction. 'This way,' he said, slipping the compass away again and setting off to his left, heading down the trough of the wooded valley, away from the sound of the shooting. Few trees grew there and being on the flat after so long climbing or descending steep gradients, they made good speed, relishing the easier going.

Sooner or later, Caspasian was certain, the trough would intersect the main track. It should then be a fairly simple matter to locate where the tribesmen had left the captives and, presumably, their horses and supplies. Using speed and aggression they should be able to capitalise on the surprise of their attack and overwhelm whatever guard force had been left behind. There would be no time to conduct a reconnaissance. The best Caspasian could hope for would be a quick glimpse of the numbers involved before he and Channing closed in for the kill. By then they would be committed. There would be no second chance, no opportunity to pull back and withdraw. They would have to win through or die in the attempt. For Rachel it was worth it. He had to trust that Ganga had succeeded in drawing off the greater part of the enemy. Knowing the tribesmen's eagerness for the hunt, and judging by the whoops and shouts he had heard, Ganga had done his job. Now it was up to Caspasian and Channing to do theirs, and do it before Ganga was hunted to earth and killed. If they could only locate the captives in time.

'Here,' the guard said at last, tripping Rachel to the ground. They had burst through low hanging pine boughs and entered an enclosed space in the centre of a clump of trees that formed a small amphitheatre. It was gloomy as no light could break through from above. The air was stifling. Not a breath of wind penetrated the dense undergrowth.

The guard hurriedly unslung his rifle and tossed it aside. His fingers worked impatiently at his pistol belt. Rachel shuffled away from him, her fingers scrabbling at the dry mat of pine needles. He looked up and grinned, baring his teeth.

'Where do you think you can go?' he said, chuckling with anticipation. 'There's nowhere. Not this time, and no old fool to help you.'

The buckle of his pistol belt came loose, he slid it from his hips and let it drop heavily to the ground. He stepped towards her. Rachel kicked out. He stood back and laughed, letting her exhaust herself on the hot air. She yanked at the rope binding her wrists but it only bit deeper into her skin. In kicking, she had backed herself across the clearing until she felt the stump of a tree against her shoulders. She glanced around for a way out and as she did so he darted in, throwing himself on top of her. Rachel twisted her face away from him but could feel his hands upon her, groping. He pushed his fingers into the tear at her shoulder, clenched his fist and tugged it hard, ripping the sleeve down her arm.

Rachel put back her face and cried out, an animal cry, refusing to submit. This could not be happening. Not to her. The guard closed his mouth over hers. The taste of him made her gag. Instead, she took his lower lip between her teeth and bit as hard as she could, holding on as her jaws worked. She felt the scream rising in him from the pit of his stomach all the way up to his throat. His fingers squeezed her neck forcing her to let go, and as she opened her mouth and let him pull his head away he shrieked, blood running freely into his beard from the wound. She had bitten clean through his lip.

For a moment he sat back, examining the tear. Then his hand shot out, slamming Rachel across the cheek. The force of it knocked her backwards. Her head smacked into the stump and she felt herself sliding away, from the clearing, from the man, from her own terrified thoughts. Her vision was swimming and she knew she was about to lose consciousness. With her last ounce of willpower, she tried to draw her knees up to her chest, to roll on to her side and curl into a ball. It was impossible. Hands were pulling at her, laying her flat on her back, straightening her legs. She could feel them upon her and do nothing about them. Embracing the darkness that waited to engulf her, she fled.

The cry shot out of the trees at Caspasian's side like a wild creature breaking cover. A woman's cry. He recognised it at once as Rachel's but the nature of it terrified him. Without pausing to check whether it might be a trap, he veered towards it and ploughed a way through the web of boughs. They were thicker than he had expected and every couple of paces they snagged on his belt and the shoulder strap of the MP18. He tugged it away fiercely and pushed on, ducking and weaving like a boxer, working his way through as fast as he could.

He heard more sounds, louder now. A man's voice, suddenly baying, and then the woman again. Caspasian felt a savage rage in his blood and when at last he burst through the last screen of trees, his rage at the spectacle before him iced into pure cold fury. He had come into a clearing and on the far side he saw a tangle of limbs writhing and struggling on the needle-covered floor. A face twisted in his direction and he saw Rachel, eyes clenched shut, one of them bruised. Blood ran from a cut lip and there was a broad purple welt across one cheek from a backhand blow so clearly defined that he could see where each of the hand's fingers had struck.

On top of her, one of the village tribesmen, a big man, so embroiled in his struggle to rape that he had not noticed Caspasian's presence. His face was buried in the hollow of Rachel's neck where the blouse had torn, while his hands fussed at the waistband of her jodhpurs trying to worry them loose.

In four strides Caspasian was across the clearing, the MP18 dropping harmlessly to one side. Seizing the man, one hand on the neck of his shirt, the other on the seat of his trousers, Caspasian lifted him clear of Rachel, sweeping him into the air like a sack of rice and swinging him aside. The man fell in a muddle of arms and legs, but managed somehow to roll on through it and scrabble to his feet, dazed but spinning round to face whoever had interrupted him. There was no fear in his eyes, just hatred. He shot a glance at Rachel's helpless form, the torn clothes signalling his unfinished business there.

With a howl of rage he ran at Caspasian, not really seeing the man before him but only an obstacle to be overcome as quickly as possible. Caspasian sidestepped, helping his attacker on his way with a light grip on the sleeve that accelerated the forward motion, while at the same time he put out his foot and tripped him. As the man went down again, Caspasian noticed Channing rushing round the side of the clearing to help Rachel. He knelt at her side and hunted through his pockets for a knife to cut her bonds.

Instead of tackling Caspasian again, the Pathan had scuttled to his gun belt while Caspasian's eyes had flicked to Channing. He had the flap of the holster open before Caspasian noticed and lunged at him. Caspasian swung with his leg and kicked the pistol from the man's grasp as it was half out of the holster. It skidded across the soft pine needles, out of reach for now.

The man rose out of the crouch straight into Caspasian, grabbing hold of him round the waist and propelling them both backwards. Caspasian fell to the ground, but as he went down, he used the power of his hips to swing the man round so, when they hit the floor, both were on their sides, facing each other. The moment they landed, Caspasian lashed out with his right fist, slamming it into the man's jaw. It connected and Caspasian saw the eyes shudder. In an instant Caspasian was on his feet, but the Pathan, sensing that only one of them would end the fight alive, had summoned deep reserves of energy and swung back out of reach. He leapt to his feet and turned to face his opponent, pausing at last to take stock of this strange man who had spoiled his opportunity with the English woman. He had been planning it since he had first seen her, biding his time. The ambush had come just as he had started to lose hope. Now all of that hope had vanished. She lay only feet away, helpless until moments ago. The prospect of what might have been was tantalising and he had to black it from his mind or he knew it would cloud his new purpose, to kill this intruder.

For the first time he examined the Englishman as they circled one another, each looking for an opening in the other's guard. He was tall and looked in good shape. Very good shape in fact. His eyes were burning with rage, but it was tightly controlled. That was impressive. Dangerous. His fair hair was darkened with sweat, his lean face had been recently burnt by the sun and scratched by the tree boughs. He was clean shaven, without even the usual moustache that so many of his countrymen favoured, but there was a light stubble, perhaps a day or two old.

What interested the Pathan was the stance the man had adopted. It looked to be very well balanced. He would probably be able to shift his weight quickly in any direction. His hands were open, but only half so. The man could grasp for a throw, or equally quickly clench a fist for a strike. It was unsettling. But the

Pathan knew how to fight as well. He had grown up fighting. In the mountains it was the only way to survive. Englishmen, he knew, might well be able to fight, but it came from training. It was not second nature. What he did not know was that Caspasian had also grown up fighting, and that for him the training had been so thorough that it had become second nature – as the Pathan discovered when he pulled the knife from his sleeve and lunged.

Caspasian's reflexes produced the block before his conscious mind had registered the attack. The blade came straight in, thin, bright and very fast. Caspasian's hips twitched aside, shifting his belly out of the way of the deadly point as his left forearm jerked forward, rigid, connecting with the Pathan's wrist, deflecting it. Caspasian felt the blade slit open his shirt, and felt the touch of steel on skin. He felt the sting of a cut, but not the trickle of blood. It had been close. It was time to finish it.

Before he could act, the Pathan attacked again, this time with a diagonal backhand knife slash from high left to low right. Caspasian jumped back out of reach, drawing the man on. He came, slashing the opposite way this time. He followed it with a thrust at Caspasian's throat. Caspasian pulled out of range, slapping the hand and its blade aside with his open palm. But as he slapped, he caught his attacker's wrist and pulled, adding to the man's own forward momentum. Expecting to be pulled off balance, the Pathan braced himself. Instead, Caspasian's foot shot up, the toe of his boot driving into the solar plexus. He put the full power of his thighs behind the mae-geri front kick, turning into the blow, driving in deep and hard. The

Pathan's eyes bulged. His mouth opened but no sound escaped, all the wind driven from his lungs.

Still keeping hold of the wrist, Caspasian, reversed his grip and bent back the Pathan's arm, folding it back upon itself. As he did so, he slid his other hand underneath establishing a firm wrist lock, and then levered the man back and over. He fell to the ground almost gently, aided by a footsweep from Caspasian that knocked his legs from under him. But as the man fell, Caspasian tightened his grip on the wrist and with a sudden vicious wrench, broke the arm. The noise of the break was muffled by the man's outraged scream of agony.

Released from the grip, he hugged his useless arm to him, turning to see whether the assault was at an end. He saw his mistake when he met Caspasian's eyes. His first assumption had been correct. Only one of them would outlive the fight.

Caspasian's fist seemed to come out of nowhere, and then the Pathan was reeling. He tried to crawl away, scrabbling to his feet, but again Caspasian's booted foot slammed into him, this time powering sideways down on to the knee. The Pathan yelped. Down on all fours he scuttled for his rifle, a yard away. His fingers touched the wooden stock as he felt Caspasian's arms encircling his neck. Through the blur of pain, the Pathan was puzzled. The Englishman had not gone for his throat to strangle him as he himself would have done with a man at his mercy. Understanding came a second later, but lasted only a second more, as the grip of the head lock fastened into place, and, with a controlled jolt, Caspasian broke the Pathan's neck.

The body stiffened for a second and then went limp, slumping to the floor in death. Caspasian ran across to where Channing was trying to revive Rachel. He knelt by her side, snatching the water bottle from Channing's hand and wetting her face and neck. Her eyes opened. For a moment she did not seem to know where she was. Then she sat bolt upright.

'The guard!'

'Dead,' Caspasian said. 'It's all over. He can't hurt you any more.'

Her eyes searched his face as if to establish the truth. He tried to smile and Rachel lay back. In the distance the sound of rifle fire escalated.

'Ganga,' Channing said in alarm.

For the moment there was nothing Caspasian could do. Rachel was beside him and for now her safety was uppermost in his mind. For the moment Ganga was on his own.

Chapter Sixteen

Hunched over his delicate work like a master watchmaker, Vassily Novikov fought for breath through his mask. In front of him, a scatter of opened ammunition boxes littered the floor, the modified flare mortar rounds lying to one side of him, those awaiting conversion on the other. He worked diligently, but the more he handled the pungent viscous chemical, his heavily gloved hands operating as efficiently as they could, the more unsettled he became. Something was wrong. He had thought as much when he had heard Karpov's elaborate explanation to Prince Mahsud, and now he had had a chance to view the chemical at considerable length, something did not add up.

He glanced over his shoulder and saw standing on the far side of the large room, the guards that the Prince had posted to watch over him. Zykov and Dragov had hauled in the boxes of mortar rounds and prepared them, but once Novikov opened the top of the hollow stone, he ordered them to move as far away as they could. The Eye of the Storm was indeed hollow, and not a stone, but glass, a strong thick crystal whose numerous flat surfaces had been painted to resemble the original Eye of the Storm.

Wherever that might be, Novikov wondered, was anybody's guess.

It was remarkable how the painted scenes had survived contact with the chemical. Vassily suspected the use of some form of resin sealant, but the more he worked the more the paint began to peel from the glass surfaces, starting from the small round hole that had been hermetically sealed using a perfectly fitting bung, peeling gradually down the sides, flake by tiny flake.

He was concentrating so hard on his handling of the deadly chemical that he had little time to examine the crystal more closely. After all, if Karpov was correct, it was simply a container. A vessel and nothing more. There was certainly nothing precious about the crystal. Being hollow it could hardly be diamond, and in any case, one edge of the hole had been chipped where one of the British agents had struck it with a blunt object such as the butt of his revolver. That would hardly have been possible with anything as indestructible as diamond.

By the time Novikov had completed his task the pile of converted mortar bombs beside him had grown. In place of the original flare rounds there were now some fifty chemical weapons. Being small and hastily improvised they would be of limited use, but in the context of unsuspecting and unprotected troops caught in a valley, the effect would be devastating. The fine droplets would rain down and exposed skin would blister horrifically on contact. Novikov had seen enough of chemical weapons during the war with Germany to learn to fear them and, even though he had handled them extensively, he had never lost his respect for them. They were to be treated with the utmost care.

With the liquid exhausted and the compartment in the last of the mortar bombs securely sealed, he laid the round gingerly on top of the pile, pushed back his stool and stood up. He stretched his back until it cracked. Testing the air, he pulled off his mask but before removing his gloves he picked up the hollow crystal and peered inside it. It was empty. Only a thick residue remained like honey at the bottom of an empty jar.

He wondered what he was supposed to do with it. It was of little use now. He set it down on top of an ammunition box. Seeing him complete his task, one of the guards had ducked out of the door and a few moments later Prince Mahsud came in, peering suspiciously round the edge of the door to check it was safe. He smiled and came in.

'Well done, comrade.' He surveyed the pile of weapons. 'Jolly good. Jolly good.'

'They'll stop any attack dead in its tracks,' Novikov said grimly. He was surprised to find he felt little pride in his work. He had seen what such weapons could do and had no interest in seeing it again.

The Prince looked quickly around for the crystal. 'Ah, there it is. Can you clean it out?'

'What for?' Novikov asked. 'Might as well throw it away now for all the good it is.'

The Prince smiled again. 'I'll be the judge of that. Call it a little keepsake. A souvenir of the victory to come.' He thought a moment, as if wondering whether to take Novikov into a confidence. He glanced at his guards, still on the far side of the room, watching the bombs with frightened eyes. He lowered his voice. 'I might still have need of it to rally the tribes. These men have been sworn to secrecy. They will not reveal what they have seen. For the others, however, a certain ruse might be necessary. The Eye of the Storm, the prophet Abdul Rashid and all that. You know.' He winked conspiratorially.

'Whatever you say,' Novikov shrugged. 'It'll take a while to clean it out.'

The Prince walked to the door. 'Oh, and don't damage any more of the paint work. If I am going to convince people that I have the real Eye of the Storm, I don't want it looking too bloodshot.' He laughed and went out of the room, saying something to the guards as he left. When the door had closed behind him, they moved closer to Novikov, studying his every move. He scowled at them and waved them back. They complied, none too reluctantly, but clearly were not going to let the crystal out of their sight.

'What do we do with the bombs?' Dragov asked.

'Pack them in their boxes again. They'll need to be transported to the mortar line, wherever that is. Mahsud will have to set one up within range of the British forces.'

With the help of Zykov, Dragov set about his task, handling the mortar rounds with considerably more care than when he had prised open the boxes and unloaded them. Zykov looked up. 'Where's Alexei?'

Novikov shook off the thick gloves and wiped his sweating hands on his trousers to dry them. 'I'm just going to find him. The Prince sent him to check on the mortars in the armoury. For some reason he didn't want him in here while I was working.' He shrugged. 'Didn't want all of us blown to kingdom come if there was an accident, I suppose.'

'How considerate of him. What about Oleg and me?' Dragov sneered.

'Expendable,' Novikov answered with a grin. 'Like empty vodka bottles.'

He left the room, the Prince's guards parting before him like acolytes before the magician. Having witnessed his deftness with the weapons and the lethal chemical, they were not about to get in his way. Everyone had heard how it had injured the Prince's concubine. She was now recovering in the kitchens and, as everyone knew, would never again regain her place in the Prince's bed. The poison from the stone was not to be tampered with, and nor was such a man as Vassily Novikov who could handle it with such apparent ease.

Novikov found Karpov in the courtyard. He had got some of the Prince's men to carry four of the mortars out of the armoury and set them up in the open so he could inspect them. Novikov approached him. 'What are they?'

'Stokes' mortars. British.' Karpov bent to examine the elevation adjustment screws. All the parts were well oiled. 'They're only a few years old. They'll work well enough.' He straightened and wiped the oil from his hands. 'Well? How did it go?'

'No problem. There was enough for fifty rounds.'

'Excellent.'

'If Mahsud can stop the British and hold them in one of the valleys,' Novikov continued, 'we'll rain mustard gas down on them and they'll be begging to surrender.'

'Yes, yes.'

'We'll have to get the mortars in close though. What's the range of these?'

'About seven hundred yards if we fit the augmenting ring charges to the base of the rounds. They'll blast them out to the maximum range.'

Novikov shook his head. 'We'll have to get closer. I want to use as few charges as we can. Too many and we could blow the seal while the bomb's still in the barrel. Not a pretty sight.'

Karpov stooped to feel one of the mortar base plates, hammering it with his fist. Without looking up he asked, 'What have you done with the crystal?'

Vassily grinned. 'Funny, isn't it, how everyone's so interested in the crystal?'

'What do you mean?'

'Well, I make up the bombs, using all the juice. Then the Prince comes in and says he wants the crystal cleaned up. It's like he wants it as a bloody souvenir. What's going on, Alexei?'

'Exactly what I've said.'

Novikov sighed. 'I'm sorry you said that, comrade. How long have we known each other?'

'A long time.'

'Then give it to me straight. You know as well as I do, there's nothing special about that mustard. It's standard chemical. Who are you trying to fool?' He grinned sheepishly. 'Come on, it's me, Vassily! I saw enough of the bloody stuff in the war. We both did.'

The smell of cooking fires had appeared around the fortress and tempting aromas wafted across to them. Karpov sniffed the air like a fox. 'You have to trust me, Vassily.' He looked at him, meeting his gaze with equal confidence. 'I can't say more than that. Not yet. Just trust me.' His manner softened. 'We've been through everything together. Do you think I would let you down now?' He opened his arms to take in the surrounding walls and buildings of the fortress. 'Here? In the middle of this pig sty?'

Novikov pondered a moment and then relented. 'No. No, Alexei, I don't. It's just . . .'

'What?'

'Nothing.' Novikov smiled. 'Let's go and find something worth eating. I'm starving.'

Karpov slapped him on the shoulder. 'That's more like it. Come on.' He led the way back to their quarters. Behind him, Novikov studied his back as he went. Yes, he did trust Alexei, but he knew the man was ambitious in a way that he, Vassily, had never been. He had watched the ambition grow the higher up the rungs of promotion Karpov had ascended. And Novikov knew that as ambition grew it eventually reached a point where the blind trust of a follower was no longer justified. Which was why he had decided to keep his peace about the Eye of the Storm, and about the strange score marks he had noticed beneath the paint at the mouth of the hollow crystal.

The rope burns on Rachel's wrists, the cut to her lip and the bruising on her face were taken care of by Caspasian and Channing using the small medical pack from one of the pouches on the side of Caspasian's haversack. What concerned Caspasian far more was the hurt he could not see, the shock effect that he knew the attack must have had on her. He knew it would do little good to question her now. Apart from anything else he wanted to get clear of the scene before the Pathan's companions returned from the chase and came in search of their missing friend. He also noticed how Rachel's eyes kept flicking to the dead body lying in the middle of the clearing as if she expected him suddenly to rise up and return to the attack. She rubbed her wrists and felt her mouth with the back of her hand.

'Caspasian,' she said quietly at last. 'I'd be grateful if you kept this to yourself. Don't tell my father.'

'If that's what you want.'

Channing looked up in surprise. 'Don't you think he should know, Rachel? I mean . . .'

'Drop it,' Caspasian said sharply. 'If Rachel wants this kept quiet, then that's what's going to happen. All right?'

'Yes, but . . .'

'No buts. Just do it.'

The terse report of a rifle sounded in the distance, though not as far as previously. Channing nodded. 'Whatever you say.'

Caspasian took Rachel by the arm to help her stand up. Instinctively she pulled away.

'Can you walk?' he said. She had retreated into herself and he could see it took a great effort before she replied, 'Thank you, yes. I'm fine.' She looked up then and tried to smile. 'Really I'm fine. Or at least I will be.'

'Do you remember how to get back to the horses?'

She shook her head. 'It all happened so fast.' She glanced around at the trees, her eyes settling on the body again. She closed them and looked away, struggling for control. 'Erm, I think it was that way,' she said pointing.

'Douglas, I'll go first,' Caspasian said. 'You stick close to Rachel.'

'Right you are.'

Picking up the MP18, Caspasian checked the magazine to ensure it was still locked on to the breech, pulled back the cocking handle and flicked off the safety catch. They reached the road quickly and off to the right he saw the horses grazing contentedly.

Rachel pushed through the trees to stand beside him. 'They took the others with them. That's the way they went,' and she indicated a run of large rocks that tumbled down to the roadside from the forested heights. Caspasian racked his brain for a plan. The situation was hopeless. Split from Ganga, his firepower would be completely inadequate to take on the tribesmen by himself. Channing could help, but without the Gurkha sergeant's marksmanship any surprise attack would be doomed from the start. He would be more likely to cause harm to the captives. Furthermore, the person he cared about most was Rachel. She had already suffered enough. If Caspasian were to stand and fight it was possible that she might fall into the tribesmen's hands again. Once they discovered what had happened to their companion, there would be no telling what they would do to her. For now she was safe. Caspasian had to keep her that way.

He was just about to turn back into the trees to

lead the others away from the road and back into the comparative safety of the forest, when one of the horses whinnied. Caspasian signalled for Channing and Rachel to get down and, while they shrank back behind the screen of leaves, he edged slowly forward and knelt down, bringing the butt of the MP18 into his shoulder ready to deliver a burst along the road. Being open, it provided a clear field of fire and acted as an ideal killing ground. Anyone stepping on to it would be cut down.

Ahead, the horse stamped, its head bucking. Around it the others sensed its alarm and pricked their ears, eyes wide, nostrils flared. One of them broke away, trotting a few steps towards Caspasian before slowing and looking back to see whether the threat had yet materialised. The next moment, it did. A bush waved slightly and as calm as if emerging from a shop, Sergeant Ganga stepped onto the road. He glanced to left and right, caught sight of Caspasian's MP18, the muzzle bearing down on him, and waved cheerfully. He was holding his rifle in his right hand by the grip as if an overlong pistol.

Caspasian pushed himself to his feet and went out to meet him. 'Where did you leave the tribesmen?'

Ganga waved his left hand vaguely in the direction of the wooded slopes behind him. 'I lost them back there.' He heaved a deep sigh, part contentment, part fatigue. 'I did a big circle, drew them after me, but doubled back to get behind them. I had to slow them down somehow and I knew you would hear my shots.' He checked his magazine. It was full. 'So. Do we take them now?'

Reunited with Ganga the odds had suddenly

tippcd closer in Caspasian's favour, but a glance at Rachel raised the same old conflict. He desperately wanted to get her away from here but what was the alternative? Once the captives reached the fortress a rescue would be immeasurably more difficult, if not impossible. The rescue had to be here or not at all.

A quick check of the ground gave Caspasian the fire positions he wanted. For Ganga he located a rocky cleft that gave a good broad view of the area where he judged the tribesmen would congregate on return from their fruitless hunt. He placed Channing with him so that Ganga could keep an eye on him and direct the use of the extra rifle's fire. Channing might not be able to hit anything but at least Ganga could tell him where to put down suppressive fire.

For himself, Caspasian selected a position level with the road. There was a good view the full length of it and from where he lay he could see Ganga, exchanging messages by use of hand signals. He kept Rachel with him, ensuring they had an escape route at their backs, leading deep into the forest. He was not going to allow her to be taken prisoner again. He would either get her to safety or die in the attempt.

When Ganga had jogged away to settle himself down, Channing following hard on his heels, Caspasian took out his knife and cut several branches to improve the camouflage around his fire position.

'What can I do?' Rachel asked.

'Keep an eye on our backs. Make sure no one creeps up on me while I'm concentrating on the road.'

As he lay down, scraping a small pile of earth beside his elbow on which he could rest the drum magazine, Rachel curled up at his feet, deeper in the bushes. He turned round and looked back at her. In spite of the heat she was shivering. He reached down and put a hand on her shoulder. She looked up sharply. Her face was ashen, the shock setting in.

'Would you like some water?' Caspasian asked.

She nodded, accepting the bottle.

'I'm sorry I don't have anything stronger.'

'That's all right.' She drank deeply, a trickle of water spilling down her chin. Watching it, Caspasian felt a renewed surge of anger at the man who had tried to rape her. Rachel glanced up and met his eyes.

Although there was no accusation in her, he said, 'It's our fault. I'm so sorry, Rachel. The Brigadier and his blasted mission. I should never have gone along with it.'

She stared straight ahead, looking out through the trees to the road, white in the glare of the sun. 'My father told me. Brigadier Percival finally told him all about the Eye of the Storm.' She shook her head. 'I thought it was all just a legend.'

'I'm not sure I care what it is,' Caspasian said bitterly. 'If it's done this to you. He had no right, no damned right to trick your father like that. If he had come clean your father wouldn't have let you come and none of this would have happened.'

'It's too late for that. In any case, you tried to tell me.'

'But I didn't.'

She drank another mouthful of water and handed the bottle back to him. 'If it wasn't for you, that man back there . . .' her words trailed away.

'I wish I could kill him all over again,' Caspasian said.

Rachel forced a smile. 'I wish you could too.'

There was a thud as a rock landed out on the road in front of them and Caspasian looked up to see Ganga signalling frantically at him.

'Here they come,' Caspasian said. He reached down and squeezed her hand. 'It'll be all right.'

He couched himself behind the MP18, snuggling the butt into his shoulder and cheek, sighting along the barrel into the clearing that was going to be the killing ground.

The first person he saw was Henry Allenshaw, his hands bound behind his back. He was soaked with sweat and complaining bitterly. Behind him came the Brigadier, Bernard Spencer, Angus McCloud and the others. One of the militiamen had been injured in the frantic scramble across the rocks and was limping badly, his face racked with pain. He stumbled and fell and was kicked until he stood up. The tribesmen were clearly in no mood for compromise after their wild goose chase following the trail Ganga had carefully set for them, leading them nowhere.

The village elder appeared, mopping his brow. Spencer was remonstrating with him. Caspasian could guess what it was about. Allenshaw and the others were searching for Rachel. One of them called her name and Caspasian felt her shift at his feet, trying to see her father. The elder hunted around for the man who had remained behind with her. He shouted something. The other tribesmen gathered one by one, coming down tiredly from the rocks, their faces long with disappointment. They were gathered in a tight cluster, their hostages off to one side. It was perfect. Caspasian glanced up at

Ganga's position and saw, just between the cleft in the rocks, the muzzle of Ganga's Lee-Enfield steady and waiting. Behind it, Ganga's face, one open eye sighting down the barrel on to his selected target.

Caspasian had agreed that the signal to open fire would be his own first shot. On hearing that, Ganga and Channing would fire too. They would keep on firing until all the tribesmen were dead. If some of the hostages died as well, it would be too bad. This would be their only chance. Once inside the fortress they would be lost forever, and Caspasian was certain that the end they would meet there would be a lot slower and more painful than being caught in the crossfire of the ambush that he and Ganga were about to spring.

His finger curled around the trigger. Slowly he tightened it. He had sighted on a group of five men who looked to be the strongest and most experienced. Always hit the hardest first. He had learned his lessons the hard way until they were ingrained. Leave the old and the young for last. The trigger tightened to first pressure. Caspasian drew a deep breath, waited and exhaled. He was just about to squeeze off the first burst when out of the corner of his eye he noticed movement from Ganga's rock. He looked up and saw that Ganga was no longer sighting at the enemy but sitting up and peering hard down the road. Caspasian tried to follow the direction but from his ground level the road curved out of sight and he was blind to whatever had attracted the Gurkha's attention. He released pressure on the trigger and swore quietly. The adrenaline was pumping through his body and he was anxious to get on with the killing. To get it done and get out of there.

Then he too heard it, the sound of hooves. Lots of them. He wriggled back deeper into the cover of the trees, noticing Ganga do the same, lowering himself behind his rocks, and a minute later a large group of horsemen rounded the corner and circled the villagers and their captives. There was shouting, stamping hooves and brandished weapons, and a tall, savage looking Pathan swung down from his saddle and strode across to the village elder. Caspasian could just see how the elder had shrunk visibly in the face of this other figure, and for a moment he wondered whether this might be Prince Mahsud himself. But amongst the chatter of voices he heard the Prince's name mentioned and realised that these were only his men, sent to investigate the shooting that had been heard.

'What is it?' Rachel whispered, crawling up beside Caspasian. He encircled her with one arm and held her down.

'It seems we're too late.' And together they watched as the tribesmen and their prisoners were escorted safely and unwittingly out of Caspasian's killing ground, and led away by Ahmed to the fortress of Prince Mahsud.

Waiting anxiously at the fortress, Mahsud stared out across the mountains in the direction from which the firing had come. In the space of a day his carefully laid plans had started to unravel. Not only had he received word of the British column making resolute progress towards his stronghold, but now there was more rifle fire closer at hand, within range of hearing even. While he waited for Ahmed to return with a full report, he paced the battlements of his father's fortress, working through his options.

The tribes were not nearly ready yet to take on the British. Had they been assembled it would have been a different story, but as it was, he had only his own immediate followers upon whom to rely. He was not unduly concerned because the nature of the ground was such that they should be able hold the British at bay until the tribes were gathered. The problem was that the column had Gurkhas with it. He had never encountered them personally, although he had heard his father speak of them with respectful loathing. Ahmed too held them in high esteem. Nevertheless, Mahsud was sure they would be unable to match his own Pathans, especially when his men were fighting on their own territory.

Furthermore, he now possessed chemical weapons, admittedly not many, but on the unprotected skin of the British and Gurkha soldiers they would have an effect out of all proportion to their numbers. Fifty, Vassily had told him. That should be ample. The Bolsheviks knew how to use the 3-inch Stokes' mortars, so all that Mahsud's men had to do was to fix the British in place and leave the Bolsheviks to rain down terror upon them. Mahsud could then watch as his men went in to mop up the blistered, scarred and screaming remnants.

It was all a far cry from his original plan but for now it would have to do. The Eye of the Storm – or what remained of it – was safe. Who cared about the chemical? So much the better if it could be put to good use killing and disfiguring the forces of British imperialism, but it was the crystal that Mahsud wanted. Once the attack had been beaten off, then he would turn his attention once again to the crystal. The thought of it made him want to hurry back to his room where it lay, cleaned and freshly wrapped in new cloths. There would be no delays next time, no crippling gas seeping out. It would be his, and he would be on his way. Just as fast as he could.

It was a further two hours before one of his lookouts shouted and Mahsud climbed swiftly up to the rampart and leaned through the crenellations to spy the long line of mounted figures heading up the dusty road towards the fortress.

He frowned and reached to snatch a pair of binoculars from the sentry. Twiddling the eye-pieces until the vision sharpened into focus, he stared in amazement at the spectacle of several Englishmen and a large number of unknown tribesmen riding in under escort, Ahmed at the head, proud and erect in the saddle as if he had been the warrior lord of the fortress himself.

A huge plume of dust rose into the sky from the horses' hooves. Impatient to learn the identity of the riders, Mahsud ran down the steps to await their arrival in the courtyard. Karpov and Novikov came out to meet him and they waited together as the column cantered in through the gates and gathered in a whirling mess of dust and confusion in the courtyard.

'Who the hell are these?' Mahsud shouted, striding angrily up to Ahmed.

Before he could answer, the elder of the village ran forward and started to explain. Mahsud listened, his eyes surveying the prisoners who sat uncomfortably on their horses, spitting dust from their mouths.

When the old man had finished, Mahsud smiled coldly at him. 'I suppose you think you can go peacefully back to your little village now, don't you?'

The elder nodded eagerly. 'But we only wish to serve you, my Prince.'

'Well that's a stroke of luck, because there's a column of bloodthirsty British soldiers a few miles away and I need every man to go and fight them for me.'

At the mention of the column Brigadier Percival sat up. He and Bernard Spencer had been following the conversation as best they could, edging steadily closer to the man they took to be Prince Mahsud. The Brigadier called out. 'Prince Mahsud, I am Brigadier James Percival. I must speak with you.'

Mahsud looked up, shoving the elder aside. 'What are you doing here? This old fool says you were snooping about in his village.'

'That's not true,' Spencer interrupted. 'I am the District Political Officer and I was there to attend a jirga. We were seized and brought here against our will. My daughter was seized along with us but has disappeared. I demand that you help us find her and I demand that you release us immediately. The soldiers have been sent to rescue us.'

'Ah,' a light dawned in Mahsud's eyes. 'You must be Spencer. I remember hearing my father speak of you.' He shrugged. 'With loathing, I should add. I

312

believe you humbled him on more than one occasion.'

'I have only ever done my duty. If that brought me into conflict with your father then that was not my wish. Now I demand that you release us, and my daughter is . . .'

'You are not really in any position to demand anything,' Mahsud shouted at him. 'And as for the British troops, they are being engaged by my men at this very minute and I am rushing fresh troops of my own to the scene as we waste this precious time speaking.' He walked boldly towards the two mounted men. 'You will find I am not so easily impressed as was my father. You see, I know where you come from. I have been to your country, seen your slums, heard your corrupt politicians slander one another, read the scandals in your so-called liberal newspapers. I know all about you.' He glared at them and smiled coldly. 'To me you are just another bunch of greedy imperialists. All your posturing, political this and political that. It's all a sham, another means of subjugating a backward people. But not me, old man. Not here, and not any more.'

Bernard sank back in his saddle, his fears for his daughter's safety almost too much to bear. It was the Brigadier's turn to speak. 'And what of the Eye of the Storm, Prince Mahsud? How does that square with your lofty ideals?'

Mahsud stared at him with renewed interest. 'What do you know of the crystal?'

'I know that you have it, and that you will use it to incite the tribes to war the whole length of the frontier.'

A great hoot of laughter burst from Mahsud. 'Oh, wonderful, wonderful.' He clapped his hands. 'You really should be on the stage. Such convincing indignation. Such shocked outrage. And all of it so very, very transparent.' He wagged an amused finger at the Brigadier. 'I can well imagine how much His Majesty's government would love to get its hands on it.'

Shaking his head with merriment, Mahsud turned away from his prisoners and ordered his men to take them to the cells. He called back over his shoulder, 'I have to go now and annihilate your friends. When I've finished I'll come back for you. Think about the manner of your death while I am away. I promise you it will be different.'

As he walked away, Karpov and Novikov turning to follow him, the Brigadier called after him, 'Mahsud, we can do a deal. I want the Eye and I can pay handsomely for it. Name your price.'

In answer Mahsud put back his head and roared with laughter again. Karpov too was smiling, though privately. Only Novikov, who had managed to follow the conversation, was wondering at the exchange. He feared that his suspicions were correct. He would have to be on his guard. If he was right, then he was probably in as much danger as the captured Englishmen.

Chapter Seventeen

It was a simple enough task to follow the tracks left by the horsemen once they had left with their prisoners. The real problem, Caspasian well knew, would be to do anything about the capture once they reached the fortress. Apart from being renowned as a formidable stronghold, it would be fully manned. Nevertheless, at the very least he had to locate it so he could return later with more troops and win their release that way.

Ganga and Channing scrambled down from their eyrie in the rocks and the four of them set off. Caspasian forced the pace as much as he dared, but with Rachel as well as Channing now accompanying them, he and Ganga had to hold themselves back. It was Rachel who first noticed what they were doing. She said nothing but lengthened her stride until she drew level with Caspasian, gradually pushing ahead and forcing him to keep step with her. He glanced at her out of the corner of his eye and smiled to himself. Staring fiercely ahead, her jaw was set and her arms swung as if she was on a route march, the one torn sleeve hanging round her elbow.

During a brief pause beside a stream to recharge the water bottles, she tried to mend the tear, but without cotton and thread it was impossible. Giving up, she tore it clean off, considered the effect for a moment and then ripped the other sleeve from her arm as well. She nodded proudly. 'There. That's better. I was beginning to feel like a lopsided scare-crow.'

Her pack and all her belongings had been taken with the other captives by the Prince's men. While it meant that she could walk faster without a load to carry, she missed the reassuring presence of spare clothes. She was hot, tired and covered in dust. Even so, the hard physical exercise helped her recover from the ordeal in the wood. Every step she took increased the distance between herself and the man who had attacked her. She thought of his broken body lying in the stifling heat of the clearing and felt neither remorse nor satisfaction. His fight with Caspasian had been a blur, but she could remember being revived by Douglas and seeing Caspasian close for the kill. His ferocity had been chilling but looking at him now she felt safe in his care. She stepped closer to him as they walked on, trying to match her pace more closely to his, but his longer legs outstripped her with ease.

Caspasian had cut away from the track and was leading them on a parallel course. The going was much harder but he could not risk an encounter with the Prince's men. They were a long way from safety, without horses and with limited weapons, ammuni-tion and supplies. In any confrontation they would be bound to come off worst.

After some two hours hard walking they ap-proached a rock escarpment jutting from the trees in front of them. Ganga scouted ahead and signalled back a moment later that all was clear. Caspasian led the others forward and they mounted the rock to find themselves looking across a wooded valley. On the far side, towering above the treetops, was the fortress of Prince Mahsud. It sat on top of a ridgeline that ran down from a mountain a mile behind it. While it was impossible to see the valley on the far side of the ridge, Caspasian could see the mountains that rose beyond it, similarly wooded on their lower slopes as were those across which they had just marched.

The fortress walls were of stone, sheer, bleak, but old. He knew the legends surrounding it and in spite of their circumstances, could not resist a brief moment of wonder as his imagination conjured an image of battle-weary Greek soldiers marching through the very same passes that they themselves had just come, shields slung across their backs, spears over their shoulders, following their war leader Alexander at the end of his journey of conquest.

'Oh, God,' Douglas Channing said bluntly, giving vent to an overpowering weariness. He stared at the stronghold and shook his head in dismay. 'What the devil do we do now?'

'Well at least we know where it is. That's one thing,' Caspasian said. He dug into a pouch on his pack and pulled out his binoculars. 'The first thing to do is have a better look at it.'

He lay down and wriggled forward on his stomach to the edge of the escarpment. He trained the glasses on the distant walls. Under magnification they were, if anything, even more impressive, but a slower, more deliberate scan revealed places where an agile person might be able to scale them.

'What are you thinking, saheb?' Ganga asked, a cautionary note in his voice. He swapped glances with Channing who groaned.

'He's not?' Channing asked incredulously.

For reply Ganga laughed. He pulled off his broad-brimmed hat and scratched his scalp, his fingers rasping on the black bristles of his shaved head. 'I think we are going to become goats, saheb,' he said cheerfully to Channing.

'Goats? We'd need to be birds to get up that.'

To his relief Caspasian lowered his binoculars and shook his head. 'No. It could be scaled, but even if we got inside, while the full garrison's there we'd just be walking into a death trap. We might as well march up to the gates and surrender.' He sat back and studied the fortress, arms clasping his knees. 'The first thing to do is to get a bit closer.' He scanned the intervening ground between themselves and the fortress. 'We'll establish a secure camp and then Ganga and I will go forward to do a close reconnaissance.'

'What does that involve?' Rachel asked. She had come this far and was reluctant to leave the place where she knew her father was being held.

'Quite simply, we do a complete circuit of the fortress, looking at it from all sides, and, if I reckon it's worth it, at one or two selected points we'll go in closer for a proper inspection. It's like the spokes of a bicycle wheel. The fortress is the hub, the outer rim is the circle Ganga and I will make around it, and at various points on the way round, we'll move in for a close look, see if we can detect weaknesses and so on. Those are the spokes.'

'How long will all that take?' she asked.

He thought for a minute, gazing across at the stronghold and studying the surrounding landscape. 'Most of tonight. There's probably enough cover to do it in daylight, but I want to get in really close.'

'Isn't that just exposing us all to needless risk?' Channing asked. 'I mean, we know where the place is now. Surely the best thing to do is to get out of here and come back with a battalion of soldiers.'

'The more information I can give them when we get back, the better. It'll help decide exactly what we need for an assault. And in any case, I don't want to leave until I'm absolutely sure there's nothing more we can do to help the others.'

After a short rest and some food they pressed on, heading down the hillside beyond the escarpment and towards the Prince's stronghold. As they re-entered the trees they lost sight of the fortress and had to follow a compass bearing that Caspasian had taken. He was anxious to find a secure location where he could leave Channing and Rachel. The more he thought about it however, the more un-settled he became. What if he and Ganga were compromised? What if they were captured or killed? Channing would have little chance of getting Rachel to safety. Caspasian would be sentencing her to capture as surely as if he left her on her own. But what were the alternatives? He could hardly take all of them with him on the close recce. They would make far too much noise and give the game away.

He considered doing the recce by himself, but a partner was useful if only to watch his back while he himself focused on the objective. Even Douglas could do that.

When they finally reached a suitable spot for the hide, Caspasian told them that he had changed his mind and that Ganga would stay behind with Rachel, while Channing accompanied him on the close recce. They stared at him in surprise. Ganga started to object but it was Rachel who was the most vociferous.

'Why doesn't Douglas stay here with Ganga and I'll come with you?'

'Because Douglas has a rifle and I might need . . .'

'I can use a rifle. In fact, I'm probably a better shot than he is,' she said. She knew what Caspasian was trying to say and pre-empted him. 'Just because I'm a woman doesn't mean I'm not as fit as Douglas, and if you're worrying about what happened back there, with the Pathan, well don't.'

She also wanted to say that she felt safest with him but she left it at that.

'Please, Rachel, I'd like you to stay here. It's not that you're any less fit, or that you're a woman . . .'

'Yes, it is. What else could it be?'

Caspasian looked to Ganga and Channing for support but neither of them was going to help him. Ganga stood back enjoying the spectacle of Caspasian meeting his match, and Channing was simply in awe of Rachel and thought it best not to contradict her. He stepped forward and held out his rifle.

'I believe you'll be needing this.'

'Now just wait a minute,' Caspasian interrupted. 'I'm in command here . . .'

'Not over me, you're not,' Rachel said, taking the rifle and quickly hiding the fact that it was far heavier than she had expected. She had been firing her father's hunting rifle since she was a girl but that was as light as a feather in comparison to this cumbersome implement of war. No wonder Channing had been struggling behind them all the way, and yet the diminutive Gurkha sergeant somehow managed to heft it with apparent ease.

She beamed happily at Caspasian knowing she had won. 'Shall we go then?'

He tried once more to change her mind, but seeing that he was wasting his time he said, 'If you're going to come with me then at least take a revolver and leave that thing behind. I don't mean to be unkind but you look ridiculous with it. The recoil would probably break your shoulder.'

Rachel inspected the ferocious looking brass butt plate and handed it back to Channing with a shrug. 'All right then. Pistol it is.'

'Revolver,' Caspasian corrected, as Channing swapped the Lee-Enfield for his Webley. He patted his Mauser. 'This is a pistol.'

'Yes. Of course. I knew that.'

Channing handed her a couple of spare clips of ammunition. She held the heavy pieces of metal uncertainly in the palm of her hand.

'Those are Prideaux speed-loading clips. it means you don't have to reload the chambers one by one.' Caspasian held his mounting irritation firmly in check. 'Look. Give them to me.' He took the Webley

321

and pressed a lever on the left side of the hammer with his thumb. The revolver broke open. He tipped the bullets into the palm of his hand and pocketed them. Then, using the Prideaux spring clip, he slid home the six new .455-inch bullets, snapped the revolver closed again, and spun the reloaded chamber. 'See? Easy. To fire . . .' He cracked open the revolver again, emptied the chamber, closed it, and aimed the gun at a tree, '. . . pull back the hammer with your thumb, aim and fire.' He pulled the trigger and the hammer slammed forward on to the empty chamber with a crack as loud as a breaking bone. Rachel jumped. The gun seemed enormous. He re-cocked it and went through the drill twice more. 'Pull back the hammer, and fire. Pull back the hammer, and fire. Got it?'

Rachel nodded diligently. 'Doesn't it re-cock itself after each shot?'

Caspasian forced a smile. 'No. That's the Webley Fosbery self-cocking revolver. Nice, but expensive and it jams. The Webley Fosbery also has a safety catch which this one doesn't. So don't pull back the hammer until you want to shoot someone. If you do, and you trip, you'll fire the damned thing, and I don't want to be in front of you when that happens. All right?'

She nodded again.

'One last thing, if you have to use it, hold it with both hands. And, don't shoot until your target's virtually up against the muzzle. The .455 bullet will blow a hole in him the size of my fist, but unless you're used to using a handgun of this size and weight, you'll be inaccurate beyond ten yards.' He sized her up, noting the slender arms and wrists. 'Make that five yards. And aim for the centre of the body.' He put his finger against the base of his sternum. 'Here. Nowhere else, the biggest possible target area. That way, if your aim wavers you're still likely to hit something.'

For the hide he had chosen a sheltered spot in a narrow defile. It would be easy to find it again by following the natural grain of the hill, and he reckoned that from there it would be a short march to cross through into the neighbouring valley, putting as much distance as possible between themselves and the fortress in a short space of time. He hoped that any withdrawal would be out of contact with the enemy, but he wanted to be prepared for the worst.

Before he set off he gathered the others around him and ran through the various standard drills that they were to follow. While it was all second nature to Ganga, Channing and Rachel listened intently. Only when he was satisfied that they understood what he wanted of them, did he break up the meeting and carry out a final quick check of their weapons and equipment. The packs would be left with Ganga and Channing. Apart from their weapons and spare ammunition, Caspasian and Rachel would take a water bottle each and a small haversack with an emergency food ration, Caspasian's army issue pullover for Rachel, and his own small survival kit that he had compiled over the years, each item selected from bitter past experience.

As darkness set in he declared them ready. Ganga and Channing wished them luck and they set off.

In addition to the Webley, Rachel had borrowed the big leather holster. She had fitted it to the left-hand side of her belt and as she walked she kept one hand on the pommel of the revolver which otherwise knocked heavily against her hip. She could imagine the bruise that would be there by morning.

Caspasian had been unhappy with her white cotton blouse and her bare arms, saying they would show up in the starlight. So Ganga had given her the spare shirt from his pack, saying that he was the closest to her size of any of them. It was collarless grey flannel and scratched abominably. She had rolled the sleeves to just below her elbows but the overall effect was demoralising. She was sure she looked a frightful mess and was grateful for the modest shield of nightfall.

It took a while before she became accustomed to the darkness. It seemed all wrong, being out, prowling through the forest at night. To start with she stared hard at the ground, watching her every footfall, but eventually she looked up and marvelled. The trees were old, their tall thick trunks disappearing up into the night sky like cathedral pillars. They were more widely spaced than before and in between their gently waving tops she could see patches of sparkling light where the brilliant stars glinted like sequins. Caspasian had said that the moon would rise later in the night and that while it would help him to recce the fortress, it would also make them more visible to the enemy. But now, as the night stretched out its early wares for her to inspect, Rachel walked with face uplifted, the shimmering spectacle wiping all fear from her mind. The treetops almost seemed to be dancing, swaying in time to the cool night breeze. Later it would become cold, but for now she revelled in the night walk.

The next thing she knew, she walked smack into Caspasian who had halted to check his compass bearing. Staggering forward, he whipped round just in time to catch her before she lost her balance and fell. Even in the night she could see the expression in his eyes. He glanced down and his sigh of relief was audible when he saw the revolver safely in its holster. He put his mouth close to her ear.

'I'm not sure this is such a good idea.'

She pulled away from him and shooed him forward. With shaking head he turned and continued on his way, glancing back after a few paces to check that she was still with him. When he did so Rachel could see that he was smiling.

By the time they came to the base of the ridge on which the fortress stood, they were both hot from the march. Rachel could feel her perspiration soaking into the thick wool of the shirt which smacked softly against her back. They rested for a couple of minutes.

'Are you all right?' Caspasian whispered into her ear.

She nodded exaggeratedly. He pointed up the steep ridge, shrugged an apology, and set off. In places the climb was almost sheer and they needed both hands to pull themselves up the rocks. When they did, Caspasian slung the MP18 over his shoulder by its strap. As he reached each secure footing, he stretched back, clasped Rachel's hand and helped her up to join him. The pace was agonisingly slow. It seemed an age before they left the trees and the undergrowth behind them and emerged out onto bare rock. Looking up, they saw the fortress walls towering high above them. As she craned her head back to gaze up Rachel lost her footing and slipped. Caspasian grabbed her by the scruff of Ganga's shirt and hauled her up again. Her feet touched solid ground, she threw her arms around Caspasian's waist and held on tight. With her face against him she could feel his heart beating inside the rough leather jerkin.

Caspasian shifted to his right and sidled along the narrow ledge until they reached broader ground. He leaned close to her.

'The wall continues on up the slope. Can you make it?'

Rachel reached up and whispered. 'Do I have a choice?'

'Frankly, no.'

They continued to edge around the base of the fortress walls that seemed to go on for ever. It was when they were at the highest point of the ridge that Caspasian stopped and signalled for them to crouch down.

'This looks the most promising so far,' he whispered.

'For what?'

He mimed the actions of climbing. Rachel's mouth dropped open.

'Don't worry. You're going to stay here. I'll be back in about fifteen or twenty minutes.'

'How long?' she asked, her eyes wide with alarm.

He patted the big Webley at her waist, then unfastened the holster for her and drew the gun from her belt. He put it in her fists, closing her fingers around the cold hand grip. 'No one's going to harm you. Not while you've got this beast.'

She looked at the gun unconvinced but reminded herself that it had been her own decision to go with him. She could hardly complain now.

She nodded bravely and settled herself with her back to a rock, facing outwards in the direction that anyone would have to come who happened to be out for a walk in the middle of the night on the top of a precipitous ridge. The thought comforted her.

When she next glanced round, Caspasian had vanished. It was only when he had gone that she remembered she did not have any way of telling the time. Her watch had been in her pack that had been taken by the tribesmen.

The minutes dragged by. Her backside grew numb and she shifted her position. She looked up at the sky but clouds had swept in and obliterated most of the stars. The moon had still to rise and it was suddenly a lot darker than before. Where the clouds parted, brushed aside by winds swirling silently thousands of feet above her, stars winked at her like conspiratorial passers-by. Strangely, she never seemed to see the same ones twice. At each gap in the clouds, a different segment of the night sky would appear, never the whole of any one particular constellation. The overall effect was highly disorienting.

She judged that she had been waiting for at least an hour and was becoming frightened when she heard the noise. It was coming from directly in front of her, but some way off, the opposite direction from the way Caspasian had gone. Rachel froze. Every limb stiffened in terror. She had lain the big revolver on the ground at her side but now reached over and picked it up, horrified again at the weight. Cradling the gun in her lap, she wedged the cold metal of the barrel between her knees and angled herself in the direction of the sound. Her eyes strained into the darkness.

There was a cough. Hard and hacking. Then she heard the feet. Whoever it was, they were stepping carefully, gingerly, and heading straight for her.

She put her thumb on the hammer and pulled back. It would not budge. She looked down at it in shock and pulled again. It was rock solid. She braced herself, setting her back firmly against the rock, and with both thumbs this time, heaved at the hammer. Slowly it moved, but she was terrified that if it slipped from her tenuous grip it would slam forward and fire the gun prematurely, giving away her position and alerting the whole fortress. Ratcheting further and further back, she finally felt it lock in place. Silently she cursed Caspasian who had made it look so effortless.

The steps came closer still until there was only one thick bush separating them from her. Sweat trickled into her eyes and she blinked, feeling the salt sting. Both hands were closed around the butt of the gun, both moist with fear. She extended her right forefinger and laid it over the trigger, curling it round the cold smooth metal.

The bush moved. A branch shuddered. Her finger tightened. The branch twitched again and she pulled hard. As the hammer slammed forward there was a blur of someone's arm in front of Rachel's eyes and the edge of a man's hand chopped down from behind her as fast as lightning, wedging its flesh between the hammer and the base of the bullet lying ready in the chamber.

Rachel jumped to her feet, her mouth opening to scream but a second hand whipped over her mouth, clamping her scream within her. She bucked and kicked but was held fast in an iron grip. As she raged silently, she twisted her face round and saw Caspasian holding her.

'Shh!' She heard his voice as the terror subsided. Her heart felt as if it was going to pound its way out of her ribcage. Her stomach convulsed and for a moment she thought she was going to be sick. He took his hand from her mouth and reached down to take the Webley. He pulled back the hammer and removed his other hand, biting away the blood where the hammer had pierced his flesh. Carefully he eased the hammer forward and disarmed the gun.

Rachel was about to scream at him but remembered the footsteps. She spun round and saw the bearded face of a goat earnestly considering her from the centre of the bush. Halfway between tears and rage, she sank to her knees cradling her head in her hands. Her body trembled and she suddenly realised how cold she was.

When she could trust herself to speak she said, 'I thought you said you'd only be fifteen or twenty minutes? You've been at least an hour.'

Caspasian looked puzzled. He checked his watch, tilting the face towards the brightest part of the sky. 'Eighteen minutes,' he said. 'Look.'

Rachel put her hand over her heart, trying to calm

the thumping. Seeing her shiver, Caspasian dug into the haversack and dragged out the light woollen pullover.

'Here. Put this on.'

He slid the revolver back into her holster and fastened the flap for her. She stood up, her legs wobbling and let him slip the woollen over her head. She stretched up and felt for the arms, sliding into them. As her head popped out, Caspasian leaned forward and kissed her. Rachel stood there, her legs weak, her heart still pounding from fear, and slowly sank forward against him. His arms encircled her and he held her tightly. She folded her arms behind his neck and pulled him closer to her, returning his kiss. The goat bleated, a disapproving witness, while behind them the fortress walls reared into the night, its battlements fingering the passing clouds as they swept past, combed of stars now that the moon had risen.

Progress had not been good, Colonel Gibson considered. He was alarmed by the increasing ferocity of the Pathan resistance. They were drawing in ever greater numbers of men by the hour, and the pickets were under continuous pressure. The two Gurkha companies had performed superbly and continued to do so, but Colonel Gibson recognised the signs of fatigue. He had been forced to slow the column to give them a breathing space, but that only presented the tribesmen on the surrounding hills with sitting targets.

The mountain artillery had also been in action,

lobbing their shells across the ridges on to any concentration that the Gurkha picket commanders judged worth engaging. He had to ration the number of fire missions however, in order to preserve the stocks of ammunition for the harder fight that would come if they eventually closed with the fortress of Prince Mahsud. He did not expect anything as dramatic as a siege. Not these days. A few well-placed shells inside the fort, some concentrated fire from the .303-inch Vickers medium-machine guns, and then a bit of negotiating by the political types. That should just about do it.

The thought of political animals reminded him of Sir Oswald. He had not seen him all day. The fellow really was proving to be a misery. Not enjoying a tussle with the Pathans at all.

A fresh burst of gunfire brought him to his senses and he raised his binoculars to survey one of the picket positions. The Adjutant had just ordered its withdrawal but they were obviously having difficulty breaking contact. It was a treacherous time. He could just make out the tiny figures. At their backs, below their picket position, they had laid out a bright orange marker panel on the ground. This indicated their position to the mountain gunners who could then range in on the Pathans, safe in the knowledge that they had an accurate fix on their own forces. There were enough casualties as it was without suffering more from the fire of the supporting guns.

Up at the position, the picket commander was a young Gurkha jemadar, newly promoted. Unlike his lieutenant counterparts in the British regiment in the valley below, the newly promoted jemadar, like all

Gurkha jemadar platoon commanders, had worked his way up through the ranks. It had been a journey of many years, through lance-naik and naik – the corporals of the Gurkha regiments – through havildar – the sergeants – and then through the ranks of warrant officer. With numerous frontier operations under his belt, he was not going to let his platoon suffer casualties, having already fought off several ferocious assaults by the Pathans. The picket had held securely, guarding the position as the column passed below unmolested. Now that it was clear, the rearguard commander down in the valley ordered the signal for withdrawal to be sent. Instantly, the signallers sent the message using the heliograph, the equipment flashing out the message with its mirror. In darkness its lamp would have been used instead. The jemadar laid his plans and briefed his section commanders accordingly.

At his hand signal, the platoon withdrew by sections to the edge of the ridge, using the standard fire and movement drill, one section putting down fire on to the enemy while the other sections moved quickly back. Once they had gone firm, they provided similar suppressive fire for the first section which then pulled back past them, and so on, leapfrogging backwards until contact with the enemy had been broken.

Withdrawal from a picket position presented the added complication of the descent over the ridgeline. Once the last man had dipped out of view, there would be no suppressive fire to dissuade the Pathans from rushing forward to the ridge and shooting down into the retreating backs of the Gurkhas.

The jemadar remained behind with the last section while the other two disappeared behind the ridge and began their descent. He had kept two of the Lewis light-machine guns with him and used these to rake the Pathan positions. Even so, the tribesmen had crept perilously close and he could see them massing in readiness for the rush the moment his back was turned. He waited until the two lead sections, out of sight of the enemy now, had halted their descent of the mountain and turned to set up a fire line about fifty yards below the ridge.

The jemadar ordered one final burst from the last section. Each rifleman rattled off five rounds rapid fire, and the Lewis guns each emptied half of their forty-seven bullet radial magazines. With a full magazine, the Lewis gun weighed thirty pounds, and their Gurkha handlers were delighted to blaze away at the Pathans, each bullet fired lightening the load they would have to carry off the mountain.

'Now!' he shouted, the second the rapid fire had finished. The men were up and away, skipping from rock to rock with the sure footing of mountain goats.

Seeing them go, the Pathans gave a blood-curdling cry and rushed forward as one, closing up to the ridge ready to shoot down the hated Gurkhas as they ran away. The yards fell away beneath the Pathans' feet as they sped forward. And then they were there. They poured over the edge of the ridge and started down the mountain after the Gurkhas, readying themselves for the slaughter. The second they cleared the ridgeline they were met by a wall of lead slamming into them from the assembled fire-power of the complete Gurkha platoon less than fifty yards away. Instead of racing down off the mountain the Gurkhas had turned to meet the Pathan onslaught. Rifles and Lewis guns chattered, the bolts of the Lee-Enfield rifles pumping home as the Gurkhas poured out rapid fire. Colonel Gibson, watching from below, grinned from ear to ear.

'Show 'em boys. Show 'em.'

The Pathans fell in swathes until at last they stopped coming. Without pausing to check for wounded, the jemadar screamed out the next command. As one, his platoon turned and cascaded off the mountainside. Lines of Gurkha riflemen streamed down through the rocks, whooping as they went, their faces bright with victory, smiles on every face. The action had been a success.

Colonel Gibson slid his binoculars back into their pouch and prepared to ride forward to rejoin the advance guard. The one thing that bothered him as he steered his horse away, was that the Pathans clearly had little concern for the number of their casualties. They were pouring men into the attack with a frenzy that sounded an alarm in his mind. They clearly had no intention of calling off their attack. As he rode up the column he decided he had better check on his own casualties at the regimental aid post. Being deep into the mountains he had no choice but to carry his wounded forward with him. With just a few casualties, the doctors could cope. If they had large numbers of wounded however, the situation could become dire. As he approached the aid post he saw the Adjutant spurring towards him with a report. The advance guard had run into trouble. At the head of the column the

Pathans were throwing large numbers of men into the attack and the pickets were in danger of being swamped. The column had been stopped in its tracks.

Chapter Eighteen

The first intensifying pallor was appearing along the rim of the eastern horizon by the time Caspasian and Rachel had completed their circuit of the fortress. For most of their reconnaissance they had been forced to parallel the towering walls fifty or more yards back for fear of being spotted. There were few guards, the Prince obviously feeling secure in his mountain fastness deep within his own territory, but from inside the walls Caspasian and Rachel could hear all the sounds that indicated a garrison of substantial size.

In fact, the level of activity throughout the night surprised Caspasian and hinted at preparations of some sort. Lights shone from many of the windows and continued to burn until shortly before the approach of dawn which was when Caspasian decided it was high time to return to the hide.

He had completed his reconnaissance near the main gate to the fortress. He and Rachel had crawled into a thicket on top of a rockfall that abutted the road leading out of the fortress. Less than twenty yards from the road, the position also gave a clear view of the main gate some two hundred yards away. At their backs a covered withdrawal route led deeper into the forest and back to the hide where Ganga and Channing were waiting.

Rachel had been borne along for most of the night by excitement and fear, but at last, hours after they had set out, Caspasian saw that she was exhausted and told her to sleep. At first she had resisted, saying that she should remain awake to keep him company, but eventually she succumbed to fatigue. Curling into a ball beneath the thicket she allowed herself to relax, her eyelids flickered shut, and the next moment she was breathing deeply, fast asleep. Caspasian wriggled out of his jerkin and drew it over her shoulders. He took the canvas haversack and gently eased it under her head as a pillow. In her sleep she gathered the cover around her, muttered something, and was quiet again.

As the light strengthened the fortress appeared in greater clarity like a photograph swimming into print in a tray of developing fluid. After the night's reconnaissance he felt he knew it reasonably well. He had located a place where he believed an assault force could climb the walls, and had identified the best approach routes to it. It was a formidable stronghold but for a force armed with modern weapons it should not be impossible to storm. The problem would be getting such a force through the passes to reach it. He knew them from past experience. They could be sealed by relatively few men who could delay a force many times their own size with resolute sniping. With more aggression still, such a force could be entirely wiped out. It had happened before.

He let Rachel sleep for the best part of two hours

and was wondering how much longer he could allow her before setting off for the hide, when the huge gates of the fortress suddenly opened. He had heard the noise of activity for the last hour so when the gates swung open and horsemen appeared, he was ready with his binoculars. He had initially expected little more than a hunting party, but as he watched with growing alarm, he saw scores of men riding and marching out of the fortress and down the road towards his position.

He reached down and shook Rachel awake. She sat up with a start. He put his finger to his lips and showed her the approaching column of tribesmen. Her face turned pale.

'We'll be fine so long as we keep down,' he whispered. While the rockfall tumbled all the way down to the edge of the road, the thicket itself had taken root on top of a boulder some fifteen feet above ground level. Caspasian was confident that if he and Rachel lay flat, the column would pass by beneath them unaware of their presence. He wanted to get a rough estimate of their numbers to see what any future assault force would be up against.

As the head of the column approached the road below him, Caspasian flattened himself against the rock and crawled forward to the edge.

'What are you doing?' Rachel hissed from behind. He could hear the urgency and panic in her voice.

'It's all right. I know what I'm doing.' He looked back and saw that his reassurance had done little to soothe her strained nerves. Her eyes brimmed with fear and she looked ready to turn and run.

The first Pathans strode past below, chatting

amongst themselves. Then came a group of horse-men. Some of them were singing. All were armed to the teeth, swathed in belts of ammunition, brand new Mauser rifles slung across their backs. To his amazement Caspasian saw Madsen light-machine guns which he had not see since the western front. There were several Lewis guns, presumably cap-tured from previous raids against the Indian Army, or bought in the arms bazaars of Kabul.

Of most concern were snippets of conversation that he heard. Piecing the bits together, he under-stood that the column led by Lieutenant Colonel Gibson had not only already left Peshawar, but was being engaged at that very moment several miles distant. Caspasian looked at the ever continu-ing stream of heavily armed fighters emerging from the fortress and imagined the destruction and slaughter they would wreak when they arrived on the battlefield.

Keeping his face close to the cold rock, he looked up at the main gate just as a fresh group of horsemen rode out. He looked, and then stared again, hard. Four white men had appeared with a train of pack-horses. Behind them, surrounded by a group of tribesmen, was a pale-skinned Indian dressed in a tweed Norfolk jacket, jodhpurs and highly polished brown riding boots. Prince Mahsud and his Bolshe-vik advisors. What most caught Caspasian's atten-tion however was the load strapped to the flanks of the packhorses. He could just make out mortar barrels, four of them, and a glimpse of a base plate and bipod identified them as British Stokes' mortars.

In themselves these were alarming enough, but it

was the ammunition boxes that Caspasian stared at. From the number of boxes he estimated there to be about four to five dozen mortar rounds, but the markings on the boxes were for parachute flare illuminating rounds. Caspasian checked again as the packhorses drew closer and saw that he was correct. A heavy guard of tribesmen had been placed around the boxes and they were riding slowly as if the ammunition was unstable.

As the group rode beneath his position, it entered Caspasian's head that with the MP18 he could probably kill all four Bolsheviks and Prince Mahsud from where he lay. Suicide was not on his agenda for the day however, and certainly not with Rachel lying close behind him.

He strained to hear whether the Bolsheviks or Prince Mahsud were speaking but they appeared to be riding out to battle in stoic silence. Mahsud looked pleased with himself. His face was softer and fuller than Caspasian had imagined. He had only seen the Prince's father once, some years ago, and he remembered a cruel hook-nosed face with a savage look in the eyes. The son, in stark contrast, looked soft, effete almost, but there was something unsettling in his manner and expression. Caspasian did not doubt that he was capable of cruelty. Being the offspring of his father that was hardly surprising.

Amongst the Bolsheviks there was a small man with cold eyes. He rode close behind Mahsud and Caspasian judged him to be the leader of their party. A large formidable looking Cossack figure with handlebar moustache bounced along behind on a horse that was too small for him, and accompanying the packhorses came two more Bolsheviks, both of them big men, hard and pitiless.

The column went on and on. Caspasian had been hoping to get away soon after the Prince had ridden by, but he was forced to lie where he was while tribesmen continued to pour out of the fortress. Caspasian shook his head in wonder. Poor Colonel Gibson was about to have the fight of his life.

Finally the torrent dried, the last horsemen bringing up the rear cantering past. The gates closed, the column disappeared out of the valley and all was silent once more. Caspasian looked back at the gates and wriggled his way back under the thicket from where Rachel looked out at him with big round eyes.

'He's got a whole army!' she whispered.

Caspasian nodded. Rachel could see that he was deep in thought.

'What is it?'

'I was just thinking. Everything's changed. I didn't know Gibson was already on the way.'

'Who?'

He explained about the briefing in Peshawar and the column that had been placed on call to assist them.

'Hadn't we better go and warn them?'

'It's too late for that. Besides, we'd never get through. We've got the whole of Prince Mahsud's force between us and Gibson's column.'

Caspasian's mind was on the ammunition boxes but, try as he might, he could not pin down the unsettling feeling he had about them. He pushed them from his mind and looked back at the fortress. 'Of course now that the Prince and his merry men have gone out to fight, that leaves the fortress un-guarded. Perhaps a small token force, but it can't be more than that. He won't be expecting any kind of attack on it while he's away. As far as he's concerned the big threat is the British column and he's gone to take care of that in person, aided by his Red allies.'

Rachel stared at him in amazement. 'You're not suggesting what I think, are you?'

'Why not?' Caspasian shrugged, his eyes danger-ous. 'That's where your father is. I think it's time we went and got him out.'

They made good time back to the hide. Ganga came out to meet them and had prepared some food for their arrival. They sat down and ate ravenously. When they had finished and Caspasian had briefed Ganga and Channing on his recce and on his plan to enter the fortress, Channing shook his head doubt-fully.

'You want me to climb the fortress walls? You're mad. I can't do it!'

Rachel cut in. 'You can. I've seen them. Honestly. Once you look close up you can see that there are footholds everywhere.'

'The fortress was built centuries ago, Douglas,' Caspasian said. 'There are shrubs and branches growing in the cracks, you'll be fine. I'll lead the way, and Ganga will bring up the rear.'

Channing was still unconvinced. 'Can't Rachel and I wait outside the gates. You and Sergeant Ganga could climb over and open the gates for us.'

'Sorry. I'm going to need every gun we've got once we're inside. Any guards that have been left will be concentrated around the main gate. That's the last place I'm going to go. If I can, I want to locate and release the others before we tackle the gate.' He reached out and patted Douglas Channing on the back. 'Sorry, old man, but you're coming too.'

Ganga started to stuff the blankets, tins and spoons into the packs. Channing stared at him. 'We're not going now, are we? In broad daylight?'

'Can't afford to wait until dark,' Caspasian said. 'Besides, from the noise of preparations we heard in the fort last night, any guards left behind will be sleeping it off. Night is when they'll be most alert. Think about it. The boss has just gone, everything's quiet. They've had a busy night. What better time to get their heads down for a nice long nap?'

Ganga grinned at him, fastening the last of the straps. 'I'm convinced, saheb.'

'Right then. Let's go.'

Caspasian led the way back to the wall, threading through the trees. At the point where they crossed the road they left their packs in a hide from which they could retrieve them later. The fortress loomed before them, seemingly dead. The sun was climbing and already the day was heating up. Caspasian glanced up at the sky and wondered what it was like for Gibson and his men. The pickets would be having a hard time of it, climbing the mountainsides in such heat.

'Here,' Caspasian said when they reached the spot he had selected for the climb. Channing stared up at the wall towering overhead and swallowed hard, but as he looked, he could see that what Caspasian and Rachel had said was true. Furthermore the wall was not vertical, but sloped gently inwards. The surface was heavily pitted as though at some point in its long history it had been pounded with missiles. Where cracks and holes pocked the irregular surface, whole shrubs grew, some of them as big as small trees.

'All right,' he said more calmly. 'I'll give it a go.'

Caspasian slung his sub-machine gun across his back. 'In the absence of a rope, I suggest you don't fall.'

He searched around for the first hand-hold and set off. Pulling himself up the wall's face, he selected each toe-hold and finger-hold before moving on to the next stance. Rachel went next, keeping close behind him. As long as she kept looking up she knew that she would be fine. Behind her came Channing, cursing the dead weight of the Lee-Enfield banging against his shoulders. Ganga brought up the rear, checking behind him to ensure they had not been seen or followed, before starting on the ascent himself.

The going was hard but just manageable. Caspasian passed the halfway point, did a quick check behind him and pushed on up. Rachel forced a smile as he looked back and, intending to pass his encouragement back down the line, looked beneath her. The ground swam blearily far below. Her vision blurred and she felt her arms and legs weaken.

'Oh, God,' she gasped, feeling herself go faint. Caspasian looked down and saw her face as grey as ash.

'Don't look down, for God's sake! Look up.'

She did not move.

'Look up!' he hissed. She raised her face, hanging

on for dear life, her fingers quaking in their tenuous holds on the rockface.

'Look at me,' Caspasian commanded. 'In the eyes.'

She did so, blinking hazily, her stomach churning.

'Focus, Rachel. Now!'

Summoning all her willpower, she looked at Caspasian and fought back the vertigo that threatened to pluck her from the wall and dash her to the ground far below.

Gradually the feeling passed. From below, Channing edged up to her, his own fear forgotten now that he saw her in trouble. He climbed round to come up level with her. Though unable to help physically, he spoke quietly, encouraging and urging her on. Ganga came up beneath. He was not sure whether he would be able to support her weight if she fell, but he could not think what else to do. He set his shoulders beneath her feet until she felt the reassuring press of them against the soles of her boots.

She shook her head to clear it. 'I'm all right,' she said at last. 'Really I am. You go on ahead.'

'You must be joking,' Channing said. 'I'm petrified!'

She looked up at him and smiled. 'Thank you.'

'No, really. I am.'

'Have you two finished mucking around,' Caspasian hissed back at them. 'For God's sake get a move on.'

Channing glared up at him. 'Caspasian, shut up!'

Moving slowly, from hold to hold, Rachel inched her way up, not daring to look down again, but rather staring hard at each next hand- and foot-hold. That way the fear was manageable. Just.

At the top Caspasian pulled himself up towards

the base of the battlements, slipped one hand over the top, and hauled up between two of the crenellations. He checked that everything was clear, and slipped through, easing himself down on to the rampart. He was desperate to check on Rachel but knew that his first priority was to ensure their entry into the fortress was secure and that they had not been seen. If they were spotted, then it would not matter whether Rachel made it to the top of the wall or not. They would all be dead.

Twenty feet below him, a small courtyard lay beneath the ramparts. A stone staircase led down to it. On the far side, an arch led into what appeared to be a much larger courtyard. Caspasian guessed that the main gate lay somewhere beyond that. To either side of him, buildings rose, topped by towers. There was no one in sight. He had been correct. Confident in his own territory, the Prince had left only a token presence in the fort. The question was, where was it, and how strong?

He leaned back over the wall and reached down for Rachel. She was only a couple of yards below the battlements now. Looking down, Caspasian saw the ground a long way down, the bushes and track horribly dwarfed. It was little wonder she had almost lost consciousness at the sight of it. He stretched his hand down as far as he could. Rachel reached up, her fingers clawing for his palm, and grasped it. He almost crushed her hand in his grip as he hauled her up, hoisted her through the crenellations, and on to the rampart. The moment she set foot on firm ground her knees gave way and she sank against him.

'Sit down. Keep an eye out,' he said.

He reached down for Channing who glared back at him, knocking aside the offered hand. He pulled himself up and over.

When he had his breath back he panted, 'You really are a bastard. Do you know that?'

'Actually, yes,' Caspasian said coldly, helping Ganga over the wall.

They unslung their weapons and cocked them, flicking off the safety catches. From their packs they had brought a haversack of hand grenades, a mix of No. 27 white phosphorous grenades for smoke and incendiary effect, No. 5 Mills grenades, and the lighter No. 34 egg grenades with less destructive blast and splinter effect, but greater range because of the lighter weight. Ganga loosened his kukri in its scabbard and tightened the chin strap of his hat. He grinned at Channing. 'Mustn't lose my hat or Caspasian Saheb will put me on a charge.'

'I bet he bloody would too.'

'Stop bitching,' Caspasian said. 'Come on.'

He went for the stone steps. They were well worn, their surfaces concave from years of use. Rachel had drawn her Webley and held it warily in both fists, not daring to yank back the vicious hammer but drawing some comfort from the feel of the big metal gun. Channing came next, cradling his rifle, scanning about him, aping Caspasian's professional stealth. At the rear, Ganga held his Lee-Enfield with the butt in the shoulder, the muzzle angled slightly down, ready for a snap shot. His eyes had narrowed to slits as he cast about him with the casual intensity of a starved cobra.

To get to the far side of the courtyard, Caspasian led the party round the edge, keeping his back to the wall. On the way they passed two solid wooden doors, both of them locked. They had just passed the last of these and were closing on the archway when a man walked smartly round it from the far courtyard. He caught sight of them and shrieked as Caspasian's foot shot out and kicked him hard in the pit of the stomach.

Caspasian rushed on to him, laying aside the MP18, grabbing the man from behind, one hand under the chin, the other on the back of the head, twisting the neck. He put his lips by the man's ear and whispered. Rachel could see the man's eyes register understanding. For a moment he hesitated but a yank from Caspasian's hands brought a torrent of garbled words. Caspasian listened carefully and then punched the man viciously on the side of the neck with the rigid edge of his open hand. The body went limp and crumpled to the earthen floor.

'He says the prisoners are in the cellars beneath the main tower.' He scooped up the MP18 and jerked his chin at the archway. 'Through here.'

Up close beside the ancient stonework, Caspasian peered round the edge and then moved. He had not gone three paces when there was a shout of alarm, a single rifle shot, followed by the throaty chatter of Caspasian's sub-machine gun. With secrecy gone he shouted for the others to follow him.

Ganga called for Channing to watch their backs while he ran past and took his place at Caspasian's side. The immediate threat was now in front of them. That was where they needed to concentrate their limited firepower. As he rounded the side of the arch, Ganga saw the body of a man lying on the far side of the courtyard. There were several doors standing open and tribesmen were running out of one of them. Caspasian dropped to one knee, tucked the butt of the MP18 into shoulder and cheek, and fired a series of short, controlled bursts straight into the doorway. The Pathans tumbled back into the darkness inside, leaving two of their number dead in the sand.

Ganga scanned the windows above. It was a terrible spot. They were overlooked by at least a score of windows from any one of which a sniper could engage them. He swept the muzzle of his rifle across them, almost in the aim now, staring hard over the top, both eyes open wide for the snap target. Then it came. A face blurred in one of the windows, the barrel of a Mauser flashed, but Ganga was on to it. His rifle swung round, stiffened into the aim, and he fired. The Mauser clattered out across the stone sill, followed a second later by the firer, cart-wheeling down into the courtyard.

With Ganga covering him, Caspasian sprinted forward, plucking a hand grenade from his pocket as he ran, a heavy No. 5 Mills bomb. He pulled the pin and lobbed it through the open doorway into which the Pathans had retreated. At one and a half pounds the Mills grenade was cumbersome but it had what Caspasian needed at that moment. Killing power. The green band around its fat waist denoted a dense filling of Amatol explosive and, packed around it, the scored metal casing. He spun to the side of the door and flattened himself against the wall. There was a cry of alarm inside the room, a momentary scrabble of panic, cut dead a second later by a deafening roar as the grenade detonated. Splinters of wood, flesh and bone sprayed out of the door in a gust of flame and the stench of explosive.

Caspasian whipped round in front of the open doorway and fired a burst from the MP18 into the smoking darkness, aiming low to sweep the floor where anyone might have been able to take cover.

He turned towards the tower where he had been told the prisoners were being held. Channing and Rachel were already at its door struggling with the lock. Caspasian signalled to Ganga and the two of them ran across to join them, backing the last few yards to check round the courtyard for fresh adversaries.

'What's the problem?' Caspasian shouted over his shoulder.

'It's locked,' Channing replied.

'You've got a rifle. Bloody well use it!'

Channing looked uncertainly at the big Lee-Enfield in his hands as if the thought of actually having to fire it had never occurred to him. He muttered something to himself, stood back, levelled the muzzle at the lock, closed his eyes and pulled the trigger. The rifle blazed and almost jumped out of his hands like a scalded cat. He opened his eyes to see an enormous hole where the lock had been and the door starting to swing open on loudly straining hinges.

'I hit it!' Channing said, marvelling at his handiwork.

Caspasian pushed past him, belted the door wide

with the flat of his boot, and strode in, sweeping the muzzle of his gun from left to right, finger on the trigger, ready. He flicked the drum magazine of the MP18 with his middle finger, the tone of the ring telling him the rough number of rounds left inside. The more hollow the ping, the fewer the rounds. A solid 'thunk' bounced back at him. Plenty yet. The adrenaline was pumping through his body now. He could feel it. His senses were wide awake, taut as a drum skin, and he felt ready to take on the world.

The ground floor of the tower was one enormous room. Steps led to a mezzanine that ringed it, doorways and further staircases leading off that. Opposite him, another door stood open, steps descending into darkness. Caspasian was tempted to roll a grenade down them but it would hardly be a good idea if the captives were there. Still, it might just wake up Henry Allenshaw. He strode across the room, the others coming in behind him.

'Ganga, stay by the door and keep watch on the courtyard,' he barked over his shoulder, never taking his eyes from the door in front of him. 'Douglas, watch the mezzanine. Rachel, follow me.'

Douglas scanned the floor above doubtfully. 'What do I do if anyone comes?'

'Challenge them to a game of bridge. What the hell do you think? Blast them!'

'I'm not sure I can.'

'That's up to you. Let them shoot you if you want, but keep them off my back or I'll shoot you myself.'

Channing knew that he meant it and set his back to the wall, aiming his rifle hesitantly at the upper floor, praying that no one showed.

Caspasian reached the doorway and started down the steps, Rachel following behind. Here again, the stone had been worn into deep half-moons, their surface so smooth it was as slippery as ice. He stumbled down the last few to find himself in a narrow passage, another open door in front of him. As he reached it a huge Pathan emerged, so tall he had to duck to get out. Caspasian pulled the trigger of the MP18. The gun jammed. The drum magazine had a capacity of thirty-two rounds, but that also meant thirty-two opportunities for a stoppage.

'Shit.' He swung wildly with the butt. The giant ducked aside, surprisingly nimble for a man of his enormous size. His hands were like two sides of beef and he darted forward and snatched the sub-machine gun from Caspasian and tossed it aside. With no time to draw his pistol Caspasian lunged at the man, but the brute casually slapped aside the thrusts like troublesome mosquitoes. With that familiar leaden feeling in the pit of his stomach, Caspasian realised he had a serious fight on his hands.

Without room to circle, his options were severely limited. The giant crouched, arms outstretched, huge fists open, fingers curled to grab, hold, gouge or crush. His face leered, teeth bared in sheer delight at the prospect of deliberate slaughter.

Caspasian forced himself to deepen his breath. Slow it down. Focus. Everyone had a weak point. There was an opening in every defence. He just had to find it. He backed away. The giant came on. Ah. Interesting. He backed again. The man advanced again. Caspasian liked that. He took three fast steps backwards, keeping his eyes on the giant at all times. The giant rushed in to close the gap. As he did so, Caspasian spun round, pivoting on his right foot and driving straight out with his left. The ushiro-geri back kick drove in under the giant's guard and found his gut. Caspasian gave it the full drive of his hips, slamming it home. He felt muscle and gut. He screamed the kiai, focusing on the kick. Spinning back on guard he faced the giant again. Badly winded, the giant shuddered, fought for breath. No time to pause. Caspasian knew it was now or never. He closed in.

A right upper cut took the giant on the chin. Caspasian felt the neck jar but it was as thick and as strong as a young tree. He went in with a left upper cut to the same spot. Same result. He pulled back his right fist, clenched it to stone and drove it in below the chin. The knuckles powered into the giant's windpipe just below the Adam's apple. Once again Caspasian put his hip and shoulders behind the punch, following through, focusing not on the windpipe but on the back of the man's neck, propelling the blow all the way through.

It worked. His opponent went down. As he did so, Caspasian put his hands behind the giant's neck and brought his knee up hard into his face. He felt the cartilage fold. There was blood. Lots of it. He repeated the blow, once, twice more. The giant creased and fell with a grunt and a long drawn out wheeze.

From beyond the doorway he and Rachel heard a shout. It was Angus McCloud. Stepping over the body of the giant, they ran to the solid wooden door from behind which the shout had come.

'Stand back.' Caspasian shouted. He pulled out his Mauser, levelled it at the lock and fired. The bullet blew the lock asunder and he kicked in the door. First to feel his way out of the darkness was Brigadier Percival, followed by Bernard Spencer. Rachel rushed into his arms. Angus McCloud and Henry Allenshaw stepped out, both of them blinking in the gloom of the passageway.

'Well done, Caspasian,' the Brigadier said. He smiled. 'Took your time but glad you made it. At last.'

'Gibson's already on the way,' Caspasian said.

'I know.'

'There's something funny though, Brigadier. The Prince has got mortars but there's something odd about the rounds. I saw . . .'

Brigadier Percival cut him short. 'Never mind about that. Where's the Eye of the Storm?'

Caspasian stared at him puzzled. 'That hardly matters now, surely. The fighting's started. Gibson's column's going to be slaughtered. The Eye is irrelevant.'

'I'll be the judge of that,' the Brigadier said, pushing past him. He came to the giant, inspected him with distaste and stepped over him. 'You have been busy.'

There was a commotion from behind as Allenshaw and McCloud released the two militia soldiers, the porters and groom from their cell.

'Get us some damned weapons,' Allenshaw complained. 'It's all very well for you, Caspasian. Armed to the teeth as usual. What about us?'

'Perhaps you shouldn't have surrendered them so

readily in the first place.' Caspasian answered acidly. He stooped and picked up the MP18, working the blockage free. He cocked the handle twice, and when he was ready led the way back up the steps.

Entering the large room he was stopped in his tracks by the sight of Douglas Channing, rifle on the ground at his feet, with a knife being held against his throat by a woman.

'Caspasian,' he rasped, wincing as the woman dug the blade threateningly deeper. 'She came at me from behind. Through that blasted door. I didn't hear her. Honestly.'

Out in the courtyard the stiff reports of a rifle told them that Ganga was holding off a fresh assault. It was impossible to tell how many, but from the rapid rifle fire Caspasian guessed that the Gurkha was under pressure. He took a step towards the woman and held out his hand.

'Give me the knife,' he said calmly in the tribal language. She bared her teeth at him and drew blood. Channing screamed.

'Stay where you are, Caspasian,' Channing shrilled. 'Brigadier, for God's sake control him!'

Caspasian noticed that the woman's other hand was heavily bandaged. He pointed at it. 'This man here,' he said indicating McCloud, 'he's a doctor. He can help you.'

'No one can help me,' the woman snarled. 'It was the stone. It is accursed.'

At the mention of the stone the Brigadier stepped forward causing another streak of blood to bead at Channing's throat. 'You are right,' the Brigadier said.

'The Eye of the Storm is accursed. But the illness it causes can be cured. We can cure it.'

A flicker of doubt shadowed the woman's face. 'How?'

Angus McCloud held out his hand. 'First give us the knife, and then I'll look at your wound.'

'We won't hurt you,' the Brigadier urged. 'We only want to see the stone.'

As they had been talking, Caspasian had edged round to the side. For one second the woman hesitated, considering their offer. The pain in her hand was agonising. She desperately wanted help. That one second was all Caspasian needed. He darted in and knocked the knife to the ground. She swung at him wildly but he caught her by the wrists and held her firmly. Angus McCloud rushed forward to help, while Rachel and her father went to Channing who had whipped his handkerchief from his pocket and was dabbing at the thin cut on his throat, eyes still wide with terror.

McCloud slowly unwound the dirty bandage from the woman's hand. It was stained with blood, pus and something else. The smell of it filled their nostrils. McCloud frowned. 'What the devil could have caused that?' he said, staring at the horrific disfigurement in disbelief.

Caspasian took one look and felt his blood run cold. 'Mustard gas,' he said tersely. He gripped the woman's free hand. 'How did this happen?'

'I touched the Eye of the Storm.'

Brigadier Percival came up to inspect her hand. 'Dear God,' he muttered. 'What do you mean? You touched it?'

She looked from Caspasian to him and back again. 'Does he not believe me? Go! Touch it yourself!' She waved her burned and blistered claw in his face. He shrunk back, wrinkling his nose against the stench. She shrugged, hugging her hand against her, fighting back the tears of pain. 'But it is all gone now. They emptied it of its poison. I heard the guards say so. The evil has been taken away.'

'How do you mean, taken away?' Caspasian asked her, hardly daring to hear the answer.

'The white strangers emptied the stone. They have taken the poison to kill the British soldiers.'

'The mortar bombs,' Caspasian said, getting to his feet. He looked round at the Brigadier. 'They've got mustard gas. I saw them leaving with mortars. Four of them. Stokes mortars. There were boxes of flare rounds.' He smiled bitterly as the pieces fell into place.

'What are you talking about?' the Brigadier asked.

Caspasian pointed at the woman's hand. 'In Flanders I saw men whose whole bodies were covered in such burns. Exactly the same. When the Germans were low on stocks of regular ammunition, they would doctor para-illuminating rounds, filling them with the chemical. That's what the bastards have done. They're going to use chemical weapons on Gibson. The poor devil won't have a chance, not unless we can stop them before they can deploy the mortars.'

Spencer, Allenshaw and the others moved towards the door but a fresh burst of firing stopped them in their tracks. Ganga backed through the door into the room, rattling off a further two rounds.

'Henry, you and your men help him!' Caspasian shouted. Allenshaw blinked at him in consternation, opened his mouth to protest, but obeyed. He ran forward, snatched up Channing's rifle, and rushed to Ganga's side, while his men ran about the room gathering the few items of furniture to construct a barricade across the open doorway. Caspasian knelt beside the woman who was crouched on the floor, cradling her hand.

'Is there another way out of here?'

She looked at him with stony eyes. 'Why should I help you?'

'Because if you do you can come with us. We can take care of your wound.'

She thought for a moment, then gestured to one of the doors on the mezzanine. 'That leads into the kitchens. You can get out through there.'

Instantly Caspasian was organising the withdrawal. He and Ganga would have to act as a rearguard. Get the others out first. He started giving out orders but the Brigadier interrupted him. 'Aren't you forgetting what we came for? The Eye of the Storm?'

Caspasian felt his irritation rising. Gibson's column was in mortal danger unless the Bolsheviks could be stopped first. 'I've been over that, sir,' he said sharply. 'It's irrelevant now.'

'Well I'm not going without it.'

Caspasian racked back the cocking handle of the MP18 as he prepared to move. 'Then stay here and enjoy it,' he said, adding, 'sir' as an afterthought.

The Brigadier barred his path. 'Don't cross me, Caspasian.'

'Don't cross me, sir,' Caspasian said levelly, his voice quiet, controlled.

Rachel stepped between them. 'For God's sake, aren't we in enough trouble without you two going for each other's throats?' She turned to Caspasian. 'Let him get his stone. Then let's get out of here.'

The woman led them to the Prince's bed chamber and there, in the new leather pouch, they found the Eye of the Storm. She told them that it had been guarded by the giant, but when the firing started he had gone down to check on the prisoners, thinking that they had broken free.

Tentatively, the Brigadier unwrapped the cloths that bound it and rolled it out on to the Prince's mattress. Cleaned of the chemical, the paintings were still largely intact. The bung rolled free from the hole and lay beside the stone wreathed in mauve velvet.

The Brigadier gazed at it, reached out, but pulled his hand back just in case. 'Wonderful,' he murmured.

'What's so wonderful about it?' Spencer asked, peering over his shoulder. 'It's a fake. What good is it?'

The Brigadier wrapped it again in the cloths and slipped it back into the leather pouch. He smiled with self-satisfaction. 'No good at all. I'm taking it, all the same. Call it evidence, if you like.'

He tied the pouch securely to his belt and went with the others back down to the mezzanine and the door that led into the kitchens. He cursed Caspasian silently. How much better if, with the Prince distracted by the column, they simply slipped away. With horses from Mahsud's stables they could be back into British territory before Mahsud realised they had taken the stone and escaped. But Caspasian clearly had the others on his side, and on his own the Brigadier knew he would stand little chance of getting away. He sighed. He would have to play along with Caspasian's tedious heroics a bit longer.

With the barricade in place, Caspasian hurriedly rigged a booby trap using four of the heavy Mills grenades and a tripwire improvised from a snare he found in the kitchens. Mixed in with them he placed a further four white phosphorous grenades. The first Pathan through the barricade would activate the trap and while the Mills bombs would kill, the white phosphorous grenades would set the tower alight. The wooden floor of the mezzanine, tinder dry after the centuries, would burn well, cutting off any immediate pursuit. With luck, by then the small garrison would have had enough and would leave them to make good their escape.

As he finished his task and prepared to join Ganga, giving one final burst out of the door with the MP18, all he could remember was the expression on the Brigadier's face when he had seen the stone. All he could see was the naked greed. That and a mark on the crystal which he recognised as part of a letter. A letter in Cyrillic script.

Chapter Nineteen

The sounds of the battle were like music to Mahsud as he drew nearer to the valley where the British column had been trapped like rats in a barrel. His experience of combat was limited, but he was starting to think it was an activity he could happily have become used to if, that is, the extraordinary Eye of the Storm had not come into his possession to change all of that. Now that he had it, he knew his life was about to change. All of this unpleasantness would soon be a quaint memory. All he had to do now was to eliminate the British troops and get back to the fortress without harm. The Bolsheviks posed a slight problem, but he was pleased with the way he had handled them. He did not want to antagonise them more than he had to. He would need allies to realise the full potential of the Eye in due course. Why not them? He was particularly proud of the game of bluff he had played with Alexei Karpov, and won. The smug little Communist thought that Mahsud was ignorant of the Eye's true worth. Mahsud smiled to himself. They would see who had the last laugh.

'There, my Prince.' Ahmed pointed to a single horseman who waited patiently ahead of them. 'He is the scout to lead our men forward.'

'Good. Let the men go on. I want you and a handful of men to come with me and our comrades to see the mortars into action. We will watch the battle from that vantage point.'

In a long continuous stream the Prince's men filed past him to where the scout was waiting. As they went they waved and cheered him. He sat back on his horse acknowledging their praise, feeling the blood of his father surging through his veins. So this was how it felt. This was the life his father had led. It was not bad. Not bad at all. With a resolute shake of the head, Mahsud wiped away the feeling. It might well have been his father's mode of existence but it was not his. He had other plans.

When the last of his men had gone, disappearing triumphantly over the ridge in the direction of the battle, Mahsud smiled at Karpov. 'Ahmed has located a perfect site for the mortars. Our time has come, comrade.'

Karpov returned the smile, infecting it with as much artificial warmth as he could summon. 'Let's get on with it then. The sooner this is done, the better.' As he followed Mahsud, Ahmed and their guards all he could think of was the Eye of the Storm, racking his brain all the while for a means of getting his hands on it. It really was too bad the way things had turned out. Nevertheless, the race was not over yet. A battle was a confused and dangerous affair. There was every chance that the Prince might succumb to a stray British bullet. That was the nature of warfare, after all. Uncertainty and danger. He and Vassily knew that all too well. Mahsud on the other hand, judging by his display of naive glee at all the excitement, had yet to be enlightened.

The ride to the site that Ahmed had selected was longer than any of them had expected and when they got there, Mahsud inspected it dubiously. The sound of the firing seemed uncomfortably close, even though there was no one else to be seen. Noticing the Prince's expression Ahmed said, 'The Russian told me how close we had to place the mortars to be effective.' He turned to Novikov for support.

'That's right, sir. The mortars' range is only seven hundred yards and we still have to be able to hit deep into the enemy column. If we sit too far back we will only be able to drop bombs on their advance guard. That wouldn't be enough to achieve the full effect I am after.'

Mahsud studied him suspiciously but eventually had to agree that he was correct. Besides, the Bolsheviks were there to advise. What did he know about it? Military tactics and the characteristics of weapons had not featured large in his studies at Oxford. His only regret was that he had not ordered more of his men to stay with him. It was too late for that now however. Already he could hear the sound of the firing intensify. Their lead elements were obviously already in contact with the British.

With a grudging signal from Mahsud that he was content with the arrangements, Novikov swung off his horse and, with Zykov and Dragov, set about deploying the mortars. As he worked, he planned his attack. He would fire a couple of ordinary high explosive rounds from each mortar to bed them in and dig the base plates firmly into the hard ground.

Then, with the firing platforms stable, he would use a further couple of HE rounds from each barrel to get the approximate range and bearing to his target, the column itself. Once he was happy that the rounds were going to fall where he wanted them to, he would load and fire the mustard gas. Then they would see how the British withstood the forces of Prince Mahsud. It would be a slaughter.

It was Brigadier Percival's suggestion that they stop by a stream to rest. At first Caspasian was all for pressing on. They could hear the firing now and the volume and ferocity indicated that a substantial battle was in progress. Looking at the others however, he could see that a rest would do them all good, giving them a pause to gather themselves before whatever lay ahead. He was most concerned for Rachel. Caspasian had urged her to go with her father, Allenshaw and the militia soldiers and head back for the border. She had refused, despite the Brigadier's sudden and enthusiastic intervention. She had argued, with justification, that if Caspasian located the mortar line he would need all the firepower he could muster, even if that meant taking her along. She had also said that her medical skills would be useful to Angus McCloud to deal with the large numbers of casualties that there were bound to be. As ever, Caspasian had found himsel' agreeing with her and admiring her courage and willpower at the same time.

They dismounted at the edge of a broad bu shallow river. Allenshaw posted a sentry while the rest of them left the horses with the groom and picked their way across pebbles to the fast flowing, crystal clear water. Coming from higher in the mountains it was beautifully cold. Caspasian had noted with some satisfaction how Allenshaw had become subdued now they were approaching a real fight. He sat by himself, checking the load in his revolver. Caspasian recognised the symptoms. He had seen them often enough on the Western Front before men had gone over the top. Preoccupation. Withdrawal. To his surprise, Caspasian found himself feeling sorry for the man. His dislike of Henry Allenshaw had not diminished over the past days, but no one deserved to feel what the fellow was now feeling.

Rachel and her father sat with Douglas Channing and Angus McCloud, chatting quietly. Caspasian and Ganga did a quick count of their available weaponry and ammunition. When they had finished and Ganga had moved down to the river to drink, Caspasian was about to join Rachel when he noticed the Brigadier. Like Allenshaw, he too had gone off by himself, but further upstream and was now crouched by the water, working busily at something in his hands. Caspasian could guess what it was and decided to join him.

The Brigadier heard him coming and to Caspasian it looked as if he had been about to hide what he was doing. He decided against secrecy however and, sure enough, when Caspasian reached him he saw that the Brigadier was busy washing the Eye of the Storm in the river. He had been using the wet sand from the river bed to scour the hollow crystal of its covering of paint. He held it up proudly to Caspasian.

'See? Bright as a button.' The exquisitely painted scenes from the prophet's life had all but vanished. In place of the old Eye of the Storm the Brigadier now held a sparkling hollow crystal the size of a large tennis ball. When he saw Caspasian looking at it closely he buried it quickly in the water again, working free the final chips of paint.

'So what is it then?' Caspasian asked. 'Let's have a look at this magnificent Eye of the Storm.' He made sure his sarcasm came across loud and clear.

'All will become clear when we get it back to Delhi.'

Caspasian snorted with laughter. 'Oh, sure. You and the stone will vanish like a will-o'-the-wisp and that'll be the last I ever hear of it.' He crouched down. 'Come on, sir. I think we've all earned the right to know, seeing as our lives have been put in jeopardy to get it.'

Brigadier Percival stared round at him while his hands continued working beneath the water. 'Right? What right? No one has a right to anything, Caspasian. I would have thought you, of all people, would have known that. How many years were you in the trenches? A soldier follows orders. No one has any rights.'

'No?'

'No. And even if they did, they wouldn't extend to this. This is government business only.'

'And the markings on it?'

The Brigadier laughed. 'I should have known you'd notice. Observant bugger, aren't you?'

Caspasian edged closer. For a moment he considered taking the crystal by force. It would have been easy enough. He decided against it. 'I want to know, sir,' he said, his voice hardening. 'I've been dragged through the hills, shot at, men have been killed and the lot of us still might end up with our heads on platters at one of the Prince's fucking banquets. So tell me, what's Mahsud doing with a fake Eye of the Storm? Why was it filled with liquid mustard gas, and why is the surface of it covered with Cyrillic lettering and numbers.'

'Not the surface, Caspasian. The inside of it.' The Brigadier looked at it under the water, turning it this way and that. 'Quite ingenious how they did it.'

'The Chinese have been painting scenes on the inside of bottles for centuries. They use a tiny brush with an angled head.'

The Brigadier considered this. 'Presumably a similar engraving tool was used on the crystal.'

'So?' Caspasian prompted. He was damned if he was going to let the Brigadier slip away without answering him. 'What is it? The formula for a new form of mustard gas?'

'Oh, no. Much more valuable than that.' The Brigadier smiled. 'In the last days of the Tsar leading up to the Revolution, Russian scientists were working on a new energy source. The Tsar gave the project top priority, convinced that if they could only perfect it in time they might be able to turn the country around. The suffering of the people would have been alleviated and revolution avoided. Unlimited power could have been produced at minimal cost. Russia would have continued on into the twentieth century as the world's leading nation, with the Tsar and his family at its head.'

'None of which obviously happened.'

'Yes and no. The situation was too far gone to stop the Revolution, but virtually as the Winter Palace was being stormed the team of scientists were putting the finishing touches to their work.' The Brigadier pulled the crystal from the water and held it up. Water poured from it as it glimmered in the sunlight. 'This is, in effect, their message in a bottle. It was devised by the team leader who knew of the Eye of the Storm. The code, the formulas for the energy source were secreted in this ball, carved into the very crystal itself. It was painted to resemble the real Eye of the Storm and placed in the Hermitage where it would be guarded, as treasures always are, until such time as he could retrieve it. Of course he was killed along with the rest of his team, but not before a British agent in Moscow had learned of their triumph.'

Caspasian rocked back on his heels. 'Of course. The mustard gas was just a protective device. Anyone tampering with the Eye wouldn't live to tell of it. But then who would suspect an old Indian jewel in the first place?' In the palm of the Brigadier's hand, the crystal winked back at him. 'And the real Eye of the Storm? What happened to that?'

'Who cares?' the Brigadier shrugged. 'Hidden away in some storage crate somewhere in the vaults of the Hermitage perhaps. Compared to this it is a worthless trinket.'

'Not to the tribesmen here. I wonder how they'd feel if they learned that they'd been duped and that the object they revere had been abused like this.'

'Well I'm certainly not going to tell them,' the

Brigadier chuckled. He grinned at Caspasian. 'You've done well, Caspasian. Lost none of your old skills, I'm glad to see.' He hefted the crystal in his hand. 'Help me get this back to Delhi and I'll see your contribution to the mission doesn't go unrecognised. You can go all the way to the top, mark my word. I know some pretty influential people. I can make you.'

Or break me, Caspasian thought.

'With the knowledge concealed in these codes, the British Empire will never be reliant on oil. Iraq and all the rest of those Godforsaken bloody deserts can go hang, and all their nasty little despots with them. We'll rule them, but we won't need them and, by God, there's a difference. We'll have everything we need right here.' He gazed at the crystal in wonder. 'This is what those men have died for, Caspasian. Tell me now it wasn't worth it.'

In the distance there was a sound like a giant chopping wood. They both looked up in alarm, recognising the sound of a Stokes mortar. It was followed a moment later by another, and then another. Caspasian pushed himself to his feet. 'They're bedding in. Getting ready to fire the chemicals. We've got to destroy them before they butcher Gibson and his men.'

He started to run to the horses, shouting to the others to mount. The Brigadier called after him. 'The crystal must get back safely, Caspasian. We can't jeopardise its security. It's too important.'

Caspasian was already on his horse. 'So is Colonel Gibson's column. You know that as well as I do, Brigadier. We've both seen what mustard gas can do.'

371

The Brigadier walked slowly back to the horses, wrapping the crystal in its cloths and burying it securely in its pouch again. 'All right, Caspasian. But just remember what I said. This could be the making of you. Remember that. Help me see it safely home and I'll see you right.'

The first high explosive mortar round came as a nasty surprise to Colonel Gibson. He had moved forward to join the advance guard when he heard the 'thunk' of the round being fired several hundred yards away. He and Captain Underwood, the advance guard commander, stared at one another, each reading the other's thoughts.

If the Pathans had an indirect fire capability the column was in even worse trouble than they already knew to be the case. While the pickets might be able to keep the enemy beyond small arms range, thereby preserving the integrity of the main body of the column, mortars were capable of lobbing bombs clean over the top of the picket positions, striking right into the heart of the British troops, the baggage train, the medical aid post where the wounded were being gathered, the ammunition supplies and the mountain artillery. What was even worse, it would be difficult while still in the steep-sided valley for Colonel Gibson's own artillery to respond in kind. The guns lacked the high trajectory of a mortar. They did not have sufficient clearance to fire up and over the high flanking ridges. The barrels simply could not be elevated high enough, whereas the enemy could rain down mortar bombs at will. Lacking this essential counter-battery fire, the Pathan mortars would have free rein.

Sir Oswald had come forward to see what was happening. He had found himself a safe place sandwiched between two rocks and Colonel Gibson could see that it would take one of the Missouri mules to extricate him from his refuge.

'Bit off the mark, aren't they?' he observed as drily as his mounting panic would allow.

The initial rounds had spread far and wide, one bursting halfway up a barren hillside, another impacting several hundred yards in front of the advance guards most forward position.

'They're just bedding in, I'm afraid,' Captain Miller the Adjutant remarked. 'Getting the range. Once they've got it they'll be putting salt on our tails all right. You'll see.'

'Shouldn't you be doing something about it then?' Sir Oswald said testily. 'I mean, are we just supposed to sit here and take whatever battering they decide to dish out?'

Colonel Gibson was getting fed up with their unwelcome civilian guest. Sir Oswald had amply demonstrated by his high-handed manner that he had a poor opinion of soldiers, and yet it was they who had forged the Empire, who policed it and who kept it in order so that the fat cats like Sir Oswald could sit in comfort and make their fortunes. It was not that Colonel Gibson was in any way envious. He would no sooner be caught driving a desk in some smelly overcrowded city than would Sir Oswald be caught assaulting an enemy-held hilltop. Gibson loved soldiering. It had been his life. If it brought only modest returns, then so be it. When the time came he would retire safe in the knowledge that he had lived his life to the full. He would have sampled it in ways no civilian like Sir Oswald could ever understand.

He turned to Sir Oswald and said, 'Something is being done about it. The picket commanders on the hilltops will have heard the mortars just like us. They'll be using their binoculars to search for them at this very minute. The moment they sight them, if they can, they will locate and destroy them.' He was finding it difficult to keep his voice civil. 'The problem is that – as I expect you might have noticed – they're under extreme pressure. The Pathans have thrown large numbers of fresh troops into the battle and, frankly, Sir Oswald, I think we'll be lucky to get out of this alive.' He saw the look of terror in Sir Oswald's eyes and privately rejoiced.

As he had spoken, more mortar rounds had landed closer to them. Colonel Gibson dismounted from his horse and handed it to his groom to lead away. 'Gentlemen,' he said calmly to Captain Miller and Captain Underwood. 'I think it might be appropriate for us to take cover.'

A round whistled down at them. They ducked instinctively as the round slammed into the ground a hundred yards behind them. Shards of white hot metal pinged and ricocheted off the rocks. There was a moment's silence, and then a cry of 'Stretcher bearers!' They could hear a scream coming from the cloud of dust. All along the roadside as far back as the rearguard, the column had dispersed into whatever cover was afforded in the floor of the valley. Although the pickets had been doing an excellent job of keeping the larger part of the Pathan force at arm's length, an increasing number of tribesmen were slipping through the screen and sniping down at the main British force.

'They've got our range,' the Adjutant observed laconically. 'Now we're for it.'

However instead of the rain of mortar bombs that they all expected the fire stopped. Colonel Gibson scanned the ridgelines through his binoculars, trying to work out what was going on. The rifle and machine gun fire was as intense as ever. Surely now was the time for the Pathans to push home their attack.

The next round that the mortars fired made an altogether different noise. Colonel Gibson peered up into the clear blue sky wondering what was happening. In place of the usual whine and rush of a high explosive round screaming towards the earth, there was a burst of light far up. The round had burst over the advance guards' most forward position some two hundred yards in front of him. Looking at them through his binoculars, Colonel Gibson could see the men craning back to see what was about to hit them.

'A flare,' the Adjutant said in surprise. 'Broad bloody daylight and the stupid buggers are using flares.' He laughed, but without confidence. He had been fighting the Pathans for too long not to hold them in the highest respect when it came to their combat ability.

'What the devil are they up to?' Colonel Gibson muttered.

He received his answer a minute later. Looking

down the road to the troops who lay beneath the point where the flare had burst in the sky, he saw first one soldier and then another jump up. He focused his binoculars on them and was surprised to see that they appeared to be slapping the dust from themselves.

'Captain Underwood, what the devil are your men up to?'

'I haven't got a clue,' he replied, fixing his own binoculars on the spectacle. More of the soldiers were on their feet now, dancing as if barefoot on hot coals. The screams reached Colonel Gibson next, piercing shrieks of agony.

There was the sound of a second round firing and again they were surprised to see a flare round burst over the same spot in a blaze of white light. Moments later, more men were on their feet, but they were not just dancing now. They were running, back towards Colonel Gibson, and with them they brought others who, although unaffected by the mortar rounds, had been infected with the panic and were breaking ranks before they too were caught by the terrifying new weapons.

It was only when they drew near to Colonel Gibson that he realised what had happened. Blotching their arms, legs and faces, everywhere where there was exposed skin, huge sulphurous blisters had sprouted. Colonel Gibson felt his blood run cold. It had been a long time since he had seen such injuries. He had fervently hoped never to have to face such weapons again. At the top of his voice he screamed, 'Gas Gas Gas!'

But this was not the no-man's-land hell of Flanders. It was the North-West Frontier, and there was not a single gas mask or a single item of protective clothing amongst the lot of them.

In the direction from which the soldiers had just fled, Colonel Gibson heard a blood curdling yell. He looked up to see the hillside blossoming with running figures, not his own men this time, but Pathans, flooding in to swamp the positions from which their enemy had just been driven, pushing home their attack.

'Captain Underwood, rally your men for God's sake! Establish a fire line with all those still able to pull a trigger.'

As he watched his officers and sergeants grab at the fleeing soldiers and fling them into fire positions, Colonel Gibson prayed that one, just one of the picket positions might have spotted the mortars. Unless someone was able to knock them out the column was finished.

In the distance he heard the thud of another mortar firing, the same sickening sound as before. He stared up at the sky in horror as the round climbed to its pinnacle and burst in a brilliant flash of light. Another flare, and raining down from it he could see now the fine mist of spray emanating from it. He could see it because it had burst directly overhead.

The firing of the mortars was like a beacon for Caspasian, drawing him straight to them. He knew exactly what would be happening in the valley beyond his vision. He could see in his mind's eye the horror unfolding just as he had seen it a score of times previously when men had unleashed their evil creations on to their fellow men. He was not sure how he would tackle the mortars when he got there. He just knew that they had to be stopped. Undoubtedly the Bolsheviks would be there. Perhaps the Prince too. And if the Prince, then a sizeable bodyguard force. Whatever the case, the mortars would be well protected. They were the Prince's prize weapon system, the ace up his sleeve. He would not have deployed them carelessly.

At his side, Ganga clung uncomfortably to the horse he had snatched when they had fled from the fortress. It was far too vigorous for his liking but with Caspasian forging ahead he had to keep up. He suspected that Caspasian did not yet have a plan, but Ganga was unconcerned. He trusted him. They had been in any number of tight corners before and, all the gods willing, would be so again. In any case, the heat of battle was the mother of invention. Caspasian would think of something, even if it was a reckless charge into the midst of an overwhelmingly superior enemy force. And if it was, then Ganga would be at his side.

Unable to match Caspasian's ferocious pace, Rachel stayed close to her father. She was desperately worried about him. This was hardly the sort of thing that a man of his age should have been doing. Behind her, Channing and McCloud stuck as close as they could, Douglas with his Lee-Enfield across his lap. He looked so out of place to Rachel, but then weren't they all? What was supposed to have been a routine attendance at a jirga had turned into a nightmare.

She glanced over her shoulder and saw Henry Allenshaw, his militiamen, the groom and the woman from the Prince's fortress, grimacing in discomfort at the speed of the ride, wincing at the pain in her wounded hand. Allenshaw's face was white with terror as the fight drew closer.

At the back came the man whom Rachel held responsible for the whole wretched affair, Brigadier Percival. The leather pouch containing the Eye of the Storm was slung round his shoulder and every so often he would reach back and touch it like a talisman to make sure it was still safely there. Rachel could not imagine what could be so valuable as to justify such dangers. She felt a burning hatred towards him and wished only to take hold of the stone and smash it into a thousand pieces.

If there was one thing she did not regret, it was the meeting with John Caspasian. She had never met anyone like him before. When they had been in the hide close to the fortress, Douglas Channing had secretly confided to her his own opinion of the man. How had he described him? A disabled romantic, doomed by having to live in the real world, and knowing it. As Rachel watched Caspasian leading their slender column at breakneck speed, poorly armed and equipped, appallingly ill-suited to the task immediately ahead of them, all she could marvel at was the reckless courage of the man. But it was the man she admired, not the courage. In their walk beside the river, that now seemed like an age ago, she had caught a glimpse of who he really was. Douglas might be right, but if so, he was only partly right, for Rachel knew that there was much more to

John Caspasian than some blighted romanticism, even if she was not yet sure exactly what. Her one wish now was that they should both live through the next hours so that she could find out.

Their road had started to climb but Caspasian refused to slacken the pace. He could hear the mortars firing, and for the first time he had noted the distinctive sound of the flare round being fired. They were closing rapidly with the fringes of the battle and at any moment he expected to feel the familiar crack of a bullet snapping past. But as each stretch of road passed beneath them and no one engaged them with fire, he realised that the whole attention of Prince Mahsud's warriors was on the fight with Gibson's column. The last thing they were expecting was an attack from the rear, however small. In that lay Caspasian's one slim hope of success. A surprise attack might, if he was lucky, have an effect out of all proportion to the size of his tiny force. With luck he might be able to destroy the mortars, and then, and only then, would Colonel Gibson have a chance of fighting his way out of the deadly trap into which Mahsud had lured him.

The next moment he was reining to a halt, frantically waving for the others to dismount. He slid from his saddle and grabbed his MP18, the satchel of grenades and the spare ammunition, before slapping the horse away from him. Ganga dropped to the ground beside him, his rifle in his fist, and together they jogged forward, keeping low. They dropped into cover behind a low rise in the ground, fringed with thick gorse. There, barely a hundred yards in front of them, was the mortar line, the four Stokes mortars deployed side by side at ten-yard intervals. The four Bolsheviks fussed around them, and beyond them, cresting the far rise that overlooked the valley where Gibson's column was trapped, Prince Mahsud and his bodyguards sat amongst the rocks like spectators at a hill race.

Caspasian waited until everyone had joined him and then spread them out in an extended line behind the rise.

'Pick your targets,' he whispered. 'Choose your man and wait until I give the order.'

Ganga went from man to man, helping those who were unfamiliar with the captured Mauser rifles, before dropping into position beside Caspasian and tapping him on the shoulder as a sign that everything was ready. On Caspasian's other side, Rachel tucked herself close to the ground. She had drawn the big Webley revolver from its holster and clutched it to her in both fists.

With a final glance to left and right, Caspasian pulled the butt of his MP18 into his shoulder, tucked his chin against the smooth cold wood, and went into action.

Chapter Twenty

Oleg Zykov never knew what hit him. One moment he and Dragov were tugging at the lid of an ammunition box to get at the flare rounds inside, and the next Caspasian's MP18 had knocked the life out of him, the rounds thudding into his body, lifting him off his feet and tumbling him and the piled ammunition boxes in a muddled heap on the floor.

Beside him, Dragov took a bullet in the thigh. He cried out and clutched at the wound, blood pumping through his fingers. He turned to seek out their assailant, drawing his pistol as he did so. Coming from a long low mound, he saw the spurts of dust kicked up by the MP18. He levelled his pistol at it to return fire, just as a single .303 round from Ganga's Lee-Enfield smashed through his forehead and entered his brain.

Vassily Novikov hurled himself to the ground, the mortars forgotten. His eyes flashed at Alexei Karpov, cowering behind a rock some ten paces away. 'Where the fuck's that bastard, Mahsud?'

He blazed off a couple of wild rounds in the rough direction of their attackers without any hope of hitting anything, but trying at least to seize some initiative back from whoever had sprung the ambush.

From his vantage point overlooking the greater battle in the valley below, Mahsud spun round at the sudden noise of firing behind him. Ahmed dashed to his side and pushed him to the ground.

'Down, my Prince. We will deal with them.'

Gathering the bodyguards, he led them back towards the mortars, shouting at them to spread out into a skirmish line and return the fire.

Caspasian saw them coming and was ready for them. He knew that there would not be much time to destroy the mortars. Once the Prince's main force heard of the battle around their leader they would rush to help him. If Caspasian and the others had not got away by then they would be finished. First however, they had to clear the way to the mortar line, and that meant slaying as many of the bodyguard as possible.

'Henry, you and your men get some fire down on the Pathans. Leave the Russians for now,' he shouted.

Allenshaw glared back at him, his face a mixture of fear and loathing. 'Don't give orders to me, Captain. We're here to destroy the mortars. You said so yourself. That's precisely what we're going to do.'

For one moment Caspasian was tempted to put a bullet through him, but with the tribesmen closing on them he spat his curse into the dust and focused on the task in hand. At his side, Ganga was putting down rapid fire, his right hand working the bolt of his Lee-Enfield like fury, slamming home a fresh round after every shot.

To Caspasian's left, Channing had crawled forward to get a good view over the mound. He was firing well but Caspasian could see the rounds going wide.

'Pull the rifle into the shoulder with the right hand,' he shouted. 'Hug it to you. Tight into the cheek.'

Channing amended his grip and fired. A hundred yards away a Pathan was stopped in mid run and knocked backwards as if swiped aside by a bear's paw.

Off to the flank Caspasian heard Allenshaw barking out fresh orders at his men and looked up in horror to see them getting up out of cover and running forward. Behind them, Allenshaw leaned up on one arm, waving them forward.

'What the fuck are you doing?' Caspasian screamed at him. He shouted at the men to get down but it was too late. Novikov had seen their hopeless charge for the mortars. He levelled his rifle, took his time, and fired once, re-aimed and fired again. At each shot, a man went down. Before the second one had hit the dirt, Caspasian was on his feet and running at Allenshaw, heedless of the bullets now spitting along the length of the mound. Allenshaw had watched in bewilderment as his men were gunned down. He blinked, wondering what could have gone wrong, when a shadow flashed in the corner of his eye and Caspasian's boot took him under the chin, sending him flying.

Caspasian was down beside him. He grabbed him by the collar, yanked his head up and held it firmly in place while his right fist slammed into the centre of Allenshaw's face three times. Leaving him unconscious on the floor, blood streaming from his shattered nose and split lips, Caspasian ducked back to his MP18, stripped off the old magazine, clipped on a fresh one, cocked and fired from a kneeling position. He raked the oncoming line of Pathans from left to right, feeling a cry of rage rise within him. Their charge faltered and stopped. Several of their number were dead. More were wounded. Now was the time for Caspasian and the others to move, before the Pathans could recover from the shock of the sub-machine gun fire. It would take them only seconds to get into cover and put down fire of their own, but for one brief moment there was a pause, and like so many pauses in battle, Caspasian recognised it as an opportunity.

Tugging two white phosphorous grenades from the satchel, Caspasian pulled the pins and threw them as hard as he could. The instant they burst, a dense white smoke cloud billowed up into the air, spreading to form a thick screen behind which Ganga led the others forward.

As Rachel got to her feet, Ganga side-stepped up to her. 'Look, memsaheb – over there!' he shouted in her ear. Rachel spun to see what he was staring at, his eyes wide with terror. The next thing she saw was a blinding flash of stars followed by oblivion. Ganga caught her as she fell, lowering her gently to the ground and tucking her safely behind the cover of the earthen bank. He rubbed the edge of his hand where it had rabbit-punched into the join of her neck and shoulder muscle. 'Sorry, memsaheb. Captain's orders,' he said, bitterly ashamed for having struck a woman.

Together with McCloud and Channing, Ganga

jogged into the thick white smoke, pungent in their nostrils. At the back, Brigadier Percival stopped behind a rock for cover. With his Webley revolver he fired off a couple of rounds to assist Caspasian's mad charge as best he could, but if there was one thing he was not going to do, it was join in such a madcap scheme. He had waited long enough to gain possession of the crystal. Now that he had it he was damned if he was going to take a bullet just to be heroic. Let the youngsters do whatever they liked. He was going to safeguard his treasure, come what may. If the fight went against them, then he could at least get to one of the horses and try to make good his escape.

Bernard Spencer had watched in dismay as Ganga struck Rachel. For a second he turned his rifle on Ganga and had been going to shoot him, suspecting betrayal, but then he had seen Ganga signal to Caspasian, had seen Caspasian's nod of acknowledgement, and he had understood. He looked across at his daughter's body and felt a flood of pure love for her. She was curled safely as if asleep. She was a wilful daughter. Always had been. But wonderful. He could never have wished for her to be any different. Wilful, independent, but with a spirit of pure fire. He pulled back the bolt of the rifle, checked that he had a live round in the breach, and slammed the bolt home again.

'Rachel.' He said the name softly to himself, a smile on his lips as he prepared to join his friends. 'My own dear Rachel,' he said, and rose to meet the bullet from Alexei Karpov's rifle that punched clean through his heart.

From thirty yards away Caspasian watched in horror as Bernard Spencer went down. He spun to see the origin of the rifle shot and through the swirling smoke spotted Karpov, recognising the trim figure of the Bolshevik from when he had seen him ride past below his hiding place. Caspasian swung the MP18 towards him, firing as he went, but Karpov had seen him too and ducked behind cover as the bullets sang harmlessly off the rock.

Filled with anger and hatred, as much as Caspasian wanted to get at the Russian, he first had to look out for his friends. The smoke was starting to clear and they were now in close contact with the surviving Pathans. Ganga had drawn his kukri and Caspasian saw the steel blade flash down on to an arm upraised in terror. It swung again, cleaving through flesh and bone. Channing and McCloud were both firing rapidly and for a moment it seemed to Caspasian that the Pathans might have had enough. Again he sensed them falter, sensed a break in the action and knew that once more it was up to him to fill it.

He drove his hand into his satchel and drew out two egg grenades, pulled the pins and threw. He had noted that the mortar ammunition boxes were now in throwing range but the wind had shifted and a stiff breeze was blowing in his face, whipping off the ridge in front of him from where he caught a glimpse of Mahsud's frightened face popping above a rock. Instead Caspasian aimed his throw at the Pathans. The grenades landed in amongst them and detonated. Screams mixed with the sound of grenade fragments ricocheting off the stony ground. More tribesmen fell and the remainder broke and ran back towards Mahsud, their leader, Ahmed, waving for them to stop.

Ganga took aim at him but his Lee-Enfield was blown from his grasp, the stock shattering as a bullet from Novikov's rifle slammed into it. Ganga felt his left wrist go numb and threw himself to the ground as a second bullet whipped the hat from his head.

Seeing his opportunity, Caspasian ran to his left in a wide arc, sweeping round the edge of their small hilltop battlefield, right round the mortar line to come at the Russians from the flank. Karpov saw him coming but by now he had got the measure of the man and wanted nothing more to do with him. Crawling backwards, he wriggled away from his rock until he reached a dip, dropped down below ground level and then ran doubled over back towards the ridge where a furious Ahmed was trying to rally the remnants of Mahsud's bodyguard, cursing and kicking them into a line, ready to defend their Prince. Karpov could see a number of them sprinting down the hillside, though whether in flight or to fetch reinforcements, he could not tell. He gave a backward glance at the mortars and wondered for a second whether he should try to save them. A burst of fire from Caspasian's MP18 raked the top of the depression and answered the question for him. Vassily was there. That was his job. He had doctored the rounds. He could bloody well defend them from this English madman.

Out on his own now, Caspasian topped the ridge and down in the valley he could see the battle raging. To his dismay it looked as though the British line had completely broken. The Pathans seemed to have penetrated the column and in places they were embroiled in savage hand-to-hand fighting. Fresh swarms of tribesmen were sweeping down on the shattered advance guard. Further back down the road, someone had managed to rally a large group of men around the supply wagons and the aid post, but even there the Pathans had closed to within close range and a life and death struggle was being waged to prevent the British and Gurkha wounded from being slaughtered where they lay, helpless.

Caspasian hunted around for some way of influencing the battle and his eyes fell on the ammunition boxes. Somehow he had to get to them. Far away to his right he saw Ganga, Channing and McCloud putting down fire on Mahsud and the few men still with him. It was clear that the bodyguards' main concern now was the safety of the Prince, not the employment of the mortars. After all, why should they bother about those? From the look of the battle below they had done their grisly work. Ganga had taken Channing's Lee-Enfield and given him a Mauser taken from one of the Pathan dead. For one moment he looked up, checking on Caspasian's whereabouts. Their eyes met and Caspasian signalled that he was going for the mortars. Ganga nodded and returned to his work.

Keeping low, Caspasian ducked back away from the ridge and headed straight for the mortars. The bodies of the two slain Russians lay amongst the Pathan dead. The surprise attack had certainly done its job, Caspasian thought as he sped towards the pile of ammunition boxes. The important thing now was to see if there was any way he could turn the tide of the battle in the valley. It had already been turned once by the use of the flare rounds containing the mustard gas. If they could do it once, then Caspasian reckoned they just might do it again.

He reached the closest of the boxes, dragged clear Zykov's body, and wrenched up the lid. There nestling inside was a clutch of flare rounds. He laid the MP18 on the ground, gripped the rope handle at one end of the box and dragged it across the stony ground towards the nearest of the mortars. He was halfway across when there was a flicker of light at the corner of his eye. His body started to react, snapping to full alert, when the butt of Novikov's pistol hit him behind the ear and he went down.

Ganga too had seen the movement, seen the form of the big Russian rise out of the ground and strike Caspasian. He tried to turn his rifle towards the target threatening his friend but there was a sudden flurry of rifle fire in front of him and he saw that Ahmed had summoned a handful of men and was putting in a counter-attack to try and drive Ganga, Douglas and the doctor away from the precious mortars. Instantly Ganga turned back to face this more immediate threat. Caspasian would have to manage as best he could.

With his head ringing and pain flashing behind his eyes, Caspasian knew that the next seconds were vital. If he got this wrong, they would be his last. The first thought in his mind was why the Russian had not shot him. Out of ammo? Yes. An empty pistol clip lay in the dirt close by. Reloading then. Summoning all his strength, Caspasian twisted on to his back, shooting out with his feet as he did so. Sure enough, they contacted legs, solid as tree trunks. The Russian howled, the pistol dropped from his hand, the fresh clip he had been inserting in the butt when Caspasian had loomed unexpectedly in front of him, flying to one side.

Novikov staggered back out of kicking range. He saw Caspasian going for the Mauser pistol in his holster and dived on to him, drawing the knife from his belt as he did so. Enveloping Caspasian in a bearlike grip, he jerked the savage point of the knife close to his ear. Metal cut flesh and Caspasian felt the flow of warm blood down the side of his face. He yelped and brought his knee up, going for Vassily's groin. But the Russian was too high. He was circling his knees around Caspasian's waist, trying to push himself upright. If he managed to kneel astride his chest, Caspasian knew the next thing would be a knife thrust to the heart.

Tugging his right arm free, Caspasian punched upwards, going for the Russian's face. It was beyond his reach. He saw the big man grin. Stupid mistake, Caspasian thought, cursing himself. Every fragment of every second counted and he had just wasted one. Reversing his hand, he partially uncurled the fingers so the tips were tight against the bases to form kumate, the half-closed fist. He stabbed it upwards in a sharp jab at Novikov's windpipe. The Russian's grin changed to a frown as the blow struck home. But Caspasian still did not have the reach, pinned down by the heavier man's weight. Nevertheless, it was just enough to cause Novikov to pull back and hesitate. That was all Caspasian needed.

He swung again, this time turning his body with

the blow, spinning himself on to his side and using the momentum to tip Novikov off him. Instead of falling helplessly to the floor as Caspasian had hoped, the Russian rolled away, finishing on his feet, the knife still in his hand. He was good, Caspasian thought as he too jumped to his feet. Very good.

The two men circled each other, eyes locked, each gauging the other, not so much looking for an opening as seeking out a weakness in the other man's soul. That was how it was done. Both of them knew that. Find the weakness and you had the opening. Caspasian knew that. Do not strike the enemy's weapon. Strike his spirit. Musashi's *Book of Five Rings*. It had been drummed into him as a boy. Day in, day out, drummed into him in the training dojo in the backstreets of Yokohama's bustling port. But Novikov knew it too. Not Musashi perhaps, but the survival instinct of the cornered bear, and every bit as lethal.

As one moved right, the other moved left, and vice versa. Neither of them was making a mistake because both of them knew that the cost of a mistake would be instant death. Neither of them could find an opening because neither of them could find a weakness. Against his will, Novikov found admiration for the blond, rugged man before him. He was sorry that one of them would have to die. He knew his cause was duplicitous, the cause for which Alexei had led him into this God-forsaken country. Oleg and Dragov now lay dead and in a moment, either he himself or this strange, intense man before him would also be dead. Alexei had lied. He had betrayed Vassily's trust. For that Vassily would make him pay. But later. First he had to . . .

Caspasian had moved. His blow had come in like lightning as, once again, Karpov had betrayed his old friend, this time, with the distraction of Novikov's wayward thought. The punch to Novikov's midriff had not gone as deep as Caspasian had intended because, against all expectation, the Russian had managed to react against even Caspasian's most ferocious attack. Yet it was enough. Where there had been no opening, Caspasian had now created one. He followed it up hard and fast, blows and kicks raining down on Novikov. As he drove him back towards the rocks, his punches connecting now, Caspasian closed in tight and took Novikov down with a deashi-barai foot sweep. On the floor, he bent over him and slammed home a series of drop punches to jaw and face, like hammering a nail into wood, the deep dark wood of unconsciousness.

Gasping for breath, Caspasian dragged himself back to the ammunition box, tugging it the last few feet to the closest of the mortars. From his brief view of the valley he had seen the rough dispositions of the soldiers. Laying hands on the mortar's bipod, he lifted it round, aiming the barrel away from the British soldiers and towards the densest pack of the enemy. He took out a round from the box, pinched out the safety clip, and popped the bomb into the mouth of the barrel, putting his fingers in his ears in readiness for the detonation. It slid home. The cap of the 12-bore cartridge in the base of the round struck the fixed firing pin at the base of the barrel and the round fired, exploding out of the barrel and arching up into the sky. Caspasian watched as it climbed higher and higher, and then descended, disappearing over the ridge and finally bursting out of sight. But before it burst, he had seen he was on target and had already fired a further three rounds. Each one followed a similar trajectory, until from the valley beyond the ridge he heard the faint but unmistakable cries of agony, alarm and then panic. Not from the British, but this time from the Pathan tribesmen of Prince Mahsud.

Across the hillside, Mahsud watched in horror and frustration as one lone figure turned the tide of battle. Each time Ahmed tried to launch a counter-attack, their men were beaten back by the deadly accurate fire of the small Gurkha and his two companions. Mahsud screamed with rage as success slipped away while he was forced to look on. Even without the mortars he could have finished the British column, but now that the chemical weapons were being used against his men he saw that the panic was spreading and that hope was melting with every second. Even where his men were unaffected by the bombs, the panic seeped in. How could they know that they were not to be next to receive the full impact of the terrifying substance?

From mouth to mouth the word spread. The Eye of the Storm had turned against them. Somehow the British and their Gurkha allies must have taken possession of it. What else could explain the disastrous turn of events? As Mahsud watched in powerless rage, he saw his men break off the attack. Even where they had closed with the British column and where they were hacking their way murderously through the helpless wounded, the Pathans faltered, turned and ran.

Mahsud stood up. All fear had gone from him now. He was filled with a rage. He had never felt anything like it before. It came straight from his ancestors, weaving down through the long generations of bandits and warlords, each generation more powerful than the last, culminating in Mahsud's father, and now, in him. He felt it in his blood, his Oxford-educated sensibilities sloughing off him with the sight of his ambitious plans being laid waste about him.

'Attack!' he screamed at the top of his voice, and rushed towards Caspasian. Ahmed and the members of his bodyguard still remaining, stared in amazement and then followed. Caspasian looked up from his mortar. He shot a glance at Ganga, Channing and McCloud, but they had fallen silent, their ammunition exhausted. Ganga drew his kukri, rose from the ground and ran towards Caspasian. Behind him, Channing and McCloud stood up. They looked doubtfully at one another, and followed.

It was then that Karpov saw his opportunity. Mahsud's back was before him, racing for the mortars. Ahmed was at his side and the rest of their little band. He raised his pistol and aimed at the Prince, his lips twisted into a cruel smile.

The knife that was plunged into his back went in low, the tip of it puncturing a kidney. Karpov roared in pain, arching his back to try and pull away from the agony. He turned on his heel, his free hand scrabbling through the rich flow of blood pumping from the gash. He stared uncomprehending at the

Pathan woman before him, and fired. She threw up a hand instinctively to shield herself from the bullet. Karpov could not help noticing that the hand was bandaged, a yellow substance like pus seeping from the cloths. He recognised her then. Saw the fierce triumph in her dying eyes. She had saved her Prince. How could he ever put her aside now?

On his knees, Karpov tried to plug his wound. The pain seared through his brain. He toppled forward, scrabbling in the dirt like a dog burying a bone. The knowledge that he was dying brought terror with it. Terror as he had never known it before. It was worse than the trenches. Worse too than the endless snow fields where he and Vassily had fled from the pursuing Tsarist officers who had been sent to hunt them down like game. There he had never really believed he would die. Against all the odds, he had always felt he would come through, climb the ladder, achieve something. Just some damned thing, or what had his life amounted to? The revelation about the Eye of the Storm, revealed to him that night by the captured White Russian officer bargaining for his very survival had given Karpov's life purpose. From that moment he had known where his future lay. Far away from the savage land of his birth. Far away too from the miseries of the October Revolution. Vassily believed he was ambitious. He was, but not as Vassily imagined. Poor Vassily. He too was probably dead by now.

Alexei Karpov slumped forward, his face driving into the dirt. His last thought was of poor Vassily, and of how he had betrayed his only friend.

Caspasian rose to meet the charge. His hand went

to his holster. It was empty. In the struggle with Novikov the flap had come loose and the gun had tumbled clear. As Ganga, Channing and McCloud rushed to his side, hats gone, panting from the long battle, Caspasian smiled briefly at them and sank into a fighting stance, ready to take on whoever came at him first. He would go down fighting. It was the only way he knew.

At the head of his men, Prince Mahsud streamed down towards him. In one hand he waved a pistol, although he had no intention of using it. He wanted to hammer the Englishman into the ground. Tear him limb from limb. Wreak upon his broken body the vengeance he had been denied in the valley. Vengeance on the British for humbling his father, and vengeance on the British for giving him at Oxford a glimpse of what his life might have been had an accident of birth not placed him in this desolate wilderness.

Prince Mahsud and his men closed to within a dozen feet of the Englishman and his three companions when they were met by a hail of bullets. To Mahsud it felt as if he had run headlong into a closed door that he had expected to be open. He shuddered to a halt, every bone in his body jarring with the shock. It was only when he felt the hammer blows continue that he looked down at his torso and realised he had been shot. Around him, his men were going down. Ahmed was on his knees, keeling over gently. The rest? What did they matter? Mahsud looked around in bewilderment. On the skyline he could just make out some vague shapes, but nothing mattered any more. Not now. To his immense surprise, he felt as if he wanted to laugh, even if his body would no longer obey him. Who would have thought it? Him, Mahsud, dying in battle. What a joke! What a wonderful hoot! His father might even have been proud of him. The bastard.

At the sound of the gunfire, Caspasian, Ganga and the others flinched, bracing themselves for the impact of bullets into flesh. Instead they saw the Pathans stopped in their tracks. Caspasian saw Mahsud go down and could swear that there was an ironic smile on his lips as he fell, his body riddled with bullets. Caspasian looked off to the right, in the direction of the fire, and saw, advancing over the side of the ridge, a platoon of Gurkhas in full battle order. Having seen the havoc being wrought on the column by the mortars, they had managed to fight their way out of their picket position and advance to locate the deadly weapons. In the centre of the extended line, their jemadar was controlling the advance to contact, half the platoon putting down a withering fire while the other half jogged stolidly forward, leapfrogging by small tactical bounds. Even after the long fight, their battle drill and fire discipline was as rigid as iron.

The last surviving Pathans turned and sprinted for their lives, pursued by the .303 bullets from the Lee-Enfields. When the jemadar saw them go, he took one look at his men, read their minds, and let them off the leash. Rifles forgotten, kukris rasped from scabbards, and like the hounds of hell they bolted after their quarry.

Caspasian sank to his knees. 'Want to go with them?' he said to Ganga, but the Gurkha sergeant just grinned and tiredly waved aside the suggestion. It was only then that Caspasian remembered the Brigadier. He scanned the battlefield, looking for him, and there, approaching out of the dust, came Brigadier Percival, smiling happily, the leather pouch safe and secure over his shoulder. If there had been a gun ready to hand Caspasian felt he would probably have shot him. Instead, he wondered what sort of disciplinary action a straightforward punch in the face would attract.

But the next moment all thoughts of that were forgotten. For beyond the smug Brigadier Caspasian caught sight of Rachel, kneeling beside the body of her father.

Night had fallen. The medical aid post was more like a charnel house. Hunched over the operating table, the Regimental Medical Officer blinked the sweat out of his stinging eyes and carried on working. In all his life he had never seen such horrific wounds. Across from him, Angus McCloud was equally busy. Immediately after being rescued by the Gurkha picket, he had made his way down to the valley along with the others and sought out the aid post, knowing full well that his services would be sorely needed there. Rachel had gone with him and now assisted, burying her own grief in her work. From time to time McCloud glanced up at her, always to find her concentrating on the task in hand. He knew that sooner or later she would have to break. She could not carry on much longer without it. Fatigue would combine with overpowering grief and the poor girl would break. Yet for now there was ample work to distract her, even if it was work of the most terrible kind.

Caspasian had stayed with Rachel all the way down from the mountain, the two of them overseeing the removal of her father's body down to the column. It would be taken, along with all the other dead, back to Peshawar and from there removed for burial.

When she had asked for the whereabouts of the aid post, he had tried to dissuade her, knowing what horrors would await her there. But she had insisted and Caspasian had finally relented. At first he had stayed with her. There was not much he himself could do to aid the wounded but he just wanted to remain close to her, to keep an eye on her and be there if she needed him. As the night wore on however, he wandered away, going in search of water.

He found a bowser amongst the supply wagons and filled a basin. The water was warm but he did not care. He rolled up his sleeves and then buried his face in it, luxuriating in the sensation. He put back his head and shook it, feeling the water run down inside his clothes. He ran his fingers through his hair and wiped them dry on his shirt. He had just started to wash his hands when he glanced to one side and saw, through the wagons, the tent that the Brigadier was now using as his headquarters. Colonel Gibson had been wounded, struck down by the mustard gas. In his absence and the absence of any other senior officer still unwounded, Brigadier Percival had taken command of the column. Only the Adjutant remained effective, in spite of his dysentery, and had been acting reluctantly as the Brigadier's second-in-command, pulling together those troops still fit for duty.

The tent flap was open, the tent empty. On a small table a single hurricane lamp burned and in its flickering light Caspasian saw the leather pouch lying beside it. Checking that there was no one around, he slipped between the deserted wagons and ducked into the tent. He looked at the pouch for a moment, wondering, and then picked it up. He could tell the moment he did so that the crystal was inside. He could feel its weight and shape. He unfastened the buckle and opened the flap, carefully taking out the bundle of velvet. Laying the pouch aside, he slowly unwrapped the cloths, wary lest the crystal fall and smash on the floor.

At last it unpeeled before him. It was a magnificent device, he had to admit. There was a canvas chair beside the table. Caspasian drew it into the light and sat down to contemplate the crystal further. Settling himself, he turned it this way and that, studying the markings on the inside of the crystal's hollow body. It had really been extremely clever how it had been done. The work of a craftsman. But there was something odd about them. Caspasian knew a little of Cyrillic lettering from his grandfather but his knowledge was rusty. The problem was that, with a few exceptions, the markings were too small to read with the naked eye. The carving was so intricate that Caspasian found he had to strain his eyes to make out even the simplest combination of letters and numbers. So this was the formula for a new energy source, was it? He smiled, marvelling at the power he held in his fist. The ramifications for the world were truly immense if the Brigadier was correct.

He drew the hurricane lamp closer, holding the crystal beside the flame. As he did so he became aware of shadows being cast behind him on the tent wall, cast by the crystal itself. He looked round in alarm and stared, amazed at the images being projected.

Ganga had been searching all through the encampment for Caspasian. He had first tried the aid post, flinching at the sights and smells that assaulted his senses when he entered. The dead had been laid to one side, row upon row of them, while the doctors continued to work feverishly on the living. He had found Rachel, but she had been intent on her work and had waved him away.

Then he had tried the makeshift armoury where the Quartermaster was making a quick inventory of the ammunition stocks. There was still a long return journey to Peshawar which would start the following day, and most of it was through hostile country. There was every chance of further ambush.

Finally, when he had exhausted most other possibilities, he was passing close beside the Brigadier's tent when he heard someone moving about inside. Knowing it was not Brigadier Percival he checked inside and found Caspasian rising from a small table, the Brigadier's leather pouch in his hand.

'Saheb, I think you should come,' Ganga said quickly.

'What is it?' Caspasian asked. Then, urgently, 'Is it Rachel?'

'No, saheb. It is the Brigadier and the other man.'

'Sir Oswald?'

'Yes, saheb.'

'What about them?'

'The Brigadier is saying they must have a firing squad. For the big Russian, the Prince's commander, and the other prisoners.'

A strange smile crossed Caspasian's face. 'I bet he does. Get rid of all the witnesses.' He felt a rage building inside him. 'Where are they?'

As Ganga led the way out of the tent, Caspasian snatched up the hurricane lamp.

'It's all right, saheb. There's no need.'

'Oh yes, there is. There's nothing like a lamp to show the way.'

Ganga went quickly. He had already spent too much time finding Caspasian and was afraid that they might arrive too late. On the way they passed groups of soldiers. Most were slumped together on the ground, sleeping. Sentries had been posted, and the pickets pulled in close to the perimeter for the night. No one really expected an attack. As Colonel Gibson had said as they carried him to the aid post, the Pathans had had the stuffing knocked out of them. He had thanked Caspasian warmly before being taken to have his wounds dressed. Brigadier Percival had sped him on his way, insisting that he have a good rest before resuming command of his battalion. In the meantime he, Brigadier Percival, would take charge. Caspasian now knew why.

They found the Brigadier and Sir Oswald consulting with the Adjutant who appeared to be remonstrating with them. Douglas Channing leaned miserably on a pile of empty ammunition crates, seeming to want no part of the proceedings. Behind him, Novikov, Ahmed, and a group of Pathans sat with hands securely tied behind their backs. Their heads were down and they stared at the ground before them. To one side Henry Allenshaw stood with arms grimly folded across his chest. His face was a mess and when he caught sight of Caspasian he pointed and said, 'And here's another bugger we can shoot!'

The Brigadier looked round and Caspasian saw his mouth tighten. Clearly Caspasian had arrived at an inopportune moment for him.

'What's all this about shooting?' Caspasian asked.

'Stay out of this, Caspasian. That's an order,' the Brigadier snapped.

Caspasian smiled. 'It wouldn't have anything to do with this, would it?' he asked, holding up the leather pouch.

'How dare you! Give that to me this instant,' the Brigadier snarled. 'That was in my tent. If you've been in there and taken it I'll have you court-martialled. You'll be sweating in a military prison so fast it'll make your head spin.'

'Oh, I did more than just take it, Brigadier. I had a close look at your precious crystal. Your Eye of the Storm.' He hefted the pouch in his fist. 'Quite a revelation. Why don't you tell the others about it?'

To one side Captain Miller, the Adjutant, stared suspiciously at Caspasian. 'I don't like this any more than you do, Captain Caspasian, but I think you're outranked here. I suggest you leave this to the Brigadier and me. I don't want a firing squad any more than you do but the Brigadier is the senior officer present.'

'And don't forget the honourable Sir Oswald Masterman.' Caspasian turned towards Sir Oswald who had backed into the shadows the moment he had appeared. 'I suppose you're in on this too.' He stared at the rotund, sweating figure backed against a wagon. 'Yes. Of course you are. How stupid of me not to realise.'

Channing stepped forward. 'In on what? What the devil are you talking about, Caspasian?'

'You too I suppose, Douglas? Or were you just the bag-carrier?'

'Listen Caspasian . . .' Channing began but, without taking his eyes from Caspasian and the leather pouch, the Brigadier snapped, 'Shut up, Douglas. Stay out of this.'

Caspasian chuckled. 'Poor old Douglas.'

'He might be a bag-carrier, as you put it,' the Brigadier said, 'but at least he knows how to obey orders. Now I'm going to give you an order. Hand over that pouch.'

'First I think we should have a little slide show, don't you?'

'Caspasian, I'm warning you!'

Before the Brigadier could stop him, Caspasian slammed down his hurricane lamp on the pile of ammunition crates, brushing aside Channing's protests. He unclipped the glass top and flipped it open. Freed from the confinement, the pale yellow paraffin flame leaped from its wick and flickered in the darkness, casting eerie shadows on the wagons and tents around them.

'Behold, the magic lantern,' Caspasian said. With a flourish of the hand, he pulled the crystal from the pouch and popped it neatly over the flame. The Brigadier made a move but Caspasian spun to face him.

'Don't tempt me, sir,' he said viciously. 'I'd love nothing more.'

The Brigadier looked into Caspasian's eyes and backed away. He knew all too well what the man was capable of.

There was a murmur from the prisoners and Novikov pushed himself unsteadily to his feet. On the wagons, the tents, the ammunition boxes, on the faces and clothes of everyone around the lamp, the crystal cast its shadows, not blurred shapes any more, but sharp and clear, whole series of numbers and letters, names and details. From the multitude of surfaces on the crystal, the tiny carved markings yielded their secrets.

'A lens,' Channing murmured, staring wide-eyed at the mass of information being cast on all sides. 'It's a blasted lens.'

Caspasian watched the Brigadier. He and Sir Osvald were looking distinctly uncomfortable all of a sudden.

'All right, Caspasian. You've had your fun. Now and it over.'

'So this is your new energy source, is it Brigadier? This is what we've all been fighting for? This is going to keep the Empire independent of other fuel requirements, is it?' He turned to Novikov. 'Tell me, comrade. What does this information look like to you?'

Vassily shuffled forward. One of the British soldiers went to push him back but the Adjutant waved him aside.

'Here, let me make it clearer.' Caspasian picked up the lamp and held it close to the side of a tent, turning it slowly in his hand, projecting a whole array of the magnified codes onto the screen, revolving one by one.

There was a choked cough and the big Russian shook his head in dismay. 'Bank accounts.'

Caspasian smiled encouragement. 'Louder, please.'

'They look like bank account details.'

'I'd say that's a pretty fair guess, wouldn't you, Brigadier?'

But while everyone's attention had been fixed on the slide show, the Brigadier had been busy. When Caspasian turned to him again there was a revolver in his fist, the muzzle pointing at Caspasian's chest. Beside him, Henry Allenshaw clutched a rifle and was clearly dying to put a bullet through Caspasian's heart. Taking courage from his companions, Sir Oswald had stepped out of the shadows while remaining behind the Brigadier, peeping round uncertainly, his eyes rarely leaving the precious crystal.

'When I was a boy,' Caspasian said, 'I worked for my grandfather in Yokohama in his business as a ships' chandler. We had a lot of Russian vessels as customers. The Japanese war with Russia was over and trade had resumed. Amongst other things, I used to help out with the book-keeping.' He waved a hand at the projections on the tent wall. 'And I saw plenty of these.' He twisted the lamp and pointed out bank after bank, some of them Swiss, but others in London, in Paris, in New York. 'The question is, why?'

'That's none of your business. Now hand over the crystal or I will be forced to shoot you.'

Captain Miller stepped forward. 'Just a minute, sir. I don't know what's going on here but I can't allow . . .'

'The Romanov treasure.'

Everyone turned to Vassily Novikov. He was shaking his head in disbelief, a sad smile on his bruised face. When he looked up there were tears in his eyes. 'I thought it was just a stupid rumour. All this time, this was what Alexei was after. He knew all along.'

'Shut him up!' the Brigadier screamed. Allenshaw stepped towards him, raising the butt of his rifle.

'Leave him alone, Henry.'

Standing beside Caspasian, Rachel held the big Webley in both fists. The hammer was cocked, her finger on the trigger. 'Go on,' she said to Novikov.

'There was a prisoner. A White Russian officer. Alexei handled the interrogation himself. He insisted on complete privacy. I should have known, but I trusted him. Afterwards, there was a rumour. I don't know how it started. The man must have spoken to someone else before he was shot.'

'And what did he say?'

'Something about the Romanov treasure. Some-thing about it having been smuggled out of the country in the early days of the Revolution. That's all I know. I never believed it. Not until now.'

'Brigadier?' Rachel said, shifting her revolver on to him, ignoring the gun in his fist. Her eyes were glass, the exhaustion and shock beginning to tell. She was capable of anything.

Slowly he lowered his gun. 'All right. It's nothing to be ashamed of. This is a government-sanctioned mission with authority from the highest level.' He glared at Caspasian. 'And I do mean the highest level.' He glanced at the shadows on the tent wall and then continued.

'When the Tsar finally saw that revolution was inevitable, he managed to get a large part of his fortune out of the country and into foreign banks. Most of it, in fact. He was adamant that records of it should be kept to the minimum, fearful lest others should get to it before he and his family escaped. Of course they never did. The crystal was the Tsarina's idea, and a brilliant one too. The crystal was fashioned and engraved by a master craftsman.' He sneered at Caspasian. 'Not some Chinese bottle-washer, but a Swiss watchmaker actually. The chemical agent was a protective device to ward off the inquisitive. When the crystal fell into the hands of the White Russians and they discovered what they had, they offered it to British Intelligence, using it to bargain for arms.'

'Which is where you came in,' Caspasian said.

'Exactly. Prince Mahsud complicated the process and of course he also knew the real nature of the so-called Eye of the Storm. Knowing his lineage, British Intelligence had watched his every move at Oxford. It was while he was there that he also heard the rumours of the Romanov treasure from Russia exiles. One of them had mentioned the Eye. Mahsud took it from there.'

Ahmed jumped to his feet. 'This is all lies! The Prince was starting a holy war to drive you from our land!'

'I'm afraid not,' the Brigadier continued. 'Prince Mahsud couldn't have cared less about the lot of you. He had discovered the good life. All he wanted to do was get his hands on the treasure and return to Europe, a wealthy Prince instead of an impoverished local chieftain.'

'And my father?' Rachel said, her voice dangerously calm.

For once a flash of regret crossed the Brigadier's face. 'My dear . . .'

'Don't you dare call me that!' Rachel shouted at him, raising the revolver.

'Rachel, put down the gun,' Allenshaw urged gently. 'You don't know what you're doing.'

'Oh yes, I do. I've never been more clear about anything in my life. The great Brigadier Percival is responsible for my father's death. He lied to us from the start and my father died as a result.' She looked at the soldiers and prisoners around them. 'How many others have died because of this piece of glass?'

Caspasian put the lamp down and lifted the crystal from the flame. He toyed with it in his hands. 'And all for what? Money.' He tossed the crystal lightly in the air and caught it. 'Do you hear that, Captain Miller? What do you think Colonel Gibson will have to say about that?'

'Caspasian, I'm warning you,' the Brigadier said, his eyes riveted to the crystal. 'This mission was completely official. The money wasn't for me or Sir Oswald. It was for the government.'

Caspasian tossed the crystal higher and caught it again, this time with one hand. 'I wonder what the press and the public would have to say about that?'

'The men who sanctioned this operation own the press. The public will believe whatever they're told. They always do.' He stood back, relaxed now, casually sinking his hands in his pockets. 'So go on, drop the crystal. I can have it repaired. You can't erase the markings from the glass itself. We'll still get the money. If only a handful of the markings survive, we'll still have more than enough. Shatter it into a dozen pieces if you like.'

'Only a dozen pieces?' Caspasian said, a dangerous twinkle in his eyes. He tossed the crystal again, but when he caught it this time there was a strange metallic sound. In the flicker of the unprotected flame all the Brigadier and the others could see was a blur in Caspasian's hands. The next thing they knew he was holding the crystal out to them, offering it. 'You want the crystal? Here you are then. Take it.'

The Brigadier stared warily into Caspasian's eyes as he reached out and accepted it. He felt the crystal in his fingers, but it was strangely heavy. Far heavier than he remembered. He looked down at the treasured object and gasped as if he had found himself clutching a poisonous snake. Plugged into the heart of the crystal Caspasian had inserted an egg grenade.

'Is this what you're looking for?' Caspasian asked, dangling the pin between forefinger and thumb. He moved his body in front of Rachel to shield her. 'Tel me, sir, can you remember the fuse time of the No. 34 grenade?'

'You fucking . . .!' The Brigadier struggled furiously with the crystal but the grenade was wedged fast. Caspasian had twisted it into place and the seconds were running.

Around him there was a sudden stampede as Channing, Ganga, Captain Miller, Vassily, Ahmed, the soldiers and prisoners bolted, ducked and dived for cover. Caspasian gently eased Rachel away from the panic-stricken Brigadier, while he himself remained to watch, a broad smile of satisfaction on his lips.

The Brigadier tried to dislodge the grenade once more and failed. He tossed it to Sir Oswald. 'You try.'

The terrified civil servant shrieked as he caught the crystal, the deadly black heart locked at its core. He tossed it like a red hot coal to Allenshaw. Allenshaw caught it, bungled, juggled and slipped it back to the Brigadier. With a scream of outrage and terror, the Brigadier hurled it at Caspasian.

'Blast you to hell, Caspasian!'

Caspasian calmly caught it, drew back his arm, and rocketed the crystal high into the night sky, arching it far above the camp. Up and up it climbed, over the wagons, the aid post, the dismantled mountain guns, the dead and the wounded.

Out in one of the picket positions, a Gurkha sentry looked up startled as a brilliant white explosion cracked above the resting column like a bright firework.

Beneath the point of blast, the Brigadier, Sir Oswald and Henry Allenshaw picked themselves up from the ground as a rain of debris pattered lightly about them, metal fragments from the grenade and a spreading cloud of the tiniest slivers of glass, not one any larger than the tip of a pin.

Epilogue

Rachel was in her bedroom when she heard the sound of a car engine. She left the scattered suitcases, the half-filled packing boxes, the bags and wrappings, and went over to look out of the window. The car drew to a halt, dust swirling around it, and the door opened. She leaned out of the window and waved.

'I'll be right out.'

Standing in the drive, Caspasian took off his hat and slapped the dust against his leg. It had been a long drive from the railhead. He walked round to the side of the bungalow and gazed from the terrace out towards the distant hills. It was late afternoon and shadows were starting to stretch lazily across the paving stones. Behind him a door opened and he turned to see Rachel hurrying towards him. It was the first time he had seen her in the three weeks since their return from the expedition. She came up to him and kissed him. He wanted to hold her for longer but she pulled away, uncertain how the ordeals of the past days might have affected him.

'Come and sit down. Can I get you a drink?'

'Yes,' he said. 'Some lime juice and soda would wash away the dust.'

She called the houseboy and ordered the drink. 'So. Tell me what's been happening?' she said when the boy had gone.

'First tell me about you. I've thought about you all the time. How have you been?'

Rachel shrugged. She drew her feet up under her and looked out across the lawn. 'It's been hard coming back here, but someone's got to put everything in order.'

'You're leaving then?'

She nodded. 'Too many memories here.'

Caspasian shifted awkwardly in his chair. The houseboy returned with a pitcher of iced lime and soda and two tumblers. He set them down on a low table and went to pour but Rachel smiled her thanks and sent him away, pouring the drinks herself. She handed one of the glasses to Caspasian.

'Where will you go?' he asked.

'Back to England. I should be able to get a job easily enough. Join a practice somewhere and find a place to live.'

'Why not stay out here? You were born and raised here. This is where you belong.'

She smiled at him. 'No, I don't. When I first returned here I wondered whether I did or not but our little outing helped me clarify my thoughts about that.'

'Yes, but England, of all places.' Caspasian thought of his own experience there as a boy at boarding school.

'It's not that bad.'

'Perhaps, but there's a whole wide world out here that's . . .'

'That's what, John? Fun?'

'No,' he answered instinctively, but then wondered what exactly he had been going to say. 'What I mean is, I can't see you working quietly in some little village somewhere. You said as much yourself.'

'A lot has happened since then. Right now, a quiet little English village practice doesn't sound at all bad.'

Caspasian took a sip of his drink. He watched her as she gazed at the patterns the sunlight was making on the hills.

'Listen Rachel . . .' He put down his glass, wringing his hands as he spoke. 'I'm not very good with words . . .'

'So you keep saying,' she smiled.

'What I mean is, I don't like the thought of you being so far away. I mean, England might as well be on another planet!'

She laughed, a pure clear sound that made Caspasian's pain all the harder to bear. 'That's a little bit of an exaggeration, isn't it?'

'All right. So what if it is? But . . .' He fought with the words. 'What I mean to say is, I'm just not right for you. Not yet, at any rate.'

She sat back and stared at him. 'Well whatever does that mean?'

He grimaced. 'You're not making this any easier for me.'

She leaned forward and took his hands in hers. 'John, I think I know what you're trying to say and I agree. I love your company as well, but I think that – for now at least – we're better apart. Your world is too . . . exciting for me.'

Caspasian heaved a great sigh, uncertain whether it was relief or regret. But she was right. Exactly so. He wanted her to stay with him. He wanted it badly. But he knew that if she did so it would only harm her. She had come close enough to death on their last expedition. He was bad news for her and he knew it. So, it seemed, did Rachel.

'Rachel,' he said, taking courage from her directness, 'God knows, I like you.' He shook his head in exasperation. 'No, it's more than that. You know it is. Much more. But this is the only life I know, and it's no kind of life for a person like you.'

'There was a time when I'd have taken exception at that,' she said smiling. 'But not now. Maybe I'll feel differently in time but right now I agree with you.'

'You do?' Caspasian said, feeling the tension ease.

Rachel nodded. 'The new district political officer arrives in a couple of days and then I'll be on my way.' She twirled her drink in her hands, brushing away the beads of condensation forming on the glass. 'I've also heard that Henry will be resuming his post here which is another good reason for moving on. What about you? How did it all go in Delhi?'

Caspasian laughed. 'The usual whitewash of course. Ahmed and the other tribesmen were released. The last thing the government wanted was a public debate on the matter. That might have succeeded in rousing a tribal frontier war where Mahsud failed. So Ahmed has gone back to the mountains.'

'And the Russian?'

'Vassily Novikov,' Caspasian said, smiling. 'I spent quite a bit of time with him. Not a bad man at all. For a Bolshevik,' he grinned. 'He was sent back where he came from as well. There'll be a small diplomatic protest at the most. Perhaps not even that. Ganga's back with the Regiment. Poor old Douglas on the other hand gets to spend another year in the service of Sir Oswald Masterman.'

Rachel stared in disbelief. 'You mean Sir Oswald and the Brigadier get off free?'

'Why not?' Caspasian said bitterly. 'They were right, it seems. The mission did have sanction at the highest level. They get to live and plot for another day. In another time and another place they'll put other lives on the line, though not their own, I'll wager.'

The thought of that horrified Rachel, but the main worry that surfaced in her mind was for Caspasian himself. 'So you . . .' she said hesitantly. 'If you really did spoil some great master plan of the Brigadier's, however twisted and corrupt it might have been, what are they going to do to you?'

Caspasian tried to brush it aside nonchalantly. 'Oh, I'll be all right. I've got friends too.'

'Your father,' Rachel said carefully. 'Could he help?'

'What? The great Sir David Edward?' Caspasian snorted. 'I wouldn't ask him. No, he's tried to help out in the past. When I found out he'd been pulling strings I told him to stop or I'd tell his wife about a little fling he once had in Yokohama. A fling with a woman who wasn't good enough for him to marry.' He stared stonily into the distance but then relented. 'I'm sorry. I didn't mean to burst out like that.'

'That's all right. I understand. But you didn't answer me. What are they going to do to you?'

Caspasian sighed deeply. 'The Brigadier wanted to go for a court-martial. Break me completely. Colonel Gibson, God bless him, said he'd go public if that happened. In doing so he's probably put paid to any further promotion for himself.'

'What an honourable man.'

'Yes. Not many of them around.'

'So it's back to your desk job in Delhi?'

'No. Though I can't say I'm sorry. The Brigadier obviously had a word with Readman and that bastard said he wouldn't have me back.'

'And . . . ?' Rachel prompted.

'And there's a town in China with a consulate that needs a junior military attaché, an assistant to some major or other. Guess who's been nominated?'

Rachel stood up, enraged. 'John, you can't go. It's a death warrant. The country's a web of revolution and warlords.' She paced the terrace, then suddenly stopped and turned, the answer becoming clear. 'Leave the army. Resign your commission.'

'And do what?'

She waved her arms. 'I don't know. Anything. Everything. Your grandfather's business . . .'

'Closed down.'

'Then . . . then . . .'

He stood up and went to her, taking her waist in his hands and looking into her eyes. 'Rachel, that's what I've been trying to say to you, however badly This is my life. It's the only life I know. Before I wa sent back to boarding school in England, my grand father said something to me that I've never forgotter

420

He said that life is like a code that has to be broken. There's always one more layer. Just when you think you've cracked it, it surprises you with another layer, and then another. And you have to start all over again, but with the added benefit of the wisdom you've gained thus far.

'He said that while the language of the code changes from generation to generation, the code we're all trying to crack is the same, and always has been, right from the very beginning when . . . when Alexander and his men walked across those hills over there. Before him even. It's there waiting for us, my grandfather said. See what you can make of it. See what you can find in it. See what you can find through it. But at least look. This is my way of looking.' He laughed. 'It's a bit like the crystal.'

'Too bad then that you blew it to smithereens.'

'Maybe, but it didn't half scupper the Brigadier's plans. It was worth it just for that.'

He slipped an arm round her waist and drew her to him. Together they walked across to the low stone wall where a flowerbed split the terrace from the lawn, a thick line of dry dark soil.

'So you're going to go and chip away at your code in China, are you?' Rachel said.

'I think that's best, don't you? At least for now.'

She shrugged, unconvinced. 'Will I see you again?'

'You can count on it.' From the tone of his voice she knew that he meant it.

'Good.'

'In fact,' he said, 'I don't sail to Shanghai for a couple of weeks.'

She smiled. 'What had you in mind?'

'Well, when all of this started I was on my way to Simla for some leave. Come with me. After all, you've already packed.'

She leaned her head against his shoulder. 'What would all the officers and their ladies say?'

'Do you care?'

'Not one bit. Not one little bit.'